Critics praise...

Geronimo's Ponies

A beautifully told story of a few weeks in the late 1930's during which young Davey Parker takes a step toward manhood... Mr. Meyers has the enviable ability to set a scene or evoke an emotion with hardly more than a flick of his pen, and his eventful little book is filled with memorable characters.

— Burt Hochberg,
The New York Times Book Review

First winner of the National Novella Award — Jane Smiley judged the contest — *Geronimo's Ponies* gracefully situates a classic theme — coming-of-age — in an unusual setting. During the Depression, a boy named Davey leaves his home on a Navajo reservation to travel with his uncle Eph through Texas. Both sympathetic and inconsiderate characters are drawn with equal wisdom in confidently unadorned prose, successfully relying on the narrative to generate momentum.

— *Publishers Weekly*

This winner of the first National Novella Award — *Geronimo's Ponies* — is a coming-of-age story about a boy in the company of his madcap uncle. Davey participates vicariously in his uncle's misadventures and becomes street-smart... A well-paced, entertaining debut, with one revelation following another.

— *Kirkus Reviews*

Critics praise . . .

Reservations

It's a cause for celebration when an author with Meyers' storytelling skills has not only a story to tell, but an insider's knowledge—a grasp of the issues and the courage to write bare, honest realism . . . as Meyers recalls the bitter feud within the U.S. Indian Service between assimilationists and anti-assimilationists . . .

> —D.L. Birchfield,
> *Roundup: Online Magazine of the
> Western Writers of America*

A beautifully told tale of devotion—a poignant story of the idealism, faith, courage and anguish of Will Parker, an Indian Service teacher, reveals Meyers' familiarity with the realities of reservation life . . . Utterly convincing characterization and descriptive detail . . .

> —David L. Caffey,
> *Book Talk: Quarterly of the New
> Mexico Book League*

A forceful tale of a family's tenacious commitment to foster Native self-reliance and cultural survival, and to justice and social change. An epic story of changing times, presenting realistic and rounded portrayals of Indian life before World War II. Meyers knows his turf.

> —*Publisher's Weekly*

Geronimo's Ponies
a novella

and

Reservations
a novel

Harold Burton Meyers

Geronimo's Ponies / Reservations

© Copyright 2021 by Harold Burton Meyers

ISBN 979-8-9850215-0-9

Published by Steven Key Meyers/The Smash-and-Grab Press

These are works of fiction. The characters might have existed and the incidents might have occurred in the times and at the places described, but did not. Any resemblance to actual events or persons, living or dead, is coincidental.

Geronimo's Ponies was originally published in 1989 by Council Oak Books, Tulsa, Oklahoma. *Reservations* was originally published in 1999 by University Press of Colorado, Niwot, Colorado.

Chapter Two of *Reservations* is adapted from the author's short story "The Zuni Bow," which appeared in *Prairie Schooner,* Autumn 1944.

Cover: the author's mother, Sallie Key Meyers *(right)* with her friend and colleague Dorothy Mayne in Nava (now Newcomb), New Mexico, *ca.* 1930. *Photo:* Donald F. Meyers.

**SMASH
&GRAB**press

Geronimo's Ponies   *1*

Reservations   *87*

Geronimo's Ponies

*For J.A.M. and all
that followed, with love*

1.

WE FINISHED SUPPER and sat on the front steps in the cool shade, watching shadows stretch over the patch of grass my father was trying against all odds to grow in the adobe soil. A Ford V8 station wagon trailed dust past the trading post and turned down the hill toward the school. We didn't often see a strange car at Klinchee. We were far from any main road.

"Now who's this, do you suppose?" Pa said as the station wagon rattled over the cattle guard.

"It looks like Uncle Eph's old crate," I said.

Uncle Eph was my mother's brother, one of many but always her favorite. He had come to visit several times before she fell sick, something none of her other brothers had done, and he was the only one she had corresponded with, even at Christmas.

"I think you're right."

"He's got somebody with him."

"Maybe he brought Muffie, though it doesn't seem likely. Funny he didn't let us know he was coming."

Muffie was Uncle Eph's wife, a big square-faced woman who wore loose dresses that fell straight from her shoulders to her ankles. She had taken up religion late in life, along about the time Uncle Eph got out of the oil business, and she had turned batty. When we took my mother home to Texas to bury her, all Aunt Muffie wanted to talk about was tablecloths. She kept trying to pin Pa and me down as to how many tablecloths my mother had owned and whether they were for family, company, or show. It was not something either of us had given thought to.

Uncle Eph unfolded out of the car like a carpenter's rule. He was a big man, taller than my father and fifty pounds heavier. Uncle Eph had the hands of a wrestler, which he had been in his young days, when he had joined a traveling carnival and taken on all comers without ever, he said, having been thrown. He dressed like a movie rancher, Tom Mix or Buck Jones, in high-heeled boots, tight twill pants, a two-tone shirt pulled taut over the belly, and a white ten-gallon hat.

My mother used to tease him about his costume, pointing out that their father, my grandfather, had been an actual rancher and mostly wore bib overalls and common work shoes, with a straw hat to keep off the sun. Uncle Eph said that kind of garb might have been all right for his daddy, but in these modern times a man had to dress his part to get ahead, had to announce by the way he dressed what manner of man he was and what in general his line of work might be. And who knows, he added, maybe if the old man had dressed for what he was—a landowner, a gentleman, an officer and hero of the Confederate Army, instead of like just another sodbuster—he might not have lost the ranch way back then and he, Uncle Eph, might have had a stake to work with instead of having to scratch every which way for every last dollar that ever came his way.

I ran down to the car. Uncle Eph picked me up and swung me around.

"Well, Davey," he said, "you just won't stop growing, will

you? I can't hardly lift you no more. Keep shooting up like you are and before long you'll have just as much trouble as me fitting into a itty-bitty car like this. I been sitting all scooched up for so long I wasn't sure my joints was still working."

A short fat man came around from the passenger side. He was dressed like my grandfather in striped bib overalls, a blue work shirt with sweat circles under the arms, and dirt-crusted work shoes. The floppy brim of a big straw hat shadowed his face.

"Will," Uncle Eph said, "I want you to shake hands with Mr. Smart, best damned judge of horseflesh you'll ever hope to meet. Mr. Smart's from Oklahoma."

"How do," Mr. Smart said. He shook hands with me too. His hand looked and felt like a lump of biscuit dough ready to be rolled out.

"I suppose you brought Mr. Smart with you because of the horse auction I mentioned in my letter," Pa said as we hauled suitcases up the walk to the house.

"Damned tootin'," Uncle Eph said. "What you said about them horses just set my brain afire. I got hold of Mr. Smart fast as could be and jumped in the car. We drove straight through, not to waste a minute. Surprised you didn't see it yourself."

"See what?" I asked.

"Why, opportunity, boy, *opportunity.*"

About a week earlier, my father had written to thank Uncle Eph for a snapshot he sent of the stone on my mother's grave, which he'd bought with money Pa gave him after the funeral. The photograph was blurred and had been taken between the legs of a lot of people standing around the grave. We couldn't read the words on the stone, but we were glad to know her burial place was properly marked. In his letter, Pa told Uncle Eph, mostly just to fill out the page, that Washington had ordered a reduction in the number of sheep and horses on the

Navajo Indian Reservation, hoping to do something about the overgrazing that was turning the reservation into a wasteland. With nothing to hold the soil, wind devils now whirled where grass once grew as high as a horse's belly. Most of the excess sheep were already gone, and thousands of horses were to be rounded up and sold at a series of auctions, starting in the part of the reservation that Pa was in charge of.

At the time he wrote, Pa thought of the horse auction only as an interesting but harmless bit of news. He said later that he had failed to take into full account who was going to read the letter. Uncle Eph saw opportunity everywhere, and sometimes managed to grasp it. He had once made a million dollars speculating in land and built the biggest house Wichita Falls had seen up to that time. But Uncle Eph didn't know when to stop. He put everything he'd made or could borrow into buying more land just as the boom ended, wiping out both the million dollars and the house.

Something similar happened when he turned to wildcatting. He brought in a gusher about a day ahead of bankruptcy and started building a still bigger house in Wichita Falls — one so big he claimed you couldn't holler from one end of it to the other without a megaphone. When Standard Oil offered to buy his leases for a sum in the millions, Uncle Eph declared that he wasn't a man to deal with thieves. He was going to develop his oil field on his own and keep the profits himself instead of letting them flow into Rockefeller britches.

Unfortunately, about the time he and Aunt Muffie moved into their new house, Uncle Eph's second well came in dry. So did the third. He went back to Standard Oil, but before he could strike a deal his first well went dry too. Pa said poor Eph's promising new oil field petered out quicker'n a mule could snatch a mouthful of hay, leaving him with nothing but three dry holes and a pocketful of debt.

He and Aunt Muffie got to live in the new house only a short time. By the time his creditors were through with him, he wouldn't have been able to keep food on his table if my parents hadn't sent him a few dollars every month.

2.

AROUND THE KITCHEN TABLE, over a supper of scrambled eggs and bacon, Uncle Eph spelled out for us the opportunity he had spotted. Mr. Smart dropped in a "yep" or a "just the way it were" now and again without, however, adding much content to the flow of conversation.

What Uncle Eph professed to see in the Indian ponies was nothing less than a chance to bring back prosperity, not just to himself but to all Texas. Those ponies would remind Texans that they were descendants of pioneers who tamed the West on horseback. The consequent resurgence of pride would do what Franklin Roosevelt and his New Deal had been unable to do, even well into a second term: Restore confidence and make the economy hum.

Things would open up once Texans began thinking free and big again like their granddaddies, Uncle Eph said, instead of dragging around as though the overdue bills and mortgages they carried on their backs were made of solid lead. Men would go back to work. They'd have dollars in their pockets and smiles on their faces. Women would sing and children frolic. The Dust Bowl would be stopped in its tracks. And all because of those little old Indian ponies my father had told him about.

Pa poured himself a cup of coffee.

"Eph, you mind running through that again, a little slower? I bounced off your train of thought along about Lubbock and haven't caught up yet. How in hell is a bunch of broken-down horses going to do all that? Or any of it?"

"Will, just think on it a minute," Uncle Eph said. "What made Texas great? The horse. We all grew up on horseback, Will, me and you too. We was thinking big, doing big things, living well, making big money, getting rich.

"It was when we give up our horses that everything began to get all pinched-like. Little old houses with leaky roofs and cardboard in the windows in place of glass. Little old cars breaking down before they was even paid for. Little old tractors stinking up the countryside, and them breaking down too. No wonder people got to feeling hard up and lost their dreams. They just quit, was what they done—just hunkered down and let them eastern bankers and Rockefellers roll over 'em without no effort to fight back. Will, take my word for it. You just give a Texan a horse again and—"

"Eph," Pa said, "I know you and Mary were born on that ranch, but seems to me your daddy lost the place years before a car or tractor came onto it. As for me, my poor father didn't have a single horse, just a couple of mean old mules. I grew up following the wrong end of a mule down one furrow and then the next, hoping for not much more from the critter than to keep out of the way of its teeth and heels. So tell me how in God's name do you expect a bunch of Indian ponies—"

"You're not seeing it, Will, you're just not seeing it."

Mr. Smart, still wearing his straw hat as he shoveled eggs into his face, nodded his head vigorously. "Yep," he said. "Yep. Just the way it were."

It wasn't clear to me whose version of Texas's past and

probable future Mr. Smart had endorsed, but Uncle Eph backed away from the big picture and began to sketch in details, speaking slowly as though to mental defectives, doggedly trying to make my father and me understand exactly what he had in mind. His plan was to buy those Indian ponies, or at least the better ones among them, feed them up and ship them down to Texas, where he predicted he would find a vast market for them as saddle horses for children. He was going to start with Fort Worth, it being a place that had some money and still thought of itself as a cow town. As soon as Uncle Eph ran a few ads in the papers, every little cowboy and cowgirl in Fort Worth—hell, in Texas—would be clamoring for an Indian pony of his or her own.

And the parents? Well, said Uncle Eph, he knew Texas parents about as well as anybody could, being one himself, though his and Muffie's kids were all grown and gone by now. Take his word for it, Uncle Eph said, or ask Muffie, whichever we wanted, but Texas parents would leap at the chance to restore their children to honest-to-God Texashood by putting them on horseback.

"Will," he said, "all you got to do is remind them folks that despite all their troubles they are by God *Texans* and it's time they get off their knees and start acting like it. You do that and the lines of people wanting to plunk down their money for these here Indian ponies is going to stretch from Fort Worth to Dallas."

Before Uncle Eph had shoveled down the last of his eggs, his pony fever had flared to such heights that he began worrying about inadequate supplies. He sounded my father out about the chances of more horse sales being held after this first round of auctions was over. Was there any way, he wondered, for him and Mr. Smart to get in ahead of the crowd with a bid for ponies to be offered at those future sales no one but Uncle Eph had started to think about yet? Pa said he doubted it. In any case, he said, if Uncle Eph came up with a way to collude with other problematical bidders at those as yet unscheduled and unplanned auctions, he certainly didn't want to hear about it.

Next Uncle Eph pondered the possibility of hooking up with a harness maker. Every one of those ponies was going to require furnishings. Uncle Eph couldn't see why, as the benefactor who first spotted the new need for ponies and started Texas back on the road to prosperity, he shouldn't get a little something out of the saddle and bridle business that was bound to spring up in his wake all across the state.

About the time I would normally have been heading for bed, Uncle Eph offered to cut my father in on the deal. The amounts mentioned floated through the room like so many balloons, starting at five thousand dollars but rapidly deflating to five hundred dollars or even, because of Pa's special brother-in-lawly status, as little as two hundred and fifty dollars. My father said he was honored, he surely was, to receive such an offer, but his further status as a government official with at least a peripheral responsibility for the success of auctions to be held in the district of which he was the supervisor would unfortunately preclude his joining Uncle Eph in the venture, even if he'd had the money to do so, which he didn't.

He also expressed a few doubts about the economics of the venture, putting his objections gently so as not to offend Uncle Eph. He pointed out that the ponies would be mostly wild and unbroken, of unknown age and dubious physical condition. To the extent possible, the Indians would be allowed to designate which horses should be sold, and it was not in human nature for them to retain old or decrepit animals while sending young and vigorous mounts to market.

Once purchased, the horses would have to be fed and watered and driven long distances to the railroad for shipment to Texas. Uncle Eph would have to recruit and pay a large crew of Navajo cowboys, who would themselves have to be fed and watered at his expense. Stock cars would be needed for the trip to Texas, and my father's understanding was that they would have to be ordered well in advance. Swift and Armour, which wanted the horses primarily for hides and other by-products, already had cars waiting on a Santa Fe siding down near Chambers.

And what about feed and water on the trip to Texas, which might take several days, perhaps even a week or more? Finally, Pa asked, wouldn't somebody have to break those ponies to the saddle somewhere along the line? Surely Eph wasn't thinking of loosing wild broncos on the innocent children of Texas?

Uncle Eph took all this in stride. He regarded the difficulties my father pointed out as mere pebbles in the path of progress. None should be an insuperable obstacle to a man of spirit, certainly not to a true Texan, born and bred. Now and again, however, he pulled a dog-eared notebook out of his hip pocket and jotted down reminders to himself.

"Swift and Armour," he said, making a note. "Cudahy not here?"

"Oh, Cudahy's in it too," Pa said.

"Good," said Uncle Eph. "The more the merrier. I'll get together with them boys and see if we can't work it out so Mr. Smart and me take on the good stock and let them have the rest for their rendering plants. No reason we should get in each other's way, driving up prices."

"Eph, don't tell me about it. That's all I ask. Just don't tell me about it."

"Yep," Mr. Smart said. "That's the way it were."

Having Uncle Eph visit made me think about my mother even more than usual when I went to bed that night. I remembered how she had looked at me sometimes, deep in thoughts I could not fathom, her face still, her eyes on me but seeing something or someone else, beyond touch. It bothered me that she had died before I was old enough to understand what or who it was she saw when she looked at me like that.

3.

MY FATHER HAD BEEN holding meetings for months to explain to the Indians why stock reduction was necessary and how the plan would work.

The final meeting was held soon after Uncle Eph's arrival, at Hosteen Tse's place at the base of Big Mesa, near Greasewood Wash. Hosteen Tse was a great Navajo medicine man and tribal leader who had attended all the earlier stock-reduction meetings. He was very old and as a child had gone on the Long Walk to Fort Sumner, New Mexico, which the Navajos called Hwalte. That is where the Navajos were sent into exile after Colonel Kit Carson and his troops rounded them up in 1863. Thousands of Navajos died at Hwalte before General William Tecumseh Sherman, the Union general who had marched through Georgia, arrived to negotiate a treaty in 1868.

As a medicine man, Hosteen Tse was not only priest, physician, and politician, but tribal historian and archivist as well. He knew not just the ancient chants and rituals, but all there was to know of importance to his family and tribe. Stored in his old brain was everything from clan relationships to all the details of every treaty or agreement signed with

Washington since Sherman met with Barboncito and other Navajo chiefs at Hwalte.

Usually Pa wore khaki wash pants, a dress shirt buttoned to the throat, and no tie. Hot as it was, however, for this last meeting before the first horse auction he put on his good blue suit and a tie, along with a low-crowned grey Stetson he said was just a five-gallon size. I polished his good black shoes, which were made of kangaroo hide and came from the Monkey Ward catalog. He wore them only on the most special occasions.

We left for Big Mesa early in the morning because there was no proper road, only a wagon trail, leading to Hosteen Tse's hogans, and the going was slow. Pa drove his official car, a green Ford pickup truck with blue and white U.S. Indian Service license plates. Hosteen Begay, a Navajo assistant at Klinchee who was the official interpreter, rode with him. I went with Uncle Eph and Mr. Smart in the station wagon.

We got to Big Mesa a little before noon. Hosteen Tse had a large family encompassing several generations. A dozen or so log and mud hogans were scattered along the slope of Big Mesa's rocky base, along with open-sided summer shelters roofed with sagebrush and dried tumbleweeds. A little way off, half hidden, stood three small sweat houses, which served both practical and ceremonial purposes. Every so often, winter or summer, Hosteen Tse and his family heated the sweat houses with hot stones and crawled inside one or two at a time for as long as they could stand the heat. Then they piled out to cleanse themselves with sand and their own sweat, while chanting sacred songs of purification.

Ordinarily, few people would have been at Big Mesa because most Navajos had moved their flocks up into the Chuska Mountains for summer grazing. Word of the meeting had traveled over the reservation like drifting tumbleweeds, however, and for days Indians had been converging on Big Mesa. Wagons were drawn up all around the hogans when we arrived. Each visiting family had its own campfire, with a blackened tin can of coffee sitting in the hot coals. Most of the wagon teams were in a brush corral set up for the occasion, but a bunch of saddle horses dozed in the hot sun with heads drooping, reins looped over their necks or trailing in the dust. Women sat on the ground in the sparse shade of the wagons and shelters, spinning wool and tending the children who played around them. No men were in sight.

We sat for a few minutes, sweating in the hot vehicles. Then Pa got out and brushed dust off his suit coat. He and Hosteen Begay leaned against the pickup's front fenders, waiting for the men to appear. Uncle Eph, Mr. Smart and I stayed back out of the way, standing in a thin slice of midday shade beside a big boulder.

Uncle Eph worried about the size of the gathering.

"These folks look like trouble to me," he said. "Where you reckon the bucks is?"

"The old men are in the big hogan," I said, "and the rest are just staying out of sight until Hosteen Tse decides it's time to start." I had been to a lot of these meetings by then.

After a while young Indian men began drifting out from behind the hogans. They stood in a silent semicircle twenty feet or so from the pickup, legs astraddle and hands in the back pockets of their Levis. Ten-gallon hats topped angry faces, and spurs jangled as the men scraped boot toes in the dust. More men came out from inside the hogans until there were thirty or so.

Finally the elders emerged. They had come from all over the reservation, not just Pa's district, for this meeting. Hosteen Tse was the last to appear. He was hatless. His white hair was drawn back from his wrinkled old face and held in place by a dark blue bandanna, neatly rolled and wrapped around his head. He wore loose white trousers like pajama bottoms and a blue velveteen blouse cinched at the waist with a silver belt. On a chain around his neck hung a medal he had received when he and other Navajo leaders went to Washington decades earlier to meet with President McKinley. Over the years the medal had turned green.

My father did not usually smoke, but he passed around cigarettes. Each of the men took one and lit up, my father too. They smoked in silence, no one looking at anyone else. To stare directly at another person was considered rude, an act of disrespect and hostility.

As the senior Navajo present, it was up to Hosteen Tse to signal the start of the meeting. After the last cigarette was ground out underfoot, he greeted my father, calling him Mr. Tall Man American. "*Yahehteh*, Hosteen Nez Belihkahnah."

"*Yahehteh*, Hosteen Tse," Pa replied. He lifted his hat to the old man. His hair, turning gray since my mother died, was wet with sweat and plastered to his skull.

My father had been through his speech so many times that Hosteen Begay could have recited it by rote—Hosteen Tse too, most likely—but for form's sake Pa had to speak before Hosteen Begay could translate. The questions and protests that followed were familiar too, dealing mostly with charges of favoritism. For example, why were families at Klinchee being allowed to keep more horses than Big Mesa families? My father knew that was not true, but it would have been insulting for him to say so. "I do not believe that is the case," he said, "but I shall look into it and stop it if it is happening, because that would not be fair."

Hosteen Tse usually said nothing after his opening words. He listened carefully but made no comment. At this last meeting before the start of the auctions, however, he made a speech when everyone else was done talking. He spoke in short bursts. Between bursts, Hosteen Begay translated, keeping his eyes respectfully on the ground at the old man's feet.

"When I was a little child," said Hosteen Tse, "my people could fight no longer and Kit Carson took us to Hwalte and kept us there. It was a jail without bars where soldiers guarded us. Times were hard and we were poor. We had no sheep, no crops. We ran out of wood for our fires. Many people died in the cold. When they tried to go home soldiers caught them and marched them back to Hwalte, pointing guns at them but giving them no food. Then General Sherman came and promised to let us return to our homes if we promised to quit fighting and live in peace. This we agreed to do in return for sheep and schools and hospitals.

"We made promises and kept them. You made promises and did not keep them. Where are the schools for every thirty students? The teachers? The hospitals? The blacksmith shops, carpenter shops, the men who would teach us to farm? Many times have we gone to Washington to ask why you do not keep your promises. All you give us is more promises—and this."

He held up the corroded medal he wore around his neck, the medal given him by President McKinley. He waved it back and forth in front of his face.

He was silent for a long time before he went on. "We have done what we must do to live, and now you tell us we cannot keep our sheep and our horses. How are we to live when you take away our sheep and our horses? Are we to live on the promises you do not keep?"

He stopped again, waiting. My father had no answer. I had heard him say many times pretty much what Hosteen Tse had just said, but he could not say it here, not before these people for whom he was not just Will Parker, a man entitled to speak his own mind, but Hosteen Nez Belihkahnah, official representative of the U.S. Government.

Hosteen Tse looked him in the eye and spat in the dust at his feet.

That evening when we were home and talking over the day, Uncle Eph said, "Will, you hadn't ought to let that shifty-eyed old heathen spit at you like that."

"I swear, Eph," Pa said, "there's times I can't tell you from a fool."

Mr. Smart said, "Yep, that's the way it were."

4.

WE COULD SEE the dust rising miles off as Navajo cowboys drove horses to auction in bunches that grew into herds. By the day of the first sale, hundreds of horses milled in temporary corrals of brush and logs on the sagebrush flats near Klinchee.

Indian families came from all over the reservation to watch the sale, and the government put on a feed. Mrs. Tsinnijinni, the school cook, fixed beans and salt pork in washtubs and boiled Arbuckle's coffee in milk cans, which Hosteen Begay and my father helped lift on and off the stove. I opened gallon tins of stewed tomatoes and peanut butter from the school warehouse. Navajo men took charge of roasting whole sheep over open fires they built in the schoolyard, while women made bread. They tossed the dough from hand to hand to lighten it with air and then dropped it into pans of boiling mutton fat. Soon there were washtubs full of fried bread for the noon feast.

The auctioneer had been brought in from Albuquerque. He put up a big tent near the corrals and rolled up the sides to let the air through. Then he backed a flatbed truck into the tent for a platform. Plank tables and benches were set up on the truck for the auctioneer and the government officials, my father among them, who were to oversee the sale.

Before the auction began, the cowboys sorted the horses into lots of ten, each lot in a separate, numbered pen. I tagged along after Uncle Eph and Mr. Smart as they circulated among the buyers from big slaughter houses who were examining the horses and deciding how high to bid on each lot. The buyers were mostly Texans like Uncle Eph, but between their cowboy boots and broad-brimmed hats they wore business suits with dress shirts and ties. They all knew one another and joked and laughed, falling silent as we came up. It was clear that they regarded Uncle Eph, fellow Texan or not, as a rank outsider, but he acted as though the buyers were as glad to meet him and Mr. Smart as he said he was to meet them.

Each time Uncle Eph introduced himself, he commented that he had never encountered a sorrier display of horseflesh. According to him, out of all the hundreds of horses in the pens, not more than a handful deserved to be called Indian ponies, suitable for young Texans to ride. The rest of the puny critters were good for nothing but dog food, and the buyers' companies were doing a real service by being willing to take the poor brutes off the Indians' hands. It was too bad, though, Uncle Eph said, that the prices everyone would have to pay were likely to be unjustly high. He and Mr. Smart would be compelled to bid on damned near every lot, seeking that one animal or two per lot they might be justified in taking to Texas as a child's mount. A pity.

The buyers stood around like Navajos, keeping their eyes on some distant point as Uncle Eph talked, and they spoke in monosyllables if at all. But more was going on than I caught on to, because after a while the other buyers joined Uncle Eph and Mr. Smart in approaching the auction officials to seek a change of procedure. Uncle Eph was the spokesman for the group, proposing that the better horses be pulled out and auctioned in separate lots. This would not lower the value of the lots destined for the dog-food factories and rendering plants, he argued, but would mean higher prices—deservedly higher, Uncle Eph said—for the more valuable animals.

Pa removed himself from the discussion between the buyers and the officials. He took me over to the trading post to buy a bottle of soda pop.

"Damn these horses," he said. "I wish I'd never told Eph about them. He's going to have us all in jail."

By the time we got back to the tent, cowboys were sorting out the ponies pointed out by Mr. Smart and forming them into new lots. The cowboys weren't too careful in their work and some shaky old nags got included with the good horses. Nevertheless, Uncle Eph was pleased with the way things had turned out in his dealings with the other buyers.

"Most men is tight as Dick's hatband," he said, "but they'll listen to reason when it don't cost them nothing."

After the noontime feasting was over, the auction started and moved along rapidly. Each lot took only a few minutes to dispose of and each drew about the same price, a dollar or two per animal. The buyers took turns making the winning bid on each lot. It went alphabetically: Armour, Cudahy, Swift, Wilson, with other buyers fitting in according to the initial letter of their companies' names. The auctioneer joked about this happenstance, as he called it, but my father and the other government officials were not amused. They called a halt to the sale while my father warned the buyers that any question of collusion would be referred to the proper authorities. The pattern became a little more intricate when the sale resumed, but the bidding continued perfunctory and the corporate buyers still took turns being the successful bidder.

The lots made up of better horses were sold last. Up to then, Uncle Eph and Mr. Smart had been standing over at one side of the tent with me. They watched but did not say anything. Now they moved down front.

The auctioneer started the bidding at about double the price the other lots had gone for. Uncle Eph lifted his hat and resettled it on his head, signaling a bid. Then he gazed up at the top of the tent as though he'd done his all and had no further interest in the proceedings.

The auctioneer went through his spiel asking for a higher bid and was calling out, "Going, going..." when he got the new bid he had asked for. It came from the Swift man. Uncle Eph looked pained, but he lifted his hat again. Then more bidders got into it. Uncle Eph ultimately bought that lot and the others he wanted, but he wound up paying many times what he had counted on.

He felt he had been double-crossed by the other buyers but blamed himself for being taken in.

"I shoulda knowed better than trust a company man," he said. "One thing I learned from Standard Oil is that the only snake lower'n a corporation is the son of a sea cook who'll work for one."

5.

I HOPED TO GET a pony for myself from among the horses Uncle Eph bought. He argued on my behalf, even offering to give me one free.

"Will, you just ain't raising this boy like a Texas boy ought to be raised," Uncle Eph said. "I aim to let him have his pick of the litter."

Pa put his foot down and would not budge. He pointed out that any time he or I wanted to ride we had only to go up to the trading post and hire a horse, already saddled and bridled, for maybe a quarter a day from one of the Navajo men who spent their time squatting in the shade while their mounts trailed reins in the dust. If we bought a horse, we'd have not only its care and feeding to deal with, but also the problem of a place to keep it. There was no corral or stable at Klinchee Day School, and no provision in the government's planning for any. And with him having to drive from school to school most days, making sure everything in his district was running smoothly, and with me generally going along, doing my lessons there beside him in the front of his pickup truck, we had no time to spare for a horse.

To make up for denying me a pony, Pa agreed to let me go to Texas for two weeks while Uncle Eph sold the Indian horses. The night before we were to leave Pa came to my room to tuck me in. He gave me a leather billfold—my first real wallet. There were three new ten-dollar bills in it.

"I'm going to miss you, son," he said, hugging me.

"Yessir," I said. Excited as I was about getting to go with Uncle Eph, I felt a little like crying.

"The money in that billfold ought to be more than enough to live on and buy your bus ticket home."

"Yessir."

"I've got a new belt for you, too," he said, "and there's something special about this belt. It's got a secret compartment in it, and I've hidden two more ten-dollar bills in there for you."

He showed me the secret compartment and the ten-dollar bills. I had never dreamed of having so much money.

"Now, Davey, this is important."

"Yessir."

"I don't want you to tell anybody—not anybody at all—about this hidden money."

"Yessir."

"And I mean Uncle Eph too."

"Sir?"

"I mean you are not to tell Uncle Eph about the twenty dollars in your belt. If things get tight and all the money in the billfold is gone and Uncle Eph says, 'Davey, don't you have any more money?' I want you to say, 'Nosir.'"

I could hardly believe my ears.

He read my mind. "I'm telling you to lie if you have to, Davey. I don't like doing it but it's necessary, take my word for it. You can give Uncle Eph every other cent you've got, but I want you to keep this money so if things don't go the way you think they should you can walk away and get to a bus station and buy a ticket home. The one thing you are not to do is give this money to Uncle Eph or even admit you've got it. I want you to promise me that."

I promised.

"And if things get beyond you, ask Mr. Smart for help. He strikes me as a sensible man, despite getting mixed up in this bird-brained scheme of Eph's."

6.

WE ALL WENT to the railroad to help load the horses into stock cars. My father drove our old Dodge, riding alone. I settled down in the back seat of the Ford station wagon, ready for the trip to Texas, with Uncle Eph driving and Mr. Smart dozing beside him. From Klinchee to Chambers, where the loading pens were, the carcasses of dead horses littered the desert, their bloated bellies ripped open by coyotes and buzzards. Some of the animals that had died on the long run to the railroad were Uncle Eph's. He damned the government for requiring the herds to be moved off the reservation too fast, without sufficient time for rest and grazing.

"A horse has got to graze," Uncle Eph said. "Grazing to a horse is like me putting my feet up at the end of a hard day and maybe taking a little nip."

"That's the way it were," Mr. Sharp said.

The stock cars were supposed to be waiting on the siding so there'd be plenty of time to load before the midnight freight stopped to pick them up, but when we got to Chambers we found nothing on the siding but bare track. It was almost dark before a coal-burning switch engine arrived, pushing the empty cars ahead of it.

As soon as the engine chugged up, whistling and spilling steam, the horses spooked. They began milling in the log corrals and kept milling. By the time it was full dark, Uncle Eph's Navajo cowboys had not been able to prod a single horse into the loading chute and over the plank bridge into a stock car.

To cut the darkness enough for the cowboys to see a little bit of what they were doing, Uncle Eph and Pa aimed their car lights at the chute through the cracks between the logs. We could see the horses circling in the corrals, wild-eyed, hooves pounding, as alternate stripes of light and dark played over their backs. They looked like rampaging zebras. The cowboys rushed them, pushed them, roped them, whipped them. Nothing worked. Every time a pony neared the open chute it whirled away, refusing to go in.

Uncle Eph was getting desperate.

"Listen, fellas," he said, "that train's gonna be here before you know it and these horses has got to go out on it. It's time you quit fooling around and got down to business."

"No savvy," the cowboys said.

"Where the hell's the foreman?"

One of the cowboys grunted and stuck out his lower lip in a quick gesture, pointing toward the railroad cars.

"He says the foreman's over there," I told Uncle Eph.

We found the foreman asleep on the track under one of the cars. Uncle Eph pulled him out and shook him.

"Drunk," he said. "I should've knowed."

He hauled the man off the tracks and stretched him out in the ditch to sleep it off We went back to the loading chute.

"I don't know how in hell we're going to get them damned horses to climb in them cars," Uncle Eph said. He took off his hat and wiped his sweaty forehead with his arm.

"Blindfold 'em," Mr. Smart said.

Uncle Eph looked at him like he was seeing Jesus on the water.

"Of course," Uncle Eph said. "Mr. Smart, you done lived up to your name again."

He ran to the station wagon and came back with a half dozen shirts. But when he tried to explain what he wanted, the cowboys stared at him blankly. He tried it again, louder this time.

"It doesn't do any good to turn up the volume," Pa said. "Let me try." He spoke a few words in Navajo, pantomiming as he went.

The cowboys started wrapping shirts around horses' heads. One after another, the blindfolded and suddenly docile creatures marched into the chutes.

"Lucky thing you know the lingo," Uncle Eph said, "or we'd been here all night and missed the damned train."

"The men knew what you wanted done," Pa said. "They just didn't care for the way you told them to do it."

The last of the ponies entered the cars as the freight whistled in the distance. Uncle Eph paid off the cowboys and we stood by the tracks to watch the train head for Texas.

"Let's get going," Uncle Eph said. "I want to make Tucumcari by morning."

I hopped in the back end of the station wagon.

"Remember your promise, Davey," Pa yelled after me.

"I will," I yelled back. I waved out the back window as long as I could see him standing in the lights of the Dodge.

"What's the promise?" Uncle Eph asked, looking over his shoulder at me. "Be a good boy and all that?"

"Yessir," I said.

"I ain't worried about that. You just do what I tell you and do it when I tell you to and we'll get along just fine."

"Yessir."

"And the first thing I'm telling you to do is stretch out back there and go to sleep."

It seemed like only a few minutes before the sun was in my eyes. The car was stopped and when I sat up there was no one in the front seat. For a moment I was scared. I looked around and saw Uncle Eph coming out the door of a roadside cafe picking his teeth and carrying a bottle of Nehi Orange soda pop and a paper sack. Mr. Smart was heading into a Chick Sales behind the cafe.

"You all right, boy?" Uncle Eph said. He looked tired. His eyes were bloodshot and he hadn't shaved.

"Yessir," I said.

After Mr. Smart came out, I went to use the Chick Sales. It was a three-holer with no toilet paper, just a torn up Wards catalog, and the smell was awful. I got out as fast as I could. I looked around for a place to wash my hands, but there wasn't any.

Uncle Eph was already at the wheel with Mr. Smart beside him.

"Load up, boy," Uncle Eph said. "We gotta move out."

I got in the back seat and he handed me the Nehi Orange and the paper sack he had brought out of the cafe. There was a greasy hamburger in the sack, along with a piece of crumbly chocolate cake wrapped in a napkin.

"Where are we?" I asked, chewing on the hamburger

Uncle Eph was driving fast. The car's shadow raced alongside us, climbing up and down the ditch bank, whipping over sagebrush. The road curved and we drove straight into the sun. It was still only a little above the horizon.

"Past Tucumcari," Uncle Eph said, shielding his eyes with his hand, "heading to Amarillo. We're going to have our first sale there, the Lord willing, and we gotta move fast to get things organized. Got to get the sales yard lined up, an auctioneer, ads in the paper, posters out, all that kind of thing."

"I thought you said Fort Worth was first."

"Feeding them animals is expensive and moving them is more so," Uncle Eph said, "and Amarillo is a hell of a lot closer than Fort Worth."

Mr. Smart had his head thrown back and his face covered by his hat. I thought he was asleep.

"That's the way it were," he said.

7.

UNCLE EPH PULLED into a tourist court on the edge of Amarillo. "Turth's Cabins," the sign said. "$1 a night."

Uncle Eph went inside. Through the window I saw him hug a big woman with bright red hair. She looked out at the car and waved. I waved back and after a moment Uncle Eph came out with a key in his hand.

"Old friends," Uncle Eph said.

We drove down a dusty lane between two rows of unpainted cabin. In front of No. 12 Uncle Eph stopped. Inside were two double beds and a cot, along with a coal range, an empty scuttle, and a washstand with a bucket and tin basin. Over the washstand hung a calendar put out by a local undertaker. The picture on the calendar was called *The End of the Trail*. It showed an Indian warrior slumping on the back of a horse that looked near as dead as some of those we'd seen on the drive to the railroad. There were no sheets or blankets on the beds. The mattresses were stained and dirty. So was the cot.

"Toilet's across the way," Uncle Eph said. He took off his boots and stretched out on one of the beds. "Boy, while I take me a nap you go out and find a store. Buy some coffee, bread, and sliced ham. Mustard. Cheese if they got it. Milk if you want it."

I waited for him to give me some money. He closed his eyes. I looked at Mr. Smart, but he was sitting on the edge of the other bed taking off his shoes.

"What you waiting for, boy?" Uncle Eph said.

I went out and wandered around for a while. We were in a part of town without sidewalks. Mostly there were used car lots, hamburger joints, and service stations, but one of the service stations turned out to be a general store too. I got the stuff Uncle Eph asked for, along with a couple of bottles of Nehi Orange instead of milk. I spent more than a dollar. When I got back to the cabin, Uncle Eph and Mr. Smart were asleep.

Waiting for them to wake up, I sat on the front steps. It was hot, with no air moving. I could hear the whine of tires from cars traveling fast on the highway past Turth's Cabins. I was feeling pretty lonely. My trip with Uncle Eph was not turning out as I had thought it would, and he seemed like a different person when my father wasn't around.

I did not care for Turth's Cabins. I was not used to sleeping on dirty mattresses without sheets, and the people I saw coming in and out of the other cabins did not look like people I wanted to know. The men were unshaven and shaggy haired. They wore dirty overalls and ripped shirts. Their teeth were yellow and broken, or missing. The women were of two kinds—some with uncombed hair and no makeup, slumping around in dirty house dresses, and others with marcelled hair and layers of rouge on their faces, strutting by in tight skirts and high heels.

I saw only one person near my age, a girl dressed in bright pink pajamas, not the kind you sleep in but the billowy sort women used to wear to look like movie stars. She shot one glance at me as she walked past but did not say anything. She was dark and had glossy black hair flowing down her back to her waist. She looked like she might have Indian blood. I thought she was as pretty a girl as I'd ever seen.

Nobody else paid attention to me sitting there on the stoop of No. 12. I went in and got one of the bottles of Nehi Orange.

Uncle Eph sat up. He rubbed the back of his hand over his mouth.

"What time is it, boy?"

"I don't know, sir."

"Is it late?"

"Nosir."

He swung his feet onto the floor and pulled on his boots. He dug through a suitcase, brought out a set of fresh clothes, and went over to the washroom. When he came back he was shaved and his hair was wet and combed. He was dressed in tan pants and a fancy three-toned green shirt.

"Come shine me up, boy," he said. He sat on the edge of the bed and handed me a can of polish and a cloth.

I got down in front of him and polished his boots. When I finished he tousled my hair.

"Now let's eat, boy."

While Mr. Smart continued to snore on his bed, Uncle Eph slapped ham and cheese between a couple of slices of bread coated with mustard. He opened the other bottle of Nehi Orange and started eating.

I made myself a sandwich too. I was still eating when Uncle Eph finished.

"Well, let's go," he said. He stood up and smoothed his pants over his thighs.

"What about Mr. Smart?"

"Don't you worry about Mr. Smart. Ain't much for him to do till the horses get here."

We got in the station wagon and drove to a print shop.

Uncle Eph left me in the car while he went in. When he came back he was chuckling.

"If you was a few years older, boy, I could tell you a hell of a funny story," he said.

From the print shop we went to an auctioneer's office and then to the Potter County Fairgrounds, where Uncle Eph walked around with the auctioneer to look over the sales yard. Most of the time I was sitting in the car, not knowing what Uncle Eph was up to and feeling like I was getting fried through in the heat. By the end of the afternoon, though, Uncle Eph was more like his old self.

"Boy," he said, "you're going to see you a real Texas-size blowout—big stripey tents, refreshment stands, even got us a band and a parade all set up. Now all we got left to do is get them ads in the paper and posters up."

We drove back to the print shop and he sent me inside to pick up the posters. There were a lot of them, bearing big red letters on yellow cardboard:

Put Texas Back
On Horseback

BIG SALE!!
A Rare Chance to Own
GERONIMO'S PONIES!!!
Tough   *Spirited*
TAME!!
Place:_____
Time:_____
COME ONE COME ALL
Bring the family!
Refreshments!!!

The printer help me carry the posters out to the station wagon and slide them into the back end.

"That'll be three bucks," the printer said.

Uncle Eph sat up behind the wheel and dug in his pocket.

"Damn," he said. "I must of left my billfold back to the cabin. Davey, you got any money on you?"

"Yessir," I said.

"You go ahead and pay him then."

"Yessir."

I gave the printer the money. He patted me on the head as he tucked the bills into a pocket of his inky apron.

"Uncle Eph," I said, "Geronimo wasn't a Navajo. He was an Apache."

"Hell, boy, you think I don't know that? But these folks here don't know it and wouldn't care if they did. When you say Geronimo they think Injun—mean Injun—and that's what gets their attention. These ain't ordinary, run-of-the-reservation, any old Indian's ponies, boy. These here is ponies they can brag on, *Geronimo's* ponies, and you keep that in mind."

We drove to the newspaper office and radio station, where Uncle Eph arranged to run ads on credit, and then we went back to Turth's Cabins. Mr. Smart was up and gone. Uncle Eph said he was down at the railroad. The Indian ponies were due in most any time. Uncle Eph got a big black crayon and filled in the time-and-place blanks on the posters. Then we drove around town nailing them on telephone poles at prominent corners and standing them in the windows of stores and service stations.

Uncle Eph knew just where to put the posters to get the most attention. "I know Amarillo like the back of my hand," he told me, and he did. Every place we went he knew someone.

Just before we quit and headed home to Turth's Cabins, he went into a store to drop off one last poster and came out with some beer and a chunk of ice. He seemed to have found his billfold, or maybe the storekeeper extended credit, because he didn't ask me to pay for the beer.

Back at the cabin he put the beer bottles in a bucket and packed it full of ice. He took off his boots and stretched out on the bed.

"Well, Davey," he said, sitting up to take a swig of beer, "we done a good day's work."

"Yessir."

"You fix you a ham sandwich for supper, if you want, or you can go out and buy you a hamburger if you'd rather. I got me a business meeting tonight and I don't expect I'll be back much afore morning. You know about business meetings, Davey?"

"Yessir." I didn't know for sure what he was telling me, but I guessed the answer he wanted.

He left, taking the bucket of ice and beer with him. I ate a ham sandwich and sat on the stoop, batting mosquitoes off my neck and arms.

The girl in pink pajamas came by. She started to walk past and then veered toward me.

"What's your name?" she asked. "I'm Clotie."

"Davey," I said.

"You want to fuck?"

I felt myself turning red. She was staring hard at me, and I looked away. I didn't know what to say. I knew whatever I said would be wrong.

"I'd let you for four bits."

"I guess not."

"Two bits?"

"No."

She shrugged. "I told him you wouldn't," she said. I thought she sounded relieved.

"Told who?"

"Your old man."

"Uncle Eph? He's not my father."

"That's not what he said."

"When did he say that?"

"Just now. He's got my ma for all night over in No. 7, and he told me to ask you could I sleep with you."

"Well, you can't," I said. "Not with me."

"I don't have no place to sleep then. He give me a dime to stay out of the way, you see."

"There's a cot. You could have that."

"All right."

It grew dark and the mosquitoes got bad. We went in. She brought out a pack of cards and we played a few hands of blackjack, but it wasn't much fun.

We went to bed, her on the cot and me on Uncle Eph's mattress.

In a little while I heard her crying, so softly it was like breathing. I didn't know what to do. She kept on crying and finally I said, "What's wrong? Did I do something wrong?"

"I didn't want to say that to you," she said.

"That's all right," I said. "I didn't think you did."

"And I wouldn't done it if'n you'd said yes."

"I knew that," I said, though I couldn't help wondering if that was true and what it would have been like.

When I woke up the next morning, Uncle Eph was flat on his back beside me, one arm thrown across my chest. Mr. Smart snored noisily in the other bed. Clotie was gone.

My new billfold was gone too, with all the money in it.

Uncle Eph laughed. "You better go ask your little pink sweetheart about that," he said.

He took Mr. Smart and me downtown to a fancy hotel restaurant with tablecloths and bought breakfast. He paid with a new ten-dollar bill.

8.

UNCLE EPH OUTFITTED me at J.C. Penney so I could ride in the parade before the sale. He bought me cowboy boots, a big white hat, and a red kerchief to wrap around my neck. When he asked if had any money, I did like Pa told me and said no. Uncle Eph said that was all right, he'd pay for my clothes and Pa could reimburse him later.

I was to ride one of the tame ponies Mr. Smart had found among the horses delivered by the Santa Fe. "About a dozen of them animals is saddle-broke enough," Mr. Smart said, "to be rode by timid girls and pregnant mammas."

Saturday was a hot day, up around a hundred before noon. Uncle Eph put me bareback on a skinny old bay with ribs that stuck out like barrel staves.

He handed me one end of a rope that was looped around the necks of three other tame horses.

"Now all you got to do, boy, is stay on that horse," he said. "I want you to go riding along with a big grin on your face like there ain't nothing in this world you'd rather be doing than sitting on that there pony holding the rope to them other ponies, riding along after the band, having yourself a good time."

"Will the other horses be in the parade?" I asked. "The wild ones?"

"Don't worry about them," he said. "When we need 'em, Mr. Smart'll have 'em ready."

The band was late turning up. I'd been sitting on the horse in the hot sun so long that its sweat and mine had drenched my pants. I was sure everyone would think I'd wet myself.

The bandleader wanted to be paid before the parade. Uncle Eph argued a while before he discovered he'd left his wallet back at the cabin.

"Boy," he yelled, "you sure you don't have no money on you?"

"I'm sure, Uncle Eph," I said. My belt with the hidden ten-dollar bills felt like it was going to pinch me in two.

Uncle Eph threw his arm around the bandleader's shoulders and walked off with him a little way. When they came back, the bandleader had a couple of bills in his hand.

I rode through the streets of Amarillo with the band playing and majorettes twirling batons. Boys ran alongside handing out fliers about the big sale of Geronimo's ponies down at the fairgrounds. What with the posters and the newspaper and radio ads, a lot of people had turned out for the parade in spite of the heat.

I enjoyed the attention we drew, even while I worried whether the poor old pony I was on would keep going long enough to get me to the fairgrounds. Every once in a while the horse would stop and droop its head, like it was taking a quick snooze, and not start up again until I kicked it in the ribs a half-dozen times. On one corner I saw Clotie in her bright pink pajamas. I waved, but she pretended not to know me.

At the fairgrounds Uncle Eph put me in charge of the lemonade stand. He gave me a little sack of whole lemons and a big sack of lemon hulls, which he had found in the alley behind the hotel where we'd had breakfast downtown. He also gave me a sugar dispenser that had been on our table at the hotel, two big glass pitchers, and several tin cups. My instructions were simple—don't squeeze more than two lemons to a pitcher of water and go easy on the sugar. He said half a dozen lemon hulls in the bottom would be ample to give a rich look to the pitcher, not to mention a sharper flavor.

Uncle Eph opened the sale with a rousing speech about the importance of the horse in Texas's history and economy. It was about like the spiel he gave Pa and me when he first arrived at Klinchee to buy ponies, but he worked in some added licks about the character-building advantages of horse ownership for kids. The way Uncle Eph saw it, the care and feeding of a horse would teach boys and girls responsibility, keep them out of pool halls, and pretty much repair any parent-worrying aspects of thought and behavior that the schools and churches weren't getting to. Heads nodded in agreement as he went along, and he got a big hand at the end.

I didn't see much of the day's proceedings after that, but every now and again I'd leave the lemonade stand in charge of Mr. Smart, put a grin on my face, and ride a pony into the auction ring, just to remind the folks what fun a kid could have on horseback. The cowboys drove the wild horses— spirited mounts, the auctioneer called them—into the ring one by one, riderless. Anyone who happened to be nearby and on foot ducked and dodged, trying to look unconcerned about flying hooves and snapping teeth.

By the end of the day most of the tame horses, but not the old bay I'd ridden in the parade, and a number of wild ones had been sold. Uncle Eph made a speech, congratulating the crowd and himself on the success of the auction and predicting an almost immediate return of prosperity and morality now that the horse was coming back to Texas. He invited everyone to stay on for a free band concert and then a barbecue over on the other side of the fairgrounds as soon as the sun went down. The band played *The Eyes of Texas*.

Uncle Eph came by the lemonade stand and grabbed my cashbox.

"Let's go, boy," he said.

"What about the barbecue?"

"What barbecue?"

9.

FROM AMARILLO we drove through the Red River Valley to Owchita, but without the ponies, which were traveling on to Wichita Falls. Owchita was the little town where Uncle Eph lived, not far from the ranch he and my mother grew up on. On the way in we stopped by the graveyard where my mother was buried. She lay at the feet of her mother and father and beside a younger sister who had died in infancy. There was no stone on my mother's grave.

I asked Uncle Eph about it. He snapped his fingers.

"Them damned vandals," he said. "Ain't nothing sacred no more."

"You mean there was a stone there?"

"Sent you a picture of it, didn't I?"

"Yessir," I said. "I guess that's right."

We stayed only a few minutes at the cemetery and then Uncle Eph drove Mr. Smart and me out south of town to a locked gate on the dirt road leading to what had been my grandfather's spread. We leaned against the gate and looked out over an empty expanse, nothing to be seen but summer-browned grass and a couple of steers on the distant horizon. An Englishman owned all this land now, my to stay on for a free band concert and then a barbecue over on the other side of the fairgrounds as soon as the sun went down. The band played *The Eyes of Texas*.

Uncle Eph came by the lemonade stand and grabbed my cashbox.

"Let's go, boy," he said.

"What about the barbecue?"

"What barbecue?"

9.

FROM AMARILLO we drove through the Red River Valley to Owchita, but without the ponies, which were traveling on to Wichita Falls. Owchita was the little town where Uncle Eph lived, not far from the ranch he and my mother grew up on. On the way in we stopped by the graveyard where my mother was buried. She lay at the feet of her mother and father and beside a younger sister who had died in infancy. There was no stone on my mother's grave.

I asked Uncle Eph about it. He snapped his fingers.

"Them damned vandals," he said. "Ain't nothing sacred no more."

"You mean there was a stone there?"

"Sent you a picture of it, didn't I?"

"Yessir," I said. "I guess that's right."

We stayed only a few minutes at the cemetery and then Uncle Eph drove Mr. Smart and me out south of town to a locked gate on the dirt road leading to what had been my grandfather's spread. We leaned against the gate and looked out over an empty expanse, nothing to be seen but summer-browned grass and a couple of steers on the distant horizon. An Englishman owned all this land now, my grandfather's and that of a lot of other small ranchers and homesteaders. No one was allowed on the Englishman's land without permission.

"He was a great man, boy, don't you forget it," Uncle Eph said, taking off his hat and placing it against his chest. He was referring to my grandfather, of course, not the Englishman.

I was angry about the gravestone but didn't know what to do about it. I said, "Pa says when you come right down to it he was just a farmer, like Pa's daddy."

"Will Parker's a goddam liar," Uncle Eph said. "His old man was nothing but a dirt-poor nester with shit on his boots and cotton in his head, but your ma's daddy—my daddy too, your grandpa—he owned all this here land far as you can see. He was a rancher, a man of good family, a Confederate officer in the War Between the States, and a hero besides."

I didn't like him calling my father a liar. I said, "Ma said Grandpa wasn't really an officer. She said he was just a private who gave himself a peacetime promotion after he got out of the Army and married Grandma."

"Your ma didn't always speak of her daddy with the respect he deserved. He was a major in the cavalry of the Confederate States of America, boy, and you better remember that if you want me to have anything to do with you."

"That's the way it were, boy," Mr. Smart said.

At first I wondered what he knew about it, and then I realized he was warning me to drop the subject.

"Yessir," I said.

We went back through town by way of the square. In front of the courthouse stood a statue of a Confederate infantryman with a rifle almost as tall as he. My mother had told me about the statue. Her father wanted a mounted cavalryman, but the horse would have added too much to the cost, so the county commissioners sent off for a Zouave, buying it from a Yankee mail-order house in St. Joe that specialized in Confederate memorials. The soldier's trousers were just as baggy as she'd said they were.

I went over and looked closely at the statue. There were several small dents in the bronze.

"Are those from when Uncle Dunc shot at the bankrobbers?" I asked.

"What do you know about that, boy?" Uncle Eph seemed surprised that I had heard about Uncle Dunc.

"Ma said he was the town marshal but didn't have real good eyes and mistook the statue for a bankrobber."

"Your ma was a real little girl when Dunc got hisself killed," Uncle Eph said, "and I reckon that's why she didn't tell it just right. It was the robbers shot up the statue."

I didn't really believe him, preferring as I did my mother's account and trusting it more, but I listened as Uncle Eph went on.

"Dunc, he was behind the statue taking what cover he could, and it was the robbers out front of it shooting at him that put them pits in it. They was shooting like an army but didn't hit him but once, right through the eye. Over here's where they found him, not a bullet left in his gun. And out there in front was one of the robbers, so full of holes we had to wait six months for him to get well enough to hang."

My mother had told me about the robber being shot, not by Uncle Duncan but by a couple of cowhands who happened to be passing. She told me about the hanging too. The gallows was set up right in the middle of the town square and all the school children were marched over to stand in rows at one side, where they would have a clear sight of the wages of sin. She was only a first-grader, but as the sister of the murderer's victim she was given a place of honor in the front row, so close she could see sweat beading the young man's face as they blindfolded him and put the rope around his neck. The platform was built with open sides so that everyone would be able to watch the hanged man's death struggle. When the trap was sprung she turned her back and closed her eyes. The teacher scolded her there in front of everyone and made her look at the body jumping at the end of the rope.

She was still sobbing and throwing up when Uncle Eph came to carry her home. Later he stopped her other brothers from teasing her for being so tenderhearted.

Uncle Eph took me inside the courthouse to see a dusty glass case of war memorabilia: bits of uniforms and a couple of medals, along with a sword which a printed card said had been carried at the Battle of Vicksburg by Maj. Amos Gower.

"See there?" Uncle Eph said. "A major, like I been telling you."

"Yessir," I said.

On the wall beside the case was a big photograph of Teddy Roosevelt the day he came through Owchita on his way to Indian Territory for hunting.

"That was a day," Uncle Eph said. "There's your grandpa, standing right next to the President on the courthouse steps, and see whose hand Teddy is shaking? Your ma's. He looked at her, Teddy Roosevelt did, and you know what he said? Bully, he said. That's what everybody who ever looked at Mary said, you got to keep that in mind. Wasn't just him. It was anybody—that little old girl was just so pretty and sassy, bully was about the least thing you could say."

I looked closely at the picture, one of the few I had ever seen of my mother as a child and the first I had seen of either of her parents. She had told me about shaking hands with Teddy Roosevelt as a girl, but hadn't mentioned having her picture taken with him. She was about my age in the photograph, perhaps a little older, and I thought she was beautiful as she smiled up at the President. Beside her my grandfather was a towering giant in bib overalls, looming over both her and the President. A big straw hat shaded my grandfather's face. All I could make out was a black beard with a white line that might have been teeth in the middle of it, which suggested he was smiling as Teddy Roosevelt shook his little daughter's hand. I was surprised. My mother had told me my grandfather fought the War to the last day of his life, and yet here he was, caught for all time, smiling at a Yankee President, a Republican at that.

From the courthouse we drove on to Uncle Eph's house. It was an unpainted cottage next door to a second-hand furniture store that Aunt Muffie ran, trying to make ends meet while Uncle Eph was off getting rich.

Aunt Muffie got out of a rocking chair on the porch of the store as we drove up.

"Praise the Lord!" she shouted.

She came out to the car. "You, boy," she said, "I been worrying about your immortal soul. Even wrote to Judge Rutherford—"

"Now, Muffie," Uncle Eph said, trying to grab her for a kiss.

She wrestled out of his arms. "Sure as Jehovah is my Witness, like the good Judge says," she shouted, "I'm finally going to get me a answer. How many tablecloths was there, boy—family, company and show?"

Mr. Smart spoke up. "Looked into it myself, ma'am," he said, "and I can assure you it was six, two and zero."

"Praise the Lord! I just knowed that's the way it were. That no-good little girl didn't do a bit better'n I done, spite of all her airs." She hugged me, kissed Uncle Eph, and shook hands with Mr. Smart.

That evening relatives came by to see Mary's boy. I had

probably met most of them at the funeral, but I didn't really remember any of them. I had been too stricken and confused to take much note of anything or anyone. I couldn't keep the names and relationships straight. My mother had been the youngest of a very big family, and some of her nieces and nephews were years older than she. I was meeting second and third cousins and first cousins twice removed. Everybody but me seemed to know exactly how everyone was related.

Aunt Muffie planted me on a stool in the middle of the front porch, where they could all get a good look at me and debate whether I took after my mother's family, which meant after the blood relatives assembled there, or my father's. They focused on non-Gower things about me—my light hair, spindly build, and long thin face—that must have come from the other side, from my father's side, dividing me from them. Some thought I had the Gower chin, describing it as stubborn-like, but others thought mine was too pointy for a true Gower chin. Everyone agreed, however, that I had the Gower hands. "Lookit the size of them hams," they said, "and him not a man half-growed."

One cousin brought a photograph in a silver frame of Grandpa and Grandma Gower sitting in a swing on the porch of their unpainted ranch house with their nine sons and my mother, the only daughter who lived past infancy. She was a little girl in the photo, standing at her mother's knee, smiling serenely at the camera. Her brothers, already full-grown, stood in a row behind their parents, arms crossed on their chests, black-bearded faces impassive. Grandpa Gower's beard was bigger and blacker than any of the others. It reached halfway down the bib of his overalls. His legs were spread apart as he sat, crowding Grandma, and he gripped his knees with stubby fingers. His hands were huge but the fingers were short and thick. I looked at his hands and then at mine. My fingers were a bit longer and thinner, but I had the ham-like hands of my grandfather, no question about it.

Aunt Muffie had baked cookies and made lemonade—real lemonade, without hulls, sweet with sugar. The men and near-grown boys soon disappeared out toward the garage and cyclone cellar behind the house. I sat on the front porch with the women and children, eating cookies and drinking lemonade, wishing desperately to be somewhere else. We sat for long periods in silence, slapping mosquitoes.

After a while Aunt Muffle looked over at me.

"Lookit him," she said. "He don't look it in all respects, maybe, but he's a Gower, all right, just like his ma, just like all of them, itching to be somewheres else, too good for us ordinary folk."

"No'm," I said. "I'm fine."

"Oh, go on," she said. "Go on out to the garage with the rest of 'em. I'll pray for your everlasting soul but nothing more I can do for you, you being a Gower and all."

So I went out behind the house and made a discovery that perhaps shouldn't have surprised me, but did. Being a Gower—a male Gower, at least—meant being a drinker. My mother had been opposed to alcohol in all its forms, but the Gower men and most of the boys who'd disappeared so quickly from the porch were jammed in the garage with the doors half-closed, sitting on nail kegs and passing bottles back and forth in the dimness. They were laughing and easy, swapping gossip and hoorawing one another.

"Well, lookit who's here," Uncle Ben Gower said. He was my mother's oldest brother, who was already married and a father several times over before she was born. Uncle Eph had told me that Uncle Ben used to be a house builder but was now all stove-up and living on the county, augmenting his income by bootlegging. "Mary's boy. I about concluded you was going to stay up there drinking lemonade with the women."

He offered me his bottle. "No, thank you, Uncle Ben," I said. "My mother wouldn't want me to."

"A wonderful woman, Mary was, I always heard, but Temperance, I suppose," said a drinker who wasn't really a Gower, but married to one. He was a younger man than Uncle Ben, by quite a bit. He was a brakeman on the Fort Worth & Denver and had on his brakeman's cap.

"All the Gower women most generally is Temperance, but Mary weren't always a teetotaler, not in her young days," Uncle Ben said.

He handed me his bottle again. I gagged on the smell just getting it to my lips, but I tipped it up anyway, blocking the neck with my tongue. Enough of the corn whiskey got around my tongue to set me choking.

No one laughed. "Second time's easier," the brakeman said, "but watch out for that third time, that's when the world gets all topsy-turvy."

Mr. Smart was sitting off in one corner. "That's the way it were," he said. I noticed that when a bottle came to him he passed it along without tipping it up.

I crowded my way into the other corner, wedging myself against the splintery boards of the garage wall. It wasn't long before the rest forgot about me and went on talking crops and weather and local politics as pipe smoke and whiskey fumes filled the air.

"I never knowed Mary weren't always Temperance," the brakeman said.

"Oh, Mary was a handful," Uncle Ben said. He laughed and reached for another bottle. "Poor old Pa. She like to been the death of him, that wild little thing, running off with that soldier from Fort Bliss, bringing shame on the family. Time was, wouldn't nobody bet she could get herself straightened out like she done, going back to school and all and finding that sandlapper from over East Texas way to marry her. Can't think of his name all of a sudden. Skinny fella, tall enough but kinda prissy. Schoolteacher."

"Will," somebody said. "Will Parker. Prissy, like you say, but a good provider. This boy's father, Will is."

A bottle came by the corner I was in. As the brakeman said, the second time was easier. I got the swallow down without gagging, though my eyes watered and for a moment I thought everything was going to come right back up, cookies and lemonade and all.

We had always lived away from kin, and there in the garage with the drinking Gowers I felt I understood for the first time what a family is. Around me, sitting on nail kegs or leaning against the wall, drinking cheap whiskey made by one of them, or at least supplied by him, were people who knew all the things about me that I didn't know and maybe wouldn't want to know. Among them they were the Hosteen Tse of the Gower tribe.

And what these men, the Gower drinkers, didn't know, the women on the front porch did. Their collective memories held everything about my past, about people I didn't know who were nevertheless connected with me in important ways. They remembered relatives who had lived and died years ago and events that had occurred long before I was born. The shared fabric of the past would be revealed, or possibly remembered but not revealed, one painful thread at a time as they, the men in the garage and the women on the porch, passed around the liquor or lemonade.

I did not particularly like my insight into the nature of families, nor did I relish having my perceptions of the world and my place in it reordered by the emergence of old truths that to me were new. But I knew there was nothing much I could do about it. For better or worse, I was a Gower and this was my family.

In the course of the evening Uncle Eph tried to sell the others an Indian pony or two, but they weren't buying.

"Last time I was on a horse," Uncle Ben said, "was when we all went after Mary and that soldier of hers. Inside of my legs was rubbed damned near raw. Two more hours in the saddle and I'd a been bleeding into my boots. Pa, now, it didn't bother him. He was a hard-ass. He could climb on the back of a horse and stay there for days, never bother him a bit."

Uncle Eph got another bottle out of a box in the back of the garage, near where I was. One of my first cousins, once or twice removed, Jimmy Junior, I think his name was, was sitting on the box. He had to stand up so Uncle Eph could reach in for the bottle.

"I used to hear y'all cut his balls off," Jimmy Junior Gower said. "That Fort Bliss soldier, I mean."

Uncle Ben laughed. "I reckon you got it near right," he said, "but not just right." His voice was thick. He'd been tipping up the bottle a lot. "What we done was— Well, to go back a little. Mary done disappeared of a sudden and it took awhile to find out where she'd gone and who with. And so then we took out after 'em. They was seven of us still alive then, all but Dunc and Nate, and we all went. Couple of my boys wanted to go along for the sport, but Pa wouldn't have it. It was up to him and us brothers to handle our sister's shame and disgrace, he said, and no need for nobody else to mix in, not even kin. So there we went, Pa out in front, whipping up that old mare of his, riding around the clock, first dust and then rain, riding across the prairie toward what used to be Indian Territory, and him not paying no mind to nothing but the thought of his little fifteen-year-old daughter bouncing along ahead of us in a goddam buckboard with a fornicating private soldier from Fort Bliss whose daddy was said to be running sheep up there in the Territory somewheres. Oh, I tell you, that was hard on Pa, him being not just a Texan but a cowman too, and a major in the Confederate Army when he weren't twenty years old, and here his baby daughter has up and ran off with a good-for-nothing Yankee sheepherder's son who don't even have a stripe on his arm.

"We rode and rode. They had a whole day and night's start on us, and could have got away had that soldier not supposed he'd give us the slip by heading west and then south before turning back north again. So the time comes and we catch 'em. And that little girl, no bigger'n a minute—like all Gower women she was about as tiny as us Gower men is big—that little girl, she stands up to Pa, scared of him though she was.

"She says, Pa, she says, I love him and I'm aiming to marry him. And Pa says, You just bet you're going to marry him, you open-kneed little slut, because you maybe got something of his you can't give back. And we took 'em on into town, forget what town, but couldn't find us a justice of the peace to marry them, Mary and her goddam soldier. And so Pa put her in the buckboard her soldier had drove her off in, put her in the buckboard and tied her down and took her home, with her screaming and raging the whole way. And the rest of us, we—"

"Well," said Uncle Eph, standing up, "that's enough. Time to break this up. Lemonade and cookies back on the porch."

Uncle Ben kept talking but a lot of what he said was lost in the bustle of uncles and cousins by blood and marriage to the second and third remove getting to their feet and taking one last drink. I heard him say, "And when her baby come, it was born dead, buried out there with Ma and Pa like it was theirs, not Mary's, though Ma was near to sixty years old then if she was a day. And now Mary's out there too, all of 'em together."

Uncle Ben shook his head and wiped his eyes.

All my uncles were standing now, five of them—Ben and Jim, Amos, John and Eph, all the Gower boys still living. They seemed to fill the garage, tall men, beardless now and gray but still broad-faced, with heavy shoulders and drinkers' bellies. They blocked what little light there was coming through the half-closed doors of the garage, bulky figures silhouetted against the night sky.

"We don't talk about all that," Uncle Eph said, not to his brothers, of course, but to the rest of us. "We don't talk about none of that at all."

We went back to the porch. The lemonade and cookies were gone and people were leaving. Aunt Muffie was standing just inside the screen door, away from the mosquitoes, her hands folded over her chest and her lips moving, not saying a word to anyone present.

10.

I GOT UP at first light and slipped out of the house before either Aunt Muffie or Uncle Eph was stirring. I walked under a star-littered sky along the dusty road that passed in front of the second-hand furniture store. It wasn't far to the cemetery, not above a mile. The gates weren't open yet, but I crawled over the fence and found the Gower plot where my mother was buried.

There were only two headstones. The big one was for my grandparents. It was of some chalky white stone that had weathered badly. I could barely make out their names and dates. My grandfather had died years before my grandmother and the stone had been put up then, with everything filled in but the date of her death. That blank had never been filled in. I knew the date, however. My grandmother died the day I was born, and my mother had not been able to go home to the funeral.

I wondered if she would have gone had I not come along when I did. I had always supposed she would, but now I was not sure. Had she gone home, wanting to, the date of her mother's death would have been filled in. That much I felt sure of.

—GERONIMO'S PONIES—

The other stone in the plot where my mother was buried was a small slab of polished black marble. Carved on it was nothing but a name: *Nellie*. I stood for a while at the head of my mother's unmarked grave, about where the stone should have been that Uncle Eph took the money for but did not buy. I tried to remember times when she spoke of the sister—her sister—who had died in infancy, but I could not recall that she ever said much more than that there had been such a child. I wished she had told me the truth about her, had told me it was my sister who had been born and died and was buried here. I wished she had at least told me her name.

Somewhere in the distance I heard a cock crowing. Soon a couple of donkeys started talking back and forth.

I thought about my mother, about her being a wild little thing who'd been willing to take a drink as a girl, a handful who had run off with a soldier and had a baby. And I thought about that baby, buried here at the foot of my grandparents' graves, next to my mother. Her mother too. That baby, about whom I had never heard except as being my mother's youngest sister who had died at birth nearly twenty years before I was born, that baby, I knew now, was my sister, half-sister anyway, and my mother had been her mother too. Was she what my mother used to see at those times when I felt she was looking at me and seeing something or someone else? I did not know what to think about that. Or about any of it. I was viewing my mother in a light I had not dreamed of. The picture of her as a handful and a wild thing that Uncle Ben had drawn—was it true? I did not want to believe him, but what he said had been endorsed, or at least not contradicted, by Uncle Eph and her other brothers, who had known her just as well as Uncle Ben.

A wild thing? I thought about that. To me she had always seemed fully formed, a constant in my life from the earliest moment I could remember and mostly always the same. Looking back I could not remember her ever being anything except what I expected her to be—not always predictable, perhaps, but always kind and loving, always reliable, doing what I knew to be the right thing even when what she did was make me stop doing something I wanted to do. I had trouble thinking of her as having had a life without me, before me, which had left her with thoughts and memories—feelings, too—she had not wanted me to know about and had given me no hint of.

I stretched out on the ground between my mother's grave and my sister's and stared at the sky. It was getting bright now and the stars faded away. The sun would pop up any minute. I thought about the photographs I had seen of my mother as a child with her family and as a young girl with my grandfather and Teddy Roosevelt. I wondered why she had not shown those photographs to me—why, in fact she had never shown me a single picture of my grandparents and uncles. In coming after her and tearing her away from the young soldier she had never mentioned to me but must have loved, had they so embittered her that she had not wanted to see them even in a picture, had not wanted me to see them either?

I realized, in thinking back, that what she had told me about growing up were mostly comic tales. All I had learned from her about her family were the jokes, the clownish images—her father in his outlandish farmer's garb picking his teeth with his knife blade at the Sunday dinner table while her hulking brothers debated how many angels could stand on the head of a pin, finally spilling out into the yard to settle the question with their fists. Even the death of Uncle Dunc had seemed more funny than tragic as she told it—the nearsighted marshal banging away at a statue he mistook for a bankrobber while the bankrobber took deadly aim at him.

GERONIMO'S PONIES

The hanging had been uncomic, of course. She wept as she told me about it, about the horror she felt and about the cruel teacher who had forced her to watch a young man's body jerk at the end of a rope until Uncle Eph came to her aid.

More questions flooded my mind. She would have been sixteen when my sister was born and twenty-five when she met my father, ten years before I came along. How had she filled those intervening years? How had a wild little thing turned herself into the teacher whose first job was in a two-room school of which my father was the principal?

She had told me the story of her first job many times and how she managed to get fired, taking my father with her. She was a strong believer in the rights of women and organized a suffragette march in the little East Texas farm town where she met my father. Wearing sunbonnets to shield their faces from the scorn of the hooting populace, she and three other young women marched down the unpaved main street on a Saturday morning when the town was crowded with farm wagons. They brandished placards bearing inflammatory slogans, while dodging horses and wagon wheels and holding their skirts out of the dust and horse droppings.

The farm women they hoped to reach with their message of equal rights turned their faces away as the men spat tobacco juice in the dust. Only my father cheered as my mother and her friends passed by. The school board instantly convened a special meeting, firing her for marching and him for cheering. Neither of them ever got the overdue pay coming to them.

That story was one of my favorites because it presented my parents in the way I liked to think of them—together, doing the right thing regardless of consequences. I remembered riding along at night in the back seat of our old Dodge, watching them in the front seat. My father gripped the wheel with long, slender fingers, driving steadily through darkness into a saucer of light on the road ahead. My mother leaned her head against his shoulder. I could hear her saying something bur could not hear her words or what he responded. They both laughed, looking guiltily over their shoulders at me, not wanting to wake me. I knew messages were going back and forth between them, more messages than words, and I did not know what either the words or the messages were.

My parents were a mystery but I did not care. They were together and I was there in the back seat riding with them into that circle of light.

The sun was up now, rising fast in the sky. I got to my feet and my shadow stretched long over the graves.

I went back to Uncle Eph's house by way of the town square to look again at the bullet-scarred Confederate soldier in front of the courthouse.

I wondered why my grandfather had felt it necessary to promote himself from private to major, and why Uncle Eph wanted to believe in his majority and my mother did not.

She had told me Grandpa Gower was just a boy when the war started, and he had run away from home to volunteer. After the battle of Vicksburg my grandmother, who lived somewhere near Jackson, hid him until they could marry and slip off to Texas. Why it was necessary for him to hide and why my grandmother felt she was the one to do it, my mother did not say and I had never learned. They were not questions I had thought to raise with her, though I had always assumed heroic purposes lay behind Grandpa's need for hiding and Grandma's decision to hide him.

With my new knowledge of the complexity of family histories and my recently acquired awareness of the pain, anger, and grief that lay beneath the cheerful surface of the stories my mother had told me of her childhood, I could no longer assume that whatever it was my grandfather did at

Vicksburg was something I would admire. One more mystery.

I wondered if my father knew about my mother as a wild thing, about Nellie. It was a question I did not know how I could ever ask. It seemed to me that if he knew he would not want me to know, and if he did not know, I could not be the one to tell him, not now, not with Ma dead out there with Nellie. I felt burdened with knowledge that was not to be shared, like a guilty secret. I thought again of my parents together in the front seat of an old Dodge on a reservation road, following a saucer of light into darkness.

11.

IN WICHITA FALLS Uncle Eph drove Mr. Smart and me past the houses he had built in his rich days, them in the front seat, me in the back.

Neither place looked as grand as I had been led to expect. They were big houses, bigger than any I had ever been in, but not so huge that I couldn't imagine living in them or what they were like inside. Uncle Eph stopped in front of the first of the houses and pounded on the steering wheel as he described the glorious details that the modest frame exterior hid from our eyes. Fourteen-foot ceilings of carved plaster, oak floors of the highest quality, mahogany paneling, a bathroom on every floor, and a kitchen with a gas range instead of a coal stove — these, Uncle Eph protested, were what we could not see as we drove past

The house had a "Rooms for Rent" sign out front.

"Look at that," Uncle Eph said. "I can't believe it — poor white trash being invited in as paying guests. In my day folks like that would of been bowing and scraping, just going past."

His other house was all boarded up. It was brick, with a porte cochère. Shingles were missing from the roof and the wood trim needed paint. The sign out front, almost obscured by weeds, said *For Sale*.

All Uncle Eph could do when we stopped in front of it was shake his head. He was too upset to speak.

"That house," he said after awhile, "it's got a ballroom, two living rooms—call 'em drawing rooms, if you want—and a bathroom for every bedroom. I tell you, it's the latest thing, never mind it being ten years going on fifteen since me and Muffie put it up. Nothing built today can compare with what that house is. Muffie loved it. There's a linen closet on every floor, and two for the dining room."

"How many tablecloths?" I couldn't help asking.

Uncle Eph didn't hear me, or pretended he didn't. Mr. Smart waggled a finger at me warningly.

Uncle Eph drove us next into another, older part of town to show us the bungalow where he and Aunt Muffie had started their married life. He was just getting into the business world then, buying hides for a harness maker. The little house was still occupied and children played on a strip of grass in front. We stopped across the street.

"That upstairs window, that's the room your ma and grandma lived all the time she was waiting for her baby," Uncle Eph said. "She couldn't stay in Owchita, of course, her being pregnant and no husband, so her and Ma come here where nobody knowed her and we took her in, Muffie and me."

I said, "Where was the baby born?"

"Right up there. Same room. Your grandpa come over from Owchita and him and Ma, they delivered that baby themselves, right up there in that same room. They knew what to do, of course, Ma having had so many kids herself and helping with a whole lot more."

"And it was born dead?"

"That's right. Never cried once. Pa, he come down the

stairs, hands still bloody, carrying the poor little thing wrapped in a towel. Next day Ma and him went back to Owchita to bury it. Mary couldn't go, of course, not so soon after the birth. Matter of fact, she never did go back, not so far as I ever heard, not even to see Ma before she died."

"Did Grandpa kill her? Nellie, I mean?" I asked.

Without looking around, Uncle Eph reached over the seat and smashed me backhanded across the face. My nose started bleeding and my front teeth felt suddenly loose.

"Don't never let me hear you say nothing like that again," he said.

"Nosir," I said, crying, holding a handkerchief to my nose. "I'm sorry, Uncle Eph."

He put the car in gear and let out the clutch.

"It was a breech birth, you see—damned near tore poor little Mary in two. Pa, he had to reach in there and just pull it out."

I felt angry with myself for letting him make me cry, and sickened by what I was learning. But I felt I was getting to know my mother for the first time as a whole person, not just as my mother, and there were more questions I wanted answers to. Fighting to get the tears out of my voice, still holding the handkerchief to my nose, I asked my questions: What had my mother done after the baby's birth and death? Where had she stayed? How had she lived?

"She stayed with us awhile longer till she was well again," Uncle Eph said, "a real sad little girl, but she and Muffie didn't get along too good. Nobody's fault, really. Muffie was just about having our second and the house was getting pretty well filled up, so she thought Mary ought to go home again so we could have her room. Mary said she wasn't going home again ever, and she wouldn't say she repented her sin or the shame she'd brought on the family name either. One day when she was out of the house, Muffie just packed her suitcases and put them out on the front porch.

"Turned out Mary that very day had found herself a job as Mrs. Dr. Morgan's live-in kitchen maid, so she was moving out anyway, which kind of killed the joy of it for Muffie. Went back to school the same time, Mary did, and got her diploma, and then she signed up at the normal school and got her teaching certificate. She was a spunky little thing, your ma was. Too spunky, Muffie always said. 'There's such a thing as too much red pepper,' Muffie used to say. And then she was full of funny ideas that I don't know where they come from. Lost her first teaching job for putting on a suffragette march."

"I know about that," I said. I didn't say so, but I didn't think letting women vote had been a funny idea or anything more than right. I had been exposed to my mother's beliefs about the equality of men and women all my life.

I had one more question. "Who put the stone on the baby's grave?"

"Mary done that herself, long years after—had it done, that is. About the time you was born, or just before. Up to then there hadn't been no marker on it at all. Fact is, none of us knowed what that baby's name was or if it had a name, but when we took your grandma out there to bury her, there was that stone with Nellie carved on it. Nellie was Grandma Wilkes's name, your great-grandma, and Mary and her always got along real well, not like her and Ma. Mary named that poor little baby Nellie for Grandma Wilkes just like she named you David for Grandpa Wilkes and not Amos for Pa."

It pleased me to know that it had been my mother, not Uncle Eph or my grandparents, who put the marker on the baby's grave. And I was glad my name was David, not Amos.

We drove back through town to the highway we'd come in on. There were a lot of rundown tourist courts along the highway. Uncle Eph picked one out for us to stay at, if it had room. He had me go in and sign the register.

"There's people here in Wichita Falls I'd just as soon didn't know I'm in town," he explained.

"What people?" I asked.

Mr. Smart waggled his finger at me again.

Uncle Eph said, "Never you mind. Just sign your name as David Wilkes from Lubbock. Tell 'em I'm your daddy, should they ask, and Mr. Smart here is your uncle. All Wilkes. Nobody here but us Wilkes."

I did what he told me, knowing by now that in this kind of place there wouldn't be any questions, even about why my nose was all puffed up. The man behind the counter handed me a pencil on a string to sign in with. He didn't say a word until I told him I didn't know what the license number of Uncle Eph's station wagon was.

"Then go look," he said. "Can't register you without we got a license number."

Uncle Eph picked out a cabin off to the side, away from any other occupied ones. It was a lot like the cabin we'd had in Amarillo. It had stained mattresses on the beds and a dirty cot for me to sleep on. There was the usual coal stove for cooking and heating, a stand with a washbowl and pitcher on it, a rocking chair with one arm broken off, and nails to hang clothes on—even another *End of the Trail* calendar on the wall, this one put out by a local drugstore. Uncle Eph had picked up sheets at home, so at least we weren't sleeping on bare mattresses anymore. As soon as we got our stuff inside, I went over to the washroom and splashed cold water on my nose until the swelling went down.

We spent most of that day getting ready for the pony sale, putting out more of the Geronimo posters we'd had printed in Amarillo and buying newspaper ads. Uncle Eph said ideally we'd be advertising steadily for about a week before the sale, but money was running a little short and so we had to get some horses off our hands in a hurry. Otherwise there wouldn't be enough cash to ship the herd on to Fort Worth, where he already had ads running in the papers and boys spreading posters around town. Several ponies had died on the train between Amarillo and Wichita Falls—from the heat, Mr. Smart said—and we sold the carcasses to a local rendering plant for walking-around money, as Uncle Eph put it. Any place he reckoned he might be known, he sat in the station wagon, his hat pulled low over his face, while Mr. Smart and I went inside and did the business.

The Wichita Falls parade was to be considerably scaled down from the one in Amarillo. Instead of a real band, Uncle Eph went out to an old folks' home and hired what he called a cowboy trio—two banjos and a fiddle. The players were too tetched in the git-along to walk very far, Uncle Eph said, so they would sit on top of the station wagon and play as they rode. Uncle Eph was going to make himself up as a rodeo clown, so as not to be recognizable, and help out the music by banging a tambourine against the outside of the door with one hand while guiding the car with the other. I was to follow along behind on my pony with a string of horses that were leadable, if not ridable.

Uncle Eph wasn't pleased at having to pinch pennies in Wichita Falls, but he told me to hold my hat till we got to Fort Worth, where we'd have not one but two marching bands and a whole troop of U.S. Cavalry, not to mention Indian chiefs swooping about in full regalia. Uncle Eph said he felt right good about the outlook for Fort Worth.

Late in the afternoon we went back to the tourist court. Parked in front of the cabin next was a Model A roadster with rusted fenders. Clotie was sitting on the running board on the shady side with her sandals off, painting her toenails red. She was wearing her pink movie-star pajamas.

"Well, look who's here," Uncle Eph said. He picked her up and swung her around, planting a big kiss on her mouth. As he put her down he ran his hands over her, up and down and around.

She scrubbed at her mouth with the back of her hand.

"Yeah," she said. "Surprise, surprise."

Uncle Eph went inside to say hello to Clotie's mother.

"Your Uncle Eph's sure got feelin' hands," Clotie said. "He knows everything I got on or don't got on."

She sat on the running board again and I sat beside her. "How come you're here?" I asked.

"Ma and him rigged this up in Amarillo. He wants us to travel with you a while."

I thought about it. "You want to do that?"

She shrugged. "It don't matter. He's mean when he's drinking, but he ain't no worse'n some of the other guys she's hooked up with."

I held her bottle of polish for her while she got back to painting toenails. Uncle Eph had left the cabin door open and pretty soon we heard the bedsprings going. Clotie's ma was moaning and Uncle Eph was calling her dirty names. Then they were both yelling at once.

I stood up and started toward the cabin.

Clotie yanked me back by the belt.

"Something's wrong. I'm going in there. "

"Oh, sit down," Clotie said. "Ma's just working."

12.

THE WARDS STORE had a new manager who didn't know Uncle Eph, so that's where he took us to buy Clotie a cowgirl outfit to wear in the parade before the auction. The dress she got had a divided skirt made out of some kind of brown cloth that looked like leather with white spangles on it. With it came a matching vest, boots, and a white hat. Uncle Eph had wanted her to be an Indian maiden, but he wasn't able to find the right kind of dress on short notice, and there wasn't time to have one sewed. We stood by the front door while Uncle Eph finished dickering for credit with the new manager.

Clotie said she was glad she wasn't going to have to be an Indian maiden. With her black hair, olive skin, and brown eyes, people had been taking her for colored all her life and she didn't want to encourage them.

"Indians aren't colored," I said.

"Redskins? That's colored, you ask me," Clotie said.

Uncle Eph came up, the bundle of clothes under his arm, and we went out to the street, where Clotie's mother was waiting in the station wagon. Clotie was proud of how fair her mother was. She had light blue eyes with no life in them and yellow hair that Clotie said she hardly had to touch up at all.

Her face was so thin and her skin so white that sitting there in the front seat in the bright sunlight she looked like a skull with a yellow wig on and blue buttons where eyes should have been.

"I got me a real pretty outfit, Ma," Clotie said.

"Did you thank your Uncle Eph?" Her mother had a high thin voice and spoke very fast. She sounded like she was singing or saying her prayers. "Did you give him a kiss?"

Clotie leaned over from the backseat and planted a kiss on the side of Uncle Eph's face. She wiped her mouth as she sat back.

Back at the cabin court Clotie's mother lay down for a nap. Clotie put on her new clothes and Uncle Eph took us to the stockyards, where one of the cowboys Mr. Smart had hired picked out a tame-looking pony for her, a pretty white-footed pinto.

Clotie had never been on a horse before, so Uncle Eph decided he couldn't risk having her ride bareback like me.

"Spoil the whole thing if she got shook off," he said.

He talked the man who ran the stockyards into lending him a saddle, the littlest one he had. The cowboy slapped the saddle on the white-footed pinto and reached under for the cinch. The horse arched its back. The saddle slid off. The cowboy picked it up from under the horse's belly and tried again. As soon as the horse felt the saddle it took off at a full gallop, knocking the cowboy aside.

"I'd a swore that critter was broke," the cowboy said, getting up and flapping dust off his pants with his hat.

He and the other stockyard hands went sorting through the horses again, looking for one tame enough to carry Clotie without throwing her or running away or biting and kicking the spectators. The only really tame horse they could find was the ancient bay I'd ridden in Amarillo. It was probably as mean as all the rest, but lacked the strength and energy to express itself.

"You'll both have to ride Davey's horse," Uncle Eph decided. "Ain't ideal, but kind of appealing in some ways—makes a nice picture, big brother taking little sister for a ride, him in the saddle and her behind, or maybe two little sweethearts."

The cowboy put the saddle on and cinched it up. I mounted and he lifted Clotie up. She leaned against me and held on tight. The horse sank to its front knees and was headed on down until the cowboy lifted Clotie off.

"The brute says no thanks, I ain't gonna play," the cowboy said.

"Ain't there some way we can prop him up?" Uncle Eph asked.

"Not and have him move, too," the cowboy said.

"That little girl don't weigh no more'n a feather."

"That ain't what the horse thinks," the cowboy said.

I was still in the saddle, with my feet braced against the stirrups to keep from sliding down the horse's neck.

Clotie laughed at me. "You look like you're posing for one of them calendars, but I don't think that horse is going to make it to the end of the trail," she said.

I got off the horse. It struggled to its feet.

"I don't know what the hell we going to do," Uncle Eph said. "Ain't there a single other ridable pony among all them?"

"Maybe," the cowboy said. "We just ain't found it yet."

Mr. Smart said, "Put the girl on the horse. Let the boy lead her."

"Mr. Smart," Uncle Eph said, "you done it again."

We all went home, had supper, and went to bed like ordinary people, except that Uncle Eph took a couple of bottles of Uncle Ben's moonshine over to the other cabin to share with

Clotie's mother. Clotie spread a blanket in the back of the station wagon for her bed.

In the middle of the night I woke up with someone pulling my foot. I gave a yell before I realized it was Clotie.

"Be quiet, Davey, don't make no noise," she whispered. "It's just me."

"I thought you were sleeping in the station wagon."

"I was, but a minute ago I heard a noise and I sat up and there was these guys out there looking over Ma's car with a flashlight and saying, 'Yeah, this is it, all right.' And they was trying to decide what to do, whether rush the cabin right then or what, but one of them said, 'How we know for sure which cabin to rush?' And another guy says, 'Or who's in it?' So they decided to go get the police in on it."

"Is it a stolen car?"

"If it is, Ma didn't steal it. It was give to her by this fellow in Amarillo, a friend of hers."

I got my pants and shoes on and grabbed the flashlight I'd put on the floor beside the cot before I fell asleep. "Let's get Uncle Eph."

"Him? He'll go out the door like greased lightning. Ma says there's hardly a man in town of any account Eph don't owe money to. May even be a warrant out on him. Anyway, last time I seen him he was so drunk he didn't know which way was up or sideways. Ma was having a hell of a time with him. We got to do this ourselves."

"Do what?"

We were outside now and I eased the cabin door shut, so as not to disturb Mr. Smart. It was a clear night, with lots of stars.

"You know how to drive?"

"Sure," I said. "I drive all the time at home." That was true. My father had taught me to drive as soon as my legs were long enough to reach the brake pedal, on the theory that living as far from town as we did, I should be able to go for help if anything happened to him.

"We got to get rid of that car."

The key was in it. There was a little slope to the graveled alley between cabins, so I coasted a little way before I put the Model A in gear and let out the clutch. The engine caught right off, the car hardly bucking, and we wheeled out of the tourist court without lights.

Clotie said she didn't want to take the Model A far, just somewhere it wouldn't be found right away, but close enough for us to get back to the cabin ahead of the cops. Next to the wire fence that enclosed the tourist court was a rundown service station and repair shop. Some old cars were parked at one side, and I drove the Model A in among them. Clotie said we had to get the license plates off. I found a bunch of tools scattered on the floor of the back seat and took the plates off without much trouble.

"Who's it registered to?"

"I don't know," she said. "That's why I want the plates off it."

"When your ma signed you in at the tourist court, didn't she have to put down the kind of car and the license number?" I realized I was thinking like a person I didn't know.

"Hell!" Clotie said.

We ran back to the tourist court. The manager slept in a cabin just behind the office, which was left open all night with a dim light burning so anyone coming in late and wanting a room could sign in and take a key without waking him. I grabbed the register and we got down behind the counter to look at it.

Clotie's mother had signed in as Mrs. Wilkes from Lubbock, which she'd spelled with one b. For the car she'd just put down Ford. That was all right, because it could just as easily stand for Uncle Eph's Ford V8 station wagon. But there was the license number of the Model A, big as life.

She'd signed in pencil, just as I had, and the pencil was hanging by its string right beside us, eraser and all. It took about two seconds to rub out what Clotie's ma had written and write in Uncle Eph's license number.

We scooted out of there and got back inside the cabin just as the cars drove up out front. Mr. Smart was stretched out on the bed, sleeping like the dead. Clotie took off her cowgirl outfit and got over by the cot in her slip. I unbuttoned my shirt and undid my belt buckle so it'd look like I had got dressed in a hurry. I had the flashlight in my hand.

"Well, it *was* here, I'll tell you that. Wasn't it, boys? Right along in here." It was a man's deep voice.

"That's right, right along here," another man said.

"Well, it sure as hell ain't here now, so whoever was in it has done skedaddled," a third man said. "We'll put out an alarm."

"Let's just check these cabins here, find out what's what." That was the deep-voiced man.

Clotie grabbed my hand. "We gotta do something or they'll find Ma with your Uncle Eph and stick her with whoring again. One more time and she's going to be in real trouble."

I opened the door of the cabin and turned my flashlight on the men standing by a bunch of cars in front of the cabin.

"What's going on?" I said, trying to sound sleepy and confused.

The men whirled toward me. Only a couple of them were in police uniforms, but they all seemed to have guns and lights pointed at me.

"Hey!" I said, not having to fake sounding scared. "Don't point them things at me. I ain't done nothing."

"It's only a kid," one of the policemen said. "Put away your guns. He ain't going to hurt you."

"There's another one," somebody yelled.

I looked over my shoulder and saw Clotie poking her head around the door. She had a big simper on her face.

"My kid sister," I said.

"My name's Clothilda, Clothilda Ann Wilkes," she said. "Call me Clotie."

"What's your name, kid?" the policeman asked me.

"Davey. Davey Wilkes. I heard all the talking and come out to see what's going on."

"You know anything about a Model A Ford parked out here tonight?"

"There was one parked over in the next row of cabins awhile ago when I went to the restroom, but when I come out it was gone."

"Notice the license number?"

"Nosir. It was a Texas car, though, I noticed that."

Clotie spoke up. "I seen it too. Davey took me to the ladies' the same time."

The policeman said, "Well, fellas, there you are. Whatever you seen, it was in the next row over and ain't there now."

"I'd a swore—" the deep-voiced man said.

The policeman cut him off and spoke to Clotie and me. "You kids better get back in there before your folks find you out of bed and tan your backsides."

"Yessir," I said.

"Good night, officer," Clotie said.

We closed the door and leaned against it, listening to the cars leave, holding hands over our mouths to keep from laughing out loud. We heard the cars stop up at the office.

They were checking the register, but that didn't worry us. We knew they weren't going to find anything out of the way.

13.

AFTER A LITTLE, Clotie went back to the cabin next door. She said she figured Uncle Eph and her ma had long since closed up shop for the evening and she'd be able to sleep in her own bed.

It seemed like I had hardly dropped onto the cot when I heard women screaming and a man yelling. It was so loud the noise even woke up Mr. Smart. For a fat man he moved fast. He was out of bed with his overalls and shoes on by the time I was just starting to pull on my pants. I followed him as he rushed out the door and into Clotie's ma's cabin.

Uncle Eph was standing in the middle of the room with nothing on but socks and an undershirt. He was all bent over, roaring like a bull, holding himself with one ham-like hand and striking out with the other like he was in the ring with Jack Dempsey. Clotie's mother stood in front of him, naked as a jaybird, trying without a lot of luck to dodge his fist while swinging at him with a broom. Big bruises were coming out all over her.

"Out of my way, you ass-peddling bitch."

"You stay off the child, you hear?" she screamed. "You want something, come to me. Don't you ever, *ever*, touch her again."

Clotie was naked too. She hunkered down in a corner behind her mother, shoulders hunched forward and hands thrust between her thighs, trying to cover her nakedness. Blood poured from her nose and dripped off her chin onto her knees.

"I just got in my bed in my slip, Ma, trying not to wake you up," she said, crying hard, "and all of sudden he piles on me and rips off my clothes."

"Oh, you bastard. What you done to my little girl?"

Uncle Eph smashed Clotie's ma across the face. "Ain't nobody gonna kick me in the balls like she done and get away with it."

Mr. Smart jumped on his back and pinned his arms. Uncle Eph hit the floor like a bulldogged steer.

"Get sheets to cover up the women," Mr. Smart said, holding Uncle Eph down.

I tore sheets off the bed. With them came some bloodied rags that I recognized as the remnants of Clotie's slip. Clotie and her mother wrapped themselves up and clung together, sobbing.

"Poor baby, oh, poor baby," Clotie's mother said. "I didn't want this for you."

Clotie said, "I locked my feet, Ma, like you said, and that's when he hit me. I done the best I could, Ma."

"I know you did. Oh, I know you did."

"I got him good, Ma. I give him the knee twice, real hard."

Uncle Eph had passed out on the floor and Mr. Smart stood up, leaving him there.

"Less'n you mean to law him you best be out of here by morning," Mr. Smart said.

Clotie's mother agreed. "Soon's we can pack up the car, we're gonna be on our way back to Amarillo."

I told her what we'd done about the Model A. Mr. Smart

thought we'd done the right thing in getting rid of it, but Clotie's ma wasn't so sure. She said it was the first car she'd ever had free and clear and she didn't know where in this world or the next she'd get another. Besides, she didn't have money to buy bus fare back to Amarillo, and after the beating Uncle Eph had given her she didn't know when she'd be able to earn it.

"Listen," I said, "I'll get some plates off another car and put them on the Model A, and then you can maybe drive it back to Amarillo."

It was not the kind of thing I'd ever have thought of a week earlier, but now the idea just seemed to pop into my head, like stealing a new set of plates to put on a stolen car was the natural thing to do.

I walked along the rows of cabins until I found an old Plymouth parked a little aside in some shadows and switched its plates with those Clotie and I had taken off the Model A earlier. I took the new plates over to the service station and put them on Clotie's mother's car. It was almost morning by then, but still dark. Making sure no one was around, I cranked the starter and drove back without lights.

Clotie and her mother were dressed and almost packed. Both of them had black eyes, puffed-up noses and split lips. Uncle Eph was sprawled out on the floor, sound asleep. I threw one of the bloody sheets over him. I didn't like looking at him.

When the bags were ready, Mr. Smart and I took them out to the Model A. Without anyone seeing me, I undid my belt and dug out the two ten-dollar bills Pa had hidden there. He'd said I wasn't to let anyone know I had them, not even Uncle Eph, but I was sure he'd approve of what I was doing.

Clotie came out and got in the car. She didn't speak and kept her face turned away. Her mother was already behind the wheel. I reached up and gave her the twenty dollars. I didn't want to give it to Clotie. I was afraid she would misunderstand.

Nobody said anything. Clotie's mother let out the clutch too fast and the Model A went bucking off.

I slept most of the morning. When I woke up Mr. Smart was sitting on the edge of the other bed looking at me.

"Boy," he said, "I ain't one to interfere, but if you got a mind to head for home, that's where you'd ought to head."

He shoved a bus ticket and a couple of dollars for food into my hand.

I started to cry, surprising myself. I hadn't supposed I would ever cry again.

"Now don't do that," Mr. Smart said. "Just remember folks has different ideas and different problems. Your uncle's got problems like you and me got problems, but they ain't the same problems. You understand what I'm tellin' you?"

"Nosir," I said, still crying.

"Just as well," he said. "But remember, that's the way it were."

I took the first bus out. In Amarillo I went to the Western Union office and sent Pa a telegram telling him I was coming home.

He met me at Chambers late at night.

On the long ride home in the old Dodge I sat close to him. It was good to be back, but I didn't feel much like talking. He told me everything that had gone on while I was away. Hosteen Tse had died, a trader over at Split Rock had been robbed by three young white men, and Washington had approved construction of a new classroom at Klinchee and the hiring of an additional teacher. When he fell silent we rode along with no sound but the motor and the bumping of the car springs over rough patches.

After a while he said, keeping his eyes on the road, "Did Uncle Eph tell you about Nellie?"

"Yessir," I said.

"What did you think?"

"Not much. I wondered if you knew."

"I knew."

We rode on into a saucer of light.

I asked, "What did you think when you found out?"

"Not much. Not nearly as much as she did. She was young, you see, and made a mistake."

"Did she think it was a mistake?"

"In after years, yes. At the time she was starved for affection and wanted to get away from that whiskey-swilling old father, well into his sixties by then, and her mother, who was so beat down and worn out she didn't care for anything but peace and quiet and no scandal. When a nice-looking young man came around who actually read books, Mary fell in love, or thought she did, which is pretty much the same thing at that age or any age."

"And they killed him?"

"She never knew for sure, or whether they just scared him away from that part of the country. All she knew was, he never reported back to Fort Bliss from his leave."

We rode a long way in silence.

"People grow and change, you know," he said. "She suffered mightily."

"I know."

He took a hand off the wheel and put his arm around me.

"I loved her, Davey, and I think she loved me. I know she loved you."

"And Nellie?"

"And Nellie. There was never a day went by she didn't think about that little baby."

"Did Grandpa Gower kill her too? Nellie, I mean."

"Mary always thought so."

"Why didn't Grandma stop him?"

"She was an old lady then, worn out from too many kids and too little consideration."

"She could have tried."

"That's what Mary always thought. That's why she wouldn't go see her mother, even when she went home to put the stone on Nellie's grave, not long before you were born. I reckon, though, that your grandma didn't have the spunk Mary had. Or maybe she used it all up hiding your grandpa after he deserted, when she wasn't any older than you are now."

"Uncle Eph and the others said he was a major, a hero."

"Your great-grandma Wilkes told your mother the real story while Mary was growing up and not getting along very well at home. Later your ma took the trouble to look it up in Confederate Army records, and sure enough, there it was, Private Amos Gower, Deserter. He hid out for most of two years in the woods and river bottoms around your great-grandpa Wilkes's little farm, with your grandma slipping him food to live on. And when the family went to Texas after the surrender, he followed along, with her still feeding him on the sly. About the time Uncle Ben came along, maybe a little before, they were married."

I mulled over all this for awhile, thinking about different kinds of families and different kinds of love, and then I began to tell him about my trip with Uncle Eph. I told him a lot, but not all of it. I didn't mention Clotie or lying to the police or switching license plates. I did tell him, though, about there being no marker on my mother's grave, and how Uncle Eph stole my money.

"I don't much like Uncle Eph anymore," I confessed.

"I never did, much," he said.

"Why did Ma like him?"

"Because he was the only one of that whole crew who ever treated her kindly when she needed help."

With my father's arm around my shoulders, I thought about what I had learned, not just about my mother but about myself. I felt I understood at last what she saw those times she looked at me, her face still, and did not see me. I fell asleep in the front seat of the Dodge and slept the rest of the way to Klinchee.

In the weeks that followed we got an occasional postcard from Uncle Eph. Wichita Falls did not respond to his message of economic salvation through horseflesh. Neither did Fort Worth, despite a full band, the U.S. Cavalry and Boy Scouts whooping and hollering in Indian costumes. Uncle Eph and Mr. Smart took the ponies to San Antonio and Houston, on to Laredo and out to El Paso before Uncle Eph gave up on trying to bring Texas back to greatness. After he and Mr. Smart sold the remaining ponies to Swift for dog food and settled accounts, they walked away with a total loss on the venture of some $125 each.

Uncle Eph looked on the bright side as usual. "That is not much to pay for an Education like I got," he wrote.

He said he had decided to get back into the wildcatting game and wondered if my father would be interested in staking him. He never mentioned Clotie or her mother. To this day I don't know if they made it to Amarillo or if that was where they were heading.

Reservations

For

J.A.M.

and

my parents,

Sallie Frances Key (1890-1938)
and
George Lentton Meyers (1887-1961)

PART ONE

ZUÑI/RED MESA

1928-1935

DAVEY

1.

AT ZUÑI IN THE SPRING of the year I turned five, Mrs. Wewha took Andrew and me across the flooding river to the place she called Hepatina, the Middle Place, the center of the world.

Our feet drummed on loose planks as we crossed the bridge. We looked through the cracks and saw muddy water swirling and rushing. An old man passed us, riding bareback on a donkey. His legs dangled almost to the ground. He was dressed all in white and had thick white hair, bobbed at ear level like my mother's. A red bandanna, rolled and tied around his head, held his hair in place. I called him Donkey Man and made Andrew laugh. Mrs. Wewha said he was not someone to laugh at. The man was a rain priest and her uncle, Andrew's grandmother's brother.

Mrs. Wewha did not have any children of her own or any husband that I knew of. She took care of Andrew and me while my mother and father taught at the government school and Andrew's mother was busy in the school's kitchen preparing noon dinner for the Zuñi children. Andrew was my best friend.

On the other side of the river, we passed the eagle pens. Mrs. Wewha said that when a Zuñi man needed an eagle feather for a prayer stick or dance costume, he pulled it from a caged bird. The eagles were big, but the pens were small, built of old boards, tree limbs, and rusty chicken wire. They smelled bad. I held my nose and made throwing-up noises as we drew near. Andrew started to laugh and I laughed with him, but again Mrs. Wewha made us stop. She said the eagles were messengers of the gods and deserved respect.

They shrieked, flapped their wings, and poked their heads through the holes of the chicken wire, trying to get at us. They had staring eyes and vicious sharp beaks that snapped open and shut. Mrs. Wewha said she had seen an eagle strip the meat from a man's arm with one swipe of its beak. We stayed far from them and gripped her hands tightly as we passed on the dusty road.

We came to a field fenced with barbed wire that sagged between rotting posts. Only weeds grew in the field, but a mound of stones and logs marked the center of it.

"There," Mrs. Wewha said, pointing at the mound. "Hepatina. The Middle Place. There."

Andrew stood on one side of Mrs. Wewha and I stood on the other, clinging to her hands, while she told us about Hepatina. I was hearing the story for the first time, but Andrew already knew about the old days when Zuñis had tails and webbed feet and lived in darkness deep inside the earth. That was before they climbed into the sunlight, became men and women, and wandered the earth in search of the Middle Place, where the gods had told them to go. At last the Rain God of the North spread his legs and told them that they would find Hepatina where his water struck the ground.

"There," Mrs. Wewha said again, pointing. "Hepatina. That is where his water fell. There. The Middle Place."

I broke away and crawled under the fence to get a closer look. I was almost to the mound when Mrs. Wewha caught me by my overall straps and hauled me back behind the fence.

"This is holy place," she said. "You got to be Zuñi and carry prayer stick to Hepatina. Terrible things happen if you don't take prayer stick."

Mrs. Wewha took us home across the bridge. Andrew told her he didn't feel good. She felt him and said he was feverish. She put me down for my afternoon nap, but instead of putting Andrew down beside me, she took him to my mother to find out what was wrong with him.

That night I told my father I had been to the middle of the world, where the Rain God of the North peed.

"I have reservations about that," he said.

I knew what reservations were. Places apart, areas set aside. I had lived on reservations all my life.

When my father explained his use of the word, which was new to me, I was astonished at his disbelief. After all, it was Mrs. Wewha who had taken Andrew and me to the fenced field and told us we were looking at Hepatina, the Middle Place. How could he doubt Mrs. Wewha?

But he insisted that the shrine Mrs. Wewha took Andrew and me to was not where the Rain God of the North's water fell. That place was deep inside the pueblo, my father said, and so sacred that the Rain Society had built a great kiva on the spot. No one but members of the society knew exactly where inside the pueblo the kiva was or how to get to it. Only the rain priests were allowed even to speak of it. What I had seen, my father said, was a stand-in for the Middle Place—an ordinary shrine for ordinary people, a place Mrs. Wewha and other Zuñis could take their prayer sticks, a place they were allowed to point out as the center of the world to outsiders like me.

I did not think of myself as an outsider. I felt as Zuñi as anyone. If I wasn't already Zuñi, I saw no reason why I should not become Zuñi. My father said that was not the way it worked.

Andrew came down with diphtheria and died. I had been inoculated and stayed well.

Mrs. Wewha and my mother leaned against one another, crying.

"It was me took him there," Mrs. Wewha said. "I took him to Hepatina, but no prayer stick."

"That wasn't it," my mother said.

Mrs. Wewha lifted her head from my mother's shoulder. She had a round face with smooth brown cheeks that felt dry and cool when she pressed her face to mine. Usually her expression did not change much. She did not smile often, nor did she frown, but always seemed the same, alert and attentive, yet serene and somehow far away. Now her cheeks were shiny with tears and her mouth was twisted like she had bitten into a crab apple. I hardly knew her. She was looking right at me but did not seem to see me. My mother looked at me like that sometimes, as if she were seeing not me but someone else. Mrs. Wewha had never looked at me like that before. I knew she was seeing Andrew.

That afternoon, when I was supposed to be napping, I slipped out my bedroom window. At the woodpile I found a small cedar stick. It was reddish brown with a golden streak running through it. I rounded and smoothed the wood with sandpaper from my father's toolbox. To make a prayer stick I needed eagle feathers and a piece of string to tie them to it. I had string in my pocket and knew how to tie knots. But I did not know how to get the feathers. I was afraid to go near the cages outside the pueblo, where eagles waited to tear the meat from my arm.

I decided chicken feathers would have to do and went to the henhouse in our backyard, where my father kept Rhode

Island Reds. I was almost as afraid of the big old rooster as I was of the eagles, but I had learned long ago that if I picked up a rock before I went into the henhouse to gather eggs, he would keep his distance. My father said the old bird was no fool and would not attack an armed man, though he might make a show of flapping his wings and thrusting his head back and forth just to impress the hens with his bravery. This time the rooster was off scratching in the road and did not interfere as I picked feathers that looked like dried blood off the ground.

I crossed the bridge all alone and found my way to the fenced field where Mrs. Wewha had taken Andrew and me. Crawling under the barbed wire, I ran through the weeds to Hepatina. I got down on my knees to look through a small opening into the mound of stones and logs.

In the gloom inside, I made out a shallow depression littered with eagle-feathered old prayer sticks, lacy bits of tumbleweed, and a shiny Juicy Fruit gum wrapper that had blown in. I was disappointed. I had supposed I would find a bottomless pit, but I had dug deeper holes myself many times.

A shadow fell over me. It grew larger and darker and swallowed the prayer sticks, the bits of tumbleweed, and even the Juicy Fruit wrapper. I was looking into a void, seeing nothing. I stretched my arm into Hepatina and dropped my prayer stick.

"I'm sorry, Andrew," I said.

Someone lifted me by my overall straps and held me in midair like a valise. When I tipped up my head, I saw the old man I had called Donkey Man.

Keeping a grip on me with one hand, the old man knelt and reached into Hepatina to pull out my prayer stick. He carried me from the field, stepping over the fence like it wasn't there. He set me on my feet.

"Go!" he said. He struck my shoulders with the feathers of the prayer stick. "Go!"

I ran as fast as I could. The old man followed right at my heels, cackling like a hen, crowing like a rooster. The planks of the bridge shook and clattered as I raced over it.

I could not hear footsteps behind me. I looked back. He was right there, just a step behind, but his feet made no sound.

"Go!" the old man said.

I rushed on, out of breath but staying ahead of him. I reached our yard and struggled to open the gate.

The old man seized my shoulder and turned me to face him. His fingers were sharp as an eagle's claws. He brushed my cheeks with coppery red chicken feathers, first one cheek and then the other.

"You are not Zuñi," the old man said, "and can never be."

He dropped my prayer stick on the ground and danced around it, kicking dust over the feathers. He cackled and crowed and flapped his arms. After a while he leaped high into the air and flew away on eagle wings.

2.

MY PARENTS HAD BEEN teaching at an Indian Service school by the ocean when they were transferred back to New Mexico. On the day we reached Red Mesa, my mother told me to go to the trading post to buy milk. I didn't know what she was talking about. My father went instead and my mother was angry with me. She thought I was just lazy. But I had forgotten what a trading post was, just as I had forgotten what the desert was like.

I went out in the yard. There was no grass outside the white picket fence around the house and none inside either. The sun came down on me like too many blankets on the bed. Everything was hazy with heat. Whatever I looked at shimmered—the outcroppings of black volcanic rock thrusting up out of dead-white alkali flats, the distant hills that were so far away they looked like dark clouds low in the sky.

My father came back from the trading post with two loaves of bread under his arm. If I had done that, he would have said, "Don't squash the bread."

"I didn't know what a trading post was," I said.

"You were pretty young when we left Zuñi. You weren't even in school yet."

"They weren't trading posts by the ocean, just stores. That's why I didn't go get the milk for Mom. I didn't know where to go. I'm sorry I made her mad."

"She's tired and she misses trees and grass. She'll be all right after she gets used to the desert again."

"I wish there was some grass."

"We'll plant a lawn right away. I'll bring topsoil in from the mountains around Toadlena and we'll soon have a fine stand of grass. There's a good well and pump."

He looked across the desert to the hills.

"God, it's hot," he said. "Here it is still June and it feels like August."

"Don't take the Lord's name in vain in front of the child," my mother said. We had not known that she was standing in the doorway. She began to cry softly with her knuckles pressed against her lips.

My father clinked the milk bottles together and looked at them a long time. After a while my mother stopped crying. He went inside to help her unpack dishes.

I walked around the outside of the house, trying to find a shady spot where there was a breeze. But the big mesa behind the house cut off any west winds; and the only signs of a breeze were little whirlwinds that picked up dried tumbleweeds and danced them across the desert floor.

A woman in a nightgown and red bathrobe came out the back door of a house across a wide driveway from ours. I had not realized anyone lived there. Her house was just like ours, except for a small addition at the side. A faded sign over the door said *Clinic*. A big *Closed* sign stood in the window. The woman's bathrobe gapped over her stomach but dragged behind her like a foot-long train. She carried a good-sized white dog with long matted hair. When she put the dog down, it tried to lift its leg but tumbled over. The woman righted it

—RESERVATIONS—

and supported it while it got its leg up.

As she turned to go back in the house, she looked over at me.

"You, boy," she said.

"Yes, ma'am?"

"You leave Bozo alone, hear?"

"Yes'm."

I went around to the front of our house. It stood in a line at the base of the mesa with the other buildings, except for the schoolhouse, which sat by itself across the road. All the buildings were covered with clapboard siding painted white with green trim around the doors and windows and at the corners. There wasn't much left of the trim. The green paint was peeling.

Our car was parked out front. Everything was still in the two-wheel trailer we had pulled from Washington, except for some bedding and the dishes. I climbed into the car and left the doors open. Air passing through the open doors made it seem as if there was a breeze. I liked that better than standing in the shade of the house, where I felt no movement of air at all.

My father came out.

"We had better carry some of this stuff inside," he said.

"I don't like this place," I said. "How long will we be here?"

"Till they get ready to move us again, I guess. But don't complain. It's a job, and we're lucky to have it."

"I'll never like this place."

"Well, give it a chance."

He handed me a bread box to carry. I followed him inside.

My mother was sitting at the kitchen table, wiping sweat off her face. "I hate to think about it, but I guess I'll have to ask you to build a fire so I can cook supper," she said.

"We could have sandwiches," my father said.

"Davey needs more than that."

"No, I don't," I said. "I'd rather have sandwiches. It's too hot to eat."

"With milk, sandwiches would be enough for him," my father said.

We ate the sandwiches on the screened porch behind the kitchen, hoping for a breeze that didn't come. But the sun was down now and it was starting to seem cooler. We could see the bright red of sunset overhead and in the east, but the mesa behind the house cut us off from the real thing. As we sat on the back porch, we looked out on the coal bin, the chicken coop, and the steep, grassless face of the mesa. The chicken coop was empty.

"Rhode Island Reds," my father said. "That's what we'll get—Rhode Island Reds. Good layers and a wonderful bird for eating, fried or roasted. You can't beat a Rhode Island Red." He was talking to cheer us up.

After we had eaten, I helped my father make beds. My bow and arrows had been wrapped in the bedding. I was glad to have them again. They had belonged to an old Zuñi chief who had given them to me when we left Zuñi. He said it was a bow he had used when he was young. Its wood was worn shiny-smooth by all the hands that had rubbed it over the years. Its string was deer hide, my father said, very strong, and the arrows had hammered-steel points and eagle-wing feathers. The bow was still too big for me and hard to draw. My father didn't let me play with it often.

But this time when I asked, he said all right and drew the bowstring taut for me. I took the bow into the yard and shot arrows without taking aim, just seeing how far they would go. With nothing in their way and no wind, it seemed to me the arrows went farther than they had in Washington. I watched

—RESERVATIONS—

carefully to see where they fell and ran to get them as soon as I shot. I didn't want to lose them.

It started to get dark. I sat on the porch steps and watched the white picket fence dissolve in the dusk. My mother and father were talking inside and I could just hear their voices. What they said didn't sound like words at all. It was a hum like you hear if you stand under a telephone wire, only deeper. But I knew everything would be all right when I heard my mother laugh.

A boy came into the yard. He had his hands in the hip pockets of his Levis and was wearing a cowboy hat. He had a gun in a holster on his hip. For a minute I thought it was real.

"Hi, kid. I hear you just got here," he said.

"We got here today."

"Your old man the new principal?"

I nodded. I didn't like to have my father called old man.

"My old man's the trader. He runs this place."

"He won't run the school," I said.

"He will if he wants to."

"My father'll tell him to mind his own business."

"Yeah? If he tries that, my old man'll talk to Washington and your old man'll be out on his fanny."

I didn't say anything. He was a lot bigger and older than I was—ten, at least. Taking the bow and arrows out of my hands, he twanged the bowstring and bent the arrows back and forth. I was afraid he would break them, but I still said nothing.

"Where'd you get 'em"

"An old Zuñi man gave them to me."

"Let's go shoot this bow."

"It's too dark. I don't want to lose any arrows. You can shoot it tomorrow, though."

"Aw, it's not very dark. Come on."

He walked out of the yard, carrying my bow and arrows. I got up from the steps and followed him. I didn't want him to shoot my bow, but I didn't know how to stop him.

"What's your name?"

"Davey. What's yours?"

"That's a sissy name. Mine's Bill."

"It's not a sissy name!"

"I said it was. What I say goes, see?"

I followed him across the road and around to the other side of the schoolhouse.

"This'll do. You draw a circle on the wall." He pulled a black crayon out of his pocket.

"We better not mark up the schoolhouse. My father won't like it."

"My old man'll tell him to go to hell. Go ahead."

I took the crayon and drew a big circle on the white side of the schoolhouse. It was hard to do because the crayon jumped from one board to the next.

"Okay," Bill said. "We'll shoot at that circle, and the one who gets the most arrows in it gets the bow and arrows."

"Not for keeps," I said.

He didn't answer and paced off a long way from the building.

"I can't shoot that far," I said.

"What's the matter? You a weakling?"

"No. But I can't shoot that far."

"Go ahead, shoot."

He handed me the bow and three arrows. I stuck two of the arrows in my belt and fitted the notch of the other to the string. I couldn't see the circle at all. It was almost dark.

"What're you waiting for? Christmas?"

"I can't shoot that far."

"Go ahead. Shoot!"

None of my arrows even hit the building. They fell short and skimmed through the sand before they stopped.

He took the bow and put an arrow against the string, drew back and let go. The string twanged loudly. The arrow hit hard and splintered. He laughed and took another. This one landed in the target and stuck. So did his last one. He picked up the three arrows I had shot and pulled his two out of the schoolhouse.

"Where's the one that bounced off?"

"It's no good," he said. "It's broke."

I found it and picked it up.

"Well," I said, "I better go in. Give me the bow and the rest of the arrows."

"Like hell."

"It's not yours. It's mine."

"We said it belonged to the one that got the most arrows in the circle. You didn't even hit the schoolhouse."

"I said not for keeps."

"Yeah. You said not for keeps. I didn't say it, and what I say goes, see?"

"But that's my bow and arrows."

"They're mine now. I don't want you messing with 'em."

He ran up the road with my bow and arrows in his hand, making derisive sounds as he ran.

My father didn't even wait until morning. He went right up to the trading post and was back in a few minutes with the Zuñi bow and arrows.

"I feel sorry for the kid," he said. "His mother tried to get the bow and arrows without her husband knowing, but he heard us talking. The old boy's drunk as a coot and mad as a hornet. I heard the kid starting to yell before I was off the porch."

I didn't feel a bit sorry for him.

3.

ON A SATURDAY afternoon in the heat of August, Hosteen Tse came to call, accompanied by his sister Mrs. Tsinnijinni and her grandson. He pulled open the screen door and, in the Navajo fashion, marched into our living room without knocking. My parents and I were reading, half-asleep after a big noon meal.

As we got to our feet, Hosteen Tse spoke. Mrs. Tsinnijinni's grandson translated. "Hosteen Parker, I come to talk."

It was a time of drought. Corn shriveled in the husk. Squash and melon vines crept budless over cracked ground whitened by alkali. Gaunt sheep wandered over grassless plains that should have been green from summer rains. At the one time of year when food was usually abundant, Red Mesa Navajos were starving, kept alive mainly by the beans, flour, canned mutton, and other relief commodities my father handed out at the school once a week.

As I later learned, Hosteen Tse was a revered medicine man and spokesman for his people. He lived at Klinchee, across the mountains from Red Mesa. As a half-naked boy he had been among the far-ranging Navajos starved into submission in 1863 by Kit Carson and his New Mexico

Volunteers, who destroyed their crops and sheep and exiled them to Fort Sumner in eastern New Mexico, almost to Texas.

They were put on a barren reservation at Bosque Redondo, named for a clump of cottonwoods. There was no wood for fires or shelters. Water was scarce and alkaline. Crops would not grow. Over the next few years, three thousand Navajos died—three hundred in a smallpox epidemic, a hundred of dysentery after eating spoiled bacon issued by the army, many more of exposure and malnutrition.

In 1868 General William Tecumseh Sherman came to Fort Sumner to negotiate peace terms. He sat at a highly polished table under an open-sided canvas shelter set up to protect him from the burning sun. Hiding near the shelter, Hosteen Tse watched and listened as Barboncito and other Navajo leaders stood before Sherman and pleaded with him to let the *Dineh*—the People—go home to what Barboncito called "the happy land."

"After we get back to our country," Barboncito told Sherman, "it will brighten up again, and the *Dineh* will be as happy as the land. Black clouds will rise and there will be plenty of rain. Corn will grow in abundance and everything look happy."

In return for Barboncito's pledge that the Navajos would give up raiding and turn to farming, Sherman made many promises. Hosteen Tse heard him offer to let the Navajos keep their land forever, with sheep, seeds, tools, hospitals and doctors, schools with a teacher for every thirty pupils, and much more. It had happened long ago, but Hosteen Tse remembered it all, Barboncito's plea and Sherman's promises.

Thirty years later, Hosteen Tse had become an important Navajo leader himself. He traveled to Washington with a delegation to ask President McKinley to keep the promises Sherman had made at Bosque Redondo. President McKinley made new promises and gave Hosteen Tse a gold medal bearing George Washington's image to wear around his neck. Hosteen Tse remembered McKinley's promises, too.

Old and frail though he had become, Hosteen Tse was still an imposing figure when he came to call on my parents, bringing with him the pleasantly pungent smell of cedar smoke. He was erect and proud, elegantly dressed. Despite the heat, he had a heavy Pendleton blanket draped over his shoulders. Under it he wore a dark red velveteen blouse, circled at the waist by a belt of many silver conchas strung on a leather strap. His trousers were white and looked like pajama bottoms, loose and flowing. His hair, white as his trousers, was drawn into a knot and tied with a leather thong. Necklaces of bone, shell, turquoise, and silver hung around his neck, along with President McKinley's gold medal. Over the years the medal had turned green.

Hosteen Tse had been summoned to Red Mesa by Mrs. Tsinnijinni. She had also been at Bosque Redondo. Now one of her great-grandsons was dying of what my mother said was a combination of malnutrition and tuberculosis. The boy had been in a government hospital, but the doctors had given up hope of his recovery and allowed him to return home to die. Hosteen Tse was holding a sing over the boy, trying with chants and sand paintings to exorcise the *tchindi* that caused him to be sick.

Mrs. Tsinnijinni was poor and careless of her appearance, lacking the elegance and dignity of her brother. She swathed herself in shawls, which she did not take off though it was sweltering in the house, and wore layers of torn and dirty skirts. Her hair, more dingy gray than white, escaped the knot on her neck and straggled in lank strands around her face. She smelled of sweat, urine, and the rancid mutton tallow smeared on her hair.

Her grandson was the sick boy's father. Dressed in a bright rodeo shirt, boots, and Levis, he was there to translate, though Hosteen Tse knew English and my father enough Navajo to get by. This was a state occasion, which required both Hosteen Tse and my father to speak in their own tongues. It would be demeaning for Hosteen Tse to speak in a language not his own and condescending for my father to attempt it. Both knew that Hosteen Tse's visit would change nothing, but it was important for him to remind Washington through my father that there were promises to be kept.

Hosteen Tse took a seat in a rocking chair, but Mrs. Tsinnijinni sat on the floor beside the front door, a shawl drawn across her face. Only her eyes showed. Most of the time she seemed to be staring at the floor. But she missed nothing. If anyone glanced her way, her head snapped up and she glared back. Above the shawl her eyes were black coals lined with red, ready to burst into flame.

The grandson also refused a chair. He stood behind Hosteen Tse, feet apart, head down, clutching a ten-gallon hat by the brim with both hands. His hands rolled and rerolled the brim. They were the only part of him that moved.

For a long time Hosteen Tse sat silently. He rocked slowly, smoking the cigarettes my father offered him, sipping coffee my mother served, and fingering the tarnished medal among his necklaces. His lined old face was serene, withdrawn.

After three or four cigarettes and several cups of coffee, Hosteen Tse loosed a torrent of words in Navajo, shaking the medal at my father. What the old man said passionately, Mrs. Tsinnijinni's grandson droned out tonelessly, without emphasis.

"Hosteen Tse, he say, 'General Sherman, he promise *Dineh* land, sheep, tool to grow crop. Promise school, teacher every thirty children. Doctor, medicine, hospital. *Dineh* need thing

General Sherman, he promise.

"'General Sherman promise like President McKinley gold medal. No good. Teacher come, not enough. Doctor come, not enough. Trader come, too many. Bootlegger come, too many. White man cattle come, eat *Dineh* grass. Once grass high as horse belly. Now grass gone.

"'*Dineh*, they promise. They keep promise. President McKinley, General Sherman, they promise, not keep promise.'"

The grandson fell silent, but before my father could respond, Hosteen Tse spoke again.

"He say, 'Black cloud don't rise. Rain don't fall. Corn don't grow. Land, it not happy.'"

My father started to speak.

Hosteen Tse cut him off in English. "Sick boy die soon."

He rose and turned his back. The grandson wrapped Hosteen Tse's Pendleton blanket around him and helped the old man out the door.

Mrs. Tsinnijinni got up but did not follow. She ducked her head, averted her hot-coal eyes, and made little chuckling sounds, smiling toothlessly. She pulled a saddle blanket from under her shawls and held it out. On one side it was brightly patterned with bright zigzags of white and red-dyed wool. But on the other Mrs. Tsinnijinni had woven long strands of Angora wool into the blanket so thickly that the design was hidden. On the floor the little rug looked like an Angora fleece, all white except for a glossy patch of black in the middle. It was the kind of rug you knew would feel good under bare feet on a cold morning.

"Dollah," the old lady said. "One dollah."

My mother liked the rug instantly. She handed over the money. Mrs. Tsinnijinni scuttled off after Hosteen Tse.

My father sniffed the glossy patch in the Angora strands

and touched it with his finger.

"It's not stove blacking," he said. "I don't know what it is. Smells god-awful."

He carried the rug to the trading post.

"Caught you, did she?" Mr. Oates said. "The old lady's one of the best weavers around. I'd pay her three times what she gets from folks like you if she'd leave off the blacking. But that don't stop her. Every time she spots a greenhorn—"

"I'm no greenhorn," my father said. He had been teaching in the Indian Service for fifteen years by then. This was his second tour on the Navajo Reservation.

"—she'll mix soot into mutton tallow and smear it on a rug and sell it cheap. Nothing'll take that spot out. Whole rug turns dirty-looking."

"Why would she do a thing like that?"

Mr. Oates laughed. "To strike back at the enemy, I reckon."

"We're not the enemy," my father said.

Mr. Oates laughed again. "Try telling that to Mrs. Tsinnijinni."

4.

I SPOTTED THE MAN at the side gate. "Here's another," I said.

My father drained his coffee cup. Then he said what he said with every tramp's arrival, never finishing it. He said it like a groan or a prayer. "There but for the grace of God . . ."

Almost every day a lost soul or two wandered down U.S. 666 across the barren wastes of the Navajo Indian Reservation to stand at the upended barrel by the back gate. It always turned out that the tramp was passing through Red Mesa on his way to Gallup to ride the 'rods to sunny California. Every one of these penniless wanderers seemed to believe that the Santa Fe Railroad would gladly carry them for nothing to a land where all comers could find work and eat free oranges right from the tree.

"I'll fix a plate," my mother said. Almost from the day we got to Red Mesa, she had kept a pot of pinto beans and salt pork on the back of the stove, ready to serve with thick slices of her home-baked bread to sop up the bean juice. If it was close to baking day and we were running low on bread, she would send me to the trading post for a store-bought loaf.

The man stood by the side gate, bareheaded in the fierce

sun. He had a greasy canvas pack strapped on his back and looked like a heap of filthy rags about to collapse. Layers of dust and a week-old beard covered his face, but we could see that he was dreadfully sunburned. His lips were split and coated with dried blood. He tried to speak but managed only a croak.

I ran inside to get a pitcher of water and a tin cup.

My father reached over the fence and held the cup to the man's mouth, letting him take just a sip at a time. "Easy now, old fellow. Not too fast."

In a little while the man was able to hold the cup himself. He cleared his throat a couple of times and said, "I like to not made it. Never seen such a dry country. And hot? B'Jesus, it's hot."

"That's a bad burn you've got. Don't you have a hat?"

"Hat?" he said, looking puzzled. He put a hand to his head. "Had a hat. Don't know what in the world—lost it, I reckon."

He took another cup of water.

"You want a shower? You can do up your clothes, too, if you want. There are washtubs and a scrub board. I'll give you soap."

My mother came out the kitchen door, carrying a tin plate heaped with beans and bread.

"Mister," the man said, "I think I just died and gone to heaven."

"You eat that plate of beans," my father said, "and I'll show you the bathhouse."

The man ate slowly, smacking his lips to show appreciation. He did not say a word until the beans were almost gone. Then he looked around him and said, "No offense, hut what're folks like you doing in a place like this?"

"We're teachers. You're on the Navajo Reservation, and this is a United States Indian Service school."

"I be damned! Them people passing me by in their rickety old wagons was Injuns? And me begging for a lift or at least a little water? Never looked at me. Never said a word."

"The reservation's not easy country for anyone," my father said. "What possessed you to travel down this way?"

We knew what the answer would be. Every tramp told much the same story. Only the details differed. These were not prince-of-the-road hobos, who would have known better. They were hardworking men who had once had jobs and lost them, once had families and lost those, too. Hard times and hard luck had knocked right out of their heads whatever good sense they'd started with back home in Pittsburgh or Detroit or Gary. Befuddled now, heading for California and all those free oranges they had begun to believe in, they got as far as Denver or Colorado Springs and saw the Rockies looming. At a flophouse or mission or a Hooverville down by the railroad tracks, they learned—perhaps from some 'bo who looked like he ought to know or from a Bible-spouting soup ladler who claimed that he, too, had once been down on his luck and had made the very trip himself—that they could save a lot of time and miles by hopping a freight on the Denver & Rio Grande Western narrow-gauge to Durango. From there they could hitchhike down U.S. 666 to the Santa Fe main line at Gallup.

"Fella at the mission claimed it was easy," the man eating at the upended barrel said. "'Nothing to it,' the fella told me. 'Just cut cattywampus over the mountains to Durango on the D.&R.G.W, and you're practically to the Santa Fe.'"

He shook his head.

"Don't know what I was thinking, falling for that malarkey. Fella was just wanting to get me out of town. Even said the D.&R.G.W. bulls was the easiest to deal with he ever seen. Said just stay outa sight the best you can and they won't give you no trouble."

—*RESERVATIONS*—

The man sopped up bean juice with bread.

"*Mean?* I never seen railroad bulls to match them fellas on the D.&R.G.W. They didn't clear us off the freight when it stopped in town, which they easily coulda done. No, sirree. They waited till we was high in the mountains somewheres before they booted us off—middle of nowhere, middle of the night. Shoved us off and laughed. Barely had time to grab my bindle"—he gestured at the pack on his back—"afore I went rolling down a cliff, bouncing off rocks and trees. Lucky not to got bad hurt. That's when I found out D.&R.G.W. don't after all stand for Denver & Rio Grande Western. Them letters stand for Don't Ride, Gotta Walk."

With the bean-soaked bread halfway into his mouth, he stopped. He shook his head.

"And this here 666. I thought it was a U.S. highway."

"It is, but the big one is 66," my father said. "This is the one they call the Devil's Highway."

"Yeah. Well, didn't nobody tell me the difference. This here ain't nothing but a trail, not even graveled to speak of, and no more traffic than you'd find coming out of hell. I liked to died afore I got here."

He scrubbed the plate clean with a final crust of bread and wiped his lips on the back of a sun-blackened hand.

"I do surely thank you, ma'am," he said. "First thing I've ate in two days."

After his shower the man came back to the barrel. His clothes were dripping wet but scrubbed clean. He looked a different person. Shaved and with his hair combed, he seemed much younger than before. Not much more than thirty, if that, my father said later.

My mother brought out another plate of beans, along with more bread and a big mug of coffee.

Sipping coffee, the tramp asked, "You got any kids more'n

this here boy?"

"No, just Davey. About as much as I can look after, as it turns out."

"Well, that's the thing. It's you looking after them and them looking after you. What's hard, I tell you, is when you can't. When things is wanted and nothing you can do."

"I think about that a lot," my father said.

The tramp said, "We was doing good, me and the wife and kids—two big boys and a girl. Prettiest little girl you ever seen."

He stopped eating long enough to dig in an inside pocket until he found a little oilcloth bag with a drawstring neck. From it he pulled a rumpled photograph showing a woman flanked by two boys about three and four years old, both in long trousers. In front of her stood a tiny girl in a flowered bonnet and a white dress with a flaring skirt.

The photograph was too dim for us to distinguish any features. But as my father handed it back, he said, "A handsome family."

The man returned the picture to the oilcloth bag, which he tucked away. He spooned up the last of the beans.

"Then Mr. Ford laid me off." He burped loudly and patted his stomach. "And one night the wife and kids is asleep and I hear my little girl crying. When I go see what's wrong, she's crying in her sleep, the poor little tyke—sound asleep, crying—and I know she's hungry. My baby girl is starving and not a scrap of food in the house or money to get any. I go and get the butcher knife—"

I jumped and my father took a step backward. The man did not notice. Still patting his stomach, still talking, he seemed to be staring at something far distant.

"—and I hold the knife over that sweet baby crying in her bed, thinking to kill her and them all and then myself. But I

—RESERVATIONS—

can't bring myself to do it. I can't stand for her to cry either. So I walk me out the door and start for California. There's still jobs out there, or so I'm told, good paying jobs. And oranges to pick right off the trees. I can't hardly wait to sink my teeth in one of them oranges."

"You mean you just walked off and left your family like that? What are they living on?"

"I don't know," the man said. "Something, I expect. One of these days I'll send for them when I'm settled. It'll be all right then."

He picked up his canvas pack. He had scrubbed it, too, before he filled it with his wet clothes.

"Well," he said, "I got to get me a move on so's I can grab on to one of them A.T.&S.F. freights and get on my way to *Ca-ley-forn-eye-ay*. You know what them initials stand for, A.T.&S.F.?"

"Atchison, Topeka, and Santa Fe, I'd suppose," my father said.

I said, "I've heard, All Tramps and Suckers Free."

"That's it." The man's cracked lips drew back, showing surprisingly white teeth. I realized he was smiling. "Best 'road in the country, or so I'm told. Tramps and suckers. I ought to do fine, either way."

My mother gave him sandwiches and a jar of water to tuck into his backpack. My father found an old straw hat, which the man slanted at a jaunty angle.

"Well, I thank you," he said, shaking hands all around. "I'll think most kindly of you poor folks stuck in this here hellhole when I'm out there in sunny California enjoying them free oranges."

5.

WELL BEFORE ENROLLMENT DAY arrived, my father spread the word as widely as he could. He posted notices in every trading post and mission within twenty miles of Red Mesa, figuring that families who lived too far for their children to walk to school might have nearby relatives or clansmen who would take them in. If these too-distant families could not enroll their children in a day school like Red Mesa, they risked having them dragooned for off-reservation boarding schools. None of them wanted that. They knew their children would come back to them as strangers unprepared for reservation life but unwelcome in the off-reservation world.

My mother teased him about putting up written notices to reach people for whom the written word was as foreign as we were. He defended his approach. Most Navajos, able to read or not, were alert and curious people, he said, and quick to spot change. A new notice appearing in a familiar place was bound to attract attention. Those who could read it would inform those who could not of its contents. The word would spread by grapevine—"Navajo telegraph," my father called it.

He was sure of a crowd on enrollment day because he promised a free meal for everyone who appeared, parents and grandparents, aunts and uncles, people with children too young to enroll or no children at all—everyone. There was nothing in his budget to cover this community splurge and no authorization for it from his superiors at Fort Wingate, much less Washington. But he felt that the expenditure was justified because it would help him get to know the Red Mesa Navajos more quickly than he otherwise could.

He said he wanted to be able to connect names and faces to the numbers in his weekly reports. Just as important, the Navajos would get a chance to meet the outsiders who were asking to be entrusted with educating their children in the white man's ways.

People came in wagons, on horseback, on foot. By eight o'clock on the morning of enrollment day, at least two hundred men, women, and children were encamped around the school. Some had been there all night, and some had come from as far as Sanostee, well beyond Red Mesa's reach. Hosteen Begay, the school policeman and my father's chief assistant, said he had never seen a bigger crowd around Red Mesa, except maybe for a celebration marking the end of a medicine man's sing over a rich patient.

My father's promise of a free meal drew more people than the school kitchen was equipped to feed. Hosteen Begay organized the willing crowd to help out. Men built campfires in the grassless yard outside the kitchen for women to cook over. Pots of beans and salt pork that wouldn't fit on top of the big kitchen range nestled in hot coals, over which three sheep turned and browned and dripped fat. Nearby waited a wagonload of watermelons, the crowning treat of the day's feast. Hosteen Begay had traded six old buckets and some used lumber for the sheep. What he had traded for the watermelons, which had probably been stolen from the irrigated fields of Mormon farmers on the banks of the San

Juan River just north of the reservation, my father said he didn't care to know.

When enrollment started, right on time, Hosteen Begay stood at the schoolhouse door, directing returning students to my father's classroom, new students across the hall to my mother's.

It didn't take long to process even a new pupil. With the help of Mrs. Begay, who was Hosteen Begay's wife and the school matron, my mother got each child's family name and assigned American first names to those who did not have one suitable to appear on Indian Service rolls. She sought to make parents understand that the child had an obligation to appear every school day, on time, and tried to give them an idea of the schedule. She wanted to make both children and parents feel at ease, or at least not threatened. She smiled a lot, spoke slowly and softly, and gave Mrs. Begay plenty of time to translate and expand on whatever she said. She waited patiently while the parents, one or both, considered her offer to answer any questions they might have. Rarely did anyone ask a question, but they did not want to be hurried.

One of the last new students to appear was the niece of Mrs. Nez, the school cook and a sister-in-law of Hosteen Begay, who explained that she hadn't brought the girl over earlier only because Mrs. Nez had been busy getting things organized for the big noon meal.

Mrs. Nez said her niece was twelve years old but was late starting school for the usual reason—she had been needed at home to herd the family's sheep until younger sisters and brothers were old enough to take over the flocks. Now, Mrs. Nez said, the girl was being sent to school for a year or two before marriage. But her family lived north of Canyon de Chelly and there was no school near her home, so she had come to stay with Mrs. Nez at Red Mesa.

My mother said there would be other pupils the age of Mrs. Nez's niece in her classroom and she was glad to sign her up, though the girl might have trouble fitting into a first-grade desk. She was a big girl, tall and well-fed, richly dressed in billowing cotton skirts that reached to her high-topped shoes. Her form-fitting blouse of dark red velveteen was adorned with cone-shaped buttons made of silver dimes. The amount and quality of the turquoise-and-silver jewelry she wore—a concha belt, several bracelets, and a squash-blossom necklace—proclaimed that she came from a well-off family, a rarity around Red Mesa. Most of the students were dressed in little more than rags and came to school as much for free clothing and a daily meal as for education.

"What's her name?" my mother asked.

"She a Benallyi, but she got no name," Mrs. Nez said, meaning that the girl was a member of the Benallyi family but lacked a Christian name.

"We'll give her one," my mother said.

She looked closely at the girl, seeking a name that would suit her. The U.S. Army had begun the custom of assigning Indians names that a soldier could get his tongue around. The Indian Agents and eventually teachers who took over from the army to administer tribal affairs continued the practice. Now it was so ingrained a custom that my mother hardly found it strange to be looking at Mrs. Nez's niece while trying to decide which name of a Biblical, historical, or literary figure to bestow on her. Her class roster was already replete with Marys, Marthas, Dollies, Ruths, Sarahs, and Claras.

She liked what she saw and felt the girl should have a special name. Mrs. Nez's niece gave an impression of serenity coupled with alert intelligence and controlled energy. The girl had probably never before been in a man-made structure larger than a mud-chinked log hogan, except possibly a trading post, but she was not at all overwhelmed, merely curious.

While my mother pondered a name for her, the girl studied my mother's desk, with its papers and books, and my mother, too. She spent a long time examining the blackboard, where my mother had chalked in large block letters, "WELCOME TO RED MESA DAY SCHOOL." Under the words, my mother had drawn a smiling caricature of herself, glasses, bobbed hair, and all. In a balloon coming out of her mouth, she was saying, "My name is Mrs. Parker. I am your teacher."

Mrs. Nez's niece looked from the caricature to my mother several times, evidently satisfying herself that they were one and the same. She even seemed to weigh the curious marks in the balloon. Her cheek twitched in a way that hinted at amusement, at a smile waiting to happen. Looking at the furtively busy eyes arid twitching cheek, my mother saw warmth, wit, and wariness.

"Nellie," my mother said, pointing at the girl with her flat-topped orange fountain pen. I knew Nellie was my mother's favorite name, my great-grandmother's name. I didn't know then or for a long time afterward that it was the name my mother had given her first child, who had died at birth. I didn't even know then that I'd had a sister.

"Nell-ee," Mrs. Nez said. She repeated it several times, nodding her head.

Mrs. Begay also tried the name on her lips, liking it. The girl looked at Mrs. Nez blankly.

"You Nell-ee," Mrs. Nez said, continuing in Navajo.

Now the girl understood. She cocked her head to one side and pulled her shawl across the lower part of her face to conceal a smile. After a moment she let the shawl drop and turned the smile on my mother, not at all shyly.

"Nell-ee," she said, pointing to herself.

My mother seized the chance to instruct. "Nellie," she wrote on a fresh page of the tablet before her, saying it aloud as she did so and again pointing with her pen. In a few swift lines she drew a Navajo girl festooned with necklaces, her hair drawn tightly over her skull into a knot at the base of the neck, just like Nellie.

"Nell-ee," my mother repeated, pointing to the pad, first to the sketch and then to the name. She tore the page out of the tablet and gave it to the girl before starting to enroll another student. Mrs. Nez guided Nellie to a desk in the front row, where the newest pupils sat, and showed her how to squeeze herself into the seat, which had been designed for a small child, not a husky girl like Nellie. Then Mrs. Nez returned to her kitchen.

Nellie studied the drawing of herself on the yellow sheet she had been given before turning her attention to my mother's likeness on the blackboard. She nodded as she glanced back and forth from the blackboard to my mother.

After a time Nellie began exploring her desk. She ran her fingers over the polished wood and around the iron filigree of the frame. When she pulled the cork out of the ink bottle and poked in a finger, my mother seized a cloth and wiped off the ink before it dripped. Mrs. Begay scolded the girl for getting into the bottle, but Nellie ignored her. She pointed at the inkwell and looked questioningly at my mother, who brought a pen and a tablet and showed her how to dip the pen in the ink and make lines on the paper.

Nellie quickly mastered the art of using the pen without leaving blots. At first she drew only simple straight lines, but gradually she became more daring. She turned corners and curved her lines. My mother gave the other enrolled children paper and pens, too, but she could not coax them to draw. They were too timid, so frightened of her they trembled if she touched their shoulders.

By ten o'clock about thirty new first-graders had turned up, a good haul—my father's posters had done their work—but my mother knew that perhaps half would disappear as soon as the danger of being shipped off to boarding school was thought to have passed. When they left school, they would take with them not only some new clothing but also, as my father said, a few weeks' nutritious hot meals, which could do their general health no harm. They would also have had a useful exposure, however brief, to the white man's world, with which their own tribal world would have to coexist, like it or not.

Now the next stage of enrollment began. My mother and Mrs. Begay introduced the new girls to the mysteries of the washhouse. My father and Hosteen Begay took care of the new boys.

First, however, the children were conducted to the warehouse, where they were each measured by eye and given their new wardrobes—for many of them, the best reason of all to enroll in school. They each got a heavy wool sweater, a wool stocking cap, two pairs of socks and underwear—long johns for the boys, bloomers and woolen vests for the girls—and a pair of high-topped shoes, black for the boys, brown for the girls. In addition the boys got two pairs of bib overalls and two blue denim shirts. The girls got two cotton dresses apiece.

Each child would be required to shower once a week on a specified day and change to a clean set of clothing. A laundress, assisted by boys to keep fires going and girls to scrub and iron, did the washing and any necessary sewing. Clothes were marked with the owner's name and the extra set stored when not in use inside a locked cage built of two-by-fours and chicken wire at the washhouse.

Most of the new pupils had never before seen water that

began to run with the turn of a faucet, or a toilet that was more than a clean spot behind a bush. My mother said she remembered very well what being in a real bathroom for the first time was like. She had screamed when my grandmother turned on a faucet and water gushed forth. Even more sharply she recalled being put on the flush toilet instead of using the two-holer out back or a chamber pot in the house. My grandmother pulled the chain to flush while my mother was still on the toilet. The noise and a splash of cold water on her bottom so startled her that it was months before she would go into the new bathroom alone.

My mother said that as soon as she started showing the new students how to turn on a faucet, Nellie Benallyi pressed forward. A few drops spattered on the girl. She clapped both hands over her mouth. Her eyes looked like saucers, my mother said, but you could tell that under her hands was a big, unbelieving smile.

My mother invited the girls to put a hand in the stream of water. Nellie was the first to do it. After a hesitant try, she thrust both hands in. When my mother showed the girls the toilets, describing how they were to be used, Nellie was again right at her side and was the first to accept her invitation to flush one. Throughout the washhouse tour Nellie soaked up information, reveled in it, and was bold enough to ask Mrs. Begay a question or two. She had a soft, husky voice and gave the Navajo sounds a musical lilt. By the time my mother had demonstrated the shower, she felt sure that Nellie was the one child there who was ready without further instruction to use a toilet, wash her hands, or take a shower.

Before showering, the girls had their heads inspected for lice. The infested few were shorn on the spot by Mrs. Begay and their scalps soaked with gasoline to kill any eggs that had been laid under the skin. Then Mrs. Begay showed all the girls, those with lice and those without, how to soap themselves. As she shoved them one by one into a shower, most resisted — none more so than Nellie, who put up a furious struggle. Her eyes flashed lightning the whole time, my mother said, and her expression was so stormy you could almost hear the thunder. Mrs. Begay was as soaked as Nellie by the time she had the girl under the shower. But the tears soon ended, and Nellie held her face up to the water as though she were basking in the sun. She refused to leave the shower until Mrs. Begay reached in and pulled her out.

Each girl was allowed to pick which of her new dresses she would wear first. Nellie had one pink and one green, both in a flowered print. She instantly picked the pink. Looking in the single small mirror over the sinks, she preened, stretched, and turned from side to side in an open display of pleased vanity.

After the girls were dressed, they were sent out to my father and Hosteen Begay, who had set two stools in the shade of a cottonwood outside the washhouse and were clipping hair. A boy's cut took only a moment. My father or Hosteen Begay upended a shallow bowl over the child's head and chopped off any hair that showed below the rim. A girl's haircut, done without the bowl, took a little longer.

Perhaps because of their new dresses and all that had recently happened to them, none of the girls, not even Nellie, protested as they climbed docilely on the stool, to have their hair bobbed at mid-ear level. Every fifth child on each stool was handed a broom and told to sweep the fallen hair toward a pile that Hosteen Begay would later bury in some secret place. He did that, he said, to confound witches, who might otherwise use the clippings to work evil spells over those whose hair it was.

Promptly at noon, under the watchful eyes of Hosteen Begay and the rest of the school staff, the feeding began,

Tables for dispensing the food had been set up under struggling cottonwood trees in front of the dining hall. Hosteen Begay moved families whose children had been enrolled to the front of the line, displacing the many who, having come only for the food, had been able to stake out advanced positions. If someone disputed a ruling, Hosteen Begay had only to tap the shiny star on his chest.

The people knew the ropes. Most had brought their own pots, tin plates, or cans to load with food, but Mrs. Nez had saved empty No. 10 cans for families that lacked anything to put their food in. No one minded dropping chunks of mutton and ears of corn into a mix of boiled beans and stewed tomatoes. Tableware was no problem. Pocketknives, which every man carried, would cut meat. Fingers picked up beans and corn almost better than forks. For coffee and anything else too liquid to handle easily, Mrs. Nez offered small cans with the tops cut out. Warnings to watch out for sharp edges were not needed. Many people used cans like these as dishes at home. Mr. Oates at the trading post called them Navajo china.

The socializing between family groups ceased while the food was devoured. Each family settled down on the ground in some comfortable place under wagons or in the shade of buildings or trees to concentrate on the business at hand. Hosteen Begay was quick to head off any greedy folks who tried to go through the line more times than he regarded as seemly. By the time everyone was sated, not a scrap of food remained—not a bean or strip of mutton or taste of watermelon. There was no crumb left of the jawbreaker biscuits known as hardtack, no trace of peanut butter, no morsel of stewed tomato or remnant of fried bread to sop it up with. Everything was gone, and within minutes so were all the people, including the shorn children in their new finery.

From enrollment day on, Nellie Benallyi was my mother's

favorite—the brightest pupil she had ever taught, even back home in Texas. My mother never had to tell Nellie anything twice. The girl took to English as though she were being reminded of a language she had always known. Sometimes children who had never seen a written word or a book would take two or three years to grasp what reading was all about and then never get far beyond rote. Not Nellie. She saw almost instantly that the written words were constants, with fixed meaning she could grasp and apply to things around her.

My mother had become a teacher hoping to change the world and make it better. She had believed that education could unlock the natural goodness of her pupils, that the more adept they became at the three R's, the clearer would be their thinking, the more rational their behavior, the kinder their treatment of one another.

After years of teaching, she had given up on changing the world. Now she only hoped that sometime her teaching would make a difference, however slight, in the life of just one student. Just when she was beginning to despair of achieving even so small a triumph, Nellie came along.

As time passed, my mother gave Nellie more and more attention, justifying the special treatment with the thought that Nellie would put whatever knowledge she could impart to use. She felt she was enriching the girl's life and prospects to a degree that had not been true of any other student she'd had.

Nellie was quick not just in book learning. The school had several old foot-operated Singer sewing machines on which my mother and Mrs. Begay gave the girls lessons. Nellie became an expert seamstress with no apparent effort. She quickly developed a knack for pumping the treadle at just the right speed to keep the needle flying through her fabric.

The few clothes the children got at the start of a school year were all that the government issued. But it did provide bolts of material for school sewing projects. Nellie was the only first-grader, even among those as old or older than she, who worked fast enough at the strange craft to complete more than one new dress during the year. Thus she got more than her share of free material. My mother felt she deserved it.

As the end of her third year in school neared, Nellie was reading well beyond the fifth-grade level. By rights she should long since have been passed along to my father's classroom. But my mother persuaded him to let her keep the girl. She argued that the special rapport she had with Nellie was a useful teaching aid.

Nellie was not just eager to learn—she was wide open to knowledge. She would come frowning to my mother's desk when she had difficulty with an arithmetic problem, and suddenly the frown would disappear as she grasped the solution. She enjoyed turning the pages of *The Ladies Home Journal* or *Good Housekeeping*, studying advertisements for products unlike any she had ever seen. She listened raptly as my mother talked about the world away from the reservation, and the towns and cities where white people lived.

My mother began to think of Nellie as a daughter and dreamed of a wonderful future for the girl. There was no reason, she told my father, why Nellie could not eventually be sent to one of the better off-reservation Indian Service high schools—Phoenix, Albuquerque, or perhaps Riverside in California. It was one of the few times I ever heard her, or my father for that matter, mention the off-reservation boarding-school system in a positive way, except perhaps as a last-ditch refuge for orphaned or destitute children. Sometimes, dreaming, she even mentioned the possibility of college for Nellie and a career as a teacher. What better thing for Navajo children than a teacher of their own race? And a woman teacher in particular?

And yet. Another side of Nellie gave my mother pause—a still, listening, observing, withdrawn side, so private and inward, she said, that she doubted whether anyone who was not Navajo could hope to understand it. Even when that broad smile warmed her plump face, Nellie's eyes said she was waiting, pondering, making up her own mind out of some deep tribal consciousness that no non-Navajo could hope to probe. My mother loved her, wanted so much for her, could see all the wonderful possibilities in her. But some part of the girl was forever Navajo—distant, wary, beyond reach.

And then there was the dark cloud on Nellie's horizon that my parents never brought up in my presence but that I sometimes overheard them discussing. Sex. At recess, the older boys showed off for no one more than for Nellie.

The favorite game of Red Mesa boys of whatever age or size was tin-can hockey, which lent itself to showing off. It was a rough game, hard on shoes and knees—and sometimes backs, heads, and arms—but my father allowed it because he believed that boys needed a rowdy release after being cooped up in a stuffy classroom. We played this dry-land version of ice hockey on skates we made by stomping on Carnation evaporated-milk tins from the school kitchen until the stiff ends of the cans folded around the soles of our shoes, forming clamps. Then we staggered over the hard-packed ground, flailing at the puck—a flattened Carnation can—with a cedar branch, a broken broom handle, or anything else that would reach from our hands to the ground with reasonable rigidity.

While we boys played hockey, the girls skipped rope and played ring-around-the-rosy at the other end of the playground, under the supervision of my mother and Mrs. Begay. My mother said it was astonishing to see how often a Carnation-can puck would land at Nellie's feet with a couple of sweating, shouting boys tumbling after it.

I often heard my mother tell my father how much she worried about Nellie and the older boys. She tried several times to discuss the subject with the girl's aunt, Mrs. Nez, with no luck. Mrs. Nez shook her head as though her quite adequate knowledge of English had suddenly failed her.

One afternoon just before the end of the school year, my mother tried again to bring up the boy question. Sitting on a high stool in the school kitchen, having a companionable end-of-the-day cup of coffee, she confided, "Mrs. Nez, I am concerned about Nellie."

"Nellie, she all right."

"Yes, she's fine. But does she know about—ah, boys?"

"Boys?"

"You know, boys—ah, babies and—and all that."

"All that?"

"I wouldn't want Nellie to get in trouble."

"Trouble?"

"She's such a bright girl. She could go so far."

"Far? She a Navajo. Why she want to go someplace?"

"I don't mean go away for good. But she could go away to school, maybe even college, and come back as a teacher."

Mrs. Nez took her half-finished cup of coffee to the sink and rinsed it out. She hung her apron neatly on the pantry door.

"I go home now," Mrs. Nez said.

As my mother told my father, not knowing I could hear, she knew she had overstepped. Still, she was worried. Lately my mother had noticed clusters of boys loitering along in Nellie's wake as she headed home to the Nez hogan.

One day she asked Nellie to stay after school. When the other children were all gone, Nellie came up to her desk, smiling, but with that familiar wariness in her eyes.

"Nellie, my dear, I don't think you should walk home

alone with boys."

Nellie tilted her head to one side. Her smile faded. She looked as she did when she was struggling with arithmetic.

"Walk home?"

"After school I mean. I'm not sure you understand everything that might happen."

"Happen, Mrs. Parker?"

"I mean happen between a girl and a boy, between a man and a woman."

Nellie's cheek twitched, the way it did when she was holding back a smile. Remembering that a Navajo hogan was generally a one-room affair and families slept cheek-by-jowl on sheepskins around a center fire, my mother realized that the girl probably knew at least as much as she about relations between men and women. But she persevered.

"You have so much promise, Nellie—"

"Promise?"

"You could be so many things. A teacher. A nurse. You could go away to school—"

"I don't want to go away."

"Not for good. Just for training, and then you could come back and—"

"I don't want to go away."

The next fall Nellie did not appear on enrollment day. Mrs. Nez said she had married a hard-working young farmer at Canyon de Chelly who was well off and had no other wives. Her mother had given her a large herd of sheep and goats as a dowry.

"Nellie, she lucky girl," Mrs. Nez said.

My mother said, "I'm sure you're right."

That night I heard her crying as she told my father she felt cheated.

"I wish I'd called her Sarah," she said.

6.

BEFORE WOMEN WON the vote, my mother had been a marching suffragette back home in Texas, so she was delighted when she learned that a woman had become president of the Farmington National Bank.

She got the news in a clipping sent to her by one of her old marching buddies, who was now the secretary of a small-town bank president in Texas. It was the same small town from whose school system my mother had once been fired for parading down Main Street on market day carrying an inflammatory poster suggesting that women might—just might—be the equal of men in intelligence, probity, and civic awareness and hence worthy of a role in the arena of public affairs. My father was discharged by the same school district for applauding as she and her friends passed.

At the time my mother got the news about the woman bank president in Farmington, she and my father kept separate checking and savings accounts in Gallup at the State Bank of Commerce, which advertised itself as *The Bank Where Your Money Is Safe*.

The State Bank of Commerce was a noisy, bustling place. The tellers were all men and so were most of the customers.

Loitering ranchers wearing big hats and shiny boots leaned against walls that bore bunting-draped portraits of Presidents Harding, Coolidge, and Hoover. Any rancher who did not have a wad of tobacco bulging his cheek like a toothache was rolling or lighting a loose-packed cigarette that smelled like burning manure when lit.

But mostly they chewed and spat. No customer was ever more than a few feet from a spittoon at the State Bank of Commerce, though I never saw a rancher hit one. My mother, a rancher's daughter herself, said it was a wonder to her how those men made a living. All they ever seemed to do was stand around, drop burning butts on the floor to sizzle in spit, and make disparaging remarks to one another in loud voices about women who bobbed their hair, held jobs when men were out of work, and on top of that maintained their own bank accounts instead of handing their pay over to their husbands as God intended.

The Saturday after my mother learned about the woman bank president in Farmington, we drove there instead of to Gallup to buy groceries. My father was reluctant to shop in Farmington. He said he was perfectly willing for my mother to bank where she liked. After all, she worked as hard for her money as he did for his and got paid less. But shopping was a different matter. Gallup, with a population of over five thousand, was five times the size of Farmington and had ten times more stores. On top of that, Gallup was closer than Farmington to Red Mesa, and its prices were better. It was on a main-line railroad, while goods had to be trucked to Farmington—generally from Gallup, my father noted, and right past Red Mesa—which increased their cost. Going to Farmington instead of Gallup would mean a bigger grocery bill, not to mention the cost of the additional gasoline required for the longer trip.

—*RESERVATIONS*—

My mother countered by declaring that principle was worth something. Once her Farmington National account was set up, she could do her banking by mail and we could continue to shop in Gallup.

We left for Farmington early in the morning to avoid the worst of the day's heat. While my father stocked up on groceries at the Piggly Wiggly, my mother headed to the bank. I went with her. Farmington's main street was unpaved and dusty. A few establishments, such as the Postal Telegraph office, had crude sidewalks out front made of loose boards laid end to end. Only the bank boasted a sidewalk of poured concrete. The bank had not just the usual hitching post but also a brim-full watering trough for the teams that farmers drove to town. Any good businessman might have installed a hitching post for the convenience of customers, and most did, but in that watering trough my mother felt she divined a woman's sensibility.

The Farmington National Bank was built like a fortress. It had a flat roof and barred windows, and its walls were solid stone, two feet thick. Stepping inside out of the hot sun on that bright September morning was like entering a cool cave where ceiling fans gently churned the air. Globe-shaped lamps of gleaming brass topped by fringed shades of age-yellowed parchment cast circles of golden light here and there in the welcome dimness. One lamp stood on the high table where customers filled out deposit slips, and others lighted the two tellers' cages. One teller was a woman, my mother pointed out. There was not a cuspidor or Herbert Hoover poster in sight. The customers were mostly Mormon farmers—straw hats, bed-ticking overalls, scuffed boots caked with dried mud— who neither smoked nor chewed. They took off their hats as they entered and spoke politely, if at all.

Behind a gleaming wooden railing still another brass lamp

spread its light over an account book and a vase of roses on a polished mahogany desk, at which Mrs. Tolliver sat. She was a small woman, older but no taller than my mother, dressed in a black suit with a flowing skirt that barely cleared the floor when she stood. My mother soon learned that Mrs. Tolliver had also been a suffragette. In no time the two were sipping tea and reminiscing about battling for the vote. They were like two old acquaintances picking up the threads of friendship after a long separation.

With such an auspicious start, the banking business was transacted as though preordained. My mother transferred her checking account and her two savings accounts from the State Bank of Commerce to Farmington National. She also arranged to deposit her government paycheck by mail. It would amount to about $80 a month, she told Mrs. Tolliver. Ten dollars was to be deposited in each of the savings accounts, and the balance of $60 was to go to checking. The total, she added, was shamefully less than the government paid my father for work not markedly different from hers.

"Women are always shortchanged," Mrs. Tolliver said. "I worked right at my husband's side in this bank for thirty years, but I wouldn't be president if he hadn't left me his stock. Even then, I had to insist on taking charge. But why do you have two savings accounts? Why not just one?"

My mother explained, after turning to me with a reminder.

"Now, Davey, this is a secret and you are not to say a word about it to anyone." One savings account was for my education, and the other—this was the secret—she had opened to send my father to the Chicago World's Fair of 1933.

"Mrs. Tolliver," she said, "my husband grew up on a hardscrabble little farm in Texas and has always been poor. He is a good man, and hardworking. He has never been able to do many of the things he might have liked to do, but I have never heard him complain. When we first learned about the World's Fair, I heard him say that he would give anything to go. He said it in a way that told me he thought it was just another of those impossible dreams, like seeing New York or the Parthenon. And I determined that he should go. Ever since, I have been putting $10 a month aside without his knowing it so that he can be there when the World's Fair opens next year in Chicago."

"Will you and the boy go with him?"

"No," my mother said. "There won't be enough for that, but for once in Will's life a dream will come true, and I shall have the pleasure of knowing that I had a part in bringing it about."

"Hurrah for you," Mrs. Tolliver said. "And count on it—your money will be safe with me. No depositor in Farmington National Bank has ever lost a dollar, or ever will."

"That's what the State Bank of Commerce says," my mother said.

"But I mean it," Mrs. Tolliver said.

On the way home, I stretched out on the backseat among bags of groceries while my father drove through the night into a little saucer of light that we never quite reached. Beside him my mother murmured something, an account of our meeting with Mrs. Tolliver, I supposed, but surely not the whole of it. They were a mystery to me, those two in the front seat—one mystery, not two. I knew that even if I could hear what she was saying, there would be messages going back and forth between them that I would not be able to fathom. I was both a part of that mystery they shared and outside it.

After a while my hand fell on the stiff spot in the green velour upholstery that was a memorial to the time when the old car was new and I was small and had thrown up in the backseat. I scratched at that mark of unforgotten disgrace—

unforgotten by me — until I fell asleep.

The winter following the election of Franklin D. Roosevelt was the coldest that anyone in that part of the reservation could remember, with the deepest snows and the worst blizzards. The drought had finally broken, but the resulting weather was disastrous. To find grass for their flocks, the Indians burrowed through snow with shovels, sticks, even bare hands. At night they took as many sheep as they could into their hogans to keep the animals alive. When firewood ran out, they burned corrals, their wagons, and even logs from the hogans.

Each week more and more people came to claim the government rations of beans, stewed tomatoes, and canned mutton, sometimes with peanut butter and flour or hardtack, that my father and Hosteen Begay handed out down at the warehouse. Often the supplies were gone before the last person in line reached the storehouse door. Then it was time to go to our own pantry. Because of the extra food my parents bought to give away, their bank accounts shrank week by week, month by month — all the accounts, that is, except my college fund and the secret World's Fair fund, which my mother added to each month no matter how hard it was to do.

In the evenings my father cranked the old Kohler generator that supplied our electricity. We read until just before nine o'clock, when we gathered around the radio, an old battery set that because of atmospheric interference brought in only static during daylight hours. After dark, with much spinning of dials, my father could tune in to Station KOB, Albuquerque, *The Voice of the Great Southwest*. We strained to hear a faint voice reading the news, me lying on the floor in front of the radio, my head practically in the speaker, and my parents leaning forward side by side on the couch. What we heard in those dying days of the Hoover administration were reports of closing factories, growing unemployment, lengthening bread lines, and failing banks. The news seemed only a confirmation of the disaster we could see around us.

When my father stood up to snap off the set, which he did as soon as the news ended, so as not to run down the batteries, my mother would say, "Once Mr. Roosevelt takes office, things will change." She said it night after night, not so much in hope as despair, knowing that any change had to be for the better.

The coming inauguration and the Chicago World's Fair were about all we had to look forward to that winter. My mother and I pointed out every newspaper and magazine story on the fair that we could find. To drum up travel business, the Santa Fe Railroad printed brochures extolling the marvels being prepared in Chicago. My father devoured every word, relaying tidbits to us as he read.

A Century of Progress, the fair was called. It promised displays of all the wonders that America's greatness had brought forth — wonders of science, technology, manufacturing, agriculture. There would be crowds, lights, laughter. A car that changed colors before your eyes. Hot-air balloons and a zeppelin. A demonstration of an amazement called television that was said to carry pictures through the air as a radio carried words. A descendant of Balboa would fly — *fly!* — from Rome to visit the fair.

As my father passed along bulletins from his reading, I was often tempted to give away my mother's secret. I never did. Sometimes in the evenings while she was preparing supper, she and I whispered gleefully about how surprised he would be when he learned that he was going to the World's Fair to see for himself the glorious changes a hundred years had made in America. Our great country had gone from wagons and coaches to railroads, airplanes, and automobiles; from candles to electric lights; from Pony Express to telegraph, telephone, and radio; from outhouses to indoor plumbing. The list of changes to celebrate seemed endless.

As March 4, Inauguration Day, drew near, my parents decided to dig deep into their dwindling resources to buy a new radio. It would be one that worked off the Kohler's electricity instead of batteries—one that would be powerful enough to overcome daytime static so that we could hear Mr. Roosevelt's address as he spoke. After much study of catalogs and advertisements, my father ordered a Grunow Majestic from the Gallup Mercantile Co. It was the most powerful set he could find at a price we could afford and had only one drawback. It required alternating current, while the Kohler delivered direct current. We could get around this with a converter, which by some magic would suck in DC power at one end and emit AC power at the other.

The next time the Red Ball freight truck came past Red Mesa, it brought the Grunow Majestic and the converter. The driver, a hard-drinking little man named Foxey, refused my father's State Bank of Commerce check but was willing to accept my mother's, drawn on the National Bank of Farmington. My father asked Foxey what he had heard to make him turn down a check on the biggest bank in western New Mexico. Foxey said Mrs. Tolliver was the only honest banker he knew of in any part of the state.

I helped my father string an aerial to the water tank on top of Red Mesa. It was still light when we finished and plugged the converter into the wall socket and the Grunow Majestic into the converter. KOB came in so strong and clear that it easily drowned out the converter's hum. The first thing we heard was a bulletin from Gallup. The State Bank of Commerce had closed its doors that afternoon to stop a run by depositors demanding their money. Suddenly we had nothing

—RESERVATIONS—

to live on but my mother's small checking account with Farmington National, which she had virtually emptied in paying for relief food and the new radio.

The next day KOB brought more bad news. To head off a statewide panic in the wake of the Bank Commerce's collapse, New Mexico had ordered a bank holiday. All banks in the state were to close, and no bank would be allowed to reopen until examiners had gone over its books and certified that it was sound.

My father slapped the shiny top of the Grunow Majestic with the flat of his hand. "What are we going to live on when Farmington National closes?"

"Mrs. Tolliver won't close," my mother said.

She was right about Mrs. Tolliver, who told KOB Farmington National would keep its doors open despite the state order. Farmington National was sound as a dollar—perhaps, she said, the way things were going under Hoover, sounder—and no two-bit state politician could make a national bank close down, not even for a day. If any of her depositors were worried about their funds, Mrs. Tolliver declared, they could have it in currency or gold—their choice. My mother did not even think of withdrawing her money from Mrs. Tolliver's bank.

On Inauguration Day I sprawled on the floor in front of the Grunow Majestic. Looking over my shoulder at my parents sitting side by side on the couch, I felt I was seeing them as I would had we been driving along in the old Dodge with me sitting out front on the hood, facing backward and watching them through the windshield. I could see my father's long fingers tighten on the car's wooden steering wheel.

President Roosevelt's voice rang out as though he were speaking in the next room. He told us that the only thing we had to fear was fear itself, but he was declaring a bank holiday of his own nonetheless. Every bank in the country was to be shuttered while its books were examined.

Once again my mother said, "Mrs. Tolliver won't close."

"She'll have to," my father said.

He was right.

"Well, Mary," he said when we heard the news, "no Century of Progress for me."

She was crying. "I didn't think you knew," she said.

He put his arms around her. "Of course I knew."

They looked at one another. Suddenly they were laughing, maybe crying at the same time. A mystery to the end, those two, riding side by side in the front seat of an old Dodge into an ever-receding saucer of light.

7.

WE STOOD on the front porch out of the rain and watched the car slither and slide toward us. It was buried to the hubs in mud but kept moving. The rain was the first we'd had all spring, coming on top of a sudden snowmelt that had turned the roads to mush.

"T-Model," my father said. "Best mud car ever made. Look at it buck through that gumbo."

We were waiting for Mr. Staley, who had been a friend of my parents since before they were married. He had written a postcard a week or so earlier saying he was on a business trip for the Fuller Brush people and would be stopping by to see us. He and my father had once sold brushes together in El Paso, and Mr. Staley had married my mother's best friend.

My mother said, "Why do you suppose he's driving an old Ford and selling brushes again? I thought he was supposed to be doing well out there in California, selling new Plymouths."

"I'm sure he'll have a plausible explanation," my father said.

"Dick's explanations are always plausible," she said.

The Model T turned off onto the school road and pulled up at our gate. A barefoot man wearing only muddy BVDs unsnapped the isinglass side window and crawled out over the door, which lacked a handle and was lashed closed with baling wire. He reached back in for a pair of shoes and a bundle of clothes and then rushed up the sidewalk through the rain, bending over the clothes to keep them dry as best he could while holding them away from the mud on his underwear.

"Lord God," he said when he got to the porch, breathing hard. "I never seen such a country. Dust one minute, mud the next. Worse'n Texas."

His arms and legs and even his hair were coated with red mud. Rivulets of rainwater bright as fresh-drawn blood ran down his face.

My parents laughed and talked all at the same time, trying to welcome him. Mr. Staley was busy looking for a dry place to put down his clothes.

"Forgive me appearing before you in my underwear," he said, "but I have to protect my working garb or I'm out of business."

My mother took his clothes. "I'll dry these and press them, too, Dick. Don't worry."

"Here, young fella," Mr. Staley said. "Show me your pump. I got to wash this goddamn mud off. It ever hardens on me, I won't be good for nothing but standing on a pedestal for a statue."

"We can do better than a pump," my father said. "We may be out in the middle of the Navajo Reservation fifty miles from town, but one thing we've got plenty of is running water. How'd you get so all-fired muddy?"

"Somebody must've went and sold the bottom out of your road. I was told it was a U.S. highway, but it ain't even graveled. Lord God, I high-centered three times since I left Gallup and had to dig out."

—*RESERVATIONS*—

We put on slickers and took Mr. Staley to the school washhouse, where there were showers. He was too muddy for our tub.

"Lord God, Lord God," Mr. Staley muttered, looking around as we went. "The end of the world. Oh, Lord God. Why hast Thou brought me to the end of the world?"

While he showered, the rain let up. My father and I hauled Mr. Staley's suitcase in from the Model T. We brought in his Fuller Brush case, too. It was big and black, maybe three feet square and six inches thick, but not heavy. Its sides were made of some stiff material that might have been only cardboard but gave the impression of being something more substantial, like steel, or at least plywood.

Mr. Staley came back to the house smiling, his hair slicked down. My father's shirt and pants fit him pretty well, though he'd had to leave the top button of the pants open and turn up the legs. He had washed out his BVDs, which my mother took to the kitchen to dry. She came back with a cup of coffee.

He took a sip. "A little more cream, Mary? And maybe a spoon more sugar? Maybe two spoons?"

"Of course," she said. "I couldn't remember how you like your coffee. It's been a long time, Dick."

"A precious while," he agreed. He reached over and grabbed my ear, yanking hard enough to hurt. "Long before this young fella here was even a gleam in his daddy's eye. Last time I seen you, Mary, was about the time you folks decided fame and fortune wasn't to be yours and you'd rather teach Indians for Uncle Sam than work for a living."

"We work hard," she flared.

"Now, Mary, he's just joking," my father said. "You always could get her goat, Dick."

"I'm sorry," she said. "I forget what a tease you are. But tell me—how are Ella and the girls? You didn't say a word about them on your postcard."

"Oh, they're fine, just fine, I'm sure," Mr. Staley said. "Living the life of Riley out there in Modesto, most likely, which'll be just fine till Riley gets home."

"I was hoping they'd be with you," my mother said. "It's been so long since I've seen Ella or even heard from her."

"Well, with the girls in school, you know, she keeps pretty busy with her sewing and all."

"My last letter to her came back marked 'No such person at this address.'"

"Which address is that?"

"The one you've had for—goodness, I don't know how long."

"I can't understand that. Lord God, no, I can't understand it. That address is good as gold."

My mother asked when he had gone back to selling Fuller brushes. He did not seem to hear. He wrapped both hands around his coffee cup and lifted it to his face, breathing in the steam.

At supper my mother brought out her good china and even her grandmother's silver serving spoons. While we ate, my father reminisced about selling brushes with Mr. Staley in El Paso after he and my mother lost their teaching jobs because she had marched in a suffragette parade. That was before they were married. Mr. Staley had gotten him the Fuller Brush job, which he said he kept just long enough to learn that there were two kinds of people in this world, salesmen like Mr. Staley and non-salesmen like himself. Mr. Staley, he said, was as good a door-to-door salesman as ever put a foot in a door.

"I remember one time we made a bet," my father said. "You remember, Dick? You came up right after me to knock at doors where I was turned away and the bet was that if you didn't get inside and sell two out of the first three of those places, you'd buy me a brand new Stetson hat."

Mr. Staley had not been doing much talking. He was busy shoving food into his mouth—fried chicken, canned corn, stewed tomatoes, mashed potatoes and gravy, hot biscuits with honey. Now he paused while dishing up more corn. It was the creamy kind, my favorite. He hefted the serving spoon in his hand and shook his head, smiling. "I remember, Will. Three out of three I sold. I wore that fine Stetson you bought me for, oh, I imagine, ten years."

"And one of those places was a widow lady whose husband had died that very day," my father said. "I never did understand how you made that sale. All I could think to do was apologize to her for intruding on her grief and skip off the poor woman's front porch fast as I could. But you sold her."

"Pass me that there plate of biscuits, young fella," Mr. Staley said. "The honey, too."

Smiling, shaking his head, he broke open a biscuit, spooned honey over it, and stuffed it into his mouth, talking around it.

"Will, that was about the easiest sale I ever made. You're just too soft. You looked at those brushes you was trying to sell and that's all you seen—a brush to do this, a brush to do that—and you tried to tell the customer that this one or that one was just such a brush as she needed.

"What you got to do is forget what's there in front of you and make the customer see something more'n what's there, so's they'll convince themselves they can't do without it, whatever it is. You got to help the customer dream a little, and that's what you was always too persnickety to do. Take that widder lady."

He paused to smear honey on another biscuit and went on talking with his mouth full.

"When you heard about her recent loss, her husband not even in his coffin yet, you swallowed hard and skipped off her porch like you said. What I done was stay and commiserate with that poor lonely widder lady until I seen a chance to remind her that while from then on it was going to be up to her to scrub her own back in the tub, at least she was going to have her late husband's insurance money to spend as she liked, with no one to say no. And I asked if in her hard-earned grief could she think of any one thing more comforting to spend part of her new wealth on than a nice back scrub? I not only sold her a bath brush—you remember the kind, with the long pink celluloid handle, thirty-six cents, I think they were then—so she could scrub her own back with ease and pleasure, I sold her a vegetable brush, too. And all because it wasn't just a brush I was selling. It was comfort for a grieving woman."

"I thought those vegetable brushes were supposed to be free, a gift you gave people just for letting you in the door," my mother said.

"Fortunately the widder lady didn't know that," Mr. Staley said. "I made an extra fifteen cents off her and had no choice but to keep it all. Lucky me. I'd a been fired in a minute had the boss found out I sold that brush instead of giving it away."

Mr. Staley let himself be persuaded to have more chicken and two pieces of lemon meringue pie. When he finally shoved himself away from the table, he made a big show of having to undo a second button of the pants my father had lent him.

"With food like that on the table, Will, I don't see how you've stayed so skinny all these years," Mr. Staley said.

"We don't have company very often," I said.

Everybody laughed.

Mr. Staley grew serious. "I suppose not. Not much company. What about neighbors?"

"Not many of those either," my father said. "The nurse

next door is another widow, still grieving for her husband though he's ten years dead. Keeps to herself. Won't answer her door anymore, even for the sick and injured. And the trader up the road a piece, Mr. Oates. His wife left him not long ago, taking their kids, and he lives with some Indian women—a regular harem. Drinks a lot. A surly sort. Over toward Big Spring ten miles or so, there's a Baptist mission. Reverend Schutte and his wife. They'll have you in the tank with water over your head before you can holler 'Fuller Brush.'"

"That's all? A bereaved nurse who don't come to the door, an Injun trader who drinks too much, and a couple of missionaries who'll want to talk souls instead of brushes? Not much business there. Who lives in the other houses I seen the other side of the washhouse?"

"Empty," my father said. "There's supposed to be a farmer, a road-maintenance man, and the like here, but the Indian Service is in a real budget squeeze, so we're short of people. Folks say it'll be different now that Mr. Roosevelt has taken office, but right now—well, we just count ourselves lucky to have jobs."

Mr. Staley tilted his face heavenward. "Lord God. And You let me come all this way?"

He sat brooding over his coffee cup. Finally he straightened up and smiled around the table at us. "Well, make hay while the sun shineth, saith the Lord."

He leaned over to my father and whispered, but I heard every word. "Will, you got anything to, ah, wet the whistle?"

My mother heard him, too. "No," she said. "Not in my house, Dick."

"Ah, yes. Temperance," Mr. Staley said. "You and Ella, both Temperance, always was. But at least you can cook. That's one deal you got the better of me on, Will. I should've took Mary and left Ella for you."

"I might have had something to say about that," my mother said.

"No offense meant," Mr. Staley said. He stood up and winked at my father. "Will, I got something out to the car I think will interest you."

My mother washed dishes and I dried. We worked mostly in silence.

After a while, I asked, "What did Mr. Staley mean, he should have taken you?"

She paused with her hands deep in suds. "There was a time when he might have thought he could choose between Ella — Mrs. Staley — and me."

"I'm glad he chose her."

"He didn't. I chose your father."

She gave me a fresh towel to dry the serving spoons, and I polished until they gleamed. She was putting the spoons away in the back of the pantry, where she always hid them, when Mr. Staley and my father came in the back door, stamping their feet and shaking raindrops off their slickers. I could smell the whiskey as soon as they came in.

"Well, young fella—" Mr. Staley said.

"My name's Davey," I said.

"David!" my mother said.

"All right, Davey," Mr. Staley said. "You are now going to have an opportunity, a rare opportunity, to see a master salesman at work and to judge for yourself what a fortune there is to be made by those who know how to sell.

"I am tonight going to spark the fires of ambition in your youthful breast by demonstrating in your presence the wonderful art of drawing money from those who do not at the outset mean to give it. I am, in short, going to show you how to plant dreams, move merchandise, and turn a buck. By the end of this evening, there will be nothing in this world you will want to be more than a salesman. And you will understand, my young friend, something of utmost importance in this crass and materialistic world in which we live and in which you, too, will have to make your way. And what you will understand is, it don't matter what you've got to sell. I've sold brushes and I've sold cars and now I'm selling brushes again, and I can tell you this—if you can sell one thing, you can sell another. Cars or brushes. It don't matter billy-damn."

Taking off her apron, my mother asked the same question he had failed to answer earlier. "Why did you quit selling cars, Dick, and go back to brushes?"

"Lord God, for the selling, of course," Mr. Staley said. "There's no selling with cars. Customer knows what he wants. Comes in when he's ready. Buys it. The salesman don't sell, he just takes the order. Oh, there may be a little haggling over price, but that ain't selling—that's just poker. Now brushes, you've got to sell brushes."

Mr. Staley led us into the living room, where his case stood against the wall. He put my mother and father in the middle of the couch and motioned me to sit on the floor in front of them.

"I really don't need any brushes, Dick," my mother said, "nor can I afford them just now. We are just barely getting by."

"Ah, but these are wonderful brushes at the very best prices."

"I still don't need or want another brush. I had about enough to do with brushes when Will was trying to sell them."

"Well, surely you wouldn't deny this young fella the opportunity to observe in action the greatest salesman who ever put a foot in a door, as my good friend Will so kindly put it?"

"Not if I don't have to buy a brush."

"Have to? There's no such thing as have to for you, Mary,

never was, though if you was to change your mind and buy a brush tonight, you would not have to wait for delivery. I'm in a position at this time to offer immediate delivery of any brush that interests you, direct from my display case."

"But isn't it against company rules to sell off your samples?"

He wasn't listening. He squatted by his case and opened it. It was hinged in the middle and opened like a book, with brushes hanging on hooks on both sides. It was like being in a store. I had never seen so many kinds of brushes, each brush in its own place, clamped to the side of the case. But I saw that at some time he had had even more brushes. There were quite a few empty places.

"Ah, Lord God, beautiful," Mr. Staley said. "Tell me straight, Will, don't you sometimes wish for your brush case, everything so new and bright and useful?"

"Can't say I do," my father said.

Mr. Staley opened a small case nestled among the brushes in the big case. Inside the small case were jars and bottles, not brushes.

"These may be new since your day, Will. Wonderful products, better than you can buy in any store—lotions, ointments, household cleansers, that kind of thing."

My father leaned forward, interested. "I didn't know Fuller Brush was branching out."

"Strictly speaking they ain't, or if they are, it don't signify. I'm no longer selling exclusively for Fuller Brush. No, an unaffiliated company has offered a few exceptional Fuller Brush representatives such as me the opportunity of a lifetime. I have, as it were, caught the eye of this unaffiliated company and am authorized to—"

"You mean you're selling something on the side without the Fuller Brush people knowing about it? I thought they didn't allow that," my father said. I realized he didn't like Mr. Staley either.

"That's one way to put it," Mr. Staley said. "But let me ask this young fella here—"

"My name's still Davey," I said. This time my mother did not scold me.

"Very well, Davey, though I will say that if you were my son, as you might have been—"

"He's not," my mother said.

"—and spoke to a guest in my home that way—"

My father said, "Mr. Staley is right, Davey. You were very rude."

"I'm sorry, sir," I said. I was speaking to my father, but Mr. Staley chose to misunderstand.

"A handsome apology, young fella," he said. "No offense intended, no offense taken. But as I was saying, can you tell me what all these different brushes is for?"

"No," I said.

"Exactly," Mr. Staley said. "Very few people do know. Many are surprised at what convenience, what labor-saving, what cleanliness is made possible by the brush displayed in this case before your very eyes."

"It's getting late, Dick," my mother said.

"There's just one thing I especially want to show you, Mary, and it isn't even a brush." He reached into the case within a case and pulled out a chamois and a white jar with a black top.

"Those serving spoons at supper—beautiful silver, solid sterling, I could tell soon as I picked them up. And I could see you spent a lot of time polishing them before placing them in front of a guest. But Mary, the fact is, those spoons do not show to half the advantage they could with a bit of real care. No, no—don't bridle like that, Mary, I am not criticizing your housekeeping. Unlike Ella, you was always neat as a man could wish."

"Dick, Ella is my friend. I don't know where she is or what the trouble between you two is, but I will not have her criticized."

"I'm not saying a word against Ella, I'm just saying that the best housewife in the world couldn't do in half an hour as good a job polishing silver as this here chamois cloth and special cleanser will do in half the time—a tenth the time. Young fella, bring me those spoons."

My father shook his head. "Davey has to go to bed."

"I'm afraid I must, too," my mother said. "Tomorrow is a working day."

"You wouldn't like your spoons polished?"

"No."

Mr. Staley shrugged. "Your loss." He closed his cases.

"Well, young fella," he said. He looked tired. "What do you say? Want to be a salesman like me?"

"I'd rather be like my dad."

"Lord God, young fella," he said, "you already are."

Mr. Staley left after breakfast the next morning to struggle back to Gallup through the mud. He said he'd made a costly mistake in thinking there might be business to be done at Red Mesa. He left wearing my father's shirt and pants. He wrote a check on a California bank for $20 in return for all the cash we had in the house.

It was the next day before my mother discovered that her spoons were missing. The California bank turned out not to exist.

8.

EVERY SO OFTEN, unmarried teachers from the far reaches of the Navajo Reservation showed up at Red Mesa for Sunday dinner with my mother.

My father and I were there, too, of course, but we were incidental. My mother was the attraction. The women came by ones and twos and threes, traveling up to a hundred miles over roads that were mostly no better than trails, bearing pots of soup, fresh-baked rolls, extravagant desserts. My father called the women Mary's Troops.

The troops were all in their twenties or early thirties, younger than my mother and, as she said, not yet resigned to spinsterhood. Most of them were southerners or midwesterners who had grown up on farms or in small towns. They regarded teaching on the Navajo Reservation as an adventurous interlude in otherwise pedestrian lives. In the old days, before President Roosevelt's commissioner of Indian Affairs, John Collier, began to reform the system, the government had not assigned single women to one-teacher day schools. Now women taught at schools once reserved for men. Mary's Troops felt that they were thumbing their noses at a male-dominated society but not renouncing it, not yet.

There were five regulars whose attendance could be counted on and about a dozen irregulars. The regulars called one another by last names. Mayne. Keith. McGehee. Schroeder. Lewis. The irregulars, failing of full membership in the sisterhood because of recent arrival or erratic attendance, were not privileged to share in the informality. They put a *Miss* in front of the names of the regulars and were themselves referred to as Miss Ryder, Miss Ehrlich, Miss Macdonald, and so on. Only my mother was known to all by her first name.

The arrival of her troops never seemed to catch my mother by surprise. She always had a big ham in the oven or an extra chicken or two from our flock of Rhode Island Reds stewing in a pot or chopped up and breaded, ready for frying.

Today it was to be chicken. I had plucked the birds that morning, with my nostrils stinging from the acrid smell of blood and wet chicken feathers. With the chicken we would have mashed potatoes, plus okra, green beans, and corn on the cob, all from our garden. I had finished shucking the corn just before Mayne drove up in her little Ford coupe.

Mayne was my mother's favorite — no bones about that — and mine, too. She was the liveliest and prettiest of the troops and one of the youngest. From Texas originally, she had grown up in a land-owning family that had once been but was no longer well off. She was blonde with creamy skin but not at all fragile-looking — a large woman, big rather than fat, with prominent teeth and a jaw that thrust forward as if ready for a bridle. She wore floppy-brimmed hats to protect her complexion from the sun and loosely flowing dresses that revealed the freckled tops of swelling breasts, which always seemed about to spill out of whatever it was that constrained them. I had a hard time keeping my eyes off her.

As soon as I saw her arrive, I ran out to the car to carry in the pot of soup she always brought. It was a different soup each time—vegetable, perhaps, or cream of chicken. She gave me a hug and pressed my face into the cleft of her breasts, from which rose an aroma headier than mere powder and perfume.

"Davey, you've grown another inch at least."

Lifting the trunk lid, she pointed out the pot she had wedged into a corner between a spare tire and a jack. She had cushioned it with an old quilt.

"Now, careful with that. Navy bean this time."

Mayne taught at Klinchee, on the far side of mountains that even from the top of Red Mesa appeared only as a hazy blue streak on the western horizon. To reach us Mayne had to drive a large U—south on an ungraded trail from Klinchee to U.S. 66, east on 66 to Gallup, north on U.S. 666, which was now graveled but not paved.

Mayne was always full of stories about goings-on at Klinchee, especially the antics of Mr. Kramer, the middle-aged trader who was courting her. I didn't think she was serious about him. She never brought him up without commenting on his bad breath and the size of his stomach, which she said flopped around under his shirt like a dying fish. He munched onions all day long, she said, because he had read somewhere that raw onions cure constipation.

Mayne had gone thirty miles out of her way that morning to collect Miss Ryder at Cottage Springs. Miss Ryder turned up only when someone gave her a lift. She had a car of her own, a new Chevy she'd bought just a year earlier, but she didn't know how to drive and couldn't seem to learn. My father had spent hours trying to teach her, letting her drive our old Dodge back and forth in front of the house after Sunday dinner.

Miss Ryder was from Mississippi. She was a tiny thing, wraithlike, with green eyes and bright red hair—so bright and red that my mother and her other troops thought it was more kin to something out of a bottle than to her hair's natural color, whatever that might have been. Miss Ryder made contentious remarks in a soft childish voice that only my mother seemed able to pick out with certainty in the gusts of conversation unleashed when the troops got together after weeks of solitude. Since Miss Ryder seldom had anything agreeable to say—my father said the only thing she was fuller of than herself was complaints—no one strained to hear what she had to say.

To Miss Ryder the world was a dark and threatening place, and the reservation especially so. If someone told of visiting Navajo families in their hogans, she was likely to gasp, *"Germs!"* A long walk over the desert looking at wildflowers? *"Snakes! Dangerous!"* Attend a nightlong tribal ceremony held outside by the light of roaring bonfires? *"Daring! Dangerous! Snakes! Mosquitoes! Germs!"* Miss Ryder seldom left her cottage except to go to the classroom. Mostly she cowered behind drawn shades.

"Every time a breeze stirs a curtain," my father once said, "she's certain that it's finally happened. A wild Indian is breaking into her house to—"

"Will!" my mother said, nodding at me.

He finished, "—to do God knows what."

I spent a lot of time wondering what Miss Ryder thought the wild Indian had in mind that my mother didn't want me to hear about.

Mayne leaped up the walk, with Miss Ryder tottering along behind her on three-inch heels and me bringing up the rear with the pot of navy-bean soup. Because of the quilt, it was still warm. After a handshake for my father and a hug for my mother, Mayne launched into her latest Mr. Kramer story.

"You know what that man did the other day? A rich lady

from Boston, her name is Miss Wheeler, comes out every summer with her maid, cook, and chauffeur to live with the Indians—well, that's what she calls it, but any Navajo who tries to get close to her is going to lose his scalp, or maybe something he values more. What really happens is that Mr. Kramer moves into his storeroom when Miss Wheeler arrives so she and her servants can have his house. This year she's got a new chauffeur, named Thomas. He's the best-looking thing I ever saw in pants—a nice person, too. And Mr. Kramer is jealous. Jealous of a chauffeur!

"Yesterday I got gas at the post, and while Mr. Kramer went in to get my change, Thomas drove up on the other side of the pump. I was chatting with him when Mr. Kramer came back with my change in one hand and an onion in the other. He rushed down the steps, waving the onion, his face the color of your Rhode Island Reds. And that belly of his! I thought he'd put an extra fish in his shirt the way—excuse my French—his tub of guts flopped over his belt buckle.

"'Thomas, I will not have you loafing around my gas pump,' Mr. Kramer yells. Cool as anything, Thomas says, 'Then I'll go to Wide Ruins to fill up.' He drives off, with Mr. Belly-Fish-and-Onions shrieking after him, 'I won't stand for it, Thomas. I won't stand for it.' And I still don't know what he won't stand for—having Thomas talk to me or going to Wide Ruins for gas."

My mother said, "Thomas sounds like he's got spunk, Mayne."

"I think he does," Mayne said.

"I don't think you should even talk to him, Miss Mayne," Miss Ryder said. "I wouldn't, not to a servant."

"I don't see the harm in it if he's a nice man," my mother said.

"Back home, servants know their place," Miss Ryder said.

"But they're probably Negro and don't have any choice."

"Well, of course. But a servant is a servant."

"I wish he weren't a servant," Mayne said, "but I'll still talk to him." She crossed her arms over her breasts and hugged herself, as she often did when deep in conversation. I had heard my father tell my mother that at these times she looked as though she was trying to keep rebellious urchins in check.

One by one other troops turned up. Keith was from Texas. She was athletic and taught her pupils football and basketball, playing right along with them. Schroeder planned to work another year or two and then return to Indiana to marry the young farmer she was engaged to. Lewis was a lanky Tennessean with a poetic bent who was learning Navajo with an eye to translating tribal chants into English. McGehee was from Oklahoma and the only one among them who wore trousers and smoked cigarettes.

That day Mrs. Wallis turned up, too. She was the senior teacher at Haystacks, east of Klinchee. But as my father said, she had no one to be senior to, because in all her years at Haystacks, no other teacher had stayed long enough to settle in. One woman assigned there had even driven her car head-on into one of the huge boulders that gave Haystacks its name, having decided that it was worth killing herself to get away from Mrs. Wallis. Fortunately the woman was thrown from her car into soft sand and only slightly injured, just enough to encourage a sympathetic supervisor to have her transferred to another school.

Mrs. Wallis was not one of my mother's troops, either regular or irregular, but was never turned away when she felt like dropping by. She was older than the rest, including my mother, and even more disapproving of the world in general than Miss Ryder was. Far back in Mrs. Wallis's past lurked a Mr. Wallis, whom she seldom mentioned. When she did bring

—RESERVATIONS—

him up, it was as though he was not and had never been a living person. She made him seem more like an echo, a deep rumble in distant hills, than someone who ate and drank and had to clean under his fingernails.

If Mayne said something funny in her presence, Mrs. Wallis might nod her head and say, "Mr. Wallis would have laughed at that." If she passed her plate for a second or even a third piece of lemon meringue pie—"Just a sliver, please"—she would explain, "Lemon meringue was Mr. Wallis's favorite." No one seemed to know what Mr. Wallis did or had done for a living or anything else about him. The trader's wife at Haystacks told my mother that she had once asked Mrs. Wallis about Mr. Wallis. Mrs. Wallis pretended not to hear.

Mrs. Wallis was always angry about something or other. Often the something had to do with the fact that she was far better educated than almost anyone else in the Indian Service and yet was still only a teacher, not even a teacher-in-charge like my father. She found it intolerable that she, an almost-Ph.D. from Columbia Teachers College, ranked no higher in the Indian Service hierarchy than my parents, who lacked any college degree and held only teaching certificates from Texas normal schools. I had heard her refer to my father—behind his back, of course—as "that Texas cowboy."

Mrs. Wallis wanted to be a principal, if not a superintendent, and kept applying for posts she didn't get. Even my mother said it was not just the Indian Service's inbred institutional bias against women that held Mrs. Wallis back. No, she said, Mrs. Wallis's problem was her famous inability to get along with people and her tendency to adamantly oppose any change in established procedures that the new Indian Commissioner proposed. She had even, illogically, criticized his recent appointment of several female supervisors, presumably because none of the promoted women was Mrs. Wallis. My father said Mrs. Wallis was so Old Guard that if she were a man, she'd trip over her beard.

The troops all crowded into the kitchen with my mother as soon as they arrived, but Mrs. Wallis cornered my father in the living room, where he and I, having completed our assigned tasks, were reading.

"Well!" Mrs. Wallis said. She seated herself bolt upright on a straight chair facing my father. She was a large woman and overflowed the seat. Her square face was capped by shiny braids of black hair wrapped around her head like a rope helmet. She looked like my idea of a hanging judge. "And what do you think of this latest rumor?"

I could tell my father wanted to sigh, but he didn't. He closed his book around the tip of a finger, keeping his place.

"Which rumor is that?"

"This idiot Indian Commissioner is saying we ought to let the children use their own language on the playground and even in the classroom."

"I see nothing wrong with that when it doesn't disrupt the teaching program. Never have. I've often wished my Navajo was better so I could tell the children what English words mean in their language."

"They'd never learn English, the lazy things!"

"I suspect they might learn it sooner."

"Sooner learned, sooner forgotten. In all my years in the Indian Service, I've never allowed a child to babble at me in another language—and besides, it's what the regulations say. Always have said."

"I understand some of the eminent professors at Columbia Teachers have been saying for a long time now that maybe it's time to change our methods, especially since we've spent fifty years proving that the old way doesn't work very well."

"Columbia Teachers is full of hacks."

"I thought I had understood from you that it is a very fine school."

"Not is, Mr. Parker. *Was*. Before these fools that Commissioner Collier is inviting to Washington changed it."

"Well, I'd like to give the new methods a try."

"You sound like Mr. Wallis," she said. She stalked out to the kitchen.

My father looked at me and winked. "I wonder if one of those new fools in Washington is named Mr. Wallis? Or more likely *Dr.* Wallis?"

The cooking smells from the kitchen drew me out to see how much longer it would be until dinner. The kitchen had grown hot and steamy from all the food roasting or boiling or baking in and on the big coal range. With so many helpers, my mother found herself with nothing to do and perched on a stool at the end of a counter. As the others had spare moments from stirring gravy or whipping mayonnaise, they would visit one by one with her.

None of the talk was deep or particularly intimate. My mother said the point was simply to have someone to talk to, someone who would listen. And she was a good listener. Schroeder relayed dismal news from her young farmer about crop prospects if the rainy spell didn't break. Lewis mused over the terrible complexities of the Navajo language and reenacted her effort to conduct a class in Navajo instead of the usual English, to the bafflement and dismay of her students. McGehee complained of the heat and dust (just as in winter she would complain of cold and snow). Keith mourned the lack of an interschool league for her teams to compete in. My mother listened, laughing with one, commiserating with another.

At table, troops sat on either side, with my father at one

end and my mother and me at the other. The troops talked shop, comparing notes Sunday after Sunday on the same old but ever fresh topics, such as the difficulty of trying to teach thirty or forty children in one classroom when half of the pupils were new in school and didn't understand a word of English or how to hold a pencil. The other half had risen at most to the third grade and were so nearly grown up they could fit in the school desks only by sitting sideways. Many stayed in school not so much to learn as to receive the hot noon meal, thus reducing the number of mouths their parents had to feet in a time of drought and economic depression.

The women swapped stories about the ingenuity their students displayed in slipping food out of the dining hall to carry home to little brothers and sisters.

One of Mayne's students won the pilferage award by acclamation. The child, a first-grader ten or eleven years old, left the dining hall dripping a trail of beans behind her. Mayne investigated and found the little girl's bloomers distended with boiled beans and hardtack, gathered in trip after trip through the serving line.

"What did you do about it?" Miss Ryder asked, her wispy voice so low that my mother had to repeat her words to the others.

"Do?" Mayne said, "I got an empty peanut-butter can and emptied her drawers into it. Otherwise, by the time she got home, she wouldn't have had a bean."

Miss Ryder said, "You should have expelled her. I would have."

Everyone but Mrs. Wallis laughed, knowing that had Miss Ryder detected the illicit beans, she would still have been trying to decide what to do long after the child and her bean-filled bloomers were gone. In the end she would have done nothing.

Mrs. Wallis said, speaking sharply, "Don't laugh. Miss Ryder's right. But I'd give that child a good spanking before I expelled her. We can't be seen to condone theft."

My mother changed the subject to a new stock-reduction plan that soil erosion experts said was necessary to allow the overgrazed range to recover but that Navajos opposed. The plan had been worked out in Washington and was stirring anger across the eroded land because limits were to be imposed on the number of sheep any one family could own, with even tighter limits on the number of horses. This was important because a man's social standing hinged in part on the number of horses he possessed—a fact, my mother pointed out, that gave a horse psychological and emotional value that no sheep could match.

"Too bad the plan was announced before the Navajos were consulted," my father said. "They know as well as we do what the problem is and should have had a chance to suggest ways to solve it. In the long run they'll all be better off, but in the meantime stock reduction is going to be hard on a lot of them. I can't blame them for being upset."

"Nonsense. Savages have to be told, not consulted," Mrs. Wallis said.

"They're like children," Miss Ryder said. "They don't know what's good for them."

A noisy debate broke out, Mrs. Wallis and Miss Ryder against all the rest. Finally Mayne said that at Klinchee the Navajos were so angry about having their sheep and horses taken from them that they were naming their dogs John Collier. If you went outside and hollered the Indian Commissioner's name, she said, a dozen mangy mutts would come a-running.

"If I had a dog, I'd name him John Collier, too," Mrs. Wallis said. "The mangier the better."

After dinner the troops pitched in to clear the table and do dishes, tasks that needed no thinking and were conducive to talk. And then they gratefully left the sweltering kitchen to doze for a while in swings and rocking chairs on the shady front porch overlooking the patch of lawn my father struggled to keep alive. The talk softened to murmurs.

Sitting on the steps, Miss Ryder played cribbage with me, which I did not enjoy because she could not remember the rules and hated to lose. After the second game, she quit.

"Back home we don't change the rules in the middle of the game," she said.

"But fifteen is always two."

"I'm sure you counted it as four when you scored your hand." She went to find my father, wanting a driving lesson.

On the porch, watching Miss Ryder drive back and forth on the strip of road in front of the house, Mayne brought up Mr. Kramer and Thomas again. The troops debated whether Miss Ryder was right in thinking Mayne should not talk to a servant.

Mrs. Wallis was firmly on Miss Ryder's side. "No good can come of it," she snapped, as though she had just made further discussion unnecessary.

"I'd talk to any man as good-looking as you say Thomas is," declared Keith, flexing the muscles of her right arm. "I wouldn't care if he was a panhandler."

"But you have to think about what you'd live on," Mayne said.

"I thought we were talking about talking, not getting married," Keith said.

"Well—" Mayne's pale skin brightened.

"What about Mr. Kramer? Has he proposed again?" McGehee asked, grinding out a cigarette under the flat heel of her shoe.

"Every time I see him," Mayne said.

"I'd take him," McGehee said. "A man who owns a trading post—that's a good business. If a man's a little dirty and smelly, you can make him bathe more often, and if he's fat, you can make him lose weight. But if a man can't earn a living, you're asking for trouble, no matter how good-looking he is. There's no way to make a lazy man work."

Mayne's laugh boomed out. "I have to say, every time Mr. Kramer asks me to marry him, he looks a little younger and a little slimmer. One of these days, I don't think I'll even notice the belly fish in his shirt or the onion on his breath. But I'm not going to quit talking to Thomas."

At the end of the afternoon, Mayne was first to leave. Waiting for Miss Ryder to finish what she described as "freshening up" in the bathroom before the long trip home to Cottage Springs, Mayne took my mother aside at the bottom of the steps, where I was sitting. I could hear every word.

"What would you think if I decided to marry Mr. Kramer?"

"I'd think you had decided to do what you felt best."

"It's such hard times, Mary. I wake up in the night worrying about losing my job or getting sick or something. I feel so alone."

"I know, Mayne. We all do that sometimes."

"But you've got Will and Davey. I don't have anybody but my parents and brothers back home, and not one of them has a steady job anymore. They're all living on what little I can send them and always needing more. And I think maybe Mr. Kramer would help."

"Times will get better, Mayne. They're bound to."

"I'm twenty-five years old. I can't wait forever."

I had never before seen Mayne look or sound less than cheerful.

My mother said, "The rest of your life is a long time."

"Am I wrong to do it, Mary?"

"I don't know, dear. What do you think?"

"I think I'm wrong, but I'm going to do it."

Miss Ryder came back. Mayne hugged my mother. I heard her whisper, "Next time we meet, I'll be Mrs. Belly-Fish-and-Onions."

I couldn't decide if the sound she left in my mother's ear was a laugh or a wail.

9.

LATE ONE SUMMER afternoon the mail truck brought notice that the archaeology students who dug on top of Red Mesa for a month every year would arrive that very day. The professor who wrote said the expedition would be larger than usual because of a generous gift from the grandmother of one of the students.

The grandmother was a rich Boston lady who had kept her money despite the Depression. She claimed to be descended from a Spanish conquistador of noble blood who historians said had fought Indians at Red Mesa back in the sixteenth century. She had agreed to underwrite much of the cost of the summer's dig on condition that her granddaughter be allowed to participate. The grandmother hoped that studying Red Mesa's past might spark some family pride in the girl, who was giving her parents a lot of trouble and not doing well in school.

The professor said the girl was a spoiled brat, beautiful but not bright. He added, however, that the expedition's leaders had decided to overlook her lack of academic qualifications in view of her grandmother's generous gift, which made possible more scholarships and a larger expedition.

Bursting with the news, I ran down to the turnoff to wait for Dumbo Taylor and Jeremy Jim to come scooting up U.S. 666 in the big yellow road grader. As I waited, Red Mesa's shadow, straight-edged as a ruler, slid toward me over the alkali flats like spilled water darkening blotting paper. The shadow had almost reached my feet by the time the grader came into view. As it rolled past the spires and chimneys and walls of the ancient lava formations that lay all around Red Mesa, the grader looked like an elongated yellow bug pulling a fat ribbon of dust behind it. It was moving so fast that I figured Bo was driving, with Jeremy standing beside him to tell him what to do. Bo was in charge, but only because he was white and had a well-placed father. It was Jeremy who understood how to operate and maintain the grader.

Deadpan as usual, my father said that old Bo must have been behind the door when God passed out the brains. Good thing he had a full head of hair, my father said, because without it he wouldn't have had a thing on his mind. Good thing, too, that Bo's daddy was an Indian Service big shot at Fort Wingate. Otherwise Bo would never in this world have been hired when he decided he'd rather operate a grader than try one more time to make it out of eighth grade.

The first day of training school, old Bo knew as much about a road grader as a newborn babe knows about warming a bottle. There were few signs that he knew any more when he got out—oh, my father said, maybe a little more, but not enough to mention. Bo still couldn't change a spark plug, which was something taught that first day.

My father added that if Bo hadn't drawn Jeremy Jim as his Navajo assistant, he would never have been able to hang on to the job, no matter who his daddy was. Jeremy was from over near Klinchee and a graduate of Phoenix Indian School. My father said there was nothing about a self-propelled road grader that Jeremy Jim didn't know or that Dumbo Taylor would ever learn, except maybe how to make it go faster than it was meant to.

All day long Jeremy perched on the shelf at the back of the cab, telling Bo which wheel to turn, what lever to pull, when to pick up the blade and when to drop it, when to gun her so that the drive wheels under the operator's cab would bite into soft ground and churn forward with mounds of dirt and gravel building up against the grader's blade, and when—most difficult call of all—to ease off power and back up to try another tack. When they had to follow survey stakes or perform complicated maneuvers, Jeremy took the controls and Bo squeezed onto the ledge, where, having nothing better to do, he kicked off his right shoe and massaged a hangnail on his big toe. That hangnail made Bo's life a misery.

The grader got to the turnoff and stopped in a cloud of dust in front of me. Sure enough, Bo was driving. Jeremy reached down and hauled me into the cab. Both of them were covered with red dust. The only place they weren't red was where goggles had kept the dust off. They looked like they were wearing Kachina masks with skin-colored circles around the eyes.

Above the clatter and bang of the grader, I told them the archaeologists were coming.

"Any girls?" Bo asked. He kicked off his shoe and rested his foot on a lever so he could massage his toe while he drove.

"I only know of one," I said, "but there's probably more. There usually are." I told him about the rich girl.

"She must really be rich. Her grandma, I mean," Bo said.

"I reckon."

Steering the grader with one hand and rubbing his toe with the other, Bo started singing. *"There was an old woman who lived in a shoe,"* he shouted, over and over.

It was all he could remember.

Jeremy nudged me.

"Hey, Bo," I said. "Want us to teach you the rest?"

"What's wrong with what I already know?"

"I just thought you'd like to learn more."

"What for?"

Jeremy and I grinned at each other. That was always Bo's answer.

We drove past the school and rattled over a cattle guard into the Road Department compound. Bo parked the grader by his old Chevy pickup truck across from the house trailer he lived in. The trailer was all unmade bed, grimy sheets, dust-drenched clothes, newspapers that Bo subscribed to for the comic strips, empty pop bottles, and calendars from Bradford's Auto Court & Wrecking Co. and the First National Bank of Gallup.

The Bradford calendar showed a pretty girl without a lot of clothes on leaning against the fender of an old Packard touring car made into a tow truck, parked in front of clapboard cottages. I recognized Bradford's tow truck and tourist cottages but not the girl. Bo claimed to know her, but he refused to tell me anything about her except that she was the sort my mother wouldn't want me to shake hands with. The bank calendar was illustrated with pictures of angels. Bo said he wasn't acquainted with any of them.

Jeremy's trailer stood next to Bo's, beside a big pile of gravel. Everything in Jeremy's trailer had its place. The bed was made, clothes were hung up, and books on automotive repair and engineering stood in alphabetical order on the shelves, along with neat stacks of clean dishes. Jeremy and Bo ate meals together. Bo could boil coffee and open cans but not much else. Jeremy did the cooking and Bo cleaned up afterward. Jeremy insisted that he wash the dishes after every meal. Bo said he didn't see the point to it when there were plenty of clean ones on Jeremy's shelves. "Just wash 'em and worry about it later," Jeremy said.

Except for the outside faucet where Bo filled the teakettle to heat water for doing the dishes, there was no running water at the Road Department compound. After they parked the grader and serviced it—something else Jeremy insisted on that Bo would rather have put off—they got towels and clean shirts and pants and headed for the showers. I walked that far with them.

Navajo women scrubbed their clothes outside the washhouse. A lot of water got splashed and spilled as they boiled laundry in old oil drums split in half and set over open fires of cedar logs that Hosteen Begay hauled down from the mountains a couple of times a year with the government truck and volunteer labor. They scrubbed and rinsed in tin-lined wooden washtubs built into a long table, using materials that Hosteen Begay had scraped up somewhere. The tubs drained directly onto the ground, which around the laundry table was always soaked. Because the water at Red Mesa was sulfurous, the rotten-egg smell was overpowering.

Bo held his nose.

Jeremy nudged me.

"Sure smells like Old Nick," I said.

"Old Nick? Only Nick I know lives in Gallup," Bo said. "He don't smell nothing like this."

"Old Nick's the Devil," I explained. "When you smell rotten eggs, you know he's somewhere around. And when it smells this strong, you got to really watch out because it means he's right here. No telling what's going on."

Bo looked around. "I don't see nothing."

Jeremy said, "The Navajo name for Old Nick is *tchindi*."

"You got him, too?" Bo said.

"Oh, we got him," Jeremy said, "but we know what to do when we smell him. We go and take us a big drink of this here water and drown that old *tchindi*."

"I always heard you got to turn around three times real fast first, to get Old Nick really dizzy," I said.

"That's what the women who were washing here today do every time they come," Jeremy said. "Turn around three times and take a big drink."

Bo spun himself around until he was falling-down dizzy and then stuck his mouth under a faucet. Water streamed down his chin. He drank until he was red-faced and choking.

"That ought to do it," I said. "What do you think, Jeremy?"

"I think that did it for him—and us, too," Jeremy said.

At supper my mother let me have a piece of the pineapple upside-down cake she had baked to welcome the archaeologists. She gave Bo and Jeremy some, too, when they came by with Bo's football. We tossed it back and forth to kill time while we waited for the archaeology students. My father said that if old Bo'd ever made it into high school and on to college, he might have been All-American—assuming he could remember signals long enough to do something about them. As it was, he was six-feet-something and two hundred muscular pounds, and he threw passes like it was always a scoreless game with time running out. Jeremy, though short, was solidly built and athletic. He could snag Bo's passes without trouble, but they always bowled me over. I didn't even try anymore. So he threw to Jeremy and Jeremy to me.

Finally a dust-covered caravan of pickup trucks, small buses, and several old Model A station wagons pulled in. While my parents handed around lemonade, met the students, and chatted with the professors, Jeremy, Bo, and I helped pitch tents on the dusty ground between the school kitchen and the bathhouse.

—RESERVATIONS—

The students were settling into the tents when a four-door Packard convertible with only one person in it came speeding past the lava formations, spewing dust. The Packard's top was down. Its backseat was crammed with suitcases and camping gear.

"Well, here's La Conquistadora," a professor said.

No one moved to help unload the Packard, so Bo, Jeremy, and I went out to lend the driver a hand. Her name was Jill. She was tall and slender, with a golden tan and teeth so white that every smile seemed to me like a celebration. Her hair was honey blonde with sun streaks in it, her eyes such a dark brown that they looked black. She wore reddish-brown riding boots, tan pants, and a man's white shirt with nothing under it. In the gaps between buttons, I glimpsed sunburned breasts.

Jill had brought her own tent. She showed Bo and me where to pitch it, under a cottonwood tree near the fence, away from the other students. She helped put it up. When she moved, her breasts bobbed beneath the thin shirt. I couldn't stop thinking about her riding along in the hot sun with the big car's top down and her shirt off.

The archaeologists made coffee in the school kitchen to go with sandwiches they had brought in big coolers from Gallup. Sitting side by side on wooden benches in the children's dining room, they talked and laughed with their mouths full and their elbows on the tables. Their lack of manners shocked me. My mother was strict about such things. Bo and Jeremy and I sat apart with Jill, and I had another piece of pineapple upside-down cake.

A professor got up to give work assignments.

"We'll be up at six, breakfast at six-thirty," he said. "You're to be at the dig with all equipment at seven. Be sure to take a full canteen of water." He paused. "Got that, Jill? At the dig at seven." He was not smiling.

Jill said nothing. She stood up and strolled out. Jeremy went on home, but Bo and I followed her. At her tent she opened a canvas-covered, tin-lined box and took out a bottle of whiskey and three Cokes. The bottles were dripping from melted ice.

"Bourbon okay?"

"Sure," Bo said. "Bourbon's fine."

"You can't drink on an Indian reservation," I said. "It's against the law. Anyway, Bo isn't old enough to drink."

"Neither am I," Jill said. "You won't tell, Davey."

It was a statement, not a question.

"No," I said, "I won't tell."

She spilled some of her Coke on the ground and poured in bourbon. She took a sip.

"Warm," she said, making a face.

"There's ice up at the kitchen," I said. I went to get it. It was dark by then. My father had the old Kohler going, and students were washing pie plates and coffee cups in the light cast by bare bulbs. I found a pan and chipped ice into it off the big block in the top of the icebox.

"La Conquistadora's newest conquest," somebody said.

They all laughed.

When I got back to the tent, the flap was closed.

"I got the ice," I said.

"Just put it down out there," Jill said. Her voice sounded muffled, a little breathless. "See you tomorrow."

The next morning I was up early and went out to feed the chickens. I looked toward Jill's tent. The pan I'd brought was still just where I'd left it. Bo came crawling out, carrying his shoes. He didn't see me. He put the shoes on and loped off, favoring his right foot, the one with the hangnail.

I scattered shelled corn over the gravel of the chicken pen.

"Here, chickie, chickie, chickie," I called.

—*RESERVATIONS*—

The Rhode Island Reds came crowding around.

I was glad Bo hadn't seen me. I had nothing I wanted to say to him.

10.

THE FIRST MORNING, I climbed the mesa with the students and helped stake out the site. Later they let me brush shovelfuls of dirt through sieves, looking for artifacts.

Jill didn't show up until after ten o'clock. Someone handed her a spade, without speaking, and she fell to work. Soon she was like the rest of us, with dust on her face and wet splotches on her shirt under her arms and along her spine. I had never seen anything like the lithe grace of her movements. Even the way she brushed sweat off her forehead with the back of her hand made me think of princesses in magic kingdoms. I decided I didn't care what she did with Bo or let him do.

On Sundays my mother invited anyone who hadn't gone to Gallup for the weekend to have dinner with us. The archaeologists talked endlessly about the ruins they had come to explore. Once, Red Mesa had been much lower, they said, but in the course of a thousand years, successive civilizations, drawn to the site by the sulfurous but ample artesian water in the valley below, had built it up layer by layer. Whole villages constructed of adobe and rock had risen and crumbled to dust, adding to Red Mesa's height. The villagers tossed their trash, and even the bodies of their dead, over the edge, and the hill grew wider. Wherever the archaeologists dug, they added a footnote, sometimes a page, to Red Mesa's history.

Back in the sixteenth century, they told us, Spanish conquistadors had stumbled on an Indian settlement at Red Mesa while searching for the treasures of the fabled Seven Cities of Cibola. Black-gowned priests and soldiers wearing shiny steel helmets and breastplates had struggled on foot and horseback for months over endless desert wastes. One day, according to a journal kept by one of the priests, they finished the last of their water just before crossing a rocky escarpment. In the distance they saw green fields at the base of a great mesa glowing red in the morning sun. It was off their intended path, but when they realized that the lushness before them was not just one more mirage, they hurried their steps. They crossed the steep-banked arroyo that some three hundred years later we called Big Wash—or perhaps one like it, because watercourses could change over time—and skirted lava deposits from extinct volcanoes. The lava took fantastic shapes and made the Spaniards think they had stumbled on the Devil's own sculpture garden.

As they neared the green fields, the weary marchers encountered a small band of Indian warriors who wore nothing but paint and loincloths. The warriors fought bravely, but their bows and stone-tipped arrows were no match for the muskets and steel blades of soldiers riding the first horses the Indians had ever seen. No native warrior remained alive by the time the conquistadors reached the red mesa. Storming on foot up the steep sides to the top, the invaders found women and children and a few old men huddled in crude mud huts. The priests baptized these survivors while the soldiers laid waste to the village, keeping an eye out for gold.

Finding none, the water-famished conquistadors returned to the base of the hill, where they discovered the artesian spring whose gushing waters had turned the desert green. The smell of brimstone was so strong, however, that the priests decided the explorers had reached the very gates of hell. They were being tempted by the Devil's own water. The priests would not allow even the horses to drink.

Near death from thirst, the conquistadors tumbled lava rocks into the spring and turned back to their former path. They took their converts with them, roped together to prevent backsliding. When a late afternoon August storm sent walls of water racing down Big Wash or its predecessor and over the surrounding plain, the new Christians unluckily drowned. Miraculously the conquistadors and their mounts were spared. They were able at last to slake their thirst with water fresh from the heavens—surely a mark of God's favor. The archaeologists laughed when they reached this point in their story.

Jill and Bo never heard any of these tales. On weekends they went to Gallup in Jill's convertible to stay at the Harvey House on Railroad Avenue and drink whiskey bought from bootleggers because the liquor stores wouldn't sell it to them. After the first day of the dig, Jill seldom had much to do with the professors or other students. She spent most of her time at Bo's trailer.

In the evenings after supper, she sat on the trailer steps, watching Bo and Jeremy and me pass the football. She drank bourbon and Coke and talked to no one in particular, complaining about being stuck in the middle of a desert where howling coyotes kept her awake at night and the water made her puke. She was angry with her grandmother for ruining her summer.

"Dotty old woman," she said. "Conquistadors! Who cares? If Grandma had any sense, I'd be up in Maine right now, or at least the Cape, instead of out here in the middle of nowhere

—RESERVATIONS—

living with savages."

Jeremy didn't like Jill's talk about savages. It bothered him that Bo wouldn't tell her to shut up.

"She don't mean nothing," Bo said.

I agreed with Bo. "It's just words," I said.

Soon Jeremy was taking the grader out alone almost every day. Bo turned up around noon, driving the Packard. He quit early, too, and day after day Jeremy finished the day's work alone. Some days Jeremy and Bo didn't say two words to one another.

On the morning the dig ended, Bo and I put the top of the Packard down and helped Jill load it with her belongings. When we were done, Bo drove the Packard to the dining hall with Jill snuggled close against him. Standing on the running board, I tried not to watch what she was doing to him with her hand.

The students had already taken down their tents and stuffed their belongings in the trucks and buses and Model A station wagons. My parents were on the porch of the dining hall. I joined them. Bo and Jill walked off a little way hand in hand. They kissed for a long time in the hot sun.

Bo said something. Jill shook her head and laughed. She couldn't seem to stop. Bo swung around and walked off fast, limping. Jill came up on the porch, still laughing.

"Dumbo Taylor just proposed to me," she said. "Can you imagine?"

She grabbed me and kissed the top of my head, holding my face against her breasts. I felt her softness beneath my lips and the beat of her heart. I smelled sweat, perfume, a hint of something more, something I could not place. I was ten, going on eleven, and felt triumphant, powerful, like a man.

"You're the one I love," she whispered. Her breath brushed my ear. "Poor little savage."

PART TWO

RED MESA

1934-1935

WILL

11.

THE NIGHT BEFORE the school buses were to come, my mind roved over the past to escape the present, all the way back to my childhood in the east Tennessee hills, to the death of my mother, who died so early I hardly knew her.

Somebody came in the night and lifted me out of bed. Wrapped a blanket around me.

"Time you come seen your ma, Willie," Aunt Emma said.

She carried me in. A coal-oil lamp sat on a box at the head of the bed. The wick burned high. The light hurt my eyes. I turned my face away. After a minute I turned back and looked. Pa and the others stood around the bed. The quilt was pulled up right to her chin. All I could see of Ma was her face and hair and one hand sticking out of the quilt, resting on the pillow beside her head. Pa touched her hand with the tips of his fingers like he was afraid of hurting. He bent over, getting his face close to hers.

I heard her whisper, breathe, soft as a leaf falling, "Not till she's gone, James."

"I won't," he said. "I promise, Mag, I won't leave your ma. Preacher, he a-ready wrote Will for me to say we ain't coming, not yet a while."

They were talking about Texas again. Pa wanted to leave Tennessee and go out to where the uncle I was named for had gone.

He had plans made to go as soon as my new brother or sister was born, but now Gramma was sick and didn't want to go and couldn't be left.

"Ain't he borned yet?" I asked.

No one gave me an answer. The lamp smoked. The glass chimney sooted up. The room darkened. I could hardly see.

"Ah, Mag," *Pa said. He pulled the quilt up, right over her face.*

THE MEMORY was painful. "But *tempus fugit*," I told myself, tossing in my bed. "*Tempus fugit.*"

And just as well. The faster *tempus fugit*ed, the better. At Red Mesa, in the depths of the Navajo Reservation, far from any town, the present was all desolation and fear. The past might be filled with terrors of its own, but at least it was fixed, made safe by the flight of time, made bearable by being over with—its hurtful truths defanged by time and turned to harmless memory, frozen at last into myth. The present, on the other hand, was an unpredictable patch of quicksand we couldn't get around and had to pass through as best we could—if we could. Like quicksand, it could suck us under at any moment, without warning.

The one bright spot the present offered was the hope of escape from Red Mesa. It all depended on the school buses that were coming after so long a time.

Early the next morning, I was at the warehouse with Franklin Begay. Franklin carried the title of school policeman and wore a shiny star on his chest, but his law enforcement responsibilities extended only to truancy. His job was to keep the school running smoothly—children fed and clean, parents happy or at least quiet, repairs made, floors swept, grounds clear of dried tumbleweeds and other debris. For me he gave meaning to the phrase "right-hand man." He was my assistant, my counselor, my interpreter, and my only friend at Red Mesa.

RESERVATIONS

On this day we were handing out relief commodities, as we did once a week, and were almost ready to start the distribution. The people who would get the food were already on hand. The men squatted on the heels of worn-out boots, smoking rolled cigarettes if they had been fortunate enough to find someone with tobacco to share. The women sat on the ground, with long full skirts spread around them, and tended their children. Babies strapped in cradleboards nursed at their mothers' breasts. Older kids played quietly nearby. Even among the boys there was little shouting or racing about.

The Navajos treated relief day as a solemn occasion. I'm not sure I ever fully understood why, but I think it may have been that they felt diminished by the need to accept charity from the very people who had played a large role in creating that need. Still, once qualified for relief, families rarely gave it up willingly, even when their fortunes improved.

Davey and his pal Sam, Franklin's son, had been ladling dried beans out of a hundred-pound burlap sack into paper bags. Joking and jostling each other as nine-year-olds will, they nevertheless took care not to lose any beans. They were almost done when Davey yelled, "The buses are coming!" He and Sam took off for the house, with Hosteen Dog frisking along at their feet.

In the distance I saw dust rising from the Gallup road. We couldn't actually see the buses yet, but there was a lot of dust, more than one car would kick up. They were still miles off, out of sight on the other side of the black lava ridge, with its strange pillars and towering peaks that snaked across the alkaline plain south and east of us. Just when you thought you were almost at Red Mesa — you could even see the mesa, easy to spot because of its color and the shiny steel water tank on top of it — the road looped far to the south again to get around the lava fields before curving circuitously back toward us.

Franklin and I kept on packaging supplies. Even without Davey and Sam helping, we had plenty of time before the buses arrived. That week we had no canned tomatoes to give out, no hardtack, and no coffee or sugar either, which would be a great disappointment for the waiting people. But we had peanut butter, beans, and flour—all great favorites. Best of all, we had plenty of strong-tasting mutton in golden tins stenciled with big black letters:

> MUTTON
> FOR INDIAN RELIEF ONLY
> NOT FOR SALE
> PROPERTY U.S. GOVERNMENT

Mutton was the Navajos' favorite food. In good times, they had sheep to slaughter from their own flocks, and money in their pockets besides. In this time of drought and economic depression, they had few sheep and no money. Their only meat came in these government tins, which looked golden because they were varnished to make the stenciled warning harder to remove. Sometimes the tins held beef or chicken, neither of which the recipients relished as they did mutton. Beef and chicken tins often turned up, warning messages and all, on the shelves of dingy stores along Railroad Avenue in Gallup, where bootleggers hung out and sensible people did not go after dark. Only rarely, however, would someone trade away his family's mutton ration, even for booze.

Franklin and I built up individual stacks of goods on the front edge of the loading platform, a stack for each family, using a list that I prepared each week with Franklin's help, showing who was to get how much of each available item. We checked off the items as we went. Every pile had its sentinel watching over it. Few of the Navajos had ever heard of an alphabet, but they knew by rote the order in which we would call names. If we moved on before completing a stack, perhaps having forgotten to bring out an extra can of mutton for an especially big family, someone was sure to protest. We would check our lists, and either Franklin or I would go back into the warehouse and get the missing tin.

With the buses coming, we hurried the line along as fast as we could, but the Navajos did not like to be rushed. And so we visited as though we had all the time in the world.

"*Yahehteh,* Hosteen Klah," I said in my serviceable but elementary Navajo as the old gentleman tottered up to get his mutton and beans. "Glad to see you this hot day."

Franklin stood beside me and translated for me when I got in too deep as I exchanged pleasantries with Hosteen Klah and others who stepped up to claim the supplies that would keep their families alive another week. Many sheep had frozen to death in the bitterly cold winter, and more had starved in the hot, dry summer that was now upon us. Cornfields had dried up and so had the grass. There was little the people could do to help themselves but accept the food we offered and stuff it into burlap bags to load on a wagon or the back of a horse. Men who were so poor that they had no horse slung the sacks over their shoulders and trudged homeward on foot. Women followed with cradleboards on their backs and older children straggling along behind.

We were just about finished when a Dodge sedan and a Model A pickup truck drove into sight, coming around the last lava tower. I knew the Dodge sedan belonged to Mr. Dawkins, the automobile dealer in Gallup who was delivering our specially built buses. The Model A pickup would be Garlen's. Other than his name and reputation—he was said to be a good mechanic but a man with a chip on his shoulder, a sorehead and bit of a bully almost impossible to get along with—all I knew about him was that he came from Oklahoma and claimed to be part Indian, though he was not carried on any tribe's official roster.

Right behind the Model A, the school buses kicked up individual ribbons of dust that soon combined into a single trailing cloud. They looked like yellow doodlebugs keeping just ahead of a sandstorm. The buses were small and rounded, with powerful engines and oversized tires, balloon tires—just the ticket, I hoped, for plowing through sand and mud to reach widely scattered families over trails that had never seen any vehicle, except possibly a horse-drawn wagon.

When all the stacks of food were gone, a young man and his wife still stood empty-handed off at one side. Two children peeked around the woman's skirts, their eyes saucered, thumbs in their mouths.

"Shouldn't Hosteen Tsosie be on the list?" I asked.

"Them Tsosies, they got food," Franklin said.

"They were on the list last week."

"Hosteen Tsosie, he got good horse. He win big race at Sheep Spring, win saddle and money. He buy all food he want, if he want."

Hosteen Tsosie came up and argued with Franklin, ignoring me. Hosteen Tsosie was a young man, tall and slender, about my height, while Franklin was middle-aged, short and squat. Even his high-heeled boots did not lift the brim of his uncreased ten-gallon hat, which sat on his head like a black stovepipe, much past Hosteen Tsosie's chin.

Hosteen Tsosie raised his voice. Franklin said little but stood his ground. He tapped the shiny tin star pinned on his denim work shirt. Hosteen Tsosie spat on the ground in front of me to show his contempt and turned away. He mounted his horse, a handsome bay with a fine new saddle, and rode off. His wife and children trailed behind on foot.

Franklin and I didn't take time to tidy up the warehouse. That could wait. We headed for the house.

By then the buses were pulling into the broad driveway between our cottage and the nurse's residence and clinic next door. Plenty wide enough for the three buses to park side by side, the driveway was flanked by a white picket fence on either side and led to a barnlike shed at the base of the mesa. A carpenter had come out from Fort Wingate to build it especially for the buses. There was a gas pump out front and a mechanic's shop at one end.

Mary told me later what happened before we got there. After Davey rushed into the house to tell her the buses were coming, she had him carry pitchers of cold lemonade out to the upended barrel we had placed by the back gate to feed tramps. The three young fellows Franklin had hired to drive the buses—his brother's boys, he said—were already waiting. She served them lemonade as they squatted against the picket fence, their hats pulled low over their faces to keep the sun off. Sam and Davey raced around shouting as the buses wheeled into the driveway, followed by the Dodge and the Model A.

"Look at them buses," Davey hollered.

"Those buses," Mary said.

"Can we get in one, Ma, Sam and me? Can we?"

"May we, but yes." Davey and Sam jumped aboard. The man who had driven the bus out from Gallup let them sit in the driver's seat and showed them the controls.

Mary was surprised to see that Garlen had a woman with him in the Model A pickup. We had not been told that he was married. Mary was pleased at the idea of another woman at Red Mesa, someone to talk to. The woman was blonde and looked young, but she kept her head turned away and a hand in front of her face, and Mary could not see her well.

"Hey, Sis, where's your old man?" Garlen yelled.

Mary was too startled to say anything. She wasn't used to being spoken to like that, certainly not there at Red Mesa.

Garlen jumped out of the Model A and stepped in front of her. It was a hot day and he was shirtless. The belt holding up his grease-stained khaki pants had a brass buckle with KKK embossed on it. A blanket of black hair curled damply over his chest. He was dark as a Navajo, but his eyes were bright blue, cold and hard as a couple of Davey's marbles. He came close to her, towering over her, so close she could smell his sweat. She stepped back.

"I asked you a question, Sis," he said, coming close again. "Where's your old man?"

"My husband is down at the warehouse, Mr. Garlen," she said. "He'll be here any minute."

She turned away. He stepped in front of her.

"Get out of my way, please," she said.

But he didn't. If she stepped back, he stepped forward. If she tried to move to the side, he moved, too. There was no sense to it that Mary could see. He said nothing, just glowered at her, and kept pressing toward her. Mary said later that he reminded her of the old Rhode Island Red rooster encountering a new hen, but she couldn't help feeling frightened—angry, too, but helpless.

Mr. Dawkins got out of his car and came over.

"Well, Mrs. Parker, we brought your buses," he said.

"Yes," Mary said. "Yes, you did." She could hardly speak.

"Wonderful machines, these buses. Not too big, plenty of power, and we've trained Mr. Garlen here so he'll be able to maintain them for you."

"Crap," Garlen said. "You didn't train me. I trained you. You didn't know shit about these buses until I showed you."

Mr. Dawkins took Mary's elbow and guided her away, over to the upended barrel where the pitchers of lemonade stood. Dropping his voice, he said, "Don't mind Garlen. He talks rough and acts rough, like he shouldn't 'round a lady, but he's a good mechanic."

"I hope so," Mary said. "That's what Will needs."

"Where is Mr. Parker?"

"He and Franklin are down at the warehouse, giving out relief supplies. We didn't expect you this early."

"We had a good fast trip. Road's in fine shape. Dusty, of course, but fast."

About then Franklin and I got there. I spoke to Mr. Dawkins and the drivers and went over to Garlen. I stuck out my hand. Garlen ignored it. He hooked his thumbs in his belt on either side of the buckle. I knew when I saw the KKK that things were not going to be easy between us. But I kept my hand out, ready to shake.

"I'm Will Parker," I said. "Glad to have you with us, Mr. Garlen."

Garlen ignored my hand and kept his thumbs in his belt. We were almost the same height, but I was skinny as a stick, while he had the shoulders and chest of a wrestler. When he moved, muscles rippled.

"Let's get it straight from the start, Parker. I ain't here with you. I'm here with the buses. I'm not a janitor, a carpenter, a plumber, or a playground supervisor. I'm here to keep them buses running and nothing else."

I dropped my hand. "That's fine with me. Just do that and we'll get along."

"I don't care about getting along. Tell me where my shop is and where to bunk. Then give me some drivers, and these buses'll go when and where you want them. Otherwise, leave me alone."

"With pleasure," I said. "Your shop's right there in the bus shed. Your cottage is down past the bathhouse, the last one at the end of the row. Your drivers are standing over there along the fence. Ben, Joe, and Archie. Franklin's nephews."

"Who's Franklin?"

"*My* assistant." I emphasized the "my" because I didn't want him trying to tell Franklin what to do.

"These fellas know how to drive?"

"Franklin says Archie does. You'll have to train the other two."

"I'll train 'em all. These buses ain't your ordinary car or truck."

I called Franklin over. The brim of his big hat barely came even with the top of Garlen's shoulders.

Garlen did not offer to shake hands. "You tell them boys of yours to be here in the morning at eight sharp."

"They be here," Franklin said. He tucked his hands in the hip pockets of his Levis and tipped his head back to stare Garlen directly in the eye. Garlen didn't know that Franklin was insulting him. Navajos didn't consider it polite to stare into another person's eyes.

Garlen turned his back and crawled under the buses one after another, checking drive trains for road damage from the trip out from town. He lifted the hoods to examine the engines.

The woman in Garlen's pickup had been sitting there all this time staring straight ahead, one hand to her face. Mary took a glass of lemonade over to her.

"Mrs. Garlen, I'm Mary Parker. Welcome to Red Mesa."

Mary said she saw right off that the woman was very young, very thin—big breasted but otherwise no meat on her. She was so thin her head looked like nothing but a skull with skin stretched over it. Her hair was blonde but showed dark at the roots. The eye Mary could see was velvety brown. The woman did not turn her head or accept the glass of lemonade.

"I ain't Mrs. Garlen."

"Oh," Mary said. "Well, welcome to Red Mesa anyway. Won't you have some lemonade and come in to rest a while?"

"Please don't let him see you talking to me. He told me not to have nothing to do with nobody. He'll be mad. He's mean when he's mad."

She turned her head and took her hand down. Her left eye was swollen shut, and a bruise like a birthmark stretched from her eye across her cheek to her jaw.

Garlen yanked open the door on the driver's side and got behind the wheel. "Listen, bitch, I told you to keep away from folks. Don't you never learn?"

He backed the Model A out of the driveway and drove down to his cottage. The drivers from Gallup had been standing around the barrel, drinking lemonade. Now they eased the buses into the shed and parked them side by side. They crowded into the Dodge sedan for the trip back to town.

As we said good-bye to Mr. Dawkins, Mrs. Reeves came out of her clinic next door. The New Mexico sun was high overhead, scorching down, but she was swathed as usual in a red bathrobe that had belonged to her husband, who died years before we moved to Red Mesa. He had been tall and thin. She was short and fat. The robe trailed along behind her and barely closed around her middle. She waddled over to the fence, carrying a lighted kerosene lamp as though she were finding her way through a dark tunnel, searching for an honest man. Mary and I had grown used to her strange behavior, but Mr. Dawkins seemed startled by the apparition.

"Don't mind Mrs. Reeves," I told him. "She's the nurse here. Just go along with her."

"Oh, I know Mrs. Reeves. Known her for years," Mr. Dawkins said, "but not like this,"

She came up to the fence. "Now see here, Mr. Dawkins.

Where's my ambulance? Dr. Dykstra specifically said you were going to bring my ambulance."

"First I've heard about an ambulance, Mrs. Reeves," Mr. Dawkins said. "Maybe next time."

"Dr. Dykstra will hear about this. No ambulance!"

She turned back to her house. "Here, Bozo," she called. "Come to Mama, Bozo."

Davey grabbed Hosteen Dog by the collar.

Mrs. Reeves looked over her shoulder, twisting her head as far as the thickness of her neck would permit. "And you, boy, I'll tell you one more time and that's an end to it. Stay away from Bozo and keep that nasty mongrel of yours away, too. I don't want any fleas on Bozo. You hear?"

"Yes, ma'am," Davey said.

Mrs. Reeves went into her house.

"Who's Bozo?" Mr. Dawkins asked.

"Her old dog," I said. "He's dead. She just tossed him under her front porch and wouldn't let me take him away, though he stunk up the place something awful. She thinks he's still alive."

"With a neighbor like her, you sure don't need Garlen," Mr. Dawkins said.

"We'll be all right," Mary said.

I hoped that was true.

12.

THAT NIGHT AGAIN I lay awake with too much to think about. Again I let my mind escape into the past.

My feet were cold. Aunt Emma said, "Be still, don't stomp around like that." We were standing in the snow under a big tree covered with shriveled brown leaves.

I watched Gramma's box go into a hole in the ground right next to the board with my mother's name carved on it. Pa had been up all night making that box for Gramma. Preacher stood at one end of the hole and Grampa stood at the other. Grampa's beard had turned white in no more time than it had taken the leaves on the tree to turn brown. He looked old and shriveled, like the leaves. Preacher prayed a while. He tossed frozen dirt into the hole. The clods hit the box. Bang. Bang. Bang. Grampa tossed in clods, too, and so did everybody else. Pa gave me a clod, but I didn't throw it. Gramma never liked noise.

Everybody sang. Way up over my head, I heard Pa singing louder than all the rest. Preacher prayed some more, and then he and another man started shoveling in dirt with a terrible clatter.

"Reckon you be leaving soon, Jamie?" somebody said to Pa.

"Reckon to," Pa said. His beard was black and his face was brown from the sun, but looking up at him I could see a white V of skin under his chin where his beard didn't grow and the sun didn't reach.

"Taking 'em all with you? This here little runt, too?"

He was talking about me. I wrapped my arms around Pa's leg and held on tight.

"Specially him," Pa said. "Willie'll make a right good Texican, onct he get his growth."

He put his hand on my head, kept it there. I felt safe.

SOMEONE SCREAMED, pulling me back to the present, back to Red Mesa.

The sound woke Mary.

"What's that?" she asked, already reaching for her robe.

"Garlen's woman, I think."

The screaming continued, came closer. Mary threw on her robe. I pulled pants on over my nightshirt. We ran out on the front porch. In the bright moonlight we saw the woman racing down the road past the school toward us with Garlen pounding after her. She was jaybird-naked and ran with head thrown back, pipe-stem legs pumping high, big breasts rolling and flipping. As she lunged along, she reached out in front of her with open hands as far as she could stretch, drawing her arms back and forth as though she were finding handholds in the air to pull herself forward. She shrieked at every step. No words came out, just wordless screams.

"Get a blanket," I said.

The woman reached the gate and plunged across the yard to the porch. I opened the screen door and she dashed into the house, still shrieking. Mary draped a blanket around her and helped her to the couch. She buried her face in the blanket, gasping for breath. The screaming died to a whimper.

Garlen stopped outside the gate, then sauntered into the yard. He had pants on but no shirt or shoes. He stood at the bottom of the steps, his thumbs tucked in his belt on either side of the KKK buckle.

"I want my woman," he said. "Send her out."

"Go on home, Garlen," I said. "She'll stay here tonight."

"Parker, you ought to know better'n to get between a man and his woman."

"That's as may be, but go home now and we'll talk about it tomorrow."

"Just won't mind your own business, will you?"

"Not in a case like this."

Garlen took his thumbs out of his belt and scratched the matted hair on his chest.

"I'm going to take that little whore out of there, Parker. If you know what's good for you, you'll get out of my way."

I held my ground. He came up the steps in one leap and knocked me aside with his shoulder. I went sliding on my back across the porch. My head hit the side of the house. I lay dazed. I could have gotten up, but I didn't want to.

He went into the house like he owned it.

"C'mon, bitch," he said, "we're going home."

"Mr. Garlen, you get out of here," Mary said. "Leave the poor thing alone."

I sat up and looked through the door. The woman had curled up on the couch and pulled the blanket over herself. Even her feet and head were covered. She didn't make a sound. It was as though she hoped that if she stayed covered up and lay still enough, he wouldn't find her.

Garlen said, "Get your ass moving or I'll kick it all the way home. Now, I said."

She stood up and dropped the blanket. There were bruises all over her face and body, even her breasts.

"I'm sorry, ma'am," she whispered. "I got to go now."

She went out the door, down the steps, and along the road like a sleepwalker, Garlen right behind her.

A little later Garlen's Model A pickup drove past. I could see two people in it. The taillight disappeared down the

Gallup road.

Long before dawn I heard a car's motor and got out of bed. It was Garlen's, coming back. As he went past our house and down the road to his own quarters, I could see that he was alone. He had not had time to go all the way to Gallup and back. I had no idea where he had taken his woman and I did not care. I was just glad to have him back.

Much as I feared Garlen, I feared losing him more. I needed him to keep the buses running.

13.

Pa loaded the furniture and the potbellied stove on a wagon. All the boxes and barrels, too. Grampa got up beside him and they went on ahead to Texas to put in a crop. In the summer, Aunt Emma took us children out on the train. It was hot. Smoke and soot blew in the windows and made my eyes sting.

Pa met us in Texas. At first I didn't know it was him. At home he had mostly worn overalls, except for funerals, but now he had a suit on. He had shaved off his beard, too. I had never seen him without one.

He had a red-faced woman with him.

"Willie," Pa said, "this here's your new ma."

"She ain't my ma," I said, and nothing he could say or do ever made me call that red-faced woman Ma.

AS TEACHER-IN-CHARGE of Red Mesa Day School—the equivalent of principal without the title or full pay—I was nominally in control of a tight little world, but I had almost no real power. The "in-charge" signified mainly that Washington had someone to blame when anything went wrong at Red Mesa or in the surrounding district.

I spent a lot of my time trying to make it appear that all was well, even when it wasn't. When a problem came up with the Navajos or at the school, I did my best to deal with it myself and hoped that my bosses in Washington would find out no more about it than I wanted to tell them. Fortunately they weren't eager to make the trek to Red Mesa to see for themselves how things were going. They were interested mainly in numbers—how many births, deaths, arrests, how many students enrolled and mutton tins dispensed. The people behind the numbers didn't matter.

Besides running the school, I taught the upper grades and gave the older boys on-the-job training in supposedly useful trades by putting them to work on keeping the school buildings in repair. Unfortunately the elementary plumbers' and electricians' and carpenters' skills I could pass along didn't have much to do with the way the boys lived. Their homes were simple hogans, more or less octagonal structures made of cedar logs chinked with brush and mud. Hogans provided practical shelter for a semi-nomadic people with a sheep-based economy. They were easy to abandon and rebuild if grass for the sheep grew scarce or someone died in one, making it *tchindi*—something akin to a haunted house.

Hogans had floors of packed dirt, no plumbing, no electricity. The people slept on sheepskins that by day were stacked around the walls. An open fire in the middle of the floor supplied both light and heat. Smoke escaped through a square hole in the roof. There were no windows, only a dawn-facing doorway closed in winter by a blanket, gunnysack, or—rarely—a wooden door knocked together of rough planks and hung on leather hinges. The nearest approach to a modern convenience might be an old washtub or half an oil barrel inverted over the fire with a stovepipe running up through the smoke hole. This arrangement not only produced more heat than an open fire but also kept the air inside the hogan a little more breathable.

Mary's title at Red Mesa was just plain teacher. She taught the first three grades and oversaw the kitchen that served the students their hot meal at noon. She looked after the girls, teaching them hygiene, sewing, nutrition—things more useful in their daily lives than the minor handyman skills the boys could pick up from me. In many ways Mary had the toughest job of all at Red Mesa, though being a woman, she wasn't paid near what I was, a fact that bothered me almost as much as it did her. Many of the first-graders she taught were twelve or thirteen years old, had no knowledge of English, and came to school mainly for the noon meal. They had never seen a book or a toothbrush before they enrolled, had never sat on a chair or a toilet.

Mary was a good teacher, patient, with a warm and friendly nature, and she had suffered enough in her own young years to feel sympathy for the fright and turmoil afflicting her students beneath their stoic exteriors. She soon overcame their shyness and found them quick to learn. They had an underlying sense of humor that allowed them to do what the white woman required while remaining invincibly Navajo. And that was fine with Mary and me. We didn't want to make them what they were not. We only wanted to give them skills, including some knowledge of English, that might help them live as they wanted to in a changing time.

For the Navajos, Franklin Begay was the most powerful government official at Red Mesa, far more powerful than I. He not only decided which families would get relief supplies but also advised me how to respond to any problems or grievances residents of the district brought to me—conveyed through him, of course. The Navajos knew as well as I that I learned only what Franklin wished me to know. I was to Franklin—and hence to them—as Washington was to me: a remote entity better left in ignorance.

Most important of all from the Navajo point of view, Franklin decided who would have jobs at Red Mesa School. He was the only Navajo on the staff who was listed as a fulltime government employee, paid monthly by Treasury check and given all benefits, such as sick leave and annual vacation days. All the rest were classified as temporary or part-time workers and received no benefits. The temporary workers—the cook, her helper, the laundress, and the girls' matron—worked full-time when school was in session but were paid every two weeks with vouchers issued at Fort Wingate. The part-time workers were paid weekly out of petty cash.

Whenever something needed doing, Franklin produced someone to do it, and I hired him or her with no hesitation. If a worker displeased Franklin, I fired the person with scarcely a question. In the Navajo tradition—and ours—he looked out first for his family and related clans in hiring people to keep Red Mesa operating. The cook, kitchen helper, girls' matron, janitors, ditch diggers, fence builders, gardeners, and now the bus drivers were all his clansmen, if not blood kin. He had said the drivers were nephews, his brother's boys, but I had no idea what the real relationship was. To Franklin, nephew was a concept with fuzzy borders, and brother was not much clearer.

Or perhaps it would be more accurate to say that Franklin knew I did not quickly grasp the complexities of clan ties, which to him were simple as breath, and so he thoughtfully kept me from befuddlement by describing all relationships in blood rather than clan terms. Thus he called the school cook his sister-in-law, though I knew she was not married to any of his brothers or related to his wife. He introduced the laundress as his aunt, when she was at most a distant cousin. I tried to tease him about showing favoritism toward relatives. "That way we get no witches," Franklin said in all seriousness.

—RESERVATIONS—

The cook's helper, Julia, was an actual niece who only recently had come home from Phoenix a high school graduate. A bright young woman who had spent years in off-reservation boarding schools, Julia was angrily aware that her education had fit her for work more challenging than washing dirty pots and pans. But there was no job for her at Red Mesa except that of scullery maid, and none better than that in the ugly little towns bordering the reservation. In those benighted hamlets, racial prejudice was so strong that Indians and Mexicans were allowed to use the municipal swimming pools for only two hours a week—the two hours before the pools were drained for their weekly cleaning.

On and on went the list of Franklin's kinsmen working at the school. His nephew Arnold kept fires going in the big coal range in the kitchen and in the washhouse boiler. On watering day an old uncle too decrepit to do much more than drag one foot after another moved a hose from one tree to the next. For this he got a quarter a week. Once I protested to Franklin about paying the old fellow to do a job that one of us could have handled just walking past.

"He need the money," Franklin said. That was enough for him—and for me. The uncle, or whatever he was, kept his job.

Other than Mary and me, Mrs. Reeves was the only white employee at Red Mesa. Luckily for her she was not under my jurisdiction. At one time she had been a skilled and dedicated nurse, but now for weeks at a time she did not step outside her cottage except to call her long-dead dog, Bozo. She no longer held clinic hours and had not treated a patient in months. When an injured or ill Navajo appeared seeking treatment, she sent the person away, telling him or her to come back when the clinic was open, which meant never. Mary and I did what we could. We dispensed simple medicines, and when that was not enough, we took the patient to the hospital at Fort

Wingate, half a day's drive. One day Mrs. Reeves refused to see a man who had been bitten by a rattlesnake. We rushed him to Fort Wingate, but it was too late. He died before we got there.

I had tried to discuss all this with Dr. Dykstra, her boss, the medical director at Fort Wingate. He said I was known throughout the Indian Service as a boat-rocker, always poking my nose into matters that were none of my concern. He accused me of mounting a vendetta against Mrs. Reeves and urged Mary and me to be better neighbors. As for the man who died of a rattlesnake bite because Mrs. Reeves would not treat him, Dr. Dykstra criticized us for interfering with his nurse's performance of her duty. The man would have lived had we allowed Mrs. Reeves to tend to him, he said—this after I told him she had refused to do so. I asked Dr. Dykstra to come to Red Mesa to see for himself Too busy, he said. Too far. And terrible roads.

I had even less control over the only other Anglo living at Red Mesa—the trader, Harry Oates. There were many traders on the reservation whom I respected. Oates was not one of them. He was a drunk, dark and sullen, with a flat face, a prominent jaw, tiny eyes, and lank black hair growing in tufts from a nearly bald skull. His front teeth were missing, and when he smiled, the fangs on either side of the gap made him look like an ill-tempered English bulldog. Oates was scornful of us do-gooders at the school and resentful of the restraints the Roosevelt administration tried to impose on his lucrative dealings with the Navajos. They had no other place to trade their wool, rugs, and jewelry for the necessities they could not grow or make themselves, such as sugar and coffee. Oates was able to set his own prices for what he bought and sold, with the result that most of his customers were deeply in debt to him. Year by year their debts grew larger.

—RESERVATIONS—

Liquor was illegal on the reservation, but Oates got all he wanted from a Gallup bootlegger who made a weekly trip through the reservation at night on U.S. 666, driving slowly and blinking his car's headlights off and on as a signal for his Navajo customers to come out to the road to pick up their booze. I did my best to have the Indian Service police stop the bootlegger, whose identity and schedule were known to everyone. But there was only a handful of professional, trained police officers on the entire reservation, none of them Navajo, and they never seemed able or willing to seize him. So the bootlegger kept making his runs. Oates and too many Navajos stayed drunk.

Oates's wife had left him shortly after we got to Red Mesa, taking their children with her. Now he lived with several Indian women, each of whom he described—always with a smirk—as his squaw and beat regularly. Fortunately for Oates none of his Navajo women was from the Red Mesa district, a happenstance that kept him out of trouble with Franklin and the other Red Mesa Navajos. Or perhaps it was not happenstance. Oates knew the Navajos well. He chose his consorts carefully, aware that though Red Mesa men would not like his fooling with Navajo women, they would regard it as none of their business if the women were from a distant part of the reservation.

When Garlen and the buses drove into our tight little world, it was because of a scheme I had come up with that I hoped would help remedy a great iniquity—one of many—in our treatment of Indians. For decades the U.S. Indian Service and its forerunners had pursued a policy of assimilation. We had worked in league with missionaries turn Indians into brown-skinned whites, good middle-class Christians like ourselves. To speed the process of de-Indianization, we removed children from their families and sent them far away to boarding schools, where we kept them until they were grown. We required them to speak only English, forbade them any contact with their families, and punished any attempt to practice the own religions. Whipping was known to be helpful in subduing pagan spirits, but punishments usually were devised less to hurt than to humiliate. Girls had their heads shaved. Boys were put into girls' dresses. In especially stubborn cases, corporal punishment might be combined with bread-and-water diets and solitary confinement in dark closets.

When their schooling ended, we returned the young Indians to reservations that by then were foreign to them. They were out of touch with the language, the religion, and the culture of their people. Like Franklin's sullen niece Julia, they were more white than Indian by the time we sent them home to harsh and hostile environments where only those who relearned Indian ways could survive.

And then we wondered why so many of them drank themselves to death. Why they hated us.

Navajo parents often hid their children when the school census was taken each year. They feared that any child deemed to live too far from a day school to walk to it would be taken from home and sent to an off-reservation boarding school, remote from all tribal influence. Each fall I sent Franklin forth to find hidden children, but the only ones he ever brought in were those whose families gave them up because they needed medical attention or were in imminent danger of starvation. I should have insisted that he chase down all the missing youngsters. I didn't. I couldn't blame the families for wanting to keep their children at home.

Since long before landing at Red Mesa, I had been protesting against abuses I perceived in an organization that was supposed to be helping the Indians but seemed more intent on destroying them. As Dr. Dykstra said, I was seen throughout the Indian Service as a maverick and gadfly, a troublemaking advocate of day schools, an anti-assimilationist no longer worthy of a plum assignment to one of the off-reservation schools where everyone thought alike and the living was easy.

For a short time during the Hoover years, I had been principal of a large Pacific Northwest boarding school, where I tried to put my views into action by ending corporal punishment and solitary confinement, encouraging home visits for the pupils, and allowing native languages to be spoken in the dormitories and on the playground. These modest reforms seemed dangerously radical to my assimilationist bosses in Washington, and they soon banished me to Red Mesa. It was the bureaucratic equivalent of putting a troublesome Indian child in a dark closet to break his or her spirit. But Mary thought as I did, and we refused to temper our views, though it meant living in desolate places and bringing Davey up far from his own kind.

Even at Red Mesa I kept hectoring my superiors with proposals for expanding the day-school system. In the dying days of the Hoover administration, the response was always that there was no money to build more schools.

So I came up with my busing plan.

I argued that small buses equipped with balloon tires and powerful motors would let us vastly extend the area served by existing schools and double or even triple enrollment at relatively low cost. I looked ahead to a day when Red Mesa would have three or four teachers, not just two. At first I was laughed out of court—buses were fine for use on established roads, but on wagon trails? And even if I could find someone to drive the buses, my opponents argued, the drivers would spend half the school day digging out of sand or mud and the other half waiting for the vehicles to be repaired.

After President Roosevelt took office and made John Collier commissioner of Indian Affairs, things changed fast. Collier had made his name battling for fairer treatment of Indians and fighting assimilationists. One of his first acts as Indian Commissioner was to authorize the purchase of three buses to test my plan at Red Mesa.

Collier also authorized hiring a mechanic to maintain the buses but specified that the mechanic had to be an Indian or have Indian blood. That represented a new—and long overdue—policy for the Indian Service, which up till then had been pretty much a white preserve. But Collier's order to hire an Indian mechanic uncovered an embarrassing fact. Our boarding schools had turned out plenty of English-speaking ditch diggers and pot washers but not many skilled workers. Besides, no qualified Indian mechanic wanted to work at an isolated place like Red Mesa.

When Garlen, an expert mechanic claiming to be an Osage and willing to work anywhere, applied for the job, the Indian Service was glad to list him as an Indian, even though the Osage nation refused to put him on its tribal roster. I was glad to accept him, too. Without Garlen, my busing scheme didn't stand a chance, and my name would be mud.

We were stuck with him.

14.

In Texas the children at school liked to make me say "help," which always came out "hep." They said I wasn't a real Texan and never would be, I was just a Tennessee hillbilly.

The red-faced woman tried to make me feel better. She said real Texicans didn't talk any different than folks from Tennessee, just put more of the sound through their noses. Those children teasing me were about as new to Texas as I was, she told me. Most likely they were nothing but Yankees, or near to it, from somewheres up north. "Don't pay 'em no nevermind," the red-faced woman said.

Even if I couldn't talk right, I knew my letters and numbers and how to read when I started school. Before long, other children, even third- and fourth-graders, began coming to me full of respect, no longer teasing, asking my help with their lessons.

I decided to be a teacher when I grew up, not a landless farmer like Pa. I didn't want to spend my life going along stickery rows of cotton with the sun hammering down while a scratchy gunnysack dragged along the ground behind me, getting heavy and pulling at my shoulder as I filled it.

WHEN THE SUN came over the horizon, Franklin's boys, wearing new Levis and two-toned rodeo shirts with mother-of-pearl buttons, were already squatting on their heels in the long shadow cast by the picket fence. They were there all the while I shaved and got dressed. After I finished breakfast, I went out to join them, just passing the time of day. A few minutes later Franklin turned up and then Garlen.

Garlen's hair, damp from a shower, was plastered against his skull. He showed no signs of his night spent driving to wherever it was he had taken the blonde woman.

"All right," he said. "What's your names?"

The bus drivers stood up one after another along the fence. Franklin answered for them.

"These boys is Begays," Franklin said. "Archie, Ben, Joe. They good boys. My brother's boys."

"They know how to drive?"

Ben and Joe looked at Archie, who translated.

"What the hell? Don't they speak English?"

"Archie, he speak English."

"Jesus!" Garlen said. "If they're too dumb to learn English, how they going to learn to drive a bus?"

"They learn," Franklin said. The drivers muttered back and forth to one another, scowling.

Garlen changed the subject. "Now look, you bohunks, you got two weeks before school starts to learn how to drive these buses my way. You forget whatever you think you know about driving and listen to me, and we'll get along. If you don't want to do it my way, I'll get me some new drivers. You got that?"

"They got that," Franklin said.

"Just be patient with them," I said. "Show them what you want them to do, and they'll do it. They're good men, quick learners."

Garlen turned slowly and looked at me. He spat in the dust.

"This is my show, Parker. You keep out of it."

It was a challenge I could not let go by, not in front of Franklin and his boys.

"Don't worry, Garlen," I said. "As long as you do your job and do it right, I'll stay out of your way. But only that long."

"I'll do my job and do it right. My way. Just leave me alone."

Franklin and each of the drivers spat in turn, aiming at the spot where Garlen's glob had hit. I felt like joining them in the insult but didn't.

That first day Garlen did not let them move a bus. He made them take turns sitting behind the wheel while he went over dials and gauges and drilled them in shifting gears with the motor off. Most of the time he yelled at the top of his lungs, as though high volume would overcome the language barrier. The second day, he allowed them to start the engine and back a bus down the driveway and then drive it up again. They went back and forth all day while he stood behind the driver, ready to turn off the engine or grab the hand brake, as needed.

On the third day, the boys were ready at last to do some actual driving. Word spread quickly. Shortly after dawn Franklin's family and friends began to arrive from far and near on horseback and in wagons, ready for the big moment. Men leaned against the picket fence, arms akimbo, hats pulled low on their foreheads. Boys ranged themselves along the fence in imitation of their fathers. Women sat cross-legged in the driveway, voluminous skirts spread on the ground around them, shawls drawn over their heads to fend off the sun. They held babies in cradleboards on their laps while toddlers played in the dust. Older girls stood in little groups near the women.

Even some longhairs turned out—men who clung to traditional ways and refused to speak English even if they knew it, which many did, having learned it as children at boarding school. They pulled their hair back and tied it with thongs. They wore rolled bandannas around their heads instead of cowboy hats, and deerskin moccasins instead of boots. Ordinarily they had as little to do with whites as possible. Their presence indicated to me that they understood the importance of the buses and shared my hopes for them.

Promptly at eight o'clock Garlen strode up the driveway like General Pershing arriving to inspect his troops.

"Who the hell are these people?" he asked Franklin.

Franklin shrugged.

"Tell 'em to keep out of the way."

"They do that," Franklin said. "They just watch."

Garlen and his drivers got aboard one of the buses. He backed it out of the driveway and into the road. Archie, Ben, and Joe lined up in the aisle behind him like altar boys attending a priest at mass. Once the bus was pointed down the road, Garlen let Archie perch on the driver's seat, both hands gripping the wheel, while Garlen stood over him and gave final instructions, with much gesturing. Joe and Ben listened intently as Archie passed on what the big man was saying. The crowd was tense and silent.

Archie sent the bus hurtling forward. Garlen, Ben, and Joe lost their balance. As they staggered backward down the aisle between the seats, they grabbed at whatever they could get hold of, trying to keep their feet.

Archie jammed on the brakes. Garlen and the two boys flew forward. All three smashed into the windshield, one, two, three. Garlen picked himself up and bent over Archie. Mary and I could see he was shaking his fists and yelling. In the crowd along the fence, we heard murmurings of the sort loving aunts emit when a favorite nephew is ruled out of a spelling bee.

On the second try Archie got the bus moving smoothly. A jubilant babble rose from the crowd. Mary and I cheered. One of the longhairs let out an earsplitting cowboy whoop. Archie drove down to the warehouse, where the road made a loop, and then turned the wheel over to Joe, who drove back. Next Ben took over.

Franklin's relatives and friends settled in. They relaxed along the fence, taking what shade they could find. Ignoring heat and dust, they watched hour after hour as Franklin's boys took turns at the wheel. The bus rolled back and forth between the driveway and the warehouse as steadily as an interurban trolley running on schedule.

Mary and I left after a while to get some work done and so did Franklin and the rest of the school staff. At my suggestion Mrs. Nez, the cook, and Julia made coffee for the remaining crowd. At noon they served up a mess of beans and salt pork out of school supplies, along with hardtack and peanut butter. It was pretty much the meal they would be serving to the children each day, once school started. I felt that a small community celebration was warranted, no matter how much my Washington bosses might frown if they learned of the unauthorized expenditure.

In late afternoon I waved the bus down and got aboard.

"I might as well learn something about it, too," I told Garlen. "Could be I'll have to drive one of these things myself sometime."

"Suit yourself," Garlen said.

He was drenched with sweat. Even with all the windows open, it was sweltering on the bus.

I got behind the wheel. The bus was geared like a truck, which was all right because I had driven many a truck in my time. I ran through the gears just for practice and then started off. I let the clutch out too fast. The bus lurched, but the motor didn't stall and we kept going.

I heard Mary yell, "Good for you, Will."

The man at the fence let out another cowboy whoop. I felt like whooping a bit myself

After a circuit or two past the warehouse, I got daring and steered the bus off the road onto the wagon track leading to Franklin's compound of hogans a half-mile or so from the school.

"I'll show you the kind of road the buses will have to go over," I told Garlen.

We bounced across a gully-cut plain of sagebrush, greasewood, and pallid-looking tufts of grass. The track went through deep sand in places and I had to drop into a lower gear, but the bus had power to spare.

Just before we got to Franklin's spread, we came to the wide, deep arroyo we called Big Wash. Most of the time it was dry. But after a storm or when a spring thaw had melted a winter's snowpack in the mountains, Big Wash ran full. On those occasions Franklin and his family could get across only by going downstream to the Gallup road, which crossed on a low bridge. Sometimes the bridge was under water at the peak of the flood, and Franklin was left stranded on one side or the other.

I stopped on the brink. The wagon track angled over the steep bank to the sandy bottom.

"Think she'll make it?" I asked.

"If you know what you're doing," Garlen said.

Again it was a challenge I could not let go by. I dropped into the lowest gear and eased the bus forward, down the bank. I heard Archie and the other boys mutter uneasily to one another. For a moment it was touch and go as to whether we would tip over sideways and roll to the bottom or dig the front end into loose sand. I fed the bus just enough gas to keep going without stalling. We made it over the edge and down the bank safely. Again I felt like cheering.

The bottom looked hard packed, but I knew that was deceptive. Under a thin crust it was nothing but loose sand. I crept forward steadily, moving just fast enough not to dig in. Thanks to the bus's balloon tires, we got across and up the other bank to solid ground without a hitch.

Though he was far better off than most because of his government salary, Franklin lived much as other Navajos did. His cornfields lay along the arroyo, where they would be watered whenever the wash ran full. On higher ground at the boulder-strewn base of Red Mesa stood three or four hogans, with sheep pens scattered nearby. At this time of year the pens were empty. The family's sheep were on summer range in the Lukachukai Mountains, part of which we could see from Franklin's place as a far-off hazy streak in the southwest. Franklin had sent only a few of his horses to the mountains with the sheep, however. Several he kept for convenience in a log corral near the hogans. The rest he had turned loose to graze, rounding them up as needed.

As we drove up, the penned horses ignored our arrival. They stood with drooping heads facing their watering trough, which was half in, half out of the corral so that it could be filled from the outside. The trough had been fashioned from large wooden barrels sawed in two and set into the ground. More barrels, whole ones, stood in the back of a nearby wagon. Franklin got the barrels from the warehouse after we emptied them of the beans or rice or flour they had once contained. He used them to haul water from an artesian spring several miles north of the school. The water that came from the school's well smelled sickeningly of sulfur, while the spring water was sweet. Mary and I got our drinking water there, too. About twice a week I took the backseat out of the old car and stuck in a couple of five-gallon milk cans to fill at the spring.

I told Garlen about the spring as we drove up in the bus,

just making conversation and thinking he might be interested.

He said, "Persnickety, ain't they? You'd think people who live like animals wouldn't be so choosy about water."

"Like all of us, when they've got a choice, they'll take the best they can get," I said.

"Well, they better keep one thing in mind," Garlen said. "These buses ain't their personal vehicles. First time I catch some navvy hauling water on a bus, I'll kick his ass from here to that fucking spring."

"Yeah, you do that," Archie said.

A pack of yapping dogs rushed out to snap at the tires of the yellow monster that was invading their territory. I pulled up in front of two side-by-side hogans where Franklin and his immediate family lived. Nearby were a couple of summer shelters, each consisting of four upright poles supporting a log-framed roof of shade-giving tumbleweeds and sagebrush. A loom of peeled logs stood in one shelter. The weaver had not gone to the school to watch the boys learn to drive. She poked her head around the rug she was working on and smiled toothlessly. I recognized her as Franklin's wife's grandmother, Mrs. Tsinnijinni.

"Gramma, she say she don't care about white-man wagon," Archie said. "She say, what wrong with horse? She stay home."

Mrs. Tsinnijinni was still looking at us, still smiling. I knew from experience that the old lady's smile was all front. She wanted nothing to do with whites. As a little girl she had been among the more than eight thousand Navajos rounded up by Kit Carson and taken to Fort Sumner at the eastern edge of New Mexico, where thousands of them died on a reservation they called Hwalte and their captors called Bosque Redondo.

Mrs. Tsinnijinni still harbored a grudge against anyone who had anything to do with the U.S. government. When we first got to Red Mesa, she had come to our house and sold Mary that beautiful rug with silky white Angora wool woven into it in loose-hanging strands and, in the middle, a glossy black square of soot mixed with rancid mutton tallow. There was no way to get the stuff out. The whole rug turned gray when I tried to clean it with naphtha.

Mary could never look at the rug without hurt and puzzlement. "What did I ever do to her?" she wanted to know.

"You were born white," I told her.

Ben took the wheel for the trip back from Franklin's compound. As we neared the wash, he stepped on the gas. We would have gone full-tilt right over the edge had Garlen not knocked Ben's foot off the accelerator and grabbed the hand brake.

"What the hell you doing? You want to kill us?"

Ben spoke in Navajo. Archie translated, "He say, gotta whip up team. Deep sand."

"Can't you idiots get it through your head? This ain't a horse and wagon."

He shoved Ben aside and drove across the wash just the way I had. For an hour he had the boys practice taking the bus down the steep banks and through the sand. After each crossing they turned around by simply circling through the sagebrush. It wasn't much rougher than the wagon trail.

When we got back to the school, it was near quitting time. Franklin was in the driveway, chatting with the dozen or so people who still squatted or sat along the fence, most of whom lived at or near Franklin's compound.

I said, "Let's give them a ride home."

"Suit yourself," Garlen said. "I got nothing else to do."

Archie yelled out the window, gesturing. Franklin was the first to accept the invitation and took a seat near the front. The others followed hesitantly, looking solemn and not talking.

They all went to the back, as far from Garlen as they could get.

I told Garlen to wait a minute and went looking for Mary and Davey. I found them at the school kitchen, where Mary was having an end-of-the-day cup of coffee with Mrs. Nez while Julia scrubbed down tables in the dining room. They all came back to the bus with me. Mrs. Nez, who lived in a different direction but wanted a ride, boarded timidly. Julia, stormy-faced as usual, popped into the front seat by the door, just ahead of Franklin. Her demeanor proclaimed that a ride on a school bus was old hat to her. I sat with Franklin. Mary and Davey were across the aisle.

Garlen stood on the step. "Okay, let's get this over with," he said.

It was Archie's turn to drive. He was the best driver of the bunch. We went along the wagon track smoothly, with hardly a bounce. Garlen paid no attention to Archie's driving, however. He had his eyes fixed on Julia. I couldn't blame him.

Despite her air of tamped-down rage—perhaps in part because of it—Julia was as pretty a young woman as you'd find anywhere. She was taller than most Navajo women, slender but full-breasted, with alert eyes and a sweet, throaty voice. Many of the older women plastered their hair with mutton tallow and drew it into tight buns. Julia's hair was clean and soft, loose around her head. Instead of the traditional long full skirt and modest velveteen blouse, a style Navajo women had copied from the Fort Sumner officers' wives, Julia wore a low-cut cotton dress with little roses on it. She had made the dress herself on one of the school's foot-powered Singer sewing machines.

Aboard the bus, she didn't seem to invite Garlen's attention nor did she speak to him. That did not deter him. He leaned over her and kept up a murmur of conversation. Close as I was, I could not hear the words. She kept her head set straight ahead and, so far as I could tell, made no response to him at all. But Franklin did not like what he saw.

As Archie eased the bus into Big Wash, Franklin spoke loudly in Navajo. Archie nodded. Everyone, including Julia, grabbed something to hang on to. Franklin leaned over to Mary and Davey.

"You hold on," he whispered. "Archie, he go fast on other side, stop quick."

"Franklin," I whispered back as Archie took us across the wash without a hitch, "that's not a good idea."

Franklin pretended not to hear. Back on the plain the bus picked up speed.

"What the hell?" Garlen said, looking around.

Archie slammed on the brakes. Thrown off his feet, Garlen hit the windshield with a thud and fell to his knees on the steps. A wave of quickly choked laughter swept through the bus.

Garlen picked himself up. With one hand he threw open the door. With the other he grabbed Archie by the collar of his green and blue cowboy shirt, twisting it until he choked. Dragging him off the bus, Garlen held him at arm's length and began punching him in the belly. Archie tried to punch back but his arms were too short to do much damage. His eyes popped from lack of air.

Franklin and his family emptied the bus instantly. It was as though their exit had been choreographed and they had practiced it for days—men first, then boys, then women and girls.

The men formed a circle around Garlen and Archie. I pushed my way through.

"Take it easy, Garlen," I said. "You've got no call to do that."

"Nobody makes a fool of me," the big man said.

He drew back his fist again.

The circle of men tightened around him. No one said a word. But Garlen didn't punch again. After a moment he let go of Archie's collar.

Franklin spoke. The men stepped back. Garlen got on the bus. He slammed the door and drove off, stranding us.

"You've got an enemy now, Franklin," I said.

Franklin spat toward the disappearing bus. "Garlen, he got enemy now."

15.

The shoes shone like glass.

"Don't you worry what they cost," Mr. Porter said. "The whole school board's chipped in for them. You're the first young man we ever had to graduate. Lots of young ladies make it through eighth grade, but you're the first young man to do it. We're mighty proud. We want you to look all spiffed up for the graduation exercises."

I took the shoes off and carried them home under my arm.

"I never thought to see no son of mine take charity," Pa said.

The red-faced woman said, "Now, Jamie, it ain't charity. It's a right nice gift for a right nice boy. Eighth grade! Think of that."

"I'm going to high school, normal school, too," I said. "I'm going to be a teacher."

"Where's the money to come from, I'd like to know? Not from me, I can tell you that. I ain't got it," Pa said.

"I'll work. I'll find me a job."

"You work? That'll be something to see."

Pa always said in all his born days he'd never seen a boy less inclined to work. But when he needed to write something more than his name, it was me he came to. And the same when he got a letter. Reading a letter was something the red-faced woman couldn't help him with.

RIGHT FROM THE START the buses performed just the way I hoped. Traveling mostly along wagon tracks but sometimes making their own roads, they brought in students from as far as fifteen miles away. Enrollment shot up, so much so that Mary didn't have enough desks in her classroom for all the new first-graders to sit down at the same time. She had her hands full just showing the children how to brush their teeth, flush a toilet, hold a pencil, and open a book. She said it was the hardest teaching she'd ever done.

Difficult as Garlen was to get along with, he did a wonderful job of keeping the buses going. He treated them like they were precious jewels and never let them go out unless they were shining from one end to the other. He raged at Ben, Archie, and Joe when they brought the buses back dusty or muddy, which was often, because of the trails they had to drive on.

Mary urged me to do something about the way Garlen abused his drivers, but I didn't know what to do. I could never forget that he was the key to making my bus scheme work. I was afraid to crack down on him. He might quit.

There was something else I should have spoken to Garlen about but resisted bringing up. That was Julia. Mrs. Nez told Mary that every time he went by the kitchen for a cup of coffee, which was several times a day, he would lean against the wall and stare at the girl. Julia was the only person he ever spoke to as he came in or left. If Mrs. Nez wasn't around, they'd get their heads together out on the back porch.

"Mrs. Nez doesn't like it and I don't like it," Mary said one night. "Garlen's not what Julia needs."

"Maybe not," I said, "but maybe Julia doesn't know that."

"There must be something we could do."

"I don't know what. Garlen's doing his job."

"I don't care if he is doing his job. If he doesn't leave Julia alone, there's going to be trouble. You know that if Mrs. Nez doesn't like what Garlen is up to, Franklin doesn't either."

I knew she was right. I still didn't see what I could do.

But when Franklin came to me and complained that Garlen had started taking Julia to his cottage after work every day, I knew I had no choice. I had to speak to Garlen.

He was standing at his workbench, bare-chested as usual, cleaning a carburetor in a can of gasoline.

"Got a minute?"

"Nope." He kept working, his back to me.

"Well," I said.

I cleared my throat a couple of times before going on.

"I want to remind you that we—you, too—are here at Red Mesa as representatives of the United States government," I said. I knew I sounded like a stuffed shirt, but I didn't know how else to go about what I had to do. "We're supposed to help the Navajos become self-sufficient so they can stand on their own feet and run their own affairs. We're not here—"

"—to fuck the girls?"

"That's right."

He turned around. The carburetor in his hands dripped gasoline. He took a lung-stretching breath and squeezed the carburetor between his palms as though he intended to crush it. The effort made his biceps and chest muscles bulge.

"Parker, I'm going to tell you something you better think about. I got Indian blood, remember. All my life I been not one thing or the other—not all Indian and not white either. The 'breed, they called me, but they let me go to white schools and learn to be a mechanic. When jobs got scarce, though, the 'breed was always first to go. What jobs there was went to white guys who didn't know half what I did. I moved away from home to a little town up in Kansas where nobody knowed I wasn't white as them. I found me a job at the Chevy garage, and pretty soon I got invited to join the Klan."

He put the carburetor down on the bench and framed his KKK buckle with both hands. He thrust it toward me.

"I figured ain't nothing more white than the Klan. So I joined and everything's going along fine. One day a guy from home happens to turn up. He says to my boss, says, 'How come you give that 'breed a job? Ain't you got any white folks wanting to work?' My boss says, 'Hell, I thought he was black Irish.' My boss says to me, says, 'You're a real good worker, all right, Joe, best mechanic I ever seen, but I got to let you go. Folks don't like somebody like you taking a white man's job.' So I lost my job and got kicked out of the Klan, too."

I didn't say anything, not knowing what to say.

Garlen wiped his hands on his pants and went over to where his shirt was hanging on a nail. He picked a sack of Bull Durham out of the pocket and rolled a cigarette. His fingers were thick as broomsticks, but he held the paper and tipped in the tobacco with surprising delicacy. He held the sack by its tag between his teeth while he rounded the cigarette, then pulled the drawstring taut before ungripping his teeth and releasing the tag. He put the Bull Durham bag back in his shirt. He licked the paper and twisted the ends, then struck a match on the KKK buckle.

I started to remind him of all the gasoline around and the danger of fire. I didn't do it. By then I was more afraid of him than of fire.

"Then Roosevelt comes in. The Indian Service goes crazy looking for guys like me—guys who got Indian blood and yet know how to do things most Indians never had a chance to learn. So what I'm telling you, Parker, is—keep out of my way. For the first time in my life, being Indian is something good to be, and Washington don't want to hear nothing bad about me, not from you nor nobody else. Far as they're concerned, they finally got them a Indian on the payroll who can do something other than sweep a floor. That's all they want to know about me. And you can't do a goddamn thing about it, Parker."

He stuck his head under the hood of a bus and started putting the carburetor back in place. The cigarette still burned, clamped between his lips.

I went back to the house.

Mary was right. Garlen was courting an explosion just as surely by fooling with a Navajo woman as by working with a gasoline-drenched carburetor while holding a lighted cigarette between his lips. But Garlen was right, too. There was nothing I could do about him and Julia.

Hell, I hadn't even been able to tell the son of a bitch to put out that cigarette.

16.

At the end of my shift, I swept out the trolley to leave it clean for the day man. My Latin book lay open on the fare box, and I memorized as I worked.

Dutch Schneider came out of the dispatcher's office and stepped slowly over the tracks toward me, moving like molasses in January.

"Tempus fugit, Dutch," I yelled. "Tempus fugit."

"You got a telegram, Will," he said. "Hope it ain't bad news."

Telegrams were always bad news. I opened it and saw it was from the red-faced woman.

YOUR PA BIT BY POSSUM DIED IN THREE DAYS COME HOME, *the telegram said.*

I started to cry. I had always meant to make it up with Pa sometime, just not yet a while.

FRANKLIN PLODDED through the crowd waiting in front of the warehouse. Usually he would stop to chat with the men like a politician at a camp meeting while the women and children stood aside listening but not saying anything. This time he spoke to no one.

He came up the steps of the loading platform with his head down. His Stetson shielded his face, and it wasn't until he was on the platform that I saw the bruises. Both his eyes were blackened and almost closed. His lower lip was puffed out like a bunion.

He didn't speak but went right to work, stacking food along the edge of the platform. When we had filled the last burlap sack and all the people were gone, he still hadn't said a word. We straightened up the warehouse in silence and were all set to leave. Franklin loitered on the platform. He was ready to talk.

"What's on your mind, Franklin?"

"Got trouble, Hosteen Parker. Big trouble."

"What kind of trouble?"

"Julia, she no do right."

"Garlen, you mean?"

"She been school, don't listen me no more. She say don't want marry longhair, live in hogan, walk behind her man."

"What's she planning to do?"

"Julia, she move in with Garlen. I go get, she don't come. Me and him, we fight."

I didn't know what to say or do. It was both a family matter I had no authority to deal with and an administrative problem that was beyond my power to resolve.

I said, "There's not much I can do, Franklin."

"You fire Garlen."

"I can't. He's doing his job."

"His job not fuck Julia."

"No, but I can't fire him for that."

"You tell Washington. Washington not like white man fuck Indian girl."

"Franklin, Washington looks on Garlen as an Indian just like you and Julia."

"Garlen not Navajo. Garlen, he no-good white."

I didn't want to debate the issue. For one thing, I thought Franklin was right.

I said, "Franklin, there's nothing I can do about Garlen as long as he's doing his job."

"Then you fire Julia, give job somebody else."

"But she's doing a good job, too. That wouldn't be fair."

The sun beat down. Looking out over the dreary brown plain blotched with lifeless white patches of alkaline soil and dotted with black lava walls and towering spires, I could see why Franklin believed in witches. The only growing thing in sight was gray-green sagebrush. All grass had long since been grazed off by sheep and horses, as well as by the vast herds of cattle that dishonest Indian Agents had allowed white ranchers to run on Navajo lands in the past. It was an empty, dead landscape.

Franklin stood at my side, short and squat, a monument of dignity with a battered face. He, too, stared out at the ominous land. I knew what he would say next and what I would have to do.

"Julia work, nobody work."

"You mean—?"

"Julia work, I quit. Cook quit. Archie quit. Ben quit. Everbody, they quit."

"All right," I said. "I'll fire Julia."

Julia took it with a shrug. Garlen was a different story. He came to the school at the end of recess. I was standing on the steps, ringing the brass handbell to call the children in.

"I want to talk to you, Parker," he said. I sent him into my office to wait while I got my pupils settled. I asked Mary to keep an eye on my classroom.

"Be careful, Will," she said.

I found Garlen sitting in my chair, reading papers he'd picked up from my desk. He didn't get out of the chair or offer to.

"Put those papers down," I said. "They don't concern you."

"Glad to see you like my work, Parker," Garlen said. He read from the paper he was holding. It was my quarterly personnel report. "'J.C. Garlen is an excellent mechanic and a diligent worker. He is keeping the buses running under difficult circumstances.'"

I took the report out of his hand. "You wanted to see me? I've got a classroom full of kids waiting."

"I want to know why you fired Julia."

"That's none of your business."

"I think it is." He pulled a Bull Durham sack out of his shirt pocket and started rolling a cigarette.

"No smoking in here," I said.

He finished making the cigarette and licked the paper, all the while sitting behind my desk like it was his.

"What about Julia?" he said. He stuck the cigarette in the corner of his mouth, let it droop there.

"How I staff the kitchen is up to me."

"I reckon you ain't happy about Julia living with me."

"It doesn't matter whether I'm happy about it or not."

"That's right. It don't matter. I'm glad you realize that. But firing Julia, that ain't fair."

"And I remind you, it's none of your business how I run the school."

"Well, Julia's my business and—"

"That's your problem. Now get out of my office. Julia's not going to work in the kitchen."

Garlen struck a match on his buckle and lit the cigarette. He dropped the match on the floor still burning and sat a moment, puffing smoke, before getting up and leaving the office. The match went out of its own accord.

I discovered I was shaking and sat down until I was steadier.

I had always prided myself on being rational. Faced with a

problem, I thought it through and then did what had to be done. I believed in rules and order, in doing the right thing, in being honest and open and not beating around the bush. Mary teased me sometimes about being rigid as a stick, stubborn as a bulldog. She said I'd make a good cop.

I didn't think I was rigid or stubborn, just principled. Until Garlen came along, I had never encountered a situation that left me baffled for so long about what was right to do. Nor had I ever before failed to do what I saw had to be done, no matter how difficult or unpleasant it was.

I knew I should fire Garlen. And I knew I wouldn't do it.

He was an angry man causing scandal and dissension in the Navajo community—the last thing my Washington bosses wanted. But thanks to him, my bus scheme was working just the way it was supposed to—working so well that the Indian Service grapevine crackled with rumors of growing support in Washington for an expanded busing program linked to a huge day-school construction program on the Navajo Reservation. I could smell the possibility of promotion and transfer and an escape from Red Mesa. Without Garlen all my hopes would go up in smoke. The buses wouldn't run and we might be stuck at Red Mesa forever.

But that was not the only reason I could not fire him. The Indian blood he claimed protected him like a suit of armor. Garlen was right—Washington did not want to hear anything bad about him. In the eyes of Commissioner Collier and other high muckety-mucks, he was no longer just an individual like any other. He had become the focus and personification of a worthy policy—an Indian who was actually qualified to fill a skilled job. No matter how questionable Garlen's Indianhood might be, it made him untouchable.

I knew I could do nothing about him, though things were bound to get worse. By firing Julia, I had made Garlen angrier than ever without mollifying Franklin more than momentarily. In Franklin's eyes I had taken only a first step toward dealing with Garlen, and not by any means the most important step. For Franklin, my firing Julia had more to do with his asserting authority over her than with revenging himself on Garlen for the beating he had suffered. Revenge was still to come. What form it would take, I could not foresee. But I could predict the circumstances that would provide occasion for it.

It was evident to me that Garlen and Julia were not destined to live happily ever after. I was sure that at some point he would abuse Julia as he had the young woman who had come to Red Mesa with him. But Julia was proud and feisty, not inclined to be submissive. She would not take his abuse passively, not for long. And when Julia broke with Garlen, Franklin and all his extended family would be fighting at her side, with by then even more wrongs to avenge. God only knew what the outcome might be.

I picked Garlen's match off the floor and dropped it in the wastebasket. For the first time since we'd been at Red Mesa, I locked the office door before going back to my classroom.

17.

She was a little thing, standing with her shoulders back and head held high, two bright spots of color in her cheeks.

"I'm the new teacher, Mary Gower," she said.

I was glad to see her. I'd been teaching all grades ever since Miss Teasdale quit to get married.

Mary Gower sat in the chair beside my desk. She looked older than most newly certified teachers straight out of normal school— closer to thirty than twenty, I reckoned. Unmarried, I knew, because Texas schools didn't hire married women.

"What's it like here?"

"It's all right," I said, "if you don't mind a one-horse town."

"I don't mind. I grew up in Owchita, which is maybe half-a-horse."

"The only thing is, the folks here don't pay very regular. I haven't been paid since the first month of school. Be patient, they say. Be patient. We'll do the right thing by you."

"But they give us room and board?"

"They keep us alive."

"You don't sound as if you like it here much."

"I don't. But you know of any jobs for teachers in towns that pay in cash?"

"No," she said, smiling, "that's why I'm here."

—RESERVATIONS—

*We sat for a moment just looking at one another.
She said, "How do you stand on the vote for women?"*

TWICE A WEEK the Red Ball Stage, a big closed truck with a red spot painted on its side, came by. The driver was a wizened little fellow called Foxey who wore a long leather apron that was split at the bottom and tied like trouser legs around his thighs. I never saw him sober. He constantly nipped at a flask of brandy he kept in the pocket of the apron. What his real name was I never knew.

Northbound on Tuesday to Shiprock and Farmington, Foxey delivered mail, groceries from the Gallup Mercantile Co., and other supplies. Southbound on Thursday, he delivered milk produced by Mormon farmers in the San Juan Valley and blocks of ice cut in winter from frozen mountain lakes above Pagosa Springs, north of Farmington. The ice, speckled with the damp sawdust in which it had been stored, kept the milk sweet in the back of the truck on the hottest days.

Foxey always went about his business the same way, stopping at the trading post and at Mrs. Reeves's cottage before coming to us. He folded back the double doors at the rear of his truck and climbed into it to chip a block of ice down to size, making sure Davey got a good big piece to suck on. Grabbing tongs, Foxey slid the ice to the back of the truck, hopped down, and eased the block off onto his leather-covered thigh. Weighing not much more than a hundred pounds himself but fueled by cheap brandy, he hauled that big chunk into the house, seemingly shoving it along with his thigh, and popped it into the top of the icebox like it was no heavier than a marshmallow. If he staggered, it was from the brandy, not the weight of the ice.

One Thursday after delivering supplies to the trading post,

Foxey went to Mrs. Reeves's. The doors were locked, and no matter how he pounded, he couldn't raise her, so he left her ice and milk inside the screened porch. On his next northbound trip, he didn't have anything for her. It was a full week before he went to her house again with ice and milk. The ice he'd left on her porch had long since melted, leaving only a little sawdust to show where it had been. The milk was still there, clabbered and poking up out of the bottles like Grecian columns. He came and got me.

Mary and I hadn't seen Mrs. Reeves for a while, but there was nothing unusual about that. Only when Foxey told me he couldn't raise her did I realize how long it had been since we had heard her calling Bozo. Foxey and I went all around her cottage, pounding on doors and windows. When she still didn't appear, I got a crowbar and pried open the front door.

The stench rolled over us. Foxey backed off the porch, reaching for the brandy flask in his apron pocket. I went through the house, opening windows. I had to swallow hard to keep from throwing up.

I found Mrs. Reeves lying in her bathrobe on the floor of her clinic, surrounded by boxes of medical supplies she had received and never got around to unpacking. Near her hand I saw a long-bladed kitchen knife and the body of a rattlesnake that had been hacked almost to bits. It was a small snake, with only a couple of rattles on its tail, but plenty big enough to have scared most anyone to death.

I rushed outside for air. Foxey was standing beside his truck. a brandy bottle tipped to his lips. He must have emptied his flask.

I told him I'd have to send the body into town with him.

"That's okay," he said, "but I ain't going to touch her."

He wouldn't change his mind, though I pointed out I could not get her on the truck alone.

I knew it was no use asking Franklin for help. A dead person was a fearful thing to a Navajo. The *tchindi* that had caused the death could move to anyone who touched the body. The only way to get rid of the evil spirit was for a medicine man to conduct a sing—chants, sand paintings, and dances, with gifts and food for all those who chose to attend. A sing like that could go on for days and bankrupt a family.

There was a further complication. When someone died in a hogan, it became *tchindi*, too. The family who lived in it knocked in the roof on the north side to warn people away and give the dead person's spirit an avenue of escape. Exceptions were made for white men's houses, so I wouldn't have to bash in Mrs. Reeves's roof. But I knew that if the clinic were ever to be used again, I would have to arrange for a medicine man to exorcise the evil spirits before Franklin or any other Navajo would willingly enter. The cost would come out of my pocket. There was no money even in petty cash for what Washington would regard as superstition.

I went to Garlen to see if he would help load Mrs. Reeves into Foxey's truck, though I was sure what his answer would be.

"She ain't my problem, Parker," he said.

I went to the trading post to see if I could get Oates to help.

"Get Garlen," he said.

"Garlen says it's not his problem."

"It ain't my problem either," Oates said.

In the end Mary helped me roll Mrs. Reeves into a canvas tarp and wrap her in it. Then we dragged her to the truck and propped her up against the back in a standing position. While Mary steadied her, I picked up her feet and tipped her into the truck. Foxey closed the doors and drove off. I dug a hole in Mrs. Reeves's backyard and buried the snake.

Foxey had been drunk as usual. Afterward he didn't

remember a thing about her death. On his next trip, he started to deliver her usual order of groceries from the Gallup Merc. I stopped him.

"Dead?" he said. "Now who'da thought it? Dead. When did it happen? Just like that? Dead!"

He reached for his flask.

For Mary and me, Mrs. Reeves's death was a turning point. Our whole outlook on life seemed to darken. When Davey was around, Mary and I forced ourselves to be cheerful. Once we were alone, however, we fell silent and started worrying, talking little because we had little to talk about anymore but problems and fears—Garlen, Julia, what Franklin might do, how it would all come out. We could see no happy ending. We could see ourselves winding up like Mrs. Reeves and leaving Red Mesa as rotting bodies in the back of a drunken freighter's truck.

18.

Mary and her three friends marched down the middle of the unpaved street right at noon on Saturday, market day, waving posters. The poster Mary carried said:

> WOMEN UNITE!
> DEMAND THE VOTE!
> IT'S YOUR RIGHT!

With one hand she held the poster high. With the other she gripped her long skirt to keep it out of the dust of the street. Under the straw hat she wore to ward off the sun, her cheeks glowed like hot coals.

The street was jammed with farm wagons. Farmers cursed and spat as they hauled at their reins, pulling their teams aside to keep from trampling the marchers underfoot. Mary and her friends did not give an inch, though dogs nipped at their heels. The farm women Mary hoped to reach with her message sat grim-faced beside their husbands on the wagon seats and turned their heads away.

I stood with a bunch of men on the steps of the hardware store. The owner was the school board chairman. He came out and watched, too.

"Lookit them damn-fool women," he said. "Ain't they a sight?"

Mary saw me standing among the men on the steps of the hardware store. She smiled and dipped her poster to me.

I cheered and applauded. I was the only one on the steps — hell, I was the only one in the whole town — not to see the scandal of it.

EVERY SO OFTEN Franklin's old uncle drove past the school, the bed of his wagon crammed with barrels, headed for the sweet-water spring a few miles north. It was an all-day chore for the old man to get there, fill the hogsheads with a bucket, and get home again.

One day, soon after the schoolbuses left to take the children home, the sky blackened and rain began to fall. Lightning danced, thunder battered our ears, and rain pelted down. It was a real gully-buster.

About the time the last bus was safely back in the shed, the old man came past the school on his way home from the spring. He hunched over on the wagon seat, drenched. By then the road had turned into a river and was deep in water. The horses, a powerful young bay and an old white so scrawny its ribs showed, put their heads down and strained to keep the heavily loaded wagon moving through the muck.

Late-fall storms usually passed quickly, but this one went on and on. Mary, Davey, and I stood on the porch, watching the downpour.

"The washes'll be running soon," I said. In that eroded land there was too little grass and other vegetation to hold the water back long enough for it to soak into the ground. It would pour into every arroyo, taking still more of the topsoil with it.

Before the words were out of my mouth, we heard a sound like a fast train in the distance. It was the sound of washes running full.

Before long Franklin came hurrying through the storm.

Water poured off the brim of his hat as he raced up the steps.

"Trouble, Hosteen Parker," he said. "Big trouble."

Franklin was mud to his waist. He wiped his face with a blue bandanna, leaving muddy streaks over his cheeks. I had never seen him so agitated.

His story tumbled out in gestures and broken phrases. He and the boys had been on their way home on the same trail I had driven when the buses first came to Red Mesa. Just before they got to Big Wash, a wall of muddy water came rushing down it, filling it from bank to bank. They saw the old man and his water wagon in the middle of the arroyo as the torrent struck and swept the horses off their feet. The wagon spun around and swept backward downstream like a boat out of control, spilling barrels and pulling the horses with it. The old man was thrown off the seat but made it safely to the bank. The horses, half-drowned, panicky, tangled in harness, didn't regain their footing until they had been carried downstream almost to the bridge on which U.S. 666 crossed Big Wash. They were trapped in a cove, unable to climb the steep bank, buffeted by the current, with the wagon tugging them back into the violent stream. Franklin said the horses were tiring and sinking fast.

"We'll take a bus, try to pull them out," I said.

That was what Franklin had come for, of course, though he knew as well as I that it was against regulations to use government equipment for private benefit, even a Navajo's. If something went wrong, I would have a terrible time explaining to the bureaucrats in Washington that when you are in the middle of nowhere and see someone in trouble, you have to help, whatever the risks.

We ran to the bus shed. Garlen was there, watching the rain come down in sheets. I told him what had happened.

"I'm taking a bus," I said.

"Parker, you're a goddamn fool. These buses is government property."

"I'll take responsibility for the bus."

"Fucking right you will. I won't."

On our way to Big Wash, we detoured by the warehouse and got some coils of heavy rope. Just before reaching the wash, 666 curved sharply and ran parallel with the bank for a little way, then made a sharp turn onto the bridge. As we drove up, I realized the storm was about over. The sky was brightening overhead. The lightning had moved to the east and rain wasn't coming down as hard as it had. But Big Wash was still deep in fast-moving water, and it was still rising.

A crowd of Navajos clustered on the bank, watching helplessly as the horses, mired in bottomless sand, half in and half out of the current, struggled to climb to safety. In a frenzy of slashing hooves and arching necks, they hammered at the muddy bank with their front legs as they tried to find footing to pull themselves to solid ground. They crashed into one another, dragged one another beneath the foaming water, fought to the surface, mouths agape, eyes wide open, only to collide once again. They gained a few inches, then slipped farther back into the stream as the wagon, swinging anchorless, was caught by a different current and snapped them off balance again. Desperately flailing, they dug their hindquarters deeper and deeper into the mud.

Great eyes rolling and nostrils flaring, the terrified beasts soon had only their heads above water. Froth swirled like dirty lace around their stretching necks.

Just short of the turn onto the bridge, I left the road and drove toward the bank at the point where the horses were trapped. I stopped well back from the edge, giving myself an extra margin of safety should the raging water undercut the bank.

Tying a rope to the front bumper of the bus, Franklin looped the free end around his shoulders and leaped into the water to try to unhitch the horses. Archie, Joe, and others held the rope to keep him from being washed away. Choking, sputtering, knocked off his feet, flying hooves chopping at him from every direction, Franklin somehow managed to unhook the harness without getting kicked.

The other men pulled Franklin, half-drowned but safe, back to the bank. Ben managed to lasso both horses, getting two loops of rope over the head of each. I tied the ropes to the front axle of the bus, put the gears in reverse and gently let out the clutch, tightening the ropes. At first the wheels spun uselessly in the mud. Franklin and the other men shoved. The bus edged back from the wash a little at a time.

The scrawny old horse had not had the strength to struggle as hard as the bay and had not dug itself in as far as the younger horse. So the white horse came out easily, clambered up the bank, shook the ropes from its neck, and plunged across the muddy plain like a terrified colt, trailing harness. The big bay, young and strong, fighting hard but unable to get a footing, had dug itself deep into the sand and was now tightly gripped. It screamed and threw its head from side to side as the ropes drew taut.

We tried again and again. It was too late. The bay weakened and gradually sank into the raging water. Its nostrils pulsed desperately. Its eyes rolled back to the whites. The men let the ropes slacken and the horse's head slipped free. After several excruciating minutes, even the eyes and nostrils were gone, leaving only swirling water. At that moment a huge chunk of bank collapsed and spilled over the spot where the horse had disappeared. Another few feet and it would have taken the bus with it.

I moved the bus closer to the bridge. Archie and Ben

transferred the ropes to the wagon, which had floated downstream and been stopped by the bridge. The men pulled the wagon right out. We didn't even have to use the bus. The water barrels had bobbed off in the flood and were long gone.

Franklin and the boys rode back to the school with me to help clean up the bus. When I finally drove it under the shed, there was not a spot of mud on it, inside or out. Garlen had gone home by then, but he would have nothing to complain about when he inspected it the next morning.

"I'm sorry about the horse," I told Franklin.

He took my hand.

"My friend," he said.

—*RESERVATIONS*—

19.

Mary and her friends were still marching past his hardware store with their suffragette posters, and I was still cheering them on, when the school board chairman said, "You're fired. And her, too. I never seen the like."

"Fine," I said. "How about the back pay you owe us?"

"You got to finish out the year for that, like your contract says."

"But you just fired us."

"For cause. Don't forget, for cause. We don't owe you a dime. Not a thin dime."

"Cause?" I said. "Why shouldn't women have the vote?"

The school board chairman looked skyward, spreading his hands.

"See?" he said, speaking not to me but to someone in the sky, maybe God. "That's what I mean. He just don't think like a white man ought."

AFTER THE STORM, you could tell by looking at their feet which children rode the bus to school and which had to walk. Many of those who lived too close to ride had been caught in the deluge on their way home. Balls of gumbo mud had formed on their feet as they slogged along, leaving their shoes misshapen when they dried out, with cracked uppers and flapping soles.

We put new shoes on as many children as we could but did not have enough for all by any means. We received only one shipment a year, and the standard sizes went fast. Children usually started out in shoes that were too big for them. When a pair fell apart or were outgrown, the child had to go barefoot or cripple along until the next year. After the storm, most of the few pairs remaining on the warehouse shelves were ludicrously small or ridiculously large. We had no money in the budget to order more. The only children who still wore decent shoes were those who rode the bus.

So I wasn't too surprised when Franklin called me out of my classroom into the hall one morning to tell me that a delegation of parents was outside, wanting to talk about shoes. By then the land had dried out. Once again we lived in a waterless desert.

"Got trouble, Hosteen Parker," Franklin said. "People, they want new shoe for kids."

"But we've given out all the shoes that will fit."

"I tell them that. Ain't happy. Now you tell them."

It was cool that day but the sun was bright. I went out in my shirtsleeves, thinking it would not take long to deal with the parents' complaint. When I stepped out on the schoolhouse porch and saw the size of the gathering, I realized that disposing of the problem wasn't going to be as simple as I had imagined. There must have been fifty people waiting for me. At least half were women, most of whom carried cradleboards in their arms and had children clinging to their skirts.

I knew perfectly well who had brought the people out. Not much happened at Red Mesa that Franklin did not have a hand in. He didn't usually bring me problems that had no solution, however, and I felt sure he would not have set up this meeting unless he had some scheme in mind that would satisfy the parents, take me off the hook, and enhance his own standing in the community.

If I simply went along with Franklin, everything would turn out fine. But would I be able to do what he wanted me to? Franklin often assumed that I had more power than I actually had. He chose to ignore what I could never forget: My authority, such as it was, came from far-off Washington and was stretched almost to invisibility by the time it reached Red Mesa.

We stood on the steps of the school in silence. The faces in front of us were stern, wary.

Franklin whispered, "You say something."

I cleared my throat. "Welcome," I said. "I am glad to see you. Is there something I can do for you?"

Franklin translated. He turned my few words into a long speech. He went on and on. For day-to-day business my Navajo was adequate, helped along by gestures, facial expression, and repetitions. But this was an oration.

After he moved past the opening words of welcome, he lost me. I caught a phrase here and there in which the words for "shoe" and "bus" figured, but the rest was beyond me. I could make no sense out of his harangue. I felt like a ventriloquist's dummy, wordless until my mentor spoke.

"Franklin," I asked when he stopped, "what are you telling them? What was all that about?"

He shrugged. "I just say Hosteen Nez Belihkahnah, Mr. Tall Man American, he happy they come."

An old longhair in the crowd stepped forward.

Franklin said, "Him, he Hosteen Tse. Big medicine man, my uncle, live at Klinchee. Very old, Hosteen Tse."

"I know Hosteen Tse," I said. "We have met before."

As he had been the first time I saw him, Hosteen Tse was elegantly dressed in pajama-like white trousers. His blue velveteen blouse was cinched at the waist by a magnificent belt with silver conchas big as saucers. Bright strands of turquoise and coral hung around his neck. His deerskin moccasins, ankle high, were closed with silver buttons. A faded red bandanna was knotted like a ribbon around his white hair.

Seeing the old man told me as nothing else could have that the mud-ruined shoes had become a larger issue than I had supposed. As an important tribal leader, Hosteen Tse would not have come all the way to Red Mesa from Klinchee on any trivial mission. He was famous all over the reservation and so old that like Mrs. Tsinnijinni, his sister, he had been on the Long Walk to Bosque Redondo, which the *Dineh* called Hwalte, in a part of New Mexico that a U.S. Army commission had once called uninhabitable.

Though he could not read or write, Hosteen Tse was a historian and walking law library — a living repository of tribal lore and the Navajo equivalent of a jailhouse lawyer. He had been present at the Creation, so to speak, and he carried in his memory every crossed *t* and dotted *i* of every treaty, proclamation, and regulation ever promulgated by the U.S. government and imposed on the Navajo people.

Hosteen Tse was said to know more Navajo chants and ceremonies than any other singer. He was one of the few medicine men still performing the full Enemy Way, which in the old raiding days was sung over returning warriors to protect them from the *tchindi* of enemies they had slain or whose dead bodies they had looked upon. The same ceremony was sometimes held for women who had lain with men who were not Navajo.

Frail as a dried twig, Hosteen Tse faced the crowd and began to talk. His was a quiet-seeming voice, surprisingly sonorous, that carried well.

"What's he saying?" I asked Franklin.

"Hosteen Tse, he tell about Rope Thrower burn cornfield, chop down peach tree, make slaves. People, they starve, die."

I had never heard of Rope Thrower. Franklin said that was the Navajo name for Kit Carson, whom I had heard of. It was Carson who in 1863 and 1864 reluctantly sent his New Mexico Volunteers, guided by Ute and Mexican scouts, to subjugate the Navajos by destroying their crops and food supplies—a strategy that was endorsed by Sherman long before he sent troops marching through Georgia.

Carson's ragtag army ravaged Navajo lands, killed sheep and cattle, cut down orchards, burned crops, stores of food, and hogans. The Utes seized some women and children as slaves and others were sold to wealthy Mexican landowners. A small band of Navajos managed to take refuge in the hidden recesses of Canyon de Chelly but were betrayed by renegade Mexican scouts, whom the Indians had welcomed as friends. This final defeat crushed the Navajo nation. It was a bitter, never-to-be-forgotten chapter in Navajo history.

Franklin went on. "Hosteen Tse, he tell about Long Walk to Hwalte. He tell about people, they die. He tell about he see General Sherman sign treaty. Hosteen Tse, he wonder why white man don't keep treaty General Sherman sign. *Dineh*, they keep treaty, why Washington don't keep treaty, he want to know?"

"Franklin, we don't have time to go through all that. I've got children waiting in my classroom. Ask him why he's here today, try to shut him up so we can move along."

"Can't do that. Hosteen Tse, he got thing to tell."

Franklin was right, of course. In typical white-man fashion, I wanted to come to the point and get it over with. I did not want to waste time chewing over the past and bringing up matters it was too late to do anything about and that in any case I had no power to deal with. But that was not the Navajo way. To the Navajo mind everything is of a piece. The past is alive in the present and still potent, not just a haven to retreat to on sleepless nights. For Hosteen Tse the incident of the muddy shoes needed to be packaged with the Rope Thrower's capture of the *Dineh*, their suffering at Fort Sumner, and Sherman's unkept promises. The long list of Washington's failures and betrayals had to be detailed in order to put this afternoon's discussion of shoes in proper perspective.

As the meeting dragged on, the sun went behind a cloud. A chilly breeze nipped around the corner of the schoolhouse and made me shiver. Every little while, Franklin would say something to me so that the people would know I was hearing Hosteen Tse's words.

"Hosteen Tse, he go Washington, talk President McKinley. President, he promise good time come."

And a minute or two later: "Hosteen Tse, he tell about white man rancher, he trespass, he drive cattle to Table Mesa, where Hosteen Dijolei graze sheep. White man rancher, he shoot sheep. White man cattle eat grass until no more grass, only dust. Nobody do nothing about white man rancher, he kill Hosteen Dijolei's sheep."

Next: "Hosteen Tse, he want know when Washington build more school like General Sherman promise, send more teacher, build more hospital, send more doctor."

Finally Hosteen Tse got around to the shoes. He turned to face me and spoke passionately. Franklin said, "Hosteen Tse, he say not right some children, they ride in bus and got shoe, some children walk in mud and got no shoe. He say that not fair. All children, they need shoe."

Hosteen Tse looked me up and down, head to toe, shaking his head. Abruptly he turned away and stepped down off the porch. It was my turn.

"Franklin," I said, "you know we don't have shoes to give

them and won't have any until we get next year's supplies. Tell them I'm sorry, but the children will just have to get along the best they can."

Franklin did not pass that along. He stood staring into the distance like a man in deep thought. I knew I was about to learn at last why he had organized this gathering of parents and what he wanted of me. I only hoped that what he came up with would be something it was in my power to do.

Finally he spoke. "If everbody ride bus, that make everbody same. If kids don't walk so much, they don't need shoe so bad. That fair. That make everbody happy."

So that was what Franklin was up to. He wanted to put all the children on the buses, even those who lived within walking distance. I pointed out that the buses were already crowded. He brushed the argument aside.

"Archie, Ben, Joe — they make more trip."

"But there's no money in the budget to pay them for the extra driving."

"Don't need money. You give boys can of mutton ever week. Boys, they like that."

"Franklin, that mutton is for Navajo relief. Your boys are working. They're not eligible for relief."

"Boys, they Navajo."

I thought about it. Franklin had known better than I how deeply the parents were upset by the fact that some children got to ride the bus and others had to walk, even in bad weather. In his eyes and the eyes of the parents, the muddy shoes had come to symbolize an intolerable inequity in the way the children were treated. The unfairness of it all was causing dissension in the community — dissension that would surely stay alive and grow, so long as children who rode buses had better shoes than those who walked.

The issue had already become significant enough to reach

across the mountains to Klinchee and engage the interest of Hosteen Tse. Before long, unless I did something quickly, word of the contretemps would reach Washington and I would have a lot of explaining to do. Washington might soon be asking, If the buses get the Navajos stirred up because some children are able to ride them and others aren't, why not get rid of the buses?

As usual Franklin had worked in a subtly Navajo way to get me to do something he felt needed doing, something that without this powwow I might have resisted, though it was within my power.

And it was something, as he said, that would make everybody happy—including me, because Washington would know nothing about it. The children whose shoes had been ruined by mud would have the thrill of riding twice a day in a white-man wagon, just like their peers in undamaged shoes. Parents would be pleased at having won more equitable treatment for their children. Archie, Benn, and Joe would have meat for their families that they could not otherwise get. Most important, Franklin would further enhance his reputation for being able to get things done for the people of the Red Mesa district.

"All right, Franklin," I said. "You win."

Franklin made a long speech, gesturing at me from time to time. I stood there nodding, pretending to understand all that he was saying, trying to look pleased.

Afterward all the men came up to shake my hand, even Hosteen Tse. The old man was so shriveled with years his hand seemed fragile and weightless. He was all memory and dignity. I told him in my halting Navajo that I was honored to see him again. Hosteen Tse said nothing.

20.

I went up the steps of the boardinghouse in El Paso two at a time.

Mary and Ella were in the front parlor, fitting Mary's waitress uniform. Ella worked in the tearoom down at Harrington's Department Store, and she had talked her bosses into hiring Mary, too.

"I got the job," I said. "Fuller Brush took me on. Dick is going to train me." Dick was Ella's friend.

"I knew he would," Ella said. "Dick's a big talker, but he's got a big heart, too."

Mary said, "Both of us working! I knew things would get better."

"Will you marry me?"

She started crying. I thought it meant she was going to turn me down.

Ella got up and left the room, closing the door behind her.

"There's something I've got to tell you, Will. I had a baby once. Her name was Nellie. I named her for my grandmother."

"That's all right. I'll adopt her."

"Nellie's dead. Pa killed her."

ONE GOOD THING came out of the storm, or so I thought for a while. The Gallup bootlegger's big black Studebaker slipped off the muddy road into a ditch and got stuck. A couple of policemen came along before he could get rid of his booze. Their natural inclination might have been to accept a few bottles as a friendly gift and drive on, not causing trouble for him or his customers. But the bootlegger's car was just about buried in the ditch, and they had no way of knowing who else might come along before he got dug out. They were obliged to arrest him and confiscate his load.

I soon learned that nothing had really changed. With the old bootlegger out of the picture and no new one yet on the scene, Oates seized the opportunity to expand his business. He struck a deal with Foxey to bring whiskey out from town on the Red Ball truck along with his other supplies. He sold spiked bottles of Coke and Nehi Orange across the counter of his trading post almost as openly as he sold Arbuckle's Coffee. The price was twenty-five cents a spiked bottle.

As usual, everyone knew what was going on and no one did anything about it. Every time I reported it, which was regularly, I was met with blank stares and lame excuses. It just didn't seem worthwhile to anyone to expend the energy it would take to head off a temporary entrant in the liquor trade like Oates. Soon enough there would be a new bootlegger blinking the lights of a fast car with overload springs along U.S. 666. Whatever was done about him now, before long Oates would be back to selling unspiked pop at a nickel a bottle, and someone else would be selling the booze to put in it.

Oates kept the trading post open until nine o'clock or so at night, not only because he wanted business but also because he used the store as a sitting room. His women stayed out of the way in his living quarters while he passed his evenings in an old leather easy chair behind the counter. If a customer came by, it was no inconvenience for Oates to serve him or her.

—*RESERVATIONS*—

Entering the trading post after dark on a winter day was like walking into a smoke-filled cave dimly lighted by a couple of hanging oil lamps with sooty glass chimneys. Oates kept trying to get permission from the Indian Service to run a line from the school to the trading post so that he could tap into the Kohler generator Franklin or I cranked every evening, but so far I had been able to head him off. The oil lamps cast grotesque shadows overhead, where dusty saddles and bridles dangled from bare rafters along with miscellaneous bulky items like wagon seats, horse collars, plows, shovels, and hoes. The walls were lined with open shelves of canned goods, bright bolts of velveteen and calico, cowboy boots and hats, Levis, and two-toned shirts.

A U-shaped counter of unpainted rough pine ran along the sides and back of the post, keeping customers from the shelves and confining them to the open well in front. Oates called this area his bull pit. In the center of it, surrounded by scuttles of coal, a big potbellied stove spilled glowing ashes onto the stone floor. Whenever the post was open in cold weather, a crowd of Navajo men squatted around the stove, chewing tobacco and smoking. From time to time the stove sizzled as someone spat tobacco juice on its hot sides.

After supper one winter day, I went up to the post to buy bread. Half a dozen Indian men were there, several with their families. Garlen sat on the counter, his knees drawn up before him, his back resting against the side of the cash register, a Coke in his hand. Oates had a Coke in his hand, too. The smell of liquor was so strong it overpowered the odor of unwashed bodies, burning lamps, and sizzling tobacco spit.

A newly woven eye-dazzler blanket, neatly folded and representing six months of work, lay on the counter at Garlen's feet. A few bills and some coins rested on top of it. That would be the amount Oates had offered for it. Over in one corner a

Navajo woman sat on the floor, staring into the distance. I recognized her as Mrs. Tahgahlchee, whose daughter Daisy was one of our first-graders. I looked more closely at the men around the stove and saw her husband on the far side, a Coke in his hand. Daisy was not there. Probably she had been left at home to look after her younger brothers and sisters.

As I entered, Mrs. Tahgahlchee was deep in thought. Slowly she rose and approached the counter. She picked up the money from the rug. A bargain had been struck. Oates tossed the rug onto a shelf behind him.

Holding the money in her hand, Mrs. Tahgahlchee silently pointed by thrusting her lower lip at coffee, flour, sugar, and other staples. Oates named the price of each item in Navajo and at the same time showed her with her own bills and coins exactly how much that was. Having determined how far her money would go, she retreated to her place in the corner and settled down again.

I stopped beside the stove and exchanged greetings with the men loitering there while I warmed myself.

After more deep thought, Mrs. Tahgahlchee rose, approached Oates with her money clutched in her hand, and pointed with her lip. Oates placed a five-pound sack of sugar on the counter. She held out her hand and he took the money needed to pay for it. While she thought about her next purchase, her husband came up and nodded at the case of open Cokes. Oates handed him a bottle. Mrs. Tahgahlchee obediently opened her hand and Oates took a quarter. Her husband returned to the stove, squatted on his heels again, and tipped up the bottle, drinking chugalug.

She pointed with her lip. Oates ground a pound of Arbuckle's Coffee to put beside the sack of sugar and took more money from her hand. She thought again. Oates selected several strips of red-and-white ribbon candy from a huge glass jar and placed them on the counter as an offering to ease the transaction along. Mrs. Tahgahlchee nodded. She picked up the candy a piece at a time, making sure there would be one for each of her children. In rapid succession she pointed at flour, baking soda, and other items, including needles, thread, and a length of deep blue calico suitable for a skirt. She had only a quarter left in the palm of her hand. She stood pondering.

"Yeah, Parker, what can I do for you?" Oates said, letting me know it was my turn.

Oates handed me my bread and I gave him a dime. As I turned away, Mrs. Tahgahlchee decided to buy a loaf of the same bread. She handed Oates a quarter. He rang it up. I said, "That bread's a dime. You charged her a quarter."

Oates pretended to look at the register. "So I did," he said.

He gave Mrs. Tahgahlchee fifteen cents. Her husband got off his boot heels and came to the counter. Oates handed him another bottle of spiked Coke.

Mrs. Tahgahlchee gave back the bread and the fifteen cents.

Oates grinned at me. The fangs on either side of his empty gums gave him the look of a snarling dog.

"I knowed this here was my money," he said, tossing the coins in his hand.

Garlen saluted with his Coke. "So'd I," he said.

There was nothing I could do. Not about Oates and his cheating. Not about his bootlegging. Not about Garlen.

Nothing.

21.

"I don't think you've got any business traveling," I said. "Not in your condition." We'd been married and in the Indian Service for years by then.

Mary laughed and put my hand on her taut belly. I felt the baby move.

"Ah, Will, you do worry so. I'll be just fine and won't be gone long. The stone's all carved and waiting for me. I'll just see it placed and turn right around, get back on the train, and come home again."

"At least let me go with you."

She shook her head. "This is something I want to do alone. Once I get the stone on Nellie's grave, I'll feel easier about her and be all ready for the new baby."

She hadn't mentioned her mother. Her brother Eph had written to say she was sick again and asking for Mary. He said she wasn't long for this world.

"If you wanted to, you could stay a few days and visit," I said.

"There's no one to visit. Only Nellie."

WE DID NOT SEE much of Julia as the winter wore on. She seldom stepped outside Garlen's cottage except at night or when she thought no one was around and then only to flit to the bathhouse to use the toilet or take a shower. There was running water in Garlen's cottage but no bathroom.

Garlen complained to me about the lack of facilities. I told him I had put a request for a bathroom in my budget, but it had been turned down. That was true. I told him I would put in the request again. That was true, too. He didn't believe me, of course.

Now and again Franklin waylaid Julia and had a few words with her. He told me she was not happy and that Garlen sometimes beat her after he came home drunk from the trading post. Whether she let this slip or Franklin deduced it I could not discover, but I did not doubt the truth of it. Often in the night we heard angry shouts and screams coming from Garlen's cottage.

"Will, you've got to do something," Mary said.

"I don't know what."

"Speak to him."

"He won't listen."

"You could try."

But I couldn't try. I was afraid of what Garlen might do, not just to me but to Mary and Davey and Julia and Franklin—to all of us. I thought of Garlen as an angry animal circling around us with teeth bared, waiting for a chance to attack.

I tried to explain this to Mary, but she would not listen. When I reached for her in bed, wanting comfort more than anything else, she shoved me away and turned her back. I lay awake listening for Julia's screams, conjuring the past.

Mary went to see Julia one winter night when we knew Garlen was still at the post, drinking Oates's bootleg whiskey. Julia would not let her in, would not even answer Mary's repeated calls. Mary could hear her breathing on the other side of the door. Otherwise she would have thought she was pounding on the door of an empty house. That night she cried in my arms and I thought everything was going to be all right between us again.

But she said, "Will, you've got to do something."

And I said, "I don't know what."

She moved away from me. Nothing had changed.

Late in January, after weeks of harsh weather, we suddenly had a spell of unseasonably warm days. The nights continued bitterly cold, but each day the bright sun melted more snow. Every afternoon the washes ran full.

The buses had gone through the snow with no trouble while the ground was frozen hard. The thaw put them to a tougher test. The trails the buses traveled over were still solid when Archie and the other drivers picked up children in the morning. As temperatures rose during the day, the ground thawed and the bottom fell out of the ruts. By the time the children were out of school, the buses had to pull in low gear through mile after mile of deep gumbo, often having to wait for the snowmelt to recede in washes running bank-full.

One afternoon Archie's bus skidded into a scrub cedar as he tried to negotiate a muddy turn. No one was hurt, and the only damage to the bus was a small dent and some scraped paint. But when Garlen saw the bus, he went wild.

Mary and I were still at the school. Davey came running to tell us that Garlen and the drivers were fighting in the driveway.

I got there at the same time as Franklin. Ben and Archie were moaning on the gravel, clutching their groins with both hands, out of action. Joe was still on his feet, but it was no contest. He was out cold. Garlen held him up with one hand and punched with the other. Franklin and I pushed and pulled, trying to get Joe away from him.

Joe's head lolled on his chest. Garlen kept punching.

Franklin picked up a rock. Garlen kneed Joe, tossed him aside, and hit Franklin in the face, one fist and then the other.

Franklin moved in as close as he could, but his arms were too short to let him reach Garlen with his rock. After a moment he dropped it. He put his hands up to protect his face and tried to back away.

Garlen grabbed him, shook him like a doll, and kneed him as he had the others. Franklin fell, face down. Garlen pulled up his head by the hair and pounded his face into the rock Franklin had dropped.

I jumped on Garlen's back. He reached around behind him with one arm and yanked me off. He threw me against the fence and kicked me between the legs. I doubled up, screaming in spite of myself. Garlen kicked me again.

I must have passed out. When I came to, I was cradled in Mary's arms and Davey was running up to us with the bottle of brandy we kept in the medicine chest. Franklin and his nephews were picking themselves off the ground. Garlen strolled down the driveway, buttoning his shirt and whistling.

I sent Franklin and the drivers crippling homeward and fell into bed, hardly able to move. When dark came I didn't feel up to cranking the Kohler. Mary lit kerosene lamps. Even before she came to bed, I heard shouts and screams from down the road, but no more than usual. Then it was quiet and I fell asleep. Much later a car motor started up, waking me. Mary was beside me. I had not heard her come to bed.

I got to the window just in time to see Garlen's Model A go past. Its lights were not on, and I couldn't see if anyone was with him. Once it turned onto the Gallup road, the car's lights came on. I watched the taillight slip and slide along the road for as long as I could see it.

"It's Garlen," I said.

Mary sat up in bed. "Where could he be going?"

"I don't know, but you'd think the dumb son of a bitch would've waited for the freeze before he took out. The roads won't set hard for a couple of hours yet and the washes are still running."

"Wherever he's going, I hope he gets stuck and never gets out," Mary said.

"But not near here," I said. "I don't want him within a hundred miles of the place, buses or no buses."

The next morning none of us was moving around very fast. Franklin's face looked like someone had used a hammer on it and so did Joe's, but the drivers took the buses out as usual.

Franklin and I went to Garlen's cottage first thing. The door was open, and it was clear that Garlen had pulled out for good. All of his stuff was gone and so was Julia's. Nothing remained but government-issue furniture that had been tossed around and wrecked. Chairs were broken, the table was on its side with one leg snapped off, the couch had rips in the upholstery, and the doors of the kitchen cabinets were pulled off their hinges. The mattress, still covered by a filthy sheet, had been pulled askew on the bed. Throughout the cottage the floor was littered with paper and empty bottles.

Blood was everywhere—on the floor, the walls, the oak front of the icebox, where a bloody hand had left a smeared print. It looked like someone had leaned against the icebox and then slipped slowly to the floor, leaving a thick puddle of blood on the cracked blue linoleum.

"My God," I said.

Franklin said, "Garlen, he beat Julia bad."

"He must have killed her."

"Julia all right. She come home."

"I hope so," I said, not understanding. I thought he meant that while she might have left Red Mesa with Garlen, she would be back sometime.

"Julia, she not go with Garlen. She home. She Navajo again. When Hosteen Tse get here, we have sing."

I understood then what Franklin was telling me. Julia had rejoined her family. Hosteen Tse would come over from Klinchee to perform purification rites that would wipe out the past. I asked Franklin what ceremony Hosteen Tse would perform over Julia.

"Maybe Mountain Chant. Maybe Enemy Way. Hosteen Tse, he decide." He looked at the horizon and shrugged. He had told me all he wanted me to know.

We left Garlen's cottage as it was for the time being and went about the daily routine. Later I saw Julia at the kitchen, back at work. Her face was bruised and her eyes were blackened. She was dressed the traditional Navajo way in a long-sleeved, high-necked velveteen blouse and long full skirts. Mary said she had quit speaking English.

During the morning, I wrote a report for Washington on Garlen's disappearance with all his belongings. I did not mention Julia or the fight, just commented that while Garlen's work had been satisfactory, his behavior off the job had been erratic and he had seemed unable to get along with the Navajo populace. I added that I could not account for his pulling out without a word to anyone. Finally I said that I didn't know how long we'd be able to keep the buses going without a mechanic. Archie, Ben, and Joe had learned a lot about routine maintenance, but if anything serious happened—a broken axle, say, or a carburetor malfunction—it would be beyond them to fix. I asked Washington to assign a new mechanic to replace Garlen.

At the end of the day, I went to Garlen's cottage again, alone this time. There had been more blood than could be accounted for by any beating Julia had received. Now it was gone. Only stains remained. Someone had scraped up the blood and taken it away.

I was not surprised. There was no doubt in my mind that

Garlen was dead. No doubt either as to why the blood was gone. To sing an Enemy Way over someone who had killed or lain with an enemy, Hosteen Tse would want some part of the foe. In the absence of the enemy's scalp, he would use hair, nail clippings-almost anything, including blood.

Knowing—even suspecting—what I did, I should have pursued the killer or killers right away and seen to it that they were prosecuted and punished. But I didn't. The action I took was to take no action. I did nothing. I said nothing, not even to Mary. Whatever the circumstances of his going, Garlen was gone.

That was enough for me.

22.

Mary held tight to my hand. The nurse told us to time the pains.

Between two bad ones, Mary said, "When Nellie was born, there was nobody but my mother and father upstairs with me. My brother Eph and Muffie were downstairs heating water. It was their house, Eph and Muffie's, in Wichita Falls.

"'You see what it's come to,' Pa said, when the pains started.

"I tried not to yell. I said, 'I don't care. I loved Jimmy. I'm glad to have his baby.'

"'Don't go talking like that, girl,' Pa said. 'You ain't had that baby yet.'

"'Pa,' I said, 'Pa, I don't want you to have anything to do with this, not after what you did to Jimmy.'

"'You don't know nothing about what happened to Jimmy, girl,' he said, 'and you remember that.'

"I screamed at him, 'You killed him. I know that, you old drunk.'

"My mother said, 'Now shush, the both of you. The neighbors will hear.'

"After that I yelled all I pleased. I wanted the neighbors to hear."

She lay still. More pains hit her. The intervals were getting short.

She said, "Nellie came and she was dead. I knew Pa had killed her, just like he killed Jimmy. And my mother didn't do a thing to stop him."

I said, holding her hand, "You can't be sure."
"I'm sure," she said.

BY THE TIME Hosteen Tse came over the mountain from Klinchee, the weather had turned cold again and the ground was frozen hard.

Wagons rolled past the school, filled with women and children huddled under blankets, headed for the sing. Iron-banded wagon wheels groaned and bumped along rock-hard ruts behind straining horses. Hooves thudded against the earth, iron on iron. Harness jangled as men rode on horseback beside the wagon teams, urging them on. The breath of men and horses fogged like smoke from mouths and nostrils.

More smoke, towering columns of it, ghosted into the sky at Franklin's compound, where the visitors drew up their wagons on the plain and built great fires to roast whole sheep and fry bread that the women leavened by tossing dough from hand to hand. The bread filled washtubs Franklin had brought from the school. It looked to me like Franklin was feeding half the reservation.

After the sing began, we did not try to hold school. There would have been no point to it. Neither Franklin nor anyone else turned up for work, and not a child appeared for classes. To help out, I let Franklin take barrels of beans and flour and cases of stewed tomatoes, creamed corn, hardtack, and peanut butter from the warehouse. This was against the rules, of course, but I justified it to myself by remembering what Franklin had said about using tins of mutton to pay his boys for driving extra trips with the buses. The food was for Navajo relief, and Franklin and his guests were Navajos. Besides, it was the food that would have gone out the warehouse door if we'd been holding school.

At Franklin's invitation Mary and I took Davey and drove

through blowing snow to the big medicine hogan he had built for the sing. We pushed aside the blanket covering the doorway and ducked into the dimly lit smoky space, which smelled of burning cedar, cheap tobacco, and many human bodies crammed close. The only light came from one kerosene lantern hung from a roof log, a few candles stuck here and there around the walls, a flickering fire smoking in an open-sided stove crudely carved from half an inverted oil drum, and the occasional flare of a match touched to a rolled cigarette. A stovepipe did little to clear the air. Now and again a snowflake drifted through the smoke hole into the hogan and melted to nothingness in midair.

I dropped a handful of change into an old mutton tin beside the door. Following Navajo custom I clanked the coins into the tin as noisily as possible to announce that we were contributing to the success of the sing, which depended in part on the goodwill of those in attendance. I turned left, or south, to the men's side and Mary turned right to the women's. Davey slipped through the crowd of seated and squatting men to stand with his friend Sam Begay against the south wall.

Beyond the fire Franklin and Julia sat cross-legged on the floor, each wrapped in a blanket. Through the close-packed crowd, we caught glimpses of their shadowed faces. Hosteen Tse and his assistants slowly built a sand painting grain by grain on the hard-packed dirt floor of the hogan.

Starting from the center and working outward, they dribbled tiny streams of colored sand between their fingers. It was slow work to create the delicate designs. Progress was slower still because Hosteen Tse was quick to detect and wipe out the slightest error. The gods would tolerate no mistake, and an imperfection could cancel out all that Hosteen Tse hoped to accomplish. It took a long time to complete the painting.

In the flickering light and swirling clouds of smoke, I had to peer over and around the silhouetted shoulders and towering Stetsons of men seated on the floor in front of me. I could see well enough, however, to identify familiar symbols—a rainbow, the sun, the moon, corn and the like, as well as a row of sticklike *yeis*, the Holy People. But my knowledge of Navajo ceremonies was too skimpy for me to tell which of the great Navajo myths Hosteen Tse recited.

His surprisingly strong voice rose and fell, accompanied by drums made of goatskin stretched over coffee cans, lightly slapped with the flat of the hand. Now and again his chanting was drowned out by a bullroarer carved from the wood of a tree struck by lightning. Whirled at the end of a leather thong by one of Hosteen Tse's assistants, the bullroarer filled the hogan with an unearthly whir. It thundered in that limited space like a cathedral's great organ. The sound, the dimness, the constantly shifting shadows playing over the domed log ceiling—all were mesmerizing.

Suddenly—had I been dozing or daydreaming?—Franklin and Julia dropped their blankets and stood on or just behind the sand painting, I could not tell which from where I sat. Franklin wore only a towel around his waist, like a man in a Turkish bath. Julia was wrapped from ankles to shoulders in a shawl.

Keening in a tremulous falsetto, Hosteen Tse touched the sacred figure of a *yei* with an eagle-plume wand and then brushed the plume over the corresponding points of Franklin's body and then Julia's to ensure that the perfection of the god's image would prevail over any imperfections that might be present in Hosteen Tse's patients. The watching people were as still as the figures in the sand painting.

In the ceremony's final passage, Hosteen Tse chanted softly. His words floated through the hogan like snowflakes, melting in my ear. As Franklin and Julia stood before him, he moved around them, daubing them with a charcoal paste, still chanting. When Julia lifted her face to Hosteen Tse for blackening, she looked at peace. Again she seemed one with the world from which she had been wrenched when she was sent off to boarding school as a child. The symbolic blackening would make her invisible to any banished *tchindi* that might seek to recorrupt her spirit.

Four dancers pushed through the doorway. Their bodies were brightly painted with wild designs. Helmet-like *yei* masks covered their heads. A path opened in the crowd. Shaking gourd rattles, the *yeis* snaked their way slowly to Franklin and Julia. They danced over the sand painting, obliterating it, before escorting the two to the doorway and out into the night, safe from any lurking *tchindi*.

Everyone stood up, stretching. People milled and chatted like a bunch of Baptists between Sunday school and church.

Hosteen Tse's assistants scraped up every sacred grain of sand used in the painting. They took the sand outside to cast into the wind so that each grain could find its way home. When that was done, Hosteen Tse started a new sand painting.

It was after midnight. Mary and I gathered up Davey and went home to bed, knowing we had witnessed something rare and important but not knowing exactly what.

The next night we went back. This time Franklin and Julia were lined up along the back wall with Archie, Joe, and Ben while Hosteen Tse and his assistants worked on an enormous sand painting to the accompaniment of chants and drums. As we entered, I again clattered coins into the mutton tin by the door, but this time we realized right away that we were no longer welcome. None of the other guests spoke to us. When I sat down, the men around me drew away more than was necessary to make space.

On the women's side, Franklin's wife's toothless grandmother, Mrs. Tsinnijinni, crowded in next to Mary, elbowing her. Overwhelmed by the old lady's smell of stale sweat and urine, Mary moved away. Mrs. Tsinnijinni moved, too, pressing close, poking, not even pretending to smile. She worked a wad of tobacco with her gums. When she spat, it was on Mary's skirt.

We left at the first break in the ceremony. Mrs. Tsinnijinni's unrebuked rudeness to a guest, rare behavior in the Navajo world, told us that we had stepped over the inviolable line the *Dineh* drew between themselves and non-Navajos—not just whites but members of other tribes, whether Zuñi, Hopi, Ute, or Apache.

Franklin's sing had turned into something far more complex and significant than the usual Night Chant or Mountain Chant or *Yeibichai,* though we supposed we had identified elements of each in the ceremonies we had observed. From his vast stock of tribal lore, Hosteen Tse was bringing forth and combining many-faceted chants and rituals that pulled taut the ties of community in ways that were too close to the bone to be shared with outsiders like us. We guessed that he was now deep into the Enemy Way, with its poignant reminders of past wrongs and triumphs.

The sing continued several days longer, but we dared not return.

On the final day, Franklin staged a great celebration with horse races and a chicken pull and sent us a special invitation. After the races, saddled and bareback, over various distances out and back, we watched as young men dashed on horseback over the frozen ground past a rooster buried alive with only its feet showing. As the horses thundered along, each rider leaned from his saddle, clinging to the horn with one hand and reaching for the chicken's feet with the other. When a rider succeeded in pulling the chicken out of the ground, other riders crowded their horses close around him, racing along at top speed, trying to snatch his trophy. Feathers flew as one rider after another managed to seize the rooster. Soon the carcass was torn apart. The blood-spattered rider who made it back to the starting line with the feet claimed the prize, a silver-worked bridle.

To wrap up the sing now that the serious business was done, there was a festive Girls' Dance, the Navajo equivalent of a debutante ball, often mistakenly called a Squaw Dance, even by the *Dineh*. We were invited but decided not to go. We had been to other such dances in the past. In the light of a huge bonfire, girls dressed in their finest and laden with silver and turquoise would run down more or less reluctant men. The girls would seize their victims by the coat and pull them slowly backward around and around the fire, refusing to let them go until they paid a dime forfeit. It was a time for clowning as well as courtship. The watching crowd roared with appreciation whenever some laughing girl danced backward into the firelight, dragging an old man with many wives who had nothing to recommend him but dimes in his pocket. The guests all knew one another, or of one another, clan lines as well as blood lines. No matter how welcome we were made, we would remain outsiders. We would feel like Elks at a Moose Lodge picnic in a town where we didn't and couldn't live.

The morning after the Girls' Dance, wagons rumbled homeward past the school. Soon the crowds were gone. Franklin, Julia, and the rest of his family came back to work, and the buses went out to bring in the children.

23.

Only after I had a son did I begin to understand my own father, my own past.

Finally, long after he was dead, I was able to acknowledge that Pa had been a good man doing the best he could to get his family safely through bad times, a hardworking but luckless man, planting corn in years when corn prices dropped and cotton when the boll weevil struck. I had blamed him unfairly for failing to do what no mortal could have done — keep my mother alive.

Hosteen Tse had it right. The past is more than just a thread. Nothing stands alone. Everything now is then and now tangled together, the past inextricably mingled with the present, part of the great living myth that all we have been and done becomes: Kit Carson, General Sherman, Hosteen Tse, Garlen, Julia, my dying mother, a rotting snake by a dead nurse, muddy shoes, Franklin's black eye, a bloody handprint on an icebox door, tobacco spit on Mary's skirt. All separate, all one. The past is right here in the fabric of today.

If we can't get away from the past, the known and unknown alike, whatever the past might have been, then the best I can see to do is try to understand the people who made today what it is and forgive them if I can.

I can forgive Pa. Even the red-faced woman. But not Mary's murdering old father. No, not old Amos Gower. Not Garlen either. Hosteen Tse would understand my not forgiving. He has forgotten nothing, forgiven nothing and no one—not Sherman, not McKinley, not me.

AFTER MORE WEEKS of snow and freezing weather, the thaw returned—a lasting thaw this time. Spring was on its way. The nights continued cold, hardening the ground as soon as the sun set, but the days were windless and sunny.

The warmth was welcome even if the thawing ground beneath our daytime feet was soupy where it was not sticky and the washes ran full again in late afternoon with melt from mountain snows. We were starting school earlier than usual, while the ground was still firm, and sending the children home right after their noon meal, before the washes filled.

One afternoon, long after the buses had returned from taking children home, Foxey's freight truck turned off the highway, coming from Gallup. It was so mud-covered I could barely make out the big red ball on its side. It headed straight for the school instead of going first to the trading post to drop off Oates's bootleg liquor, as it usually did. I was in my office working on reports and saw the truck coming. I went out on the porch.

Foxey poked his head out the window and started yelling even before the truck stopped.

"Mr. Parker, I just seen a Model A pickup near to buried in Big Wash. Looked to me like that fellow Garlen's. Didn't see nobody around, but thought you'd ought to know."

I helped him unload the supplies he had brought. He chattered away the whole time. He said Big Wash had been running so full when he reached it that the bridge was covered. He'd had to wait on the bank for the flood to subside before he dared cross. He didn't say so, but he had obviously used the wait to suck up the brandy he always had on his hip and some of Oates's consignment of booze as well. He was very drunk.

He said that about the time the bridge railings came back into sight, he had left his truck to make water, as he delicately put it. Wandering along the arroyo a little way, he looked across the raging torrent and spotted the rear end of a pickup truck sticking out of the water in a little cove of the opposite bank. The truck poked up just far enough for him to see part of a fender and read the *Ford* script on the tailgate. The rotting body of a dead horse bobbed in the water beside the pickup, blocked by a fender from floating downstream.

Foxey said he hadn't even waited for the floor of the bridge to clear the floodwaters. He eased his truck across as soon as he could do so without drowning the engine and came directly to me to report his find.

He reached into the cab of his truck and brought out a half-empty bottle of bourbon. He took a long swig right in front of me—even offered me the bottle.

I ignored it and pretended to be unimpressed by his news.

"Franklin lost a horse in quicksand there by the bridge a few months ago," I said. "It probably got washed out by the flood, along with an old wreck."

"Reckon that's it," Foxey said, tipping up his bottle again. "Just thought you'd ought to know."

He got in his truck. "Sure looked for all the world like that fellow Garlen's old pickup. Makes you wonder what happened to him."

"I'll look into it," I said.

He drove off toward Farmington, so drunk he forgot to stop at the trading post. Oates would have to wait until Foxey's return trip for his supply of rotgut.

As soon as the Red Ball Stage was out of sight, I went to the shed and got a bus, knowing my car would never make it through the mud. I headed for Big Wash, grinding in low gear through muck all the way. The water had gone down and now swirled along the arroyo no more than a foot or so deep. The remains of Franklin's horse had washed downstream a little way and lay on the sandy bottom right next to the bridge. Crows and buzzards were pecking at the carcass, so engrossed in their scavenging that they paid no attention when I drove up.

The Model A pickup Foxey had seen was sticking out of the sand, its rear wheels hanging in the air. Only its nose was still buried. Now that the water had subsided, I could see that the cab was almost filled with sand and water. Through the broken-out window on the driver's side, I could make out the arm and head of a man. The arm was swollen to twice life-size, stretching the skin taut as a pregnant woman's belly. It was green and purple and sickly yellow. It looked ready to explode at the first peck of a buzzard's beak. The man's head was stripped to the skull in places, but there was flesh enough left in the face for me to recognize Garlen.

I turned the bus around and rushed back to the school as fast as I could. I found Franklin at the school kitchen, drinking coffee with the cook and the bus drivers while Julia scrubbed down tables. Mary and Davey were there, too. It was like old times, before Garlen, when we all got together at the end of the day to drink coffee, to talk and laugh.

Everyone looked up, wondering where I had gone in the bus.

"I went out to see if the buses should roll in the morning," I said, not waiting for the question. "I think we won't have school tomorrow."

I took Franklin aside and told him that Foxey had seen Garlen's pickup.

"Me and boys, we go look," Franklin said.

"Good. Let me know what you find."

The next morning Franklin reported that he and the boys had searched all along the wash and had found only the bay horse's decomposing body. They had come across no sign of a pickup truck. I did not mention a dead man, and neither, of course, did he.

"Foxey, he seeing things."

"That's what I thought," I said. "He was drunker than a coot. Even forgot to drop off supplies at the post. He won't remember a thing when he sobers up, if he ever does."

I got a bus and we went together to the bridge, Franklin and I. Everything was as I expected. There was no water left in the wash. The dead horse, or what was left of it, was stretched out on top of the damp sand. Coyotes had ripped at the carcass during the night. Crows and buzzards were still feasting. There was no pickup, and no trace of a man's body.

Franklin and I shook hands. We had been friends and were now accomplices, bound by Garlen's blood for all time, founding members of a new clan. Squatting on his heels beside a dying fire, one day Franklin would tell about the crazy white man who had once done a right thing.

By then it would no longer matter what he said. He would be old and so would I. His words would drift like snowflakes through the cedar-scented haze and melt harmlessly into myth.

PART THREE

KLINCHEE/KEAMS CANYON

1935-1941

DAVEY

24.

ONE DAY EARLY in our first summer at Klinchee, where we moved after my father's promotion, Navajos flooded past our house in wagons and on horseback. They headed for the Jim family's hogans in the cedar-covered hills a mile or so away.

My father tried to find out what was going on. No Navajo would say. Mr. Kramer at the trading post said all he knew was that he had sold almost his entire stock of ammunition, all but some .410 shotgun shells. There were few .410s on the reservation, or those shells might have gone, too. He said he had no idea why the Jims needed enough ammunition to fight a war. He was just glad to get it off his shelves. Some of the powder was getting mighty old.

Most evenings that summer, Billy Jim came by after supper and we tossed a baseball back and forth while distant voices sang the sun down. That day he did not show up until it was almost too dark to see. It was the first time he had been so late.

Billy Jim was a younger brother of Jeremy Jim, who had been my friend at Red Mesa. An all-around athlete at the intertribal Phoenix Indian School, Billy Jim had won letters in football and basketball as well as baseball. Phoenix and Tucson sports writers called him the Navajo Jim Thorpe.

Baseball was what he liked best of all, however—especially, he told me, the moment when he, the pitcher, was just starting his windup, and around him, at the bases and in the field, his teammates stood poised, alert, every muscle drawn taut, waiting for Billy Jim to throw. The man at the plate waited, too, bat cocked, eyes intent, hoping for a homer as Billy Jim hoped for a strike. Anything and everything was possible in that brief moment before he released the ball.

Billy Jim practiced almost every evening because he wanted to play professional ball and was keeping his arm in trim for the next season, when he would be a senior. He was at least eighteen to my eleven that summer and fired his fast ball at me only because I had a catcher's mitt, something none of his Navajo friends owned. When I caught one of his pitches, which was not often, it blistered my palm. Time after time Billy Jim stuffed more padding into my glove, laughing as he did it, until the mitt looked like a pillow. My hand still stung with every catch.

The evening of the great conclave at his family's hogans, he got in only a couple of pitches before we had to quit for darkness. As we sat on the porch steps, talking, slapping mosquitoes, and drinking the lemonade my mother fixed for us, we could hear drumming and chanting in the distance.

Billy Jim told me that the gathering people were his father's clansmen. They had come from all over the reservation to decide what to do about the murder of Joe Jim, Billy Jim's uncle. I knew Joe Jim, a thin silent man who wore his hair long and always looked worried, but I had not heard about a murder.

Billy Jim said his uncle had done nothing wrong. He was just trying to take care of his family. Joe Jim had not owned any sheep, but his wife owned a big flock with a fine ram and half a dozen goats. A Hopi had sold Joe Jim grazing rights for his wife's sheep on tribal land not far from where her family lived, northwest of White Cone. The land was fenced and hadn't been grazed in years. The grass was thick and belly-high to a horse. Joe Jim paid with a silver belt and necklace, both set with fine Nevada turquoise, and two horses, the only horses he owned.

Joe Jim cut the wire and drove the sheep onto the land, then mended the fence to keep other stock out. His wife's brothers lent him two teams and wagons and went into the mountains with him to get logs for a hogan.

After the hogan was built and his wife's brothers had gone home, two Hopi policemen from the Navajo-Hopi Agency at Keams Canyon turned up in an Indian Service pickup truck. The policemen told Joe Jim that the Hopi he had bought the grazing rights from did not have any right to sell them. That was something only the Hopi Tribal Council could do, and if the council were going to let someone put sheep on the land, the someone would be a Hopi, never a Navajo.

Joe Jim agreed to take his wife's sheep off the land if the Hopi who sold him the grazing rights would return his horses and jewelry. The policemen laughed at Joe Jim. They told him he must have been eating locoweed to buy the grazing rights from somebody who didn't own them. They said there was nothing they could do for such a stupid fellow. They said he was lucky he still had his wife's sheep.

The Hopi policemen dragged Joe Jim's wife and children out of the hogan. Joe Jim begged the policemen for permission to gather up his family's belongings. Except for her sheep and goats, everything he and his wife owned was inside. The policemen laughed again and splashed gasoline all over the hogan. When one of them took a box of matches out of his pocket, Joe Jim tried to grab his arm. The other Hopi policeman drew a pistol and shot Joe Jim between the eyes.

They drove away, leaving Joe Jim dead and the fine new hogan in flames.

Billy Jim said another of his uncles, not a Jim but a nephew of his grandmother's mother—I would have called him a distant cousin of some sort, but to Billy Jim almost any older male kinsman was an uncle—happened to be at the Keams Canyon trading post when the Hopi policemen stopped by for a cold drink. One policeman bought a Coke and the other a Nehi Orange. Billy Jim's uncle understood Hopi and heard them brag about burning out Joe Jim.

"That's one Navajo ain't going to make trouble no more," the policeman with the Coke said.

"Only good navvy's a dead navvy," the Nehi Orange policeman said.

The uncle spread the news about Joe Jim's murder as fast as he could. Billy Jim said the young men meeting at his father's hogans wanted to kill the Hopi policemen right away. But the old men wanted to consult with Hosteen Tse, another of Billy Jim's uncles. The old men said Hosteen Tse would know what to do. The Navajo leader and medicine man lived near Klinchee but just then was at Chinle, fifty miles away, holding a sing over a sick child. No one could tell when he would be back. It would depend on how many chants and sand paintings it would take to cure the illness.

So the talk went on and on. Kill Hopis now? Wait for Hosteen Tse? Billy Jim said he got tired of standing around without being able to take part in the discussion and decided to get in some pitching practice.

As soon as Billy Jim went home, I told my parents about the murder.

"It doesn't sound like something Hopis would do," my mother said.

My father found it curious that Billy Jim would drop by to

pitch when it was already too dark to see the ball. He concluded that the elders doubted the report and had sent Billy Jim to let us know what was going on before the younger Jims got out of hand and some hothead decided to use Mr. Kramer's ammunition.

My father called the White Cone trading post to see what he could find out. It took a long time to get through on the party line, and then the connection was poor. Too many people between Klinchee and White Cone took their receivers off the hook to listen in. But with him hollering into the phone at Klinchee and the trader at White Cone hollering back, my father finally established that there had been no shooting.

A Navajo the White Cone trader did not know but supposed could have been Billy Jim's uncle had cut a fence and driven his sheep onto a tract of Hopi land where the Soil Conservation Service had been conducting a grass reseeding experiment for years. The trader reported the intrusion to the Navajo-Hopi Agency at Keams Canyon. A Conservation Service man came down from Keams and told the Navajo, who may have been Joe Jim, to get his flock out of there. The Navajo did it right away, with no argument.

There was no trouble of any kind. No hogan had been built or burned. The trader said he hadn't seen a Hopi policeman at White Cone in he didn't know how long. The Conservation Service man had not been armed.

My father got his Indian Service vehicle, a green Ford V8 pickup, and drove to Chinle. He wanted my mother and me to ride with him as far as Ganado and stay at the hospital there until things quieted down, just in case. But my mother wouldn't go. We'd be fine, she said, and it would just stir things up unnecessarily if it got around that the area principal's wife and son had run for cover just because a bunch of edgy young Navajos bought more ammunition than they needed for hunting. So my father went off alone.

It was the middle of the night before he got back and dropped Hosteen Tse off at the Jim place. Drumming and chanting continued for a while after that. But at first light, wagons and riders started coming past our house, heading home.

About noon I saw Billy Jim at the trading post. Joe Jim was there, too, leaning against the hitching rail with some other men, silently spitting tobacco juice. He looked no more worried than usual.

I went over to Billy Jim. "You said Joe Jim was dead."

"He was. But while he was lying on the ground with a bullet in his head and his wife crying over him, a Hopi medicine man came along. Joe Jim's wife told him what the policemen had done. The Hopi medicine man said the policemen were wrong to shoot anyone like that, even a Navajo. The medicine man used his Hopi magic to back everything up and change it to come out so the hogan didn't burn and nobody got killed. Joe Jim came on home this morning."

"A Hopi medicine man did all that?"

"It was lucky he showed up. Hopi medicine men have powerful magic. Hosteen Tse says they can do things even he can't."

"You really believe that's what happened?"

He looked puzzled. "You want me to call my uncle a liar?"

I didn't know for sure which uncle he had in mind, and I couldn't ask. It was as though Billy Jim had never thrown me a baseball and I had never caught it, my palm stinging.

25.

IN THE AFTERNOONS, Miss Wheeler took a long rest at the trading post, and I went with Thomas, her chauffeur, to a stock-watering trough a couple of hills away to wash and polish her old Packard touring car. Miss Wheeler was a rich lady from Boston who did not like dust on her possessions. She came to Klinchee every summer to collect Navajo myths for a book she had been working on for years.

Each morning, Thomas drove Miss Wheeler and Mr. Kramer, the Klinchee trader, over dusty trails to whatever destination Mr. Kramer had selected for the day. On reaching a mud-and-log hogan beside a spring or in a sheltered cove at the foot of a mesa, Mr. Kramer called forth any Navajo men who happened to be there and ordered them to stand at the side of the Packard. Sitting in the backseat with the windows rolled partway up to fend off germs, Miss Wheeler questioned the Navajos about tribal myths while Mr. Kramer stood outside the window and translated.

My friend Billy Jim said Mr. Kramer spoke only pidgin Navajo. But Miss Wheeler did not know that, and the Navajo men were glad to answer her questions, even though they did not know what Mr. Kramer would tell her they were saying.

She gave each informant a dollar, which was more cash money than many Navajos saw from one sheep-shearing season to the next. Anyone who told her a story she hadn't heard before got two dollars. Billy Jim said some of the two-dollar stories were ones no Navajo had ever heard before either.

Thomas was about thirty and had been everywhere as a truck driver and merchant seaman before becoming Miss Wheeler's chauffeur. He was tall and erect, with a powerful chest and bulging biceps. When he put on his uniform jacket and buttoned it all the way up, which he did whenever Miss Wheeler was in the car, he looked as though one deep breath would pop every button. I envied him his muscles and his uniform, especially the tan riding pants, dark brown leather puttees, and fringed driving gloves. The fringe was Miss Wheeler's concession to western informality.

Miss Wheeler told people that she came to Klinchee to live with the Indians, but that was not true. Every summer Mr. Kramer moved into a corner of a windowless storeroom. Miss Wheeler took over the trader's quarters, sprucing them up with family portraits, silk sheets, and silver egg cups that Thomas brought from Boston in the Packard. Miss Wheeler and her other servants came by train.

The previous autumn, shortly before we moved to Klinchee, Mr. Kramer had married Mayne, who was my mother's best friend. Now my mother taught the lower grades at Klinchee, Mayne the upper. When Miss Wheeler learned that Mr. Kramer had taken a new wife, she was delighted. Her cook hated the summers at Klinchee. She found the heat oppressive and was frightened by Navajos, scorpions, and rattlesnakes, in about that order. All were part of daily life at Klinchee. Just recently I had come out our front door, heard a rattle from among my mother's potted geraniums, and in one leap had gone from a standing start there in the middle of the porch to safety at the bottom of the steps. My agility had surprised even me. Now, Miss Wheeler declared, her cook could stay comfortably at home in Boston: Mr. Kramer's bride would prepare her meals that summer.

Mayne had always sung and laughed a lot. Anyone who heard her booming laugh wanted to join in. After she became Mrs. Kramer, I didn't often hear her laugh or sing, but I thought she was as beautiful as ever.

During the school year, she still played right along with the children at recess. She jumped rope with the girls and took her turn at the plate when the boys played baseball. Her breasts lifted as she raised the bat. They bounced and rolled as she swung and ran for first base. I was further along in school than any of the Navajo pupils and could not be officially enrolled anyway, being white. But I often took recess with the older children Mayne taught and could not keep my eyes off her. I spent a lot of time imagining what I might see if her breasts should break free and spring into view when she raced around the bases after hitting a homer, as she often did.

It was a mystery to me why a lively person like Mayne should have chosen to marry the trader. Mr. Kramer was a middle-aged widower, older than my parents were. Fat and bald, he had bad teeth and a sour smell of whiskey and onions on his breath. My parents had nothing but contempt for him. Like Mr. Oates at Red Mesa, he charged his Navajo customers higher prices for flour and coffee than we paid. He bought their jewelry and rugs at below-market prices, telling them that their work was substandard. He then sold the rugs or jewelry to tourists at very high prices as great works of art—which generally was closer to the truth. He yelled and swore at his Navajo employees and bragged a lot, too. To hear him tell it—also like Mr. Oates—he ran everything at Klinchee, including the school where Mayne and my mother taught.

That also was a lie and annoyed my father. Mr. Kramer had nothing to do with the Klinchee school or any of the other day schools my father supervised. I asked my mother why Mayne had married Mr. Kramer. She said it was out of panic.

When her husband told her that she would have to serve as Miss Wheeler's cook, Mayne protested that she scarcely knew how to boil his breakfast egg, which was true. She had grown up surrounded by servants on a big Texas ranch and had never learned to cook anything but soups and stews. Unfortunately her father lost his money and his land in 1929. Now Mayne was the only member of the family with a job. She supported her parents and several brothers and sisters on her small salary. She still felt out of place in a kitchen. Mr. Kramer insisted, however, and so there she was—Miss Wheeler's cook.

It had not worked out well. Nothing Mayne did seemed to please Miss Wheeler, who was demanding at table and often sent dishes back to the kitchen. Sometimes Miss Wheeler became so angry she would dine on hot milk and sugared toast, which she fixed herself. Mayne lived in terror of her. A couple of times a day, she rushed down the hill from the trading post to our house at the school in her little Ford coupe to consult my mother on recipes and cooking techniques.

One day Mayne came with Thomas and me to the stock trough. Thomas gave me a chamois and set me to work shining the Packard's chrome radiator. Miss Wheeler was particular above all about the radiator. While I rubbed off bug stains, Thomas lifted out the seat cushions, front and back, and put them on a canvas tarp he spread on the ground to protect them from the dirt. He took off his shirt and got down on his knees to beat dust out of the cushions with a whisk broom. He pounded vigorously, grunting with every blow. As he worked on the cushions, Mayne polished a side panel. They talked softly, but not so softly as they thought. I couldn't help hearing, even with the windmill rattling and groaning overhead.

"Why did you do it?" I heard him ask.

"Tommy, don't you see? I had to. He was the best chance I had."

"You had me. I asked you twice last summer."

"I know you did, and I wished I could say yes. But I couldn't."

"Because I'm somebody's servant?"

"Yes."

"I won't always be a servant, but a man's got to take the job he's offered when there ain't any other jobs."

"And a woman's got to take what she's offered."

"So now you're a servant, too."

"Tommy, don't. It's too late. I did what I felt I had to do at the time. There's nothing to be done about it now."

"I'm still offering."

"I wish you wouldn't."

They fell silent, and I think they forgot about my being there. I stepped back to admire my handiwork on the radiator and saw them locked in a kiss. They broke away from one another instantly. I was flustered, but Mayne was not. She smiled and put a finger in front of her lips. I nodded. I wouldn't think of telling on them.

After a while, Mayne left Thomas and me to finish shining up the car. She walked back to the trading post, taking a shortcut over the juniper-covered hills and through a lava-coned valley. We could hear her singing as she went. Her high sweet voice echoed in the distance. What she sang was a variation on nonsense verses that Thomas had made up to roar out endlessly when Miss Wheeler was not with him in the Packard. His first verse started:

*Heigh-le-hee, heigh-le-hee
She's my girl and heigh-le-hee.*

Mayne sang:

*Heigh-le-hee, heigh-le-hee
He's my guy and heigh-le-hee.*

When Thomas and I got back to the trading post, Miss Wheeler came out to inspect the job we had done. She reminded me of the Rhode Island Reds my father kept in a chicken coop in back of our house. She was tall and long-necked, with a heavy body, dark red hair, a beaked nose, and yellow-flecked brown eyes that narrowed as she bent over to search for smears or specks of dust.

Her maid came out to help with the inspection. Rose had been with Miss Wheeler a long time. She tended to echo whatever her mistress said and had come to resemble her, in a half-pint sort of way. She, too, reminded me of a chicken, an aging bantam perhaps, small and fretful, with flapping wings.

Rose was both nearsighted and vain. She wouldn't wear glasses and unfailingly saw what wasn't there. She would spot a rock formation at the horizon and insist it was a man on horseback. A stick on the ground at her feet would set her screaming that she'd nearly stepped on a snake. In an effort to see better, she would lean far forward to get as close as she could to whatever she was looking at. As she squinted, she bobbed her head like a feeding hen.

"Those wheels are dusty. Shine them again," Miss Wheeler said.

"Oh, Miss Wheeler, those wheels are dusty," Rose shrieked. "Make him shine them again."

She continued to *tsk* away while Miss Wheeler fussed over

gravel nicks in the front fenders.

"It's a wonder the windshield isn't pitted, too, the way you follow other cars so closely," Miss Wheeler said.

"A wonder," Rose said. She pecked her head back and forth. "Look at those pits in the fender."

Thomas stood at attention, but when Miss Wheeler looked away, he pecked his head back and forth just like Rose and winked at me. I winked back.

One day late in August, Miss Wheeler got a headache and came back early from her day's outing. When I went to the trading post at the usual time to help Thomas clean up the Packard, Mr. Kramer said he had already driven to the windmill. I took the shortcut over the hills, figuring I would be in time to help with the finishing touches.

At the top of the last hill, I saw Rose off to one side, crouched behind the twisted trunk of a juniper. She peered down the hill toward the watering trough. She stretched her neck out like a telescope and bobbed her head the way she did when she was trying to figure out what she was looking at. I crept forward and looked, too.

Mayne and Thomas were tangled together on a seat cushion beside the Packard, thrashing around. His shirt was off and his pants were pulled down to his puttees. Mayne's skirt was up and her blouse open. She was on her back and had her legs wrapped around Thomas. A breast flowed into view like a stream of white-hot lava, flame-tipped.

I wanted to see more, but I was close enough to Rose for her to make out who I was. I couldn't think of anything worse than being caught spying on Thomas and Mayne. I turned away and started home. Rose left, too. She scampered off toward the trading post, flapping her arms to pick up speed.

A couple of hours later, Thomas drove down to our house. He was alone in the car but dressed as he would have been had Miss Wheeler ruled the backseat. His cap was square on his head, and his uniform jacket was buttoned, collar and all. He had come to deliver a note from Miss Wheeler to my mother. The note asked that I be allowed to accompany Thomas so that Miss Wheeler might have a visit with me.

"A visit?" my mother said. "What is this all about, Thomas?"

"I'm sorry, ma'am, I can't say. I guess maybe she decided she'd like some company and the boy would be it."

"Well, I suppose it's all right."

She made me wash my hands and face and put on a clean shirt. I didn't know how to tell her I didn't want to go.

Thomas put me in the back and we drove off. The glass between the seats was rolled up.

I found a crank and lowered the glass.

"Listen," I said. "What's going on?"

"The old lady said not to say a word to you, Davey, and she'll fire me in a minute if she thinks I did. She may fire me anyway."

I cranked the window up again.

At the trading post, Thomas ushered me into the living room. Navajo rugs were thick on the floor, and the furniture was covered in cowhide. Miss Wheeler sat in a big chair with a flaring back. It looked like a throne. Mr. Kramer stood scowling at her side, his arms crossed over his chest, his belly sagging over his silver-and-turquoise belt buckle. Before Mayne agreed to marry him, I had heard her laughing about Mr. Kramer's stomach. She had said it was like a big fish flopping around in his shirt. I saw now that she had been right.

Mayne sat in a corner, head bowed, crying softly, with the knuckles of one hand jammed against her mouth. She had a black eye and a bruise on her cheek. She did not look at me. I knew she would not want me to see she was hurt, and after that one quick glance, I did not look at her again. Rose hunched forward in another corner, jerking her head up and down like a pullet in a corncrib.

A low footstool had been placed in front of Miss Wheeler. That was for me. I had the feeling that if there had been a window between us, she would have rolled it halfway up.

"Thank you for coming, David," Miss Wheeler said. She bobbed her head as though she were in that corncrib with Rose. "You may be seated. Did Thomas tell you why I wanted to see you?"

"No, ma'am."

"Thomas, stand behind David where the boy can't see you."

"Yes, ma' am," Thomas said.

"David," Miss Wheeler said, "something has happened for which I feel a certain responsibility. It is very important that you tell us exactly what you did and saw this afternoon."

"Yes, ma' am," I said.

"Well," Miss Wheeler said. "Go on, tell us."

"Well, after dinner—"

"Dinner?"

"Yes'm. We had dinner about noon and then I read a while and then I decided to help Thomas wash the Packard. I came up to the post, and Mr. Kramer said Thomas was already at the windmill, so I headed there."

"*Ah!*" said Miss Wheeler. "And what did you see?"

"See? Well, there was a jackrabbit on top of the first hill and a cottontail about halfway up the next one. A buzzard, too. I saw a buzzard."

"I mean when you got to the windmill."

"I didn't actually get there. When I got to the top of the last hill, I brushed up against a prickly pear and got a needle in my toe. So I decided to go home so I could take it out with tweezers."

"Did you see anyone? Tell us who else was there."

"Well, I saw Rose way off to the side on top of the last hill, kind of hunkered down behind a tree, like she was hiding. She was bobbing her head back and forth like she does when she's trying to make out something she can't see very well. I think she was trying to make out what Thomas was doing down by the watering trough."

"*Ah!* And what was Thomas doing?"

Behind me I heard Thomas draw a deep breath.

"He had his shirt off," I said, "and was on his hands and knees, using the whisk broom on the seat cushions like he always does, moving around a lot and grunting. It's hard work beating the dust out of those cushions."

Thomas let out his breath.

"Nobody else?" Miss Wheeler asked. "You didn't see anybody else?"

"No'm," I said, "just Rose and Thomas."

"Mrs. Kramer? What about Mrs. Kramer?"

"Mrs. Kramer wasn't there."

Miss Wheeler kept pecking away at me, but I had already decided that I would rather lie forever than try to describe what I had seen or admit that I had spied on Thomas and Mayne, even accidentally.

After a while Miss Wheeler gave up. "Very well, David. That will be all, thank you."

I hoped she would give me a dollar, or maybe two, but she didn't. She told Thomas to drive me home.

He let me sit in front with him. We sang:

> *Heigh-le-hee, heigh-le-hee*
> *She's my girl and heigh-le-hee.*

26.

HOSTEEN DOG did not follow me up the steps to the dark porch, which he knew was Edward's territory. He ran around in the snow at the foot of the steps, barking, as I pounded on Lucy C.'s door. Edward barked back from the other side and hurled himself at it. The door shook each time he bounced off it. In the background I heard Queenie's shrill yap. Edward was a big deep-voiced Airedale, Queenie a sort of Irish Setter.

"Mrs. Drew!" I shouted. "Heard the news?"

Lights came on. Lucy C. shushed the dogs and opened the door, pulling me inside quickly to let in as little cold as possible. Edward and Queenie climbed all over me as I unbuttoned my coat.

"What news, Davey?"

"King George is dead," I said, still shouting, though we were face to face. "We heard it on KOB."

She threw her arms around me and hugged me close. I felt her breasts yielding between us.

"Davey!" she said. "I've danced with a king!"

Holding me tight, she turned her head to look at a photograph hanging on the wall. It showed the Prince of Wales in a uniform covered with medals, sashes, and braid.

Lucy C. took my hands and waltzed me around her living room at arm's length, humming *The Blue Danube*. That was the tune the Prince of Wales had hummed in her ear in France during the Great War. Bits of melting snow fell off my boots and jacket as we whirled over the Navajo rugs.

It was on outings with the dogs that Lucy C. had told my mother and me about dancing with the prince. In the afternoons after school, my mother would leave her classroom and Lucy C. her clinic. We would shout up Hosteen, Edward, and Queenie and hike past the windmill-fed stock-watering pond toward hills covered with sagebrush and the wind-twisted evergreens that we called cedars but that my mother made sure I knew were really a kind of juniper.

If we went far enough into the hills, we came to a stand of piñon trees. In the fall I would scrape around in the needles and cones at the base of the trees and fill my pockets with nuts, being careful to avoid sheep droppings, which were the same size, shape, and color. We cracked shells with our teeth and ate the nuts as we walked. I had often seen a Navajo man tip his head back and pour a handful of nuts into one side of his mouth as empty shells streamed out the other side. When I tried this cracking-mill technique, all I got was a mouthful of shells mixed with nutmeats. There was nothing to do but spit the whole mess out. After a while I quit trying to be fancy and cracked the nuts one by one, just like my mother and Lucy C.

We did not stroll on these walks but set a brisk pace. Even so, there was lots of talk and laughter. My mother and I found it wonderful to have a traveled and sophisticated friend like Lucy C. She had grown up rich in Boston, not poor in Texas like my parents or on Indian reservations like me. But that seemed not to matter. We felt she was one of our own kind, someone with whom we shared background and outlook, however much the details of experience differed. We had

Navajo friends, but it was not the same. They treated us politely but with reserve, kept us at arm's length. We were intruders in their land and their culture—curiosities, strangers, outsiders.

Our impermanence put further constraints on friendship. For the Navajos who lived there, Klinchee was forever home. They might wander off in search of summer grass for their sheep or maybe to take an off-reservation job, but they would come back—would want to come back even when they could stay away. For my parents, however, Klinchee was just an assignment, a step on a ladder leading to better jobs and places to live. After a year or two, at most three or four, somebody else would come to run the Klinchee area schools, and we would be off to another Indian Service post or even, perhaps, into the great world beyond the reservations.

It was much the same for Lucy C. Although she had turned down every transfer offered to her over the years, she knew that unlike the Navajos she could always get away. But like them she didn't want to. She was held at Klinchee by the grave of Edward's grandfather, who was buried between her house and the clinic under a gravestone marked:

PRINCE
A HERO
1917—1930

Even after my mother fell ill—when King George died she was at a radiation clinic in Albuquerque—Lucy C. and I continued the afternoon walks with the dogs, and she continued telling stories about her life. My favorite was the one about dancing with the Prince of Wales. I never tired of hearing her tell it.

In the winter before the Armistice, she had been a nurse in

France with the American Expeditionary Force at a big field hospital so close to the front lines she could hear not just the big guns but rifles and machine guns, too. Wounded men were carried in covered with blood and mud minutes after falling in the trenches. One day General Pershing, commander of the AEF, sent word that he would be bringing the Prince of Wales to the hospital on an inspection trip. He ordered a couple of wards cleared of all but slightly wounded patients. He wanted no moaning men or bloody bandages to spoil the royal visit. Since the prince was known to be a playboy and ladies' man, Pershing specified that only young and pretty nurses were to be on duty that day. The prettiest of all was to escort the official party.

It did not surprise me that Lucy C. was chosen for this honor. Twenty years later she was still beautiful. She prided herself on using no makeup and needing none. She smiled a lot, which had left fine lines at the corners of her eyes. Otherwise her skin was soft and smooth, stretching taut and clear over the fine bones of her face. Her hair was brown, thick and glossy, just beginning to be streaked with gray. I had heard her tell my mother that she did not like turning gray but did not plan to do anything about it. She liked to face facts, she said, and couldn't stand deceit or artifice. My mother had smiled but said nothing.

On the day of the inspection, Lucy C. met General Pershing and the Prince of Wales at the door of the first ward. She saluted the general, though that was probably not required, and curtseyed to the prince. She had spent a lot of off-duty hours practicing the deep dip she had learned as a child at dancing school in Boston, and she executed the curtsey gracefully in the long starched skirts of her nurse's uniform. The prince was in uniform, too—khaki and shiny boots, but disappointingly little gold braid. He stretched out his hand

and helped Lucy C. up. He wasn't as tall as she and looked like a boy. His blue-marble eyes bulged from their sockets, but she thought he was as handsome a man as she'd ever seen. She could imagine falling in love with him.

The prince put her hand on his arm and would not let her remove it. By protocol he preceded all the rest of the party, even General Pershing—all the rest but Lucy C., whom he kept at his side, where she felt surprisingly comfortable. They went through the ward as though he were taking her in to dinner, a ceremony I had read about but never witnessed. Lucy C. put her hand on my arm and showed me what it was like.

Guiding the prince past wounded soldiers lying at attention—eyes on the ceiling, arms straight and rigid on top of the covers—she stopped now and again at the bedside of some fully recovered and well-rehearsed man who was on his way back to duty and willing to avow eagerness for more combat in exchange for one more day away from the trenches.

The wounded soldier gave name, rank, and outfit, snapping out "sir" at the end of each bit of information.

Pershing: "And what happened to you, Cavanaugh?"

Soldier: "The Heinies, sir. They sent over a shell, sir. Caught me a piece of shrapnel in the leg, sir."

"Taking good care of you, are they, ah, ah—Connolly?"

"Cavanaugh, sir."

"Of course. Cavanaugh. Taking good care of you, are they?"

"Yes, sir! The best, sir!"

"Be ready for duty soon, won't you, ah—Connor?"

"Can't be too soon for me, sir. Don't want nothing more in this world, sir, than another crack at them dirty Huns, sir."

"That's the ticket, ah, ah—soldier."

The Prince of Wales: "Good man, Cavanaugh! Good show, what?"

Lucy C. was impressed that the prince, who was famed as being lightly if at all furnished upstairs, had been able to get the wounded man's name right, while General Pershing did not take the trouble. "Ah, ah—soldier!" she said, in telling my mother and me the story. "How do you suppose that made poor Cavanaugh feel?"

A long porchlike corridor, screened on both sides, connected the two wards the dignitaries were to visit. As the prince and Lucy C. left the first ward, he seized the door from the orderly who had opened it. Slamming it behind them, the prince left the orderly, Pershing, and all the British and American aides—Lucy C.'s commanding officer, too—on the other side.

"Shall we dance?" the prince said, holding out his arms.

He waltzed her down the corridor, humming. Before reaching the door to the next ward, where another orderly stood at attention, the prince stopped humming and whispered in her ear, "My dear, you're much too beautiful to be wasted here. You should be in London with me."

"Thank you, sir," she said and curtseyed.

At Pershing's order, her commanding officer gave Lucy C. a dressing down for being forward and causing scandal. A full report of the incident was put in her service file. She didn't mind a bit.

Had she seen the prince again? There was, after all, that photograph on the wall. Lucy C. merely smiled. She admitted only that she had served six months at a hospital in England after the fighting stopped and had spent her evenings, weekends, and leaves attending fashionable dinners, balls, dances, and parties in London and at various country houses. Her account of these nonstop parties did not make clear whether she saw the Prince of Wales at them. She never said he was present but never denied the possibility either.

"You don't talk about the private affairs of royalty," she explained.

Lucy C. had feared she might be shunted onto night duty when she reported to that hospital near London because of her escapade with the prince. But the black mark on her record was offset by the fact that she had served bravely under fire at the front.

She was put on the day shift and given charge of a ward where an air ace who had shot down fourteen Germans before being shot down himself lay immobilized. His bandaged legs were suspended in slings hung from the ceiling.

The air ace's name was Thomas K. Drew—the K stood for King, a family name—and he was a Texan. Lucy C. said he was so tall that when his legs came down from the slings, the hospital had to lengthen a bed for him to keep his feet from poking out.

"What does the C in your name stand for?" I asked the first time she told me what the K in her husband's name stood for. I had wondered for a long time and never dared ask.

We were walking along the sandy bottom of a steep-walled dry wash with the dogs dashing around on the banks above us.

"My maiden name," she said.

She put her hand on my shoulder to balance herself and wrote in the sand with the toe of one shoe.

"Cabot?"

"That's right."

She scrubbed the sand with her foot, wiping out the name, and went on with her story.

On her first day in charge of the ward, she went through it to get acquainted with each of her patients. When she introduced herself to her future husband, he said, "Nurse Cabot, did anyone ever tell you you're beautiful?"

She studied his chart and did not answer. He said, "Answer my question, Nurse Cabot. That's an order."

She still did not answer, though she smiled. She went on to the next patient.

On the second day and every day thereafter, King Drew handed her a red rose as she came up to his bed. Along about the fifth day, she allowed him to pin the rose on her uniform. When he was able to leave the hospital on crutches for brief periods, they went together to the parties that filled her spare time. Before long he proposed. They were married at a church near Lyme Regis, where some of her English friends owned a country house. A hundred people attended the wedding. Among them, incognito, was the Prince of Wales.

"I thought you weren't supposed to talk about royalty," I said.

"At my wedding? That's all right."

I understood that she was telling me something, confirming something. I wasn't sure what.

As Lucy C. had supposed when he was able to buy her a fresh rose each day in the hospital, King Drew was rich. When it came time for them to go home, he refused to travel on a hospital ship or troop ship. Instead he booked passage for himself and his bride on a passenger liner, first class.

It took only a day or two aboard ship for Lucy C. to reach a terrible conclusion. Out of uniform and away from their circle of friends, King Drew was a drunken bore. That daily rose at the hospital had used up his entire store of romance. Though he was fully recovered from his wounds, he refused to dance or even walk about the decks. All he wanted to do was sit at the ship's bar and soak up gin. As he drank, his Texas drawl, which up to then she had hardly noticed, got thicker and thicker until it seemed to her that his words had become coated with grits boiled in booze. His sole topic of conversation, which he explored endlessly with the bartenders and anyone else who would talk to him, was about ways to get a drink once he landed in a nation that had voted to prohibit the sale of liquor.

King did not like Boston or her family. He said her father, who served only a single cocktail before dinner each evening, was a stuffed shirt and looked down his nose at folks from the West. He insisted that they leave almost at once for his family's ranch in Texas. They spent days on the train and another day driving over unpaved roads through the flattest, driest, dustiest country Lucy C. had ever seen. It was far worse, she said, than the Navajo Reservation.

When they got to a place that could not have been flatter, drier, or dustier, they were home.

They lived with his parents and three married brothers in an enormous house designed to look like Mount Vernon. It was next to a huge feed lot in the middle of the ranch. The sour smell of ensilage and manure hung in the air day and night, tainted the food, and permeated the sheets of her bed. A hot wind stirred the dust from sunup to sundown, while nights were breathless for lack of a breeze. Lucy C. was always sticky with sweat and covered with dust, but water was so precious she was allowed just one bath a week and was supposed to flush the toilet only after a bowel movement.

The men were out of the house all day, mostly on horseback. The women slept late and then sat around doing nothing but needlework or other ladylike tasks, chattering of hairdos and dress designs while being waited upon by German girls from the hill country around Fredericksburg. The house was full of noisy children, but the German girls took care of them, too. In the evenings after supper when the children and German girls were in bed, the men drank bootleg whisky and told tall tales. The women simpered.

Every Saturday the family was up before dawn, and the men packed the wives and children into three Pierce Arrows and a Packard and drove to Wichita Falls for the one big outing of the week. That was when the women got their hair frizzed with permanents—all except Lucy C., who wore her hair uncurled, falling long and free down her back or coiled around her head. After the beauty parlor came a couple of hours of high-speed shopping before they had to start home again.

One Saturday Lucy C. slipped away in Wichita Falls and bought herself riding pants and boots, along with a broad-brimmed Stetson like those every man in Texas seemed to wear. On the next working day, she talked a cowhand into providing her with a horse. When she rode up to join the men on their rounds of the ranch, her father-in-law flew into a rage. He was a big man, taller and heavier than any of his sons. His florid face grew purple when he saw Lucy C. in pants. He said the only women he had ever known to wear trousers were—in telling this, Lucy C. looked at me and did not use his exact words—undesirable residents of Dodge City, where he had gone on cattle drives as a boy. Both those pants-wearing women had been diseased. He ordered King to take his slut to the house and strip her bare.

That night Lucy C. packed her bags while everyone was sleeping, took a car, and drove herself to Wichita Falls. She bought another Stetson and a man's business suit big and full enough to conceal her figure. Dressed in her new suit and with her bountiful hair stuffed into the new Stetson, she was on the platform ready to board the train to Kansas City when she saw King Drew, his father, and his brothers rush grim-faced toward her, wearing gunbelts. She felt sure she was caught.

They pushed past her and accosted the porter of the Pullman car she was about to board.

"Seen anybody looks like this, George?" her father-in-law snapped. He shoved a photograph at the porter.

The porter studied the picture. "No, sir. Ain't seen no young lady like that, not on this run."

Her husband and in-laws crowded down the platform to the next car.

Lucy C. put her foot on the low metal stool the porter had placed at the bottom of the train steps for her.

"Let me give you a hand up them steps, miss," the porter said. He smiled at her.

During a layover in Kansas City, Lucy C. found a large picture of a donkey. She cut out the ears and pasted them on a postcard, which she mailed to King Drew with the message, "Are these yours?"

That did not discourage him. He followed her to Boston, where she found a job as a public-health nurse. She rejected his pleas and threats, but he would not leave her alone. For protection she bought a big Airedale, a show dog, already full grown and well trained. His official name was Champion Adelbert of Afflick but he was called Bertie. She renamed him Prince.

Prince proved his worth in her eyes almost at once by taking an instant dislike to King Drew. Any time King neared Lucy C., Prince leaped between them, baring his teeth and making ugly sounds deep in his throat.

"That dog's downright dangerous," King complained.

"That's right," she said. "He is."

One winter afternoon Lucy C. drove past a frozen pond with Prince on the seat beside her. King Drew was right behind in another car, keeping a jealous eye on her. A woman rushed up a snow-covered hill into the road ahead.

"My babies," she screamed. "My little boys."

Lucy C. saw sled tracks going down the hill and across the

ice to a patch of open water in the middle of the pond. She stopped her car. King Drew pulled up beside her.

"Please, sir, save my babies," the woman shrieked.

"I'll get help," he said. His car's tires spewed gravel as he drove off.

As soon as Lucy C. opened her door, Prince leaped out. He raced down the hill and plunged across the ice into the water. In a moment he was back at the edge, his teeth locked in a child's coat. The ice kept crumbling, but finally the little boy was close enough for Lucy C. to grab his collar. Prince dove in again. About the time Lucy C. had the first child breathing, Prince pulled out the second.

When King Drew returned with firemen in tow, both boys were bundled in blankets in Lucy C.'s car, cold but recovering in their weeping mother's arms. Lucy C. rubbed down Prince while he studied her face with adoring eyes.

A photographer and reporter from a Boston newspaper turned up. The next morning's paper carried a front-page story with big pictures of Lucy C., Prince, and the children. The headline read:

CANINE HERO SAVES TWO TOTS

Lucy C. had framed the headline and hung it over a nearly life-sized painting of Prince right next to the photograph of the Prince of Wales. Between the painting and the photograph was a medal attached to a faded blue ribbon with chipped and tarnished gold lettering:

PRINCE
IN RECOGNITION
OF VALOR

The Commonwealth Of Massachusetts
1923

Except for the one headline, Lucy C. kept Prince's clippings in a red leather album. One day she brought it out and let me read about Prince. I found it puzzling that while the photographs showed Lucy C. and the story referred to her service under fire as an AOF nurse in France, she was identified as Mrs. Lucille Carnowski Drew.

"The paper got it wrong," she explained.

To escape her husband and his unwelcome pursuit, she eventually slipped away from Boston and joined the U.S. Indian Service. She hadn't heard of or from King Drew in all the years she had been at Klinchee.

On the day King George died, we were still waltzing around the living room when the dogs began to bark up a storm, Hosteen outside, Edward and Queenie at the front door. We stopped dancing and opened the front door.

A short, stocky man came up on the porch. Bundled up in a green mackinaw, he looked soft and pudgy in the light that fell on him through the door. He stamped his feet to knock off the snow.

"Jesus, Lucille," the man said, "whyn't you ever get a dog can keep his mouth shut?"

"Oh, my God, Tom," Lucy C. said, "what are you doing here?"

"I told you I'd find you, no matter how long it took," the man on the porch said, "and I done it." He put his hand on the screen door.

Edward hurled himself at the screen. The man braced himself against the frame to keep Edward from pushing the door open.

"Go home now, Davey," Lucy C. said. "Please go home. Out the back way."

The wind had died, but snow was still coming down. The doghouse Lucy C. had built for Edward and Queenie in the backyard was almost buried, and so was Prince's gravestone. An old Ford was parked out front. The car's windshield was iced over except for a hole right in front of the steering wheel. The license plate was so plastered with snow I couldn't tell where it was from. I supposed it was Texas.

The man was still on the porch, still holding the screen door closed to keep Edward from getting at him. At the bottom of the steps, Hosteen barked his head off but stayed well away from the stranger. I grabbed Hosteen's collar and shushed him. Edward finally quit jumping at the door. I could hear Lucy C. speaking soothingly to him as she led him and Queenie toward the back to put them in the yard.

The man came over to the edge of the porch and looked down at me. "Who're you, kid?"

"Davey Parker," I said.

"You live hereabouts?"

"Yes, sir."

"Then get home, hear?"

"Yes, sir," I said. I didn't know what his accent was, but it sure didn't sound like Texas to me.

For two days the Ford sat in front of Lucy C.'s house. The sun came out and the coating of ice and snow on the car slowly slid off. It was a battered old crate with Massachusetts plates. Three worn spare tires were tied on the back end with loops of rope.

I didn't see Lucy C. or the man in all that time. She didn't open the clinic. Edward and Queenie stayed penned up in the backyard, moping in the snow and cold.

On the third morning, the old car was gone. My father said Lucy C. had come around and got him to cash a check so she could send her husband on his way. He had left in the night after the roads froze.

"I thought Mr. Drew was a tall man, a rich Texan," I said.

My father sighed. "Folks have to dream a little, Davey, some of us maybe more than others."

Lucy C. didn't open the clinic that day either. The next afternoon Hosteen and I went over to her house. In the backyard Edward and Queenie ran along the fence through the remnants of melting snow. They barked half-heartedly. I knocked on the door. After a long while Lucy C. opened it a crack.

"Edward and Queenie need a run," I said.

"You take them," she said. She stood back from the door, where I couldn't see her.

"That wouldn't be the same," I said.

After a long time she said, "All right. Don't look at me."

She came out wearing a three-striped Hudson's Bay coat with a hood that protected her face from the wind. Neither of us said a word until we were trudging through deep snow in the bottom of a sheer-banked arroyo. It felt warm there in the sun, out of the wind. Above us the dogs coursed far ahead on the bank. They barked their heads off as they chased jackrabbits through the sagebrush. We could hear but not see them.

"Tell me about dancing with the Prince of Wales," I said.

"You've heard all that."

"I want to hear it again."

We whirled over the snow in the bottom of the arroyo as she told me the story. The dogs returned and raced back and forth on the bank overhead, barking and looking for a way down to join us. I felt weightless, as though we were dancing on air. I was surprised to see how our feet packed down the snow. I had never felt so light. So free. There in the snowy bottom of the arroyo, I learned that truth and fact need not always be the same.

27.

THE DOCTOR SHOOK my hand. "Your mother's going to be just fine," he said. "Just fine."

We knew one another well. The doctor had operated on my mother twice before. Each time he had said she would be just fine.

I shook my head and did not say anything.

"Just fine," the doctor said and prayed over me. He was a missionary doctor who ran Sage Memorial Hospital at Ganado for the Presbyterian Church. My father had been brought up a Cumberland Presbyterian, which he always said was not the same thing as a run-of-the-mill Presbyterian, but he had given it up. My mother was a Methodist but didn't work at it. I had decided not to be either. I was mad at God for what He was doing to her and mad at her for letting Him do it.

"Amen," the doctor said. He went back to the operating room.

Lewis came over. She was tall and skinny and wore long flowing dresses. She was one of the regulars among the young teachers who called themselves Mary's Troops and turned up every few weeks for Sunday dinner to hear my mother tell about marching for the vote in Texas and urge them to stand up for their rights as women.

Her troops had come to her when my mother taught at Red Mesa and continued to do it now that she was teaching at Klinchee, though the roster had changed a bit. Some teachers had returned to their homes to get married and others had been transferred. My mother's favorite, Mayne, had left Mr. Kramer, the Klinchee trader she had married, to run off to California with Miss Wheeler's chauffeur. Miss Wheeler had been angry at having to hire a driver to return her big Packard to her home in Boston. She said Mayne was a sinful woman and not a good cook. My mother believed Mayne had done the right thing. So did I.

Lewis had come to Ganado from Greasewood to be near my mother during the operation. The troops were taking turns at being there while my mother was in the hospital. Because Greasewood was a one-teacher school, she had given her pupils a holiday.

"Hey," Lewis said, "how about a game of cribbage?"

I shook my head. I did not feel like playing cards.

My father came into the room. He had been with my mother until they wheeled her into the operating room. He spoke in low tones with Lewis. I saw tears roll down her face. She dug in her purse for a handkerchief while my father talked. She blew her nose.

My father came over.

"She sent her love," he said. His voice cracked. He put his arm around my shoulders, something he seldom did. "She said to be brave."

I did not say anything. I had wanted to see my mother, but the doctor had not allowed it. My father went over to a window and stared out.

We were waiting in the doctor's private sitting room, next to the office from which he ran the hospital and its school of

—RESERVATIONS—

nursing, which admitted only full-blooded Indians. He had started the school years before, when most nursing schools did not accept Indian girls. My mother said it was still the only nursing school on a reservation. The walls of the doctor's office and sitting room were covered with pictures of smiling Indian nurses he had trained. My mother said he was a great man as well as a famous surgeon.

The walls were painted light green. It was a cheerful color, I supposed. Most of the hospital was painted that same light green. But for some reason the corridors were dark green along the lower part of the walls and yellowish brown on the upper part, including the ceiling. The corridors looked grim, a little sad, as though they led to airless places.

I contemplated the pictures on the wall and the color scheme of the hospital. I pondered its smell, too. Every part of the hospital smelled about the same, even the doctor's sitting room, where fresh flowers stood in vases but made no difference to the underlying acrid mix of ether and iodine and Lysol, with just a trace of something even more unappealing — rot, perhaps, or blood, or urine. The hospital's smell made my nostrils sting, made me want to cry.

A student nurse wearing a stiffly starched blue and white uniform came over to me. I knew her. Her name was Betsy Tsosie. She had worked for my mother at Red Mesa for a while after finishing high school in Phoenix. Betsy wanted to be a nurse, and my mother had sent her to the doctor with a letter of recommendation. My mother had been very proud when Betsy was accepted. Many more girls wanted to be nurses than Sage Memorial could accommodate.

Betsy did not say anything but pressed a Hershey bar on me. After holding it for a while, I stripped the brown wrapper off and folded back the tinfoil around the softening candy. I broke the bar into pieces and ate it slowly, letting the chocolate melt on my tongue before I crunched down on the nuts. It was an almond bar, my favorite kind.

In the middle of the morning, my father disappeared. Later Lewis and I went to the staff dining room for a bite to eat. At home we called the noon meal dinner, but here at Ganado it was lunch. We each got a glass of milk, a ham sandwich, and a piece of flat-looking apple pie. I wasn't hungry and did not finish the sandwich. I didn't eat all of the pie either.

"That candy bar filled you up, I bet," Lewis said.

I nodded, agreeing, although it was not true. She had taken only a few bites of her sandwich and pie. I did not say anything about that.

After lunch my father came back.

"Let's go for a walk," he said.

We left the hospital and walked down the driveway between rows of cottonwood trees, which had already lost a lot of leaves.

"They better rake these leaves off the lawn or it'll kill the grass," my father said. His voice sounded dry and hoarse, like he was coming down with a cold.

"Maybe they're waiting for the rest of the leaves to fall," I said. I scuffed my feet through them.

"I reckon that's it," my father said.

We walked along the road to the trading post. My father offered to buy me a Coke. I said I didn't care for one. I was fond of Coke, but my mother did not think it was good for me. She thought a lot of things were not good for me.

We walked back to the hospital. By the time we got there, a strong wind was blowing and we were chilled.

"Winter's about here," my father said.

"I reckon," I said.

More troops had arrived and were waiting in the doctor's sitting room. McGehee was there, and so were Groves, Miss

Schroeder, Miss Ryder, and several others. Miss Ryder couldn't drive, and I wondered who had gone all the way to Cottage Springs to pick her up.

It troubled me to see so many of the troops. I had understood that they would come to the hospital one at a time on different days. Across the room I heard Miss Ryder explain to my father in her childlike voice, "Lewis called this morning and said it was time for Mary's Troops to muster. So here we are."

Not being a regular, Miss Ryder overstepped when she referred to Lewis by her last name alone, but no one said anything.

The troops hugged me one by one, Miss Ryder, too. They turned their faces away so I would not see the tears in their eyes.

"Yes, ma'am. Thank you, ma'am," I said, trying not to hear what they were saying.

My father went back to my mother. Late in the afternoon the doctor came and the troops gathered around him. I sat in a corner, staring at a copy of *Country Gentleman* but not seeing it. The doctor kept his back to me and spoke in such a low voice I could not hear what he said. When the doctor finished, the troops joined hands while he prayed.

Before the doctor left, I went over to him and asked to see my mother.

"Not just now, son," he said. "Maybe later."

At suppertime nobody felt like going to the staff dining room. Betsy and other student nurses brought trays and later carried the trays away. No one had eaten much.

Still later, my father returned. He put his arms around me and kept trying to say something. He could not get the words out. I had never seen my father cry before, had not supposed he could cry. Across the room the troops sobbed aloud, not bothering to conceal their tears.

My father went away again. The troops hugged me, caressed me. They were confused and alarmed when I stood stiffly and did not cry with them. They tried to get me to speak of my mother, to pray for her. They did not understand that I could not.

28.

THE WESTBOUND SUPER CHIEF rolled into Gallup right on time. We were standing among the Zuñis, Navajos, and a Hopi or two who waited to sell souvenirs to the passengers. Most of the pots, rugs, and jewelry were genuine Indian crafts created by the men and women who offered them for sale. But some souvenirs were junk from Japan or New Jersey—gaudily painted ceramic canoes, bows with rubber-tipped arrows, machine-made tin bracelets polished to look something like silver, and headdresses of dyed chicken feathers. The women peddlers spread blankets over the bricks and sat amid their goods, while the men squatted on their heels nearby or leaned against the cast-iron pillars that supported a tin roof. The bricks around each man were stained with fresh spit and tobacco juice.

Passengers eating a late lunch in the air-conditioned dining car of the silvery train turned their heads, forks halfway to their lips, to stare at us. In their dining-car finery, they looked like people in a movie—men with neatly knotted ties and dark jackets, starched white shirt cuffs just poking from jacket sleeves, and marcelled women in bright flowery dresses. I knew we looked as foreign as any Indian to them. Or for that matter, as foreign as they looked to me.

My father was tall and so thin that he could have stepped behind one of the iron columns and been lost to sight by turning sideways. He wore a wide-brimmed Stetson, khaki pants, a clean but sweat-stained shirt buttoned at the throat, and high-laced black shoes that looked about as wide as the Stetson's brim. As a concession to the eminence of the man we were there to meet, he had shined his shoes and brushed his hat, a new one he had bought a while back for my mother's funeral in Texas. He had even tried to put on a tie she had given him long ago, but he had given up after several attempts at knotting it. She had always knotted his ties for him. I didn't have a tie on either. The only time I had ever worn one was at her funeral. It had been a clip-on. My father hadn't made me put it on today. I was wearing my usual Levis and denim shirt, with sweat rings under my arms. It was a hot day.

He looked at the people on the train. "Dr. Tannenson will just have to take us as we are," he said.

Porters in white jackets jumped down and placed their little stools on the platform beneath each set of steps. A number of passengers got off, mostly to look at the curios.

Not knowing what Dr. Tannenson looked like, we went over to the train to ask for him. A portly man with a heavy gold chain dangling over his vest and two big suitcases fit our idea of what a professor at Columbia Teachers College and a consultant to the commissioner of Indian Affairs ought to look like. No, the portly man said, he wasn't no kind of doctor, just a drummer trying to make a living selling men's haberdashery.

A couple of cars away, a cluster of porters deposited a briefcase and a half-dozen new-looking Gladstone bags on the platform.

"Mr. Parker, please. Over here, Mr. Parker, for Dr.

Tannenson," one of the porters called in a deep, booming voice, a train-announcing voice.

I hung back, but my father went over. He arrived just as the porters sprang to help a little man, barely taller than I, step down from the sleeping car to the stool. Except for shiny brown boots, he was dressed all in white—white riding pants, white jacket buttoned all the way to an upstanding collar. His cork hat was white, too.

I thought of Kipling. I had read most of his books.

"Dr. Tannenson?" my father asked.

"Right," the little man said. "You must be Parker." He spoke crisply, in a high clear voice that reminded me of a tin whistle.

He did not shake hands or wait for a response. Turning his back, he handed out dollar bills to the waiting porters.

"Thank you, George," he said, each time he pressed a bill into a dark hand. "Thank you, George."

"Now, Parker," Dr. Tannenson said, picking up his briefcase, "take care of these bags. And let's be on our way. I lunched in my compartment."

I helped haul Dr. Tannenson's luggage to the green Ford pickup truck that was my father's official car. All the suitcases but one were crammed and heavy. The light one, I guessed, would be filled with souvenirs when Dr. Tannenson returned to Washington.

He did not offer to help but watched us closely. "Careful with those bags," he said. "I don't want them scratched."

When we had the bags all lined up in the back of the pickup, my father braced them with boxes of groceries we had bought earlier.

"Aren't you going to cover my luggage?" Dr. Tannenson asked. "Sun dries leather, you know. Not good for it."

"I've got a canvas tarp," my father said.

"A clean one, I trust."

"Well, it's all I've got."

Dr. Tannenson looked the tarp over carefully before allowing us to spread it over his bags. Then he opened the pickup door, briefcase in hand, and inspected the seat. He scrubbed it with his handkerchief

I started to get in the cab ahead of him to sit in the middle, with the gearshift lever between my knees.

"Here," he said. "Who are you? Where are you going?" Up till then he had not seemed to see me.

"This is my son, Davey," my father said. "He'll ride in the middle."

I put out my hand as I had been taught to do, but Dr. Tannenson ignored it.

"No," he said, "no, we'll be too crowded. Let him ride in back."

"Get in, Davey," my father said.

I got in and squeezed as close to my father as I could. There was plenty of room, even after Dr. Tannenson got in. None of us was very wide.

Dr. Tannenson opened the briefcase on his knees and took out a road map. Unfolding it, he said, "Before we start, show me just how we're to go."

My father leaned over me to show him — west on U.S. 66 to Chambers, then north on the Ganado road to Klinchee.

"Oh. I thought we might go this way." Pointing with a fingernail that was shiny with the kind of clear polish my mother had used, Dr. Tannenson traced a route that would put us on the Navajo Reservation almost all the way — north on U.S. 666, west on a feeder road past Fort Defiance to Ganado, south to Klinchee.

"Well—"

Dr. Tannenson explained, "I want to learn as much about

the Navajos as possible before making my recommendations to Commissioner Collier. It's imperative for me to see everything, not just those six schools of yours."

"It'll take a lot longer going that way."

"Nonsense. I measured both routes. There's not a lot of difference—no more than ten, twenty miles."

My father shrugged. "It's a slow road, lots of ups and downs and switchbacks. We call it going over the mountain."

"Nevertheless, that's the way I want to go."

"It's dusty. Our rainy season is late this year."

"Now, please, Parker! Do as I say."

On the way out of town, we stopped twice, once to gas up and then to buy some hamburgers to take with us.

"I told you I had lunch on the train," Dr. Tannenson said.

"We didn't," my father said.

I went into the café with him, leaving Dr. Tannenson in the pickup.

"Ride in the back?" my father said. He put his arm over my shoulder. "You just bet, in all that sun and dust. Yessirree."

We each got two hamburgers and a Coke. The hamburgers were wrapped in napkins. I put my second hamburger on the seat between Dr. Tannenson and me while I unwrapped the first. He shoved the hamburger as far from him as he could. I put it on my lap.

"Sorry, sir," I said.

My father kept his extra burger on his lap, too, and ate as he drove. He held a Coke by the neck with one hand and a hamburger with the other. He kept his Coke hand on the wheel. When he wanted a swig, he drove with his hamburger hand.

The road out of Gallup was concrete but broken and rough. It had been pounded to pieces by heavy trucks going to and from the coal mines we passed. The mines were what had brought Gallup into existence soon after railroads first crossed the West. Smoldering slag piles, some as high as the surrounding mesas, marked the mine adits and sent clouds of black smoke over the town. My mother used to say that no one ever slept on clean sheets in Gallup because those burning slag piles turned everything gray, if not black. *Ripley's Believe It or Not* had reported a few years back that Gallup's slag piles had not gone out in fifty years. You couldn't go into any store in town without seeing a clipping of that *Ripley* cartoon neatly framed and proudly displayed. Being featured in *Ripley* was the town's greatest claim to fame.

The pickup's wheels banged over the cracks in the concrete road. After a while, chewing the last of his second hamburger, my father said, "That sign up ahead there. That's where the pavement ends and we go onto the reservation. From now on, we'll be running on gravel and dirt."

"Gravel? Dirt? The map says this is a U.S. highway— U.S. 666."

"That's what the map says, all right. Lots of folks have been fooled by that into thinking it'd be a paved road. Starting here, it's not."

Dr. Tannenson sighed and shook his head. But he was on the edge of his seat as we left the pavement. "How very exciting," he said. "I'm on an actual Amerind reservation! How I envy you, Parker."

My father said nothing.

"I suppose you've heard about the movement to find a more acceptable designation than 'Indian' for our American natives?"

"Many times," my father said. "But I've never thought of them as our American natives."

He concentrated on guiding the pickup over the washboard road while making as much time as possible. Dust boiled up into the pickup.

Dr. Tannenson sneezed and coughed. "Can't you do something about this dust?"

"I don't know what."

"You could moderate your speed."

"Slow down? We've got a long way to go, and I want to be there not too long after dark."

"Don't you have headlights?"

My father didn't bother to answer. Dr. Tannenson pressed his handkerchief to his face, coughing. Soon the road smoothed out and the dust lessened. Dr. Tannenson could breathe again. He examined the passing country eagerly.

"Where are the houses — 'hogans,' I believe they're called?"

"All around. Look at that mesa over there. You can just make out a couple at its base."

"I see them! Let's run over for a better look. I'd like to visit with some Indians."

"We don't have time. That mesa's farther away than it looks, and nothing but a trail to it. There'll be a lot more hogans, a lot more Indians. From now on, Navajos will be watching every move we make, though we won't always see them."

As we topped a hill, my father had to slam on the brakes to avoid piling into a flock of sheep. Two barefoot little girls in torn skirts and cut-down velveteen blouses tried to get the sheep off the road with the help of several snarling dogs, who raced around the flock, barking and snapping. One of the children squinted up at us as we passed. I saw pus oozing from the corners of her eyes. The pus left tracks in the dust on her cheeks.

My father eased the pickup forward in low gear through the dodging herd. Clouds of dust pervaded the pickup, along with a powerful odor of manure.

Dr. Tannenson seemed no longer to notice the dust. As the flock flowed around us, he had eyes only for the children.

"Oh, beautiful," he said. "Beautiful. This is what we must preserve — their way of life. Don't you agree?"

"Well, the good parts of it, sure," my father said, "but I'd feel a whole lot better if I knew these kids would be in school this fall, with somebody else herding the sheep. And they need medical attention. That one child's got trachoma. She'll be blind in a few years if something's not done."

"How beautiful," Dr. Tannenson said. "How truly pastoral."

Soon we reached the turnoff for the feeder road that led west over the mountain. It was a narrow trail, ungraded, deeply rutted.

Dr. Tannenson said, "On the map it was a red road just like U.S. 666."

"I reckon that's right," my father said, "but we've got to drive on what's in front of us."

We went up and down steep hills, often on switchbacks that reversed every quarter of a mile or so. Now and again my father backed and filled in order to get around a particularly sharp curve. He judged his distances carefully. If he backed too far, the pickup might tumble a hundred feet down a cliff. Not far enough, and when he went forward again, the pickup would fail to make the turn and hang up on loose earth at the edge of the road, possibly touching off an avalanche that could take us with it.

At one point a rattlesnake several feet long and thicker than my arm crossed the road in front of us. To avoid hitting it, my father veered to the edge.

Dr. Tannenson gasped and hugged his briefcase to him.

"You nearly took us right off the road, Parker."

"Your window's open, Doctor. Where do you suppose that

old rattler would've landed if I'd hit it and it got tossed up by the wheel? Maybe in your lap?"

Hot as it was, Dr. Tannenson rolled up his window. He opened the briefcase on his lap and brought out a yellow pad.

"We might as well make use of this time," he said. "I have only a few days and a great deal to do. I've read all the relevant literature, of course, both pedagogic and ethnologic, and have formulated my conclusions and recommendations for reorganizing the government's educational program for the Navajos. But Commissioner Collier wanted me to take a firsthand look before turning in my report. He suggested spending a few days on the reservation with a real insider."

"Insider," my father said. I couldn't tell if it was a question or a statement.

Dr. Tannenson went right on. "First of all, I'm sure you read my paper in *Pedagogic Journal* on the conflict between primitive values and the education of primitive peoples?"

"Can't say I have."

"That surprises me. However, to get our discussion started, I'll fill you in on the principal points I made. Commissioner Collier was quite taken with the theoretical base for practical action that my ideas provide."

As we backed and filled over the mountain, Dr. Tannenson described his theories. I didn't understand much of what he was saying, though I had been around this kind of talk all my life. My father said later that he heard little that he had not heard or read many times before. Most of it was commonsensical and goodhearted. Dr. Tannenson garlanded the obvious with learned asides and scholarly footnotes, my father said, but he clearly had the best interests of the Indians at heart.

Only once did my father raise an objection. Dr. Tannenson said he would recommend that the Indian Service quit building conventional schools on the reservation. He believed classes should be held in hogans similar to those the children lived in. Each would have a dirt floor and a heating stove in the middle. He would abolish chairs, desks, and blackboards. Children and teachers would sit on sheepskins scattered around the stove so that the children would feel instantly at home.

"Well, Doctor," my father said, guiding the pickup along a hogback where the ground fell away sharply on both sides of the road, "I don't think you'd find the Navajo parents very happy about that. A dirt floor's mighty cold and drafty in the winter. The only reason hogans don't have wooden floors is that lumber is expensive and hard to come by. And dirt floor or not, if you've got a red-hot stove in the middle of a roomful of rambunctious kids, I don't care if they're Navajos or good Texas Baptists like I started out teaching, somebody's going to get burned. As for sheepskins, they're hard to keep clean and free of lice and aren't as comfortable as you might think. You'll find Navajo parents are like parents anywhere. They want the best and most modern schools possible for their children. They've sent a lot of delegations to Washington over the years, asking for them."

"Nonsense," Dr. Tannenson said.

From then on, my father drove in silence and Dr. Tannenson talked.

We came off the mountain and into Ganado about dark. It was black, moonless night by the time we reached Klinchee. Dr. Tannenson was still talking. My father stopped in front of the dining hall, where a guest room had been fixed up off the kitchen for official visitors. I had made up the bed in it that morning before we left for Gallup.

On the distant hills beyond the trading post, coyotes were beginning to sing.

"What in the world is that dreadful caterwauling?" Dr. Tannenson asked, shuddering.

"Some folks say it's the spirits of warriors killed in the Indian wars, howling for revenge," my father said, "and some say it's witches working up a spell. It's really just coyotes, of course."

"Of course," Dr. Tannenson said.

We carried his Gladstone bags into the guest room. As we moved back and forth between pickup and guest room, carrying bags, Dr. Tannenson trailed after us. He continued to discuss his educational theories nonstop. He broke off only to complain that there seemed to be no private bath for the guest room.

"The bathhouse is right next door," my father said. "Just take soap and a towel with you, and you'll find everything else you need right there. After you've washed up, come on over to the house. Davey made a pot of soup we can warm up for supper."

"You're not going to stay with me while I wash up?"

"We won't be a hundred yards away."

"But the Indians?"

"They won't bother you if you don't bother them."

"They're around?"

"Of course. They're everywhere. We're on their land."

"I don't need to wash up, as you put it. I'll just use the facilities in your cottage."

"Suit yourself."

My father and I each had two bowls of the soup, which was from a recipe of my mother's—navy beans with onions, bacon, one potato, and a carrot, finely chopped. I thought it had turned out well. Dr. Tannenson didn't touch it. He had a piece of dry toast and a cup of tea. Even with the cup at his lips, he kept talking. My father said later that he had never heard a grown man chatter away like Dr. Tannenson. It was as though he feared someone or something was slipping up on him unbeknownst, and he was throwing up a breastwork of words to shelter behind.

He talked right through the eleven o'clock news, which we usually didn't stay up for. By then he had long since quit describing the educational theories laid down in his articles and was passing along gossip circulating in the Indian Service's Washington office. I found it interesting but confusing.

We learned who was supposed to have Commissioner Collier's ear, who had lost it, and what unfavorable comments the commissioner was said to have made about a senator from New Mexico who had been critical of the Bureau of Indian Affairs. Dropping his voice and leaning close, Dr. Tannenson told us that now a Farmington lawyer who was a friend of the senator was spreading rumors that Commissioner Collier was probably a Russian and certainly a Communist. The senator was encouraging Congressman Dies of the House Committee on Un-American Affairs to investigate both Commissioner Collier and Secretary Ickes.

Dr. Tannenson said all of this had something to do with a scheme to get rid of Collier in the hope that his successor might restore grazing rights on Navajo land that Collier had taken away from some white ranchers. I didn't understand half of what he said. My eyes kept closing.

Dr. Tannenson was still talking when the new diesel generator turned itself off at midnight, as it was set to do. Lighting kerosene lamps, my father said, "Doctor, I don't want to hurry you, but tomorrow's a working day. We're scheduled to go to Haystacks Day School, and we'll need to make an early start. You should find it interesting. Mrs. Wallis is the teacher there and has views you probably won't hear from anyone else around here. Perhaps you know her. She got her master's from Columbia Teachers."

"Wallis? I've a colleague at Teachers named Wallis—good man, very sound, working with me now in Washington. But I know his wife and she's in New York. Lovely woman, younger than he, an anthropologist. What was your Mrs. Wallis's name before she married? Perhaps I knew her under that name."

"I've no idea," my father said.

We walked with Dr. Tannenson to the guest room and lit his kerosene lamp for him. The coyotes had moved in closer and were howling down near the sheep pens at the trading post.

"They aren't, ah, dangerous, are they?" Dr. Tannenson asked.

"Not as long as you're in here and they're out there. Biggest cowards in the world."

"Should I have a gun?"

"I reckon not."

As we left, my father said that he felt obliged to advise Dr. Tannenson not to walk around in the dark in his bare feet and to tip his boots upside down before putting them on in the morning, to be sure a stray scorpion or rattler hadn't found a cozy home.

"Nothing to worry about," my father said, "just something you need to be aware of."

"I see," Dr. Tannenson said.

The next morning he looked haggard. He had not changed out of his white jacket and riding pants—had not even taken off his boots or unpacked his bags. He had stretched out on top of the covers and left his lamp burning until it ran out of oil. Fortunately, he said, that had not happened until after dawn. He said that instead of going to Haystacks as planned, it would be better for him to return to Gallup as quickly as possible. He had realized overnight that the valuable insights he had already gained made additional fieldwork unnecessary. He felt it was urgent to deliver his report to Commissioner Collier at once and wanted my father to get him to Gallup in time to catch the eastbound Super Chief. He suggested that we not go over the mountain but by way of Chambers and U.S. 66, which he said he understood to be a better and more direct route than the one my father had chosen the day before.

Dr. Tannenson dozed all the way to Gallup. While we waited for the Super Chief to pull in, his spirits lifted. He bought from the platform peddlers at a furious rate. He bought not just genuine Navajo blankets and Zuñi and Hopi pottery and jewelry but also quantities of ceramic canoes, chicken-feather headdresses, and bows with rubber-tipped arrows. He packed as many curios as he could into the Gladstone bag he had kept empty for that purpose. The rest he stuffed in paper sacks that he clutched in his arms as the train glided into the station.

Another set of Pullman porters named George took charge of the Gladstone bags. Dr. Tannenson stepped aboard the Super Chief in wrinkled, dusty whites, too laden with souvenirs to wave.

We leaned against pillars amid tobacco-spewing peddlers. The train rolled eastward.

"Insider," my father said.

29.

WHEN WE WERE ready to leave for home, Hosteen Yazzie, the school policeman, came out to the pickup with us. The star on his chest gleamed in the sun. His black Stetson rode low on his forehead and shadowed his face. My father got behind the wheel, and I climbed in on the passenger side.

Hosteen Yazzie reached through the driver's window to shake hands with my father. He did not offer his hand to me. To Hosteen Yazzie a handshake was a serious matter, a sign of respect. He did not shake hands with enemies or boys.

Miss Ryder had followed us to the pickup. As Hosteen Yazzie went back to the school, she reached up and grabbed my hand. She had green eyes, greener even than the pickup, and red hair. Peering up at me she looked like a child, somebody's little sister perhaps. She sounded like a child, too. She was from Mississippi and spoke in a little-girl-lost kind of lisping whisper.

"What a big hand," she said. She measured her hand against mine. "Almost a man's hand. You'll be a wrestler when you grow up, Davey."

"No'm," I said. "I'm going to be a poet."

"You don't have a poet's hands."

She stood on tiptoe to look past me at my father behind the wheel. "I'm sure I could learn to drive if you gave me a few more lessons, Will. Maybe Sunday? Maybe you and Davey could come have Sunday dinner with me and you could teach me? I'm a good cook, Will."

"I'd get in touch with that dealer again, Miss Ryder," my father said. "He sold you the car with the understanding he'd teach you to drive it."

"He says he's taught me all he can. He says he can't keep coming all this way from Gallup just because I can't seem to learn."

"I think all you need is practice. Every nice day after school, ask Hosteen Yazzie to back the car out of the garage so you can go for a spin."

"I couldn't do that."

"He'd have you driving everywhere in no time."

"Hosteen Yazzie calls me Turquoise Girl behind my back, Will."

"He doesn't mean anything by it."

"He scares me, Will. He wears that awful black hat everywhere, even inside."

"All our school policemen wear black hats. I don't know why. It doesn't mean anything. Let him teach you to drive."

"Won't you teach me?"

"I'm afraid not."

My father let out the clutch and we drove off. I sat close beside him. He put his arm around me. "Don't pay her no nevermind, Davey. She's just a mixed-up little thing, the most helpless human being—man, woman, or child—I've come across in all my born days."

As we drove along, my father kept talking about Miss Ryder almost like he was alone and talking to himself. He said there wasn't a thing in this world that Miss Ryder knew how to do except sit around and look pretty. It was not just that she had never learned to drive the Chevy coupe she'd bought so that she could get away from Cottage Springs from time to time. She couldn't even learn to fill out the Indian Service reports on school attendance and other matters that she was supposed to file weekly, monthly, and quarterly. He had to help her with every report.

It was cruel, my father said, that the Depression had come along just in time to catch her the way it had. In almost any other era, somebody back home would have been able to look after her—a father, uncle, brother, maybe even a husband— and she'd have become what she was brought up to be, a decorative object. With times so hard, she had been forced to fend for herself as best she could. In her innocence, or maybe ignorance, she had chosen to make her living in the Indian Service, most likely moved as much by romantic dreams about the noble savage as by relatively high government salaries.

Whatever the case, her dreams could not have survived the dusty trip from the railroad to Cottage Springs. My father said nobody but a fool, a madman, or a Washington bureaucrat would have been dumb enough, cruel enough, or careless enough to assign a helpless creature like Miss Ryder to an isolated spot like Cottage Springs, where she had to live all alone among people she didn't know, didn't understand, didn't trust, and feared with all her being.

Cottage Springs was the loneliest of the six schools in my father's district. It was made up of four red stone buildings huddled high in the Chuska Mountains among pine and piñon trees. The schoolhouse had three classrooms, but only one was used. Planners in Washington who forgot or didn't know that they were dealing with a seminomadic people had decided the size of the school, using a census taken during summer months when Navajos from all over brought herds to the mountains to graze. The planners didn't realize that in winter the population shrank to a quarter of what it had been in July. Even using buses to bring in distant pupils, there were not enough children around from September to April to fill more than one classroom.

Next to the classroom building was a smaller structure with toilets and showers for the schoolchildren. Then came the kitchen and dining hall, where the pupils were treated to their hot dinner each day at noon. Last in the line of buildings, well removed from the others but connected by a covered walkway, was the teachers' cottage. It was a stone bungalow with a big living room and three bedrooms. Two of the bedrooms had never been used.

Miss Ryder's school wouldn't have operated at all without Hosteen Yazzie. Like my father's old friend Franklin Begay at Red Mesa, Hosteen Yazzie knew how to do whatever needed doing, except for filling out those troublesome forms and the actual teaching. He was called a policeman chiefly because it was he, if anyone, who maintained order and dealt with truancy. Truancy was an offense so common that it was generally ignored unless it was thought to be connected with something more serious but unprovable, such as vandalism or theft. I had never heard of him or any other school policeman being called upon to arrest a criminal.

Hosteen Yazzie took over the spoon to give the children cod-liver oil on winter mornings. The smell of the stuff made Miss Ryder ill. On days the Navajo cook didn't turn up to prepare the noon meal, it was Hosteen Yazzie, not Miss Ryder, who warmed the canned mutton stew and added water to the tins of condensed milk. He also supervised the children at play during recess, because the weather was always too hot or too cold, too dusty or too damp, for Miss Ryder to venture outdoors. Hosteen Yazzie kept the buildings clean and in good repair, the grounds neat, the electric generator and water pump running.

Most of the teachers at my father's schools became friends with the Navajo families around them. Not Miss Ryder. She was always hiding herself away somewhere. When she wasn't in the classroom, she was cowering in her cottage, doors bolted and shades drawn against a germ-ridden, danger-filled outside world. My father said that when she did venture out, she was like Miss Wheeler's maid, Rose, who couldn't tell a stick from a snake. It was not because Miss Ryder was nearsighted, but because she was so frightened and wrapped up in herself that nothing in the world concerned her but her own fears. Sometimes, though, when he leaned over Miss Ryder to show her how to fill out a form, it seemed to me that he liked her better than he said he did.

My father tried to visit each of his schools at least once a week. Because of distances and road conditions, he could usually get to only one school a day, and not always that, which meant that many weeks he was on the road every day but Sunday. Most of the time he took me with him, and I did my lessons sitting beside him as we bumped over the Navajo Reservation on unpaved trails bladed through sand and clay, around rock outcroppings, past great clumps of greasewood and sagebrush, across arroyos. Every so often we'd get stuck and I would help dig out of a sandy rut or a mud hole.

Because of the bad roads, we often arrived late in the day when we delivered supplies to Cottage Springs. I would help Hosteen Yazzie unload the pickup while my father filled out forms for Miss Ryder. When we finished unloading, Hosteen Yazzie and I spread oiled sawdust to keep down the dust and swept the floors of the school and dining hall. At one time Hosteen Yazzie had filled in for Franklin Begay at Red Mesa and had gotten to know my mother well. He used to tell my mother Navajo stories. Now he told the stories to me as we worked. I liked hearing him refer to my mother, but I didn't have anything to say about her myself. I hadn't been able to talk about her or even mention her since I found out she was dead.

One day as we pushed our brooms over the floors, Hosteen Yazzie explained why he called Miss Ryder Turquoise Girl. He said that a long time ago, at the beginning, Navajos lived in darkness inside the earth. When they finally found their way from the underworld into the sun and air, they were menaced everywhere by man-eating monsters. One day the few surviving *Dineh* came across a girl baby at the end of a rainbow. Like Miss Ryder the baby had white skin, red hair, green eyes, and a tiny voice. The Navajos took her in, nurtured her, and called her Turquoise Girl.

I asked who Turquoise Girl's parents were. Hosteen Yazzie shook his head. "That don't matter."

He said that in four days Turquoise Girl quit speaking like a child and became Turquoise Woman, ready to take charge. In another four days she gave birth to the Sun's twin sons, who killed all the man-eating monsters and made the world safe for the *Dineh*. Then Turquoise Woman established clans and repopulated the world. I asked how she did it.

"That don't matter," he said.

Except for her appearance and childish voice, Miss Ryder didn't seem to me like Hosteen Yazzie's Turquoise Girl, and even less like Turquoise Woman.

"She may look and sound like Turquoise Girl," I said, "but that's all. She hasn't grown up a bit in all the time I've known her, let alone four days."

Hosteen Yazzie nudged me. "You wait."

I didn't want to give up. "And even if she did grow up, Miss Ryder still wouldn't be Turquoise Woman. Turquoise

Woman knew how to do what she had to do, and Miss Ryder won't even try to learn."

Hosteen Yazzie nudged me again. "You wait. She Turquoise Girl, and all of a sudden she turn into Turquoise Woman. You wait."

Early on a March morning, my father and I were finishing breakfast at Klinchee. We were getting ready for a run to Haystacks with a load of oranges. I was looking forward to the trip. For a long time Haystacks had been one of my father's problem schools, but it wasn't anymore. A new teacher named Miss Horton had recently taken charge there. My father and the old teacher, Mrs. Wallis, had not gotten along, but she had recently transferred to Keams Canyon at her own request. She had frequently asked for transfers in the past, but always to supervisory posts that no one wanted to see her in. When she finally gave up hope of a promotion and asked only for an in-grade transfer, my father approved it instantly and the principal at Keams, a new man who did not know Mrs. Wallis, had accepted her without a question. Miss Horton was young, rode a motorcycle, was popular with the Haystacks families, and taught in Navajo as well as English. Mrs. Wallis had never allowed Navajo to be spoken in her classroom. Haystacks was now a model school.

The telephone on the kitchen wall rang. Two longs, a short, a long. Our ring.

My father answered. "Klinchee, Parker here," he shouted into the phone. He listened a moment.

"All right, Hosteen Yazzie," my father said. "I'll come right away. Should be there around noon or a little after, depending on the roads. Go pound on her door again, try to make sure she's all right. Otherwise do just like you've been doing. Keep the children in the schoolroom and make sure they get their dinner just like usual."

He hung up the phone and came back to the table. He scraped up the last of his fried eggs and drained his coffee cup.

"Going to be a long day, Davey," he said. "We've got to go to Cottage Springs."

The winter freeze was out of the ground, but the sun was not yet strong enough to dry the roads. Even with chains on and the back end weighted down with oranges, the Ford pickup slipped and slid all the way. A lot of the time, we were driving in low gear, barely moving through the mud. A couple of times we got stuck and had to dig out. It was midafternoon when we got to Cottage Springs. The doodlebug bus was already at the schoolhouse to take the children home.

The children, maybe thirty of them, were still in the classroom. They sat at their desks like mannequins frozen in an approved position-bolt upright, feet side by side on the floor, hands clasped and resting in the precise center of their desks, heads pointed straight ahead at a blank blackboard. Seated at Miss Ryder's desk, Hosteen Yazzie also sat bolt upright. He stared back at the children, with his arms folded over his chest, almost but not quite hiding his policeman's star. His black hat rode his eyebrows.

He and all the pupils stood as soon as we entered. Hosteen Yazzie shook hands with my father. We went out into the hall where the children could not hear. "Turquoise Girl, she stay in house, Hosteen Parker. Won't come out. Turquoise Girl ain't come out since Saturday."

"She's probably not feeling well. That happens, you know. Let the children go home. Tell them Miss Ryder will be back tomorrow and there'll be a special treat for dinner."

"What treat?"

"Oranges. We got a shipment of oranges yesterday and brought you a load. Tell you what. Go out to the pickup. Open a sack or two and give each child an orange to take home. Tell them they'll get another orange tomorrow. Show them how to peel the orange and make sure they know not to eat the peel. Take some oranges home to your family, too."

My father and I went over to Miss Ryder's cottage. Our shadows stretched ahead of us in the afternoon sun.

"Listen, Davey," he said. "You stay right with me no matter what, understand?"

"I think so."

"If she says, 'Why don't you go for a walk?' or 'Don't you want to do this or that?' I want you to say, 'No, thank you, ma'am,' and stick to me like glue. You got that?"

"Yes, sir," I said.

The window shades were pulled down as usual. We pounded on the front door and then on the back door. As we walked around the house, my father tapped at each window in turn.

He was banging on the front door again when I saw a shade quiver.

"She's there," I said. "In the living room. She's looking out."

"Smile at her. Wave."

I did. He kept pounding. She let go of the window shade, but after a moment she peeked out again. I told my father.

"I think we've got her hooked," he said.

He yelled through the door, "Doris, are you all right? We heard you weren't feeling real good and came quick as we could. Open the door, Doris."

We heard her turning locks. She eased the door open a crack. "I've been ill," she whispered. "I've hardly had the strength to comb my hair. I look a fright. Please go away."

"We're here to help you, Doris."

"I don't like you to see me this way, Will. Couldn't you come back another time?"

"No," my father said. He put his foot in the door. "Let us in, Doris. I've got to talk to you."

After a moment she stepped back from the door and we went in. The house was dark and cold.

"Remember what I told you, Davey," my father said.

Miss Ryder had on a black velvet bathrobe. There were greasy streaks down one side of the skirt. Her eyes were narrow slits in puffy flesh underlain by dark circles. But her hair was redder than ever and neatly combed. She'd put on lipstick, too.

"I'd fix you a cup of coffee," she said, "but everything's such a mess."

"That's all right. I'd like some coffee," my father said. He walked ahead of her into the kitchen.

The sink and table and countertops, even the coal range, were piled high with unwashed dishes and empty cans of Van Camp's pork and beans and Campbell's soup. My father pulled up the shades to let light in.

"I don't know what's wrong," Miss Ryder said, sounding more than ever like a little girl. "I just feel like I can't go on."

My father cleared the top of the stove and shoveled ashes from the firebox into an empty coal scuttle. I brought kindling from a pile that Hosteen Yazzie kept stacked outside the back door. He had left a couple of scuttles of coal there, too. I brought those in. My father curled shavings onto crumpled-up newspapers with his pocketknife. He struck a match and blew gently until the shavings caught, then dropped in sticks of kindling and a few lumps of coal. Smoke poured into the room before the draft began to work. I opened a window.

"Never let your fire go out," my father told Miss Ryder. "If you don't do anything else, have Hosteen Yazzie tend your fire twice a day."

"I never thought I'd be beholden to a savage." She dabbed

at her eyes with a knotted handkerchief.

"Hosteen Yazzie's no savage. He's a fine man. A gentleman."

"He's always following me around, always looking at me. He even tries to look in my windows."

"He just wants to be helpful."

"Did you know he calls me Turquoise Girl?"

"Yes, you told us."

"I don't know what he means by it. It scares me, Will."

"Don't you know the story of Turquoise Girl? He means it kindly."

"I don't think so."

The fire was blazing and my father got the coffeepot. It was full of stale grounds. He washed the pot and a couple of cups.

"You shouldn't let things go like this," he said.

"You're scolding, Will," she said. "Please don't scold."

She turned to me. Her lips drew back from her teeth. She was trying to smile.

"Davey, sweet," she said, "it's such a pretty day. You don't want to be cooped up in here with us big folks on a pretty day like this. Wouldn't you like to go for a walk?"

"No, thank you, ma'am," I said.

"Please, Davey. For me?"

I shook my head.

She pulled the collar of the black velvet bathrobe across her face. "Nice boys don't treat ladies this way back home," she said.

"I'm sorry, ma'am," I said. "I just want to stay with my dad."

My father put the coffeepot on the stove and rubbed his hands together. "What a grand fire. Won't take any time at all to get the place cozy."

He cleared the table. I found some bread and a wire toaster

and took a lid off the stove to toast the bread over the hot coals. By the time the toast was brown, the coffee was ready. My father and Miss Ryder sat at the table. I leaned against a counter and had a Coke. From where I stood, I could see the brim of Hosteen Yazzie's hat. He was leaning against the wall outside the window I had opened. He could hear everything that went on inside.

Miss Ryder buttered her toast and cut it into tiny pieces. She rolled each piece between her fingers into balls not much bigger than the lead in a .22 cartridge. She built a pyramid of toast balls beside her plate. Every now and again she took a ball off the pyramid and popped it into her mouth, then rolled another to replace it. Each time she rolled a ball, she wiped her fingers on the skirt of her robe and took a sip of coffee. She kept her head down and stared at her pyramid of toast balls.

"You've got to learn to take care of yourself," my father said. "Set a schedule and stick to it. That's what you have to do when you live alone."

"I don't want to live alone," she whispered. "I can't live alone, Will."

"Let me tell you what I can do for you, Doris, other than notify Washington that you aren't keeping classes, which would mean you'd be out of a job."

"I need this job, Will." She still kept her head down, like she was talking to her toast.

"I know you do," he said. He buried his face in his coffee cup and took a long sip before he went on. "The only thing I can do other than have you removed is to recommend an immediate transfer to a boarding school—Phoenix, maybe, or at least Keams Canyon. There's a long waiting list for Phoenix, but I hear Keams has an opening right now for a teacher in the lower grades. It's a long way from town, but there's a big staff and you would be around your own kind again."

"That's all you'll do? Just send me to Keams?"

"That's all I can do." He poured himself another cup of coffee. "I think you'd like Keams. Mrs. Wallis is there. You know her. You'll probably know some of the other teachers, too."

"It's not what I want, Will."

"It's as much as I can do for you, Doris."

"I don't have anybody to turn to, Will. No one I can count on."

"You have yourself."

"That's not enough."

Looking at my hands, I said, "My mother told me before she died—she told me if you can't count on yourself, you'll never be able to count on anybody."

Miss Ryder lifted her head and stared at me. Her eyes were cold and hard as turquoise chips.

"You keep out of this," she said. Her voice was strong—a woman's voice.

She was not Turquoise Girl anymore. But she was not Turquoise Woman either. She was just Miss Ryder out in the open.

My father pushed back his chair and stood up.

"I'll see what I can do about Keams," he said. "I want you back in that classroom tomorrow."

Hosteen Yazzie was waiting at the green pickup. He shook my father's hand. And then he shook mine.

30.

CRIPPLING ALONG on the crutches he had to use because he'd fallen off a ladder a few days earlier and broken his ankle, my father went up to the Navajo-Hopi Agency Hospital as soon as we heard that the Jim family had brought Billy Jim in. By then he—my old man, that is—had been principal of Keams Canyon Boarding School, part of the Agency setup, for several years.

    It was ironic, I thought—*ironic* had recently become my favorite word—that he should wind up his Indian Service career running a boarding school after fighting for day schools most of his life. It seemed especially ironic that his boarding school was staffed in part by teachers he'd had transferred to Keams Canyon years earlier because he didn't think they were competent enough for his day schools and he was too softhearted to fire them. It had bucked him up when he got rid of both Miss Ryder and Mrs. Wallis that way. Now he had them again. Served him right, I thought, although I didn't know why that should be true. He and I hadn't been getting on well since I'd first left home to enter high school—at a boarding school, of course. That was also about when I started thinking of him at times as my old man. He seemed an awful fuddy-duddy to me, and I resented his trying to run my life.

When he came back from the hospital, he found me out behind the house, hoeing the garden, which is what he'd told me to do. It was not yet noon, but the temperature was already hitting a hundred degrees.

"Billy Jim's dead. It's up to us to bury him," he said. "With this heat and all, we can't wait for Tom Naningha or any of the other Hopis to get back from the Snake Dance."

He leaned on one crutch and scraped connecting circles in the dust with the other.

"I won't be much help, I'm afraid," he said.

"That's all right," I said. "I can use the money."

I hadn't been able to find a job that summer. For the first time I could remember, the Indian Service was hiring Indians ahead of whites. I wasn't at the Snake Dance myself only because I couldn't afford the gas to get to Hotevilla.

I got a pickax and shovel, filled a water bag, and backed the Agency's old International pickup against the hospital loading dock. Billy Jim had been a tall man, taller than any other Navajo I'd ever known, but the nurses had folded him into a child's coffin of unpainted yellow pine. It was the only coffin available. Mr. Hendricks, the school carpenter, had made it for a little girl who had been expected to die but recovered. He had gone to the Snake Dance, too, and we couldn't wait for him to return and build a coffin that Billy Jim would fit into more comfortably.

The nurses had put the lid on the box. With my old man giving me instructions, I nailed it down. Hopping along on one foot, dragging his crutches, he helped me shove Billy Jim across the loading dock and into the back of the pickup.

I sniffed.

"Gangrene set in before his family could get him here," he said. "That's what we smell."

He drew invisible circles on the loading dock with his crutch and kept talking. Usually he didn't have much to say to me anymore, but now he couldn't seem to stop. I could tell he was upset by Billy Jim's death. I was upset, too, but I was determined not to show it.

"His boot caught in the stirrup. The stallion he was breaking rolled over on him before he could get free. Bent his legs backward and cracked both thighs. The nurses said that when his family brought him in, his heels were almost touching his shoulder blades, like he'd got himself a pair of backward-bending knees. Bones sticking out all over."

"Jesus," I said. "Poor guy."

"Three days in the back end of a wagon getting here. He never had a chance."

"Poor guy," I said again.

"His family took off as soon as they got him to the hospital, of course. They'd done everything they could for him and were afraid of *tchindi*."

"I know," I said. "I don't want to hear about it."

Being Navajo, the Jims believed dead bodies were bad luck. They feared that a dead person's spirit might turn into an owl, a coyote, a pack of dogs, or any number of other things that could follow them and cause trouble—perhaps give them the ghost-sickness, which could kill them if they didn't call in a medicine man and have him hold a sing over them right away.

The Navajo fear of *tchindi* was why Tom Naningha had the orderly's job at the hospital and buried patients who died. As a Hopi, Tom Naningha did not share the Jims' fear of *tchindi*, especially when the dead person was a Navajo. He regarded all Navajos as enemies of his people. To him, burying a young Navajo leader like Billy Jim would have been more a pleasure than a chore, even on a hot day.

"If you stop to think about it, *tchindi* makes a lot of sense," my old man said. "Not handling dead bodies cuts down on the spread of disease and—"

"I don't want to hear about it," I said. I didn't want ghosts on my mind while I buried Billy Jim up there on the mesa top.

He told me where to dig the grave.

"Wear your hat," he said. "This sun's a killer. You'll need plenty of water. Did you fill both water bags?"

"Yes, sir," I said, though I had filled only one. He was fussing over me like I was still a little boy.

"If you need any help, come get me and I'll do what I can."

"I won't need help," I said.

I found the grave site he had assigned to Billy Jim. It was a nice spot in the Navajo sector of the cemetery near the rim of the mesa and overlooked the school and hospital. In the distance mountains shimmered blue at the horizon. There were signs that earlier burials had encroached on Billy Jim's plot, but I gave that no thought. I took off my hat and shirt and started trying to break up the hard-baked adobe soil with the pick.

After a few minutes I straightened up, wiped sweat off my face, and went over to the shady side of the pickup to swig water from the canvas bag hanging on the door handle. It was so hot that water soaking through the canvas evaporated instantly, leaving the outside of the bag dry and the water inside cool. I tipped the bag above my head. Water spilled over me.

Clouds of flies buzzed around Billy Jim's coffin—so many flies that their shadows darkened it. They were the biting kind, big and black, with bulging green eyes and iridescent wings. I licked at the water dribbling down my face and looked closely at the box. It was no longer than my shovel handle. I did not relish the picture of Billy Jim all cramped up in there, his broken legs bent this way and that. Nor did I like the thoughts of *tchindi* that came to mind.

Billy Jim had been my friend when we lived at Klinchee. That was when he was a star pitcher for the Phoenix Indian School's baseball team, the Chiefs. Sometimes when he was home for the summer he would throw to me, coming out of his windup like a rattlesnake striking. My hand was always red and sore, even though Billy Jim, laughing, stuffed my mitt with extra padding.

During one school vacation, my old man hired Billy Jim to go around telling Navajo parents about the importance of education. Some of the parents were longhairs who clung to traditional ways and wanted nothing to do with whites, refusing even to hear Billy Jim's message. But most parents were glad to listen as he urged them to send their children to school at an early age instead of using them to herd sheep until they were ten or twelve years old and younger brothers and sisters were big enough to tend the flocks. That fall my old man had more students in his schools than ever before.

In Billy Jim's senior year, the Chiefs were in a playoff for the Arizona high school baseball championship. We went to Phoenix to see the game, and Billy Jim got us seats in the first row of the grandstand. As soon as we arrived, he came over to say hello. His jaw bulged with a big wad of tobacco. Every now and again he would shoot out a muddy stream of tobacco juice. He had been warming up and was sweating. He took off his cap and wiped his forehead on his arm. His black hair glistened with sweat.

His team's uniforms bore the word *Chiefs* arching in red over a many-feathered war bonnet, which was also red. Billy Jim said he did not much like the insignia. His Navajo ancestors had been brave warriors, but they had not worn feathered bonnets into battle. That was the kind of showy thing Plains Indians like the Crows or Sioux or Comanches

—RESERVATIONS—

might have done, but not the Navajos. Billy Jim didn't like the team's name either, because it led people to address the players as "Chief."

"I can't stand being called Chief," he said.

Though his coach had told him a whole bunch of scouts were in the stands, from minor-league farm clubs as well as several colleges that offered athletic scholarships, Billy Jim did not seem nervous as he visited with us. Neither did he seem to pay attention to the yells—"*Chiefs! Chiefs! Chiefs!*"—orchestrated by cheerleaders in thin white blouses and short red skirts. He just stood and chatted. He asked about this person and that back home, gave us a couple of messages to deliver to his family, and said he thought he'd like to play professional ball long enough to make some money before going on to college. He said he'd decided to be an engineer and then come home to the reservation to live and work.

Standing there talking with us, he was as easy and relaxed as if he were only taking a break from tossing the ball to someone like me. Then he went out to the mound, hitched up his pants, sprayed the dust with tobacco juice, and went into his rattlesnake windup. Billy Jim had himself quite a day, pitching a no-hitter against a Tucson team which until then had been the favorite. Right after the game, a farm-club scout signed him to play for a Class C team in southern Illinois.

The day after Billy Jim graduated from Phoenix Indian School, he left for Illinois by bus with more money in his pocket than he'd ever dreamed of having at one time.

About a month later, my father got a telegram. It was mailed out from town:

> BE ADVISED WARRANT ISSUED FELONY CHARGE CHIEF BILL JIM NO LAST NAME STOP ASSAULT STOP BREACH OF CONTRACT STOP MISAPPROPRIATION FUNDS STOP ARREST ON SIGHT STOP HOLD FOR EXTRADITION STOP

The telegram was signed by an Illinois sheriff.

"Poor Billy Jim," my father said. "I wonder what went wrong."

"Will you have him arrested if he shows up?" I asked.

"No," he said. "As far as I'm concerned, he's safe if he makes it to the reservation."

Someone sent us Illinois newspapers with stories about Billy Jim. Next to headlines about war clouds in Europe were accounts of his brush with the law. Like the sheriff, the papers called him Chief Billy Jim. The stories described him as "an Indian boy but a promising rookie." They said he had become angry on being told that he would have to stay behind when his team left for a swing through the South.

"You're a great pitcher, Billy Jim, and we'll miss you," the manager told him, according to the papers. "But no matter what, I can't take a colored player down south."

"I'm not colored. I'm Navajo," Billy Jim said.

"If I say you're colored, Chief—"

"Don't call me Chief."

"You can't tell a white man what to do, Chief."

The manager was a little fellow, the papers said. Billy Jim grabbed him by the throat, lifted him off the ground, and whirled him around a couple of times before pitching him against the wall of his office, breaking his nose.

Billy Jim never went back to the boardinghouse where the team was staying and where he had slept on a cot in the furnace room. He just disappeared. He had signed a contract promising to stay with the team a full season. The advance he had accepted in Phoenix was supposed to cover not only his travel expenses to Illinois but also his salary for most of the season. The manager claimed he had not provided the services for which he had been paid. That was where the charges of breach of contract and misappropriation of funds came in.

—RESERVATIONS—

Six weeks or so after his disappearance from the Illinois farm club, I saw Billy Jim at the Klinchee trading post. He was preparing to mount a horse at the hitching rail.

"Hey, Billy Jim," I yelled. I started to run toward him.

"No savvy," he said. He swung into the saddle.

For a moment I thought I had made a mistake. He was thin as a rope and had let his hair grow. It was already long enough for him to tie at the back of his neck with a piece of string. But it was Billy Jim, no doubt about it. I yelled at him a second time. He spurred his horse right at me. I had to duck aside.

A couple of Indian men squatting on their heels in the shade at the side of the trading post laughed. One of the men said, "Billy Jim, he a longhair now."

Billy Jim apprenticed himself to Hosteen Tse, the famous old medicine man and tribal leader he called uncle, to learn the sacred chants and ceremonies of his people. For money to live on, he broke wild horses to the saddle. His bronc-busting jobs and studies with Hosteen Tse took him all over the reservation. Billy Jim became known as the leader of a group of radical young Navajos who urged Indian parents to keep their children out of school. He also argued that whites, Hopis, Mexicans—everyone but Navajos—should be barred and forcibly evicted if necessary from land claimed by Navajos. Before long Billy Jim began to accompany tribal elders whenever they met with government officials to discuss ancient disputes over land claimed by both Navajos and Hopis, whose villages were surrounded by the Navajo Reservation.

Billy Jim never spoke at these meetings but left the floor to older men while he quietly gave counsel in the background. Like Hosteen Tse he seemed to know by heart every treaty and agreement ever signed between the Navajos and the U.S. government, as well as every law applicable to the land disputes. Billy Jim was on his way to becoming a great Navajo leader.

Wherever he turned up, however, something bad was bound to happen. Tires on a school bus at Teec Nos Pos were slashed three nights running while Billy Jim was assisting Hosteen Tse at a sing in the neighborhood. A Hopi family's new house north of Leupp burned down in the middle of the night just after Billy Jim bought flour and coffee at a nearby trading post. He was at Tuba City shortly before a herd of wild horses stampeded across fields planted by Hopis in disputed territory. He bought a side of bacon and other supplies at the Weaver Woman trading post a few days before several dozen young Navajos surrounded a car bearing two Indian Service officials who had just announced from the front steps of the post that the number of horses in the Weaver Woman district was to be cut in half. For two days the officials were not allowed to move their car or even to open a door or window, though the sun beat down, their water ran out, and one of them suffered recurring bouts of diarrhea.

Not all of the incidents Billy Jim was rumored to be connected with ended bloodlessly. He was said to have been near Table Mesa on the day that a Mexican bootlegger was found nearby, tied to the trunk of a cottonwood tree beside U.S. 666 with his throat cut and broken whiskey bottles stacked around him to the hips. The bootlegger's Buick with its overload springs was missing and never found.

A few months later Billy Jim and Hosteen Tse were conducting a sing near Jeddito when someone riddled the U.S. mail truck with bullets as it pulled through the sandy bottom of Jeddito Wash. The Hopi driver, a cousin of Tom Naningha, escaped with an insignificant flesh wound in the upper arm, but the truck was disabled. Tom Naningha's cousin had to walk ten miles through a blizzard to the nearest trading post.

He lost the toes on one foot to frostbite.

Everyone felt sure Billy Jim or his followers were mixed up in these events one way or another. But none of it was ever pinned on him—not the slashed school bus tires, the stampeding horses, the house fire, the bootlegger's death, or Tom Naningha's cousin's frozen toes—not even the interference with federal officials on lawful business at Weaver Woman, which led to a formal inquiry. Despite the sworn statements of the confined officials and the evidence of the fouled car, neither the Weaver Woman trader nor anyone else had noticed the car or Navajos milling around it during the two days that the Indian Service men claimed to have been held prisoner. Nor had anyone noticed a single untoward action, much less seen Billy Jim, or so they swore under oath.

The trader, perhaps conscious that his license to do business on the reservation might be at stake, confirmed selling bacon to Billy Jim a few days earlier. But he added that he had not had occasion to glance out the front door of his post during the two days in question and therefore could not be expected to be aware of everything that was going on around him.

The day I buried Billy Jim, the sun bore down like an acetylene torch and the temperature kept going up. Sweat poured off me like I was standing in a shower. I couldn't seem to get enough water to quench my thirst, no matter how much I drank.

I had been digging only a little while when I realized that not all the ground was hard-packed. Much of the plot had been broken up at one time or another.

Soon I struck a pine box protruding six inches or so into the hole I was digging for Billy Jim. A little deeper and I hit the rotting edge of still another coffin. And another.

I knew right away what had happened. In burying

Navajos, Tom Naningha had not taken very seriously either the surveys establishing individual plots or the convention that every grave should be six feet deep. He had dug wherever he felt like digging and quit whenever he got tired. He had stuck Navajo bodies in the ground any which way and only as far down as convenient. There was nothing for me to do but keep shoveling while I tried to keep my mind off the heat, the stench of decaying bodies, and *tchindi*.

Finally I managed to carve out what I thought would be enough room for Billy Jim. I drank the last of my water and backed the pickup to the grave. The monster flies no longer hovered over Billy Jim but clustered on his box like a restless black shroud.

As I lowered the tailgate and climbed into the back of the truck, flies left the coffin to buzz around me. I was already tipping Billy Jim into his grave before I realized I did not know whether he was going in feet or head first. I hated the thought of his being upside down even for a moment. But the only way to be sure was to open the box, which I had no intention of doing. The flies started to bite.

The corners of other coffins poking into the grave stopped Billy Jim's box from slipping in all the way. It stayed at an angle, almost straight up and down, with the uppermost end—head, foot, whichever it was—no more than ten inches below ground level. I tugged and pushed. Back and forth. Back and forth. I could hear Billy Jim shift inside.

No matter how I struggled, I could not get him past those rotting coffins so that he could lie flat. I tried to break off intruding comers by pounding with the point of my shovel. I succeeded only in chipping away bits of old planks and releasing long-sealed emanations of decomposed corpses. I tried to pull Billy Jim out of the grave. That didn't work either. He was too heavy.

—RESERVATIONS—

The sun beat down. I had no more sweat in me. My skin grew dry. My throat felt parched. Flies clung to my face and crawled over my bare back and arms. They bit viciously, raising great welts. They got in my nostrils and even my mouth. I slapped and scraped, but they would not leave me. They had evil faces with glittering green eyes. Suddenly I understood. The flies were *tchindi*—Billy Jim's *tchindi*.

Someone laughed. It was Billy Jim, sounding as he used to when he stuffed padding in my glove at Klinchee. I knew why he laughed. It was not because he had been my friend and was concerned about my sore hand. He laughed because he was Navajo and I was white and once again he had bested me.

Years before, an old man had told me I wasn't Zuñi and could never be. Billy Jim was reminding me I wasn't Navajo either. And could never be.

His box remained nearly vertical, and I still didn't know whether he was resting on his head or feet, but I shoveled dirt into the grave as fast as I could. Billy Jim laughed and laughed.

PART FOUR

KEAMS CANYON

1944

WILL

31.

I GOT BACK FROM a week-long conference at Window Rock just before four o'clock and picked up my mail at Mrs. Hendricks's house. She was the Keams Canyon postmistress. Her post office was nothing more than the living room and front porch of her cottage. Her husband, the school carpenter, had enclosed the porch, turned a window of the house into a stamp counter, and inserted a double row of mailboxes in the wall.

There were three letters from Davey. He'd written them over a period of five or six weeks, but they must all have come on the same ship. Or maybe the censors were running behind in their work, and letters from soldiers in war zones were piling up on their desks.

I opened Davey's most recent letter first to make sure he was still all right and not wounded. I sat in the car, reading letters, surrounded by the odds and ends of supplies I'd been able to scrounge from the Window Rock warehouses between meetings. It was a good haul, considering all the wartime shortages. The car's trunk was full and the backseat was piled to the roof. I even had stuff in the front seat next to me.

I missed the old days when my official car had been a pickup. You could carry more in a pickup. Still, I'd been able to pack in everything from pencils, several boxes of chalk, and a hundred-pound sack of beans to three gross of women's gray flannel, full-length nightgowns, large-size—tent-size, really. I figured we could get enough material from each gown to make three or four little girls' nighties.

I was still reading the letters from Davey when Mr. Fallingbrook rapped on the car window. He was all bundled up—gloves, scarf, and not just a stocking cap but earmuffs, too. Except for his dark complexion, he looked like a character out of *A Christmas Carol*. He was my assistant principal at the boarding school, a good man, a Cherokee.

I rolled down the window. Cold washed over my face. It had been cozy in the car. That was one thing about it that was better than the pickup. It had a heater.

Mr. Fallingbrook's words came out wrapped in foggy breath. "We've got runaways, Mr. Parker. Two of them. Little kids. Sisters. First-graders. One's six, the other seven."

"Get in."

I cleared a place as best I could on the seat beside me. He came around the car and got in.

"Heater feels good," he said. "Zero last night and hasn't got above freezing all day. I'm chilled to the bone just running down here from the office after I saw your car coming off the mesa. I knew you'd stop here first."

The school was tucked into a rocky canyon with sheer cliffs on three sides. The fourth side opened out onto an arid plain. From the plateau on top of the cliffs, the road into Keams Canyon angled steeply down the rocky face along a series of switchbacks. Nobody could come down that road to the school without being spotted.

"Tell me about the children." I already had the car moving, headed for the office.

"Mrs. Wallis—"

"Mrs. Wallis?"

"Yeah. Mrs. Wallis. She caught two little girls speaking Navajo during recess yesterday afternoon."

"What was she doing overseeing first-graders?"

"Half the staff's down with flu. I've got people doubling on everything."

"And so what if they were talking Navajo at recess? It's not against regulations anymore. Hasn't been for years and shouldn't have been then."

"Well, you know Mrs. Wallis."

"Too well."

"She figured that if she told me, I'd say, 'So what,' just like you just did, and send the children on their way with a piece of hard candy and a pat on the head. That's exactly what she told me, in fact. Her own words—a piece of hard candy and a pat on the head."

"I can hear her."

We were at the office by now, but we sat in the car with the motor running and heater on while he told me the rest of it.

"She told Juanita—"

"Why Juanita?" She was the cleaning woman at the little girls' dormitory, a Hopi, good-hearted and hard working. But her job was to take care of floors, not children.

"Flu again. Both matrons are down with it. Juanita was filling in. Mrs. Wallis told Juanita she was taking charge of the two little culprits for the night."

Mr. Fallingbrook's voice broke.

"Jesus," I said. "And poor Juanita didn't know that no one—*no one!*—'takes charge' of the children except the matrons?"

"Even if she knew, she's such a gentle soul I doubt that she could have stood up against Mrs. Wallis. I've tried to tell her it's not her fault, but she won't accept that. Been hysterical all day. Doc gave her a shot a little while ago and she's sleeping now."

"And Mrs. Wallis?"

"Defiant, of course, talking about the old days and weak-kneed administrators and our Christian duty to lift these infidels out of their heathen ways."

"She's saying this to *you*?"

"And anyone else who'll listen. Doesn't seem to realize we're talking about two little kids. They're just savages to her."

His voice broke again. After a moment he went on. "Nobody checked on the children until this morning—"

"Not until this morning?"

"—when Mrs. Begay was well enough to go back to work."

Mrs. Begay was one of the matrons, as capable as my old friend Franklin Begay at Red Mesa, though no kin to him. She was a stricter disciplinarian than I thought necessary, but fierce in defending the welfare of her wards.

"She took the roll and found the children missing. Juanita told her Mrs. Wallis had them. Mrs. Begay tore off madder'n a wet hen to find her. Mrs. Wallis told her what she'd done. She was proud of it. Still is. 'About time somebody showed some backbone around here,' Mrs. Wallis told Mrs. Begay."

"What had she done?"

"She took the children to her classroom and made them strip. Then she put them in the closet and told them to stay there until she came for them. She left them there all night. Planned to let them out this morning after breakfast was over. Said she figured that missing two meals and being naked in a dark closet all night not knowing who or what might open the door would make the point: No Navajo during school hours."

Mr. Fallingbrook took out a handkerchief and scrubbed his nose before going on.

"Mrs. Begay rushed over to Mrs. Wallis's classroom and found the closet door open. The closet was empty. Sometime in the night, the children got their nerve up and came out. Their clothes were still there in the classroom where Mrs. Wallis had left them. The kids must not have been able to find them in the dark."

"They slipped away naked?"

"A couple of old blankets that had been stored in the closet are missing. Mrs. Wallis thinks they must have taken those. Or rather, to use her word for it, they must have 'stolen' them. She's furious about that. So they're out there with nothing on but maybe a blanket in temperatures that got down almost to zero last night and haven't got up to freezing all day. No shoes, even."

"Any trace of them?"

"Not yet. We've got every employee on the place out searching. Wives and husbands, too. All the older boys and girls. Slim Thompson up at the trading post spread the word right off, and maybe a hundred Hopis and Navajos are out looking, too. Some good trackers, Navajo and Hopi both. But no sign yet. Not a thing. Ground is too frozen."

I thought a minute.

"It'll be dark in half an hour. Let's send Navajo women along every road in cars. Tell the drivers to go along very slowly, honking and blinking their lights. Tell them to stop every little way so the women can call out in Navajo, just in case the children might hear."

"They're dead by now unless somebody took them in and is hiding them."

"Let's do it anyway. Just in case," I said.

"You want to see Mrs. Wallis?"

"Not ever again. But I will see her as soon as I call Window Rock."

"Line's been out all day—this cold weather. Can't get through."

Mr. Fallingbrook went to the dining hall, where he had set up a command post. I went to the Employees' Club, where teachers without spouses lived on the second floor in two-room apartments, taking meals downstairs in a common dining room. Six doors opened off the hall, which was lighted only by two small bulbs and a window at the far end. Light was fading fast.

Mrs. Wallis was in her apartment but refused to see me.

"I have nothing to say to you," she told me through the door. "If you had run this school properly, I would not have had to take action."

It took me a couple of tries to get any words out. "You had no call to take action of any sort, no matter how much you disapprove of the way I run this school."

"I knew if I didn't, no one would."

"You could have gone to Mr. Fallingbrook if you felt there was a problem."

"Mr. Fallingbrook! Hah."

"So you've killed two children. I'll see that you answer for it."

"Nonsense. They'll turn up. These people are indestructible."

As I left the Employees' Club, the cold air hit my face like a mallet. After Mrs. Wallis it felt good.

I saw Mr. Fallingbrook running toward me, coatless. I knew at once what he would tell me. The children had been found through lucky chance in some unlikely place. Found by another child, perhaps, who peeked under the porch of one of the school buildings where, incredibly, no one had thought to look before. Or by a Navajo man, who didn't even know about the missing children when he got off his horse to relieve himself against a culvert, miles farther from the school than anyone had supposed such little girls could walk in such a short time. As he pissed, he glanced into the culvert, and there they were, curled up together for warmth. Dead, of course. Mr. Fallingbrook would tell me the children had been found, but found dead.

I will go to the parents, and we will sit on sheepskins in a crowded hogan around an open fire that sends more smoke than heat or light toward us. I will explain through an interpreter what happened, knowing that the news has long since raced ahead of me. We will sit a long time in silence.

With eyes stinging from the fire's smoke, I will wish for Hosteen Tse. He would weave the strands of this latest tragedy into his great mythic tapestry of tribal wrongs to give context, perhaps even meaning, to the deaths of two little girls driven by cruel disdain to seek warmth in a concrete culvert.

The fire dies down. The father rises. He pushes aside the faded green army blanket that serves as the hogan's door and goes outside. He returns with an ice-coated log. As he throws it on the fire, sparks glitter toward the smoke hole overhead. On the far side of the fire, the mother hides within her shawl and turns suffering eyes on me. Her eyes ask, *Why?*

www.ingramcontent.com/pod-product-compliance
Lightning Source LLC
LaVergne TN
LVHW091619070526
838199LV00044B/851